ACCLAIM FOR *Richard Bausch's*

REBEL POWERS

"Bausch reads like Raymond Carver or Andre Dubus. . . . This book is daring and masterful and shows Bausch at his best as a sublime orchestrator of his material."   —*Los Angeles Times*

"A testament to [Bausch's] extraordinary sympathetic powers of narrative. . . . [*Rebel Powers*] seems like a piece of history—personal, intimate, but nonetheless true. . . . Bausch succeeds miraculously."   —*USA Today*

"The telling of this story is the telling of a stream of small courages. Bausch's writing is so solidly detailed that the reader cannot escape his characters' pangs of anguish. . . . Bausch has given us a pathology of a family with writing that cuts to the bone."

—*Philadelphia Inquirer*

"Like Anne Tyler . . . Bausch [is] a writer's writer whose compelling work deserves a wider audience. A skilled stylist with a keen ear for dialogue, his generous heart and passionate curiosity make his characters come powerfully alive. . . . Unforgettable."

—*Seattle Times*

Richard Bausch

REBEL POWERS

Richard Bausch is the author of five other novels and two volumes of short stories, including the novel *Violence* and the collection *The Fireman's Wife and Other Stories,* his most recent works. His stories have appeared in *The Atlantic Monthly, Esquire, Harper's, The New Yorker, The Southern Review, Prize Stories: The O. Henry Awards, New Stories from the South, The Granta Book of the American Short Story,* and *The Best American Short Stories.*

REBEL POWERS

Richard Bausch

VINTAGE CONTEMPORARIES

Vintage Books

A Division of Random House, Inc.

New York

for KAREN, *with all my love*

FIRST VINTAGE CONTEMPORARIES EDITION, AUGUST 1994

Copyright © 1993 by Richard Bausch

All rights reserved under International and Pan-American Copyright
Conventions. Published in the United States by Vintage Books, a division of
Random House, Inc., New York, and simultaneously in Canada by Random
House of Canada Limited, Toronto. Originally published in hardcover by
Houghton Mifflin Company, New York, in 1993. This edition published by
special arrangement with Houghton Mifflin Company, Inc.,
and Seymour Lawrence, Inc.

Library of Congress Cataloging-in-Publication Data
Bausch, Richard, 1945-
Rebel powers / Richard Bausch. — 1st Vintage contemporaries ed.
p.   cm. — (Vintage contemporaries)
ISBN 0-679-75253-6
1. Vietnamese Conflict, 1961-1975—Veterans—Wyoming—Fiction.
2. Fathers and sons—United States—Fiction. 3. Teenage boys—
United States—Fiction. I. Title
[PS3552.A846R43 1994]
813´.54—dc20   94-17940
CIP

Author photograph © *Jerry Bauer*

Author's Note: As far as I know, there is no place in
Wyoming, near the lovely Belle Fourche River, called
Wilson Creek, nor is there a missile site near that
river, nor a federal penitentiary. I made it all up. *R.B.*

Manufactured in the United States of America
10 9 8 7 6 5 4 3 2 1

ACKNOWLEDGMENTS

To Harriet Wasserman, Sam Lawrence, Tim O'Brien,
Robert Stone, Barrett Prettyman, and Camille Hykes,
this book is offered in gratitude.

Poor Soul, the center of my sinful earth,
Fool'd by these rebel powers that thee array,
Why dost thou pine within, and suffer dearth,
Painting thy outward walls so costly gay?
Why so large cost, having so short a lease,
Dost thou upon thy fading mansion spend?

— *William Shakespeare*
Sonnet CXLVI

PART ONE

I

————

THE SETTING of a story my parents liked to tell on themselves when I was small is rather exotic in an ends-of-the-earth kind of way. Listening to them tell it, I used to get the feeling that while I was one of the major characters, and while its central event was a quarrel between them, much of its charm — not to say the real reason it was being told — had to do with the fact that it happened in northern Alaska, not too far from the Arctic Circle, in the middle weeks of the six-month darkness of winter, the freezing northern night.

That year, the year of my first birthday, we lived in an Air Force compound on the outer edge of the Seward Peninsula, facing the Bering Strait, the small channel of water separating Alaska from Siberia. We were sequestered together with several other civilian families in a barracks — a small, sealed group of supply-cluttered rooms and passageways, really — battened against icy winds and the always possible and now unwanted communications from the increasingly difficult and unpredictable former allies so close to us across the face of the ice. Obviously this was a remote duty post, and the reason Mother and I were there at all was that my father had left the Air Force. He and a pair of friends from a previous duty tour had mustered out together, and were trying to make a go of it as civilian employees in the hopes of starting up in the oil business.

It was my father's first separation from the service (he would re-enlist before the year was over), and the story takes place on the evening he and Mother celebrated my birthday. As he used to tell it, we were far away from anything familiar in the way of landscape or weather — though since Mother had grown up in North Dakota, she knew something about snow and ice — and all three of us were tremendously miserable, and hungry for sunlight. What remained of Father's mustering-out pay was running low, the work was grueling and paid almost nothing when expenses and bills were toted up; there wasn't anything shaking in the search for oil, and hopes were fading. He had found himself feeling sullen and uncommunicative with my mother and rather helplessly resentful of me, since I represented the weight of his responsibility, and since it seemed I did nothing but squawk all the lightless day and through what would be the night. When I had the decency to lapse into a restless and fidgety semblance of sleep, my poor mother was so exhausted and discouraged and sick of the dark that she couldn't take advantage of the lull. She'd developed a case of insomnia.

If she managed any sleep, the fleeting minute of welcome unconsciousness always gave way to the same dream, and I heard her describe it many times, growing up: she would see herself moving through a dim, pencil-drawn landscape with odd angles of illumination all around; she was always looking for something hidden in the areas of light, and then she was trying to find the light itself; it seemed to lie just beyond a big, shaded hill or promontory, and her lonely struggle had become only a matter of reaching the rounded crest, the gold glow there. But her legs were so heavy, and the dark was falling, and she always woke up before she reached the top. And of course when she awakened it was always night. Pitch dark at the windows, with the wind and the elements, and the sense of the whole world as being hugely indifferent, a planet, an alien surface, tossed by solar storms. Sometimes she woke in different rooms, for the dream made her sleepwalk, and one night she found herself in the common kitchen she and my father shared with his two friends and their wives.

It was out of restless, middle-of-the-night despair that she decided to have a big celebration for my first birthday.

She brought out the ingredients to make a cake, and got started right away. When the others woke, they joined in. No one noticed that she was in the throes of a sort of hysterical spell. They all worked together making bunting and decorating the room; they laughed and had a few drinks as the day went on, the party was given as planned, and at the end of the whole thing my parents had their quarrel — just the kind of near-pathological altercation between young marrieds that makes for funny stories years later. When it was over, out of all the pent-up frustration, my father put his fist through a glass pane in the kitchen supply cabinet, breaking two glasses inside with the same blow, and then, bleeding from a cut on his hand, destroyed what was left of the birthday cake and pulled down all the decorations. My mother fainted dead away on the couch, and when she woke some moments later, she said she had been dreaming of the light again. To everyone's astonishment, she had only a disconnected and scanty recollection of the entire day.

Father took home movies of the birthday party (he was always taking home movies in my early childhood), and it will doubtless be no surprise to anyone that I'm in possession of the film. I've even watched it from time to time, having inherited my father's old archival sense. I set it all up and take my place in the chair by the door; the projector clicks with its small procedural sound, pulling the black strip into the machine, and the sudden light on the wall yields up the two young people who were my parents. They set me down in the middle of a woven area rug on a spread-out bedsheet, alone with the big chocolate cake Mother had put together from scratch with such suicidal meticulousness, in what would be the normal middle of the night. I am in focus; my mother and father move in and out, a blur. But then for a flickering instant, they stand side by side, flanking me: Daniel and Connie with their baby boy, Thomas. There are the two other young couples present, with children of their own, and we catch brief glimpses of these friends — a quiet little party in Air Force housing with snow flying at the dark windows. Everyone is happy. It's impossible to believe that a domestic squabble is looming or that anyone is suffering, though in fact it's also hard to think of the scene itself as in any way domestic, even with the decorations and the smiles.

Because what one knows, looking at these youthful people, is that out in the vast, windy spaces, beyond the iced-over windows with their puny decorations in honor of an infant, the world is still reeling from the ravages of the most terrible catastrophe in its history. It shows in the something almost hurried about every gesture they make, as though they have become accustomed to the belief that they might not get the chance to continue. The hilarity is somehow desperate. And, having studied the film, I believe I can see even more than that: remembering my father's voice as he told the story, and looking at everyone in the scene, it's also readily apparent that they have set out on a venture together, an all-out attempt to score big, to pull something out of the ruin and make the future somehow safer for themselves than for everyone else they have known, and this feeling is colored by what they have seen and been through and feared. It is a venture that has already begun killing the light in their hearts, and without having admitted it to each other or even to themselves yet, they have all started gearing up their courage for the failure that is under way, a failure which — according to my memory of the way Father talked about that time — they will all remember fondly anyhow, since it happened when they were young and foolish and resilient.

"This was back when we tried to make a go of it in the oil business," he would say. I can almost hear him when I run the film, watching the faces smile and mug and look away, and now the camera returns to the baby, one year old, sitting on what looks like a patch of glossy, wrinkled snow in that room with cinderblock walls, his short, fat legs stretched out on either side of the enormous cake. The chubby, puffy-faced baby I was gazes at this mountainous confection with obvious puzzlement, to have been so blithely placed in its vicinity. Tentatively he reaches over and puts his hands to one ledge of it as though to test what the reaction might be. Now he's got some of the icing on his fingers, and he looks around in the false brightness, wondering why no one has tried to dissuade him from such messy curiosity. Gradually he gains the courage to stick one finger into the top of the cake, like Jack Horner in knitted blue boots and denim overalls. Instead of a plum, he pulls out a dollop of custard and for a moment applies it to his face, like a little clown putting on the greasepaint. Then he laughs the silent laugh of old home movies. The image flickers briefly, and he's eating the cake now, and soon he's attacking it. The tiers collapse on themselves, and crumble. He pulls one side of it apart. And a slender brown arm comes down into the picture to push the hair out of his eyes: the camera moves up the body of my mother, and there, in perfect focus for the first time, is her face. For those few seconds she stares right at you, and her clear eyes grow infinitesimally more focused with something, they narrow and seem darker, with concentration or memory — or perhaps it is just that something is being said to her.

Then the film flashes white, and we are elsewhere. It's snowing; it's some other place and the baby is older, more aware of the camera. He's wearing a miniature parka with the hood pulled tight around his face. He simply stares back.

The fact is, my father liked showing these movies as much as he liked making them, and whenever a visitor expressed even mild curiosity about Alaska, or about any of the other unusual and distant places to which his duty tours had taken him, he would almost invariably bring the conversation around to the subject of home movies. It never took more than the faintest suggestion to prompt him, and with disarming tentativeness — the kind that extracted polite, if feeble, encouragement from his embarrassed victims — he'd haul everything out. Soon the living room of whatever place we then occupied would be darkened, one white wall glimmering with images of what he had deemed worth recording for our future.

When I was old enough to understand some of the talk among the adults, and came to know the story of the birthday party fight, I recall being vaguely disturbed by it, even though it was a thing my parents had obviously got far beyond, and could laugh about with perfect ease. (Their attitude about the whole affair was almost sociological, even as they teased and chided each other and remembered; it was part of the lore between them, a perfect example of what was always understood as Father's unpredictable temper, his tendency to rage at inanimate objects when he was angry, especially when Mother was the one who caused the anger.) Even so, I remember being obscurely sorry for the baby in the grainy home movie, who must have seen something terrible: his parents screaming at each other, his big scary father destroying what was left of his half-eaten cake.

My parents had no precise memory of what had set them off, and this was always one of the more charming features of the story; they joked and goaded and recalled other fights; they were tempestuous, always going off the deep end with each other. Amid other adults, they assumed a kind of mantle: the stormy lovers. Except that this was also what they believed about themselves: they were passionate about each other, always on each other's mind. I remember sensing that the tumult which was on the other side of the whiteness of the film running out had never been quite contained. And when everything began to change for us as a family — that is, when our own peculiar history became drastic — I believe some part of me, however wrongly, felt a sort of recognition about it all, as if it had happened before, or was something I had been waiting for.

My father was sent to prison in the late spring of 1967, when I was seventeen. A military court sentenced him to two years at hard labor for stealing, and then trying to sell for profit, an electric typewriter. They remanded him to Wilson Creek, Wyoming, to the federal penitentiary there, because he was a career man in the Air Force, and the typewriter was government property. It was one of those new, sleek, expensive ones with a rotating ball instead of keys. His plan was to use the cash it brought him to pay a pressing debt — or I should say many pressing debts. He had been writing bad checks, and was trying to cover himself. He must've thought he could find a way to redeem everything, save his skin, get the typewriter back before anyone noticed it was gone. But an airman, some nervous boy fresh out of technical training school, saw him putting the typewriter into the trunk of his car, and reported him to the military police. When my father tried to sell the thing, they were watching him; they had already begun gathering the evidence they would need to prosecute him for the bad checks.

And they did prosecute, to the fullest extent of the law, though he was a good worker, a "lifer" as all the boys who had enlisted to avoid the draft called them back then, a faithful and decorated veteran of the dirty little war that was in progress on the other side of the world. (I had only recently learned about that use of the term "lifer," because Father never used it. Just before he was arrested, I had begun to spend time with a couple of the young men he supervised all day in the parachute shop, and they said the word a lot; it was not always with derision that they used it, either. More often than not it was simply descriptive, as in, "Tom's dad's a good lifer. Old Sergeant Bullock is a bad one.")

I grew up on Air Force bases. When my father met my mother in

April of 1948, he had already served two years with the Army Air
Corps, as it was called then. The Corps was in a sense his only family.
The year before he enlisted, he'd lost both parents — his father in an
automobile accident at the main intersection of the little Texas town
where he was born and raised, and his mother, through alcoholic
poisoning, a little more than a month later. He was the only child, and
he had no cousins, uncles, or aunts — at least none who would speak
to him. When he told my mother about all this, he took the trouble to
mention that his parents' deaths were not actually related: his mother's
alcoholism had been a recurring problem in the years of his growing
up; it was one of the reasons his father tried to join the Navy at the age
of forty-six; and it was the reason there were uncles and cousins and
aunts who had long refused to have any truck with that branch of the
family. Also, it was why my father seldom had anything stronger than
iced tea to drink. Mother liked the serious way he explained these
difficult facts, and she would talk about how even then she could tell
that he was, in her words, "true blue." She would also say with a
peculiarly serene smile that he was what she hadn't known she was
looking for.

They met while he was on a temporary duty assignment at Minot
Air Force Base in North Dakota. She was home for spring break, after
her second semester away, feeling restless and bored, and discovering
how desperately she did not want to return to the small New England
women's college to which her father had sent her. Her father, William
Tinan, was a federal judge who had often been touted for a run at the
state house. Until she met Daniel Boudreaux she had been in every
sense the judge's daughter, living in a big white house on a quiet street
in the center of town, calling the old man Daddy; there was a coquettish debutante's flair about her when she was with him, like a kind of
cynical flirtation, according to my father. But the story was Mother's,
really, and in her version Father was the enticing and mysterious
stranger at the gates, the dangerous young man with the French-Cana-
dian forbears, the pretty uniform, and the sea-dark eyes — the man
from distances, in possession of a smile that could change the way
blood flowed in your veins. The story is commonplace enough: the
overbearing judge bars the young man from ever coming to the house,
and so of course at the first opportunity the restless daughter runs

away. Mother loved to tell the story, right down to the ladder at the window and the car speeding off into the frosty night. The facts, though, were that she told Grandfather she was going out to a movie; she met my father at the south gate of Minot, and they took the train south. They were married in St. Louis, and soon afterward my father got sent to Japan for a year. Mother was pregnant with me, and was planning to stay in St. Louis, and while relations with the judge were smoothed over in the end — this with the inestimable help of my unexpected early arrival, and the ambassadorship of my aunt Elaine — things were never quite as they had been. I was born while Mother was living in her old room upstairs in the big white house, and so for the few months until my father's return, Grandfather Tinan had a squawking baby in the rooms to remind him.

When Father did come home, it was with plans to use his mustering-out pay to get a start in Anchorage, and thus we began our nomadic life together. If my first memories all include snow, there are also images of rooms piled high with boxes, and of strange landscapes gliding by out the windows of automobiles or trains. I remember making the erroneous assumption that everyone lived as we did, traveling from place to place, always talking about the next assignment, the next housing arrangement, though the houses were always similar and the bases were enough alike to provide a meager sort of continuity.

By the time I entered my teens, we had stood in extremes of weather in several far-flung parts of the continent, sometimes within a matter of weeks, and it seems to me now, looking back on it all, that there was always a faint sense of unreality about the daily business of the living we did, even before my father was court-martialed — though I admit the very real possibility that I could be supplying this feeling from the point of view of hindsight.

The fact is, my memory is so randomly concrete that I tend to trust its more visceral impressions. (I remember the detergent and coal-steam smell of the base laundry on icy winter evenings, and I remember breathing that same odor in the heat of a southern California noon — and thinking about how it was the middle of December. No event or series of events connects to this memory, and yet it has the power to take my breath away for its sudden visitations, like the product of

some retention in the nerves, separate from volition or simple recollection.) For us, the seasons were without much definition or meaning,
and we lived in a kind of pause, waiting for the next change. We had
been all over the country in one- to three-year stints, and my father had
served brief tours in Europe, and Korea, and in Vietnam (he was one of
the earliest to have been wounded in that conflict; John Kennedy was
still alive at the time).

In 1967, we were stationed at Andrews Air Force Base in Maryland,
rather luxuriously housed in married officers' quarters because of a
shortage of housing for married enlisted men. Plush digs indeed: tall
ceilings, spacious rooms, skylights, central air conditioning, nooks and
crannies everywhere, and — a favorite feature of my younger sister
Lisa's and mine — an intercom in the walls. When our parents were
out and I was left alone with her, I sometimes entertained her by
playing games with the intercom, speaking to her in a stentorian voice
from the farthest reaches of the house, pretending to be the soul of the
building itself or of a specific room, demanding that she come clean
me. I'd hear her piercing laugh ringing in the walls. We played hide and
seek with it, too, calling back and forth to each other.

Sometimes the adults argued or had one of their fights from separate
rooms, pushing the buttons and shouting at each other. More often
they teased that way, and it sounded like fighting.

I don't recollect a single argument, not one, teasing or otherwise,
having to do with money.

Although the amounts of the bad checks my father wrote were not
terribly serious, and there was evidence of his sincere, if cockeyed,
intention to somehow buy back the typewriter and return it, the Air
Force handed him a dishonorable discharge along with the prison
term. They wanted to make an example of him for others who might
be tempted to stretch the rules of possession, the customs of deposit
and withdrawal — and never mind that he hadn't actually tried to
defraud anyone (at least not permanently), but only to give himself
time to catch up with his payments.

I say all this not to mitigate what he did — for the law was broken, a
typewriter was removed surreptitiously with the clear aim of selling it,
and checks were written on ghost accounts (or, rather, on accounts
whose balances were all the result of bad checks drawn on still *other*

accounts, everything floating back and forth between three different institutions, as a way of stalling the inevitable, and of course any fool could see where it was all leading) — I mention these things not to excuse my father, but so that you may know something about him: he was not really a criminal in the usual sense of the word. He was a man capable of deluding himself, of misbelieving the evidence of his own eyes, and as such, you might think that he was not very different from the rest of us.

At least I hope you might.

At the time he was arrested, the situation between us — the two of us — was fairly complicated, though on the surface it probably won't sound that way. Just reciting it aloud makes me cringe slightly, since it *is* so familiar, yet you must know that at the time it was new: to me then, as I was then, it might as well have been occult. He had wanted me to play baseball, and had even talked about college scholarships and the minor leagues, but I was in the process of leaving baseball behind, trying to learn how to play electric guitar (at which, incidentally, I had no talent whatsoever) and letting my hair grow. I had been attempting to form a band with some boys at school, and failing that, had discovered that two of the airmen who worked with my father in the base parachute shop liked to play. I saw them perform at a USO dance in the local high school gymnasium, and waited to talk to them, having recognized them from the several times I had accompanied my father to work. They were good enough on their instruments, and they took an interest in me which I chose to believe was purely because of my musicianship. We took to meeting at the band hall of squadron headquarters in the evenings to jam and, because none of us was interested in covering other people's songs, to try writing some ourselves. These sessions aggravated the already deep tension between my father and me about other things, most notably the baseball, for which, I must admit with all modesty, I did have a certain aptitude. What he couldn't or wouldn't understand was that I'd never had more than a superficial interest in the sport. It had been merely something I did to fill time on summer days, and, when he was home, to be with him.

The year before he was arrested, I had led the sixteen-year-olds to their second straight county championship, and then quit as they were getting ready to compete for the state finals. He was on temporary duty in Florida, and I was tired of the grind. I didn't even like winning the games, since that was simply a matter of continuing to throw the ball with frightening velocity past the crouched, wide-eyed opposing batters, most of whom were unlucky enough to be smaller than I was. I had piled up a boring number of strikeouts because a lot of these boys would swing at anything, just wanting not to get beaned. I imagined that a lot of them didn't like baseball either. Baseball was a thing you did if you were an American boy on a military base, or else you got branded.

In any case, that early spring — the spring of 1967, with its air of rebellion and upheaval — I was in the process of throwing off the requirement that I play a game I didn't like, while my father was transforming himself from a fairly unpredictable and humorous man with a penchant for story-telling, a gregarious spirit, and a grandiose temper, into a dour, monosyllabic ramrod with a crew cut and an overzealous belief in discipline and order. The conflict went all the way to the forms of address: I had begun to feel that his regulation that we address him and my mother with the terms "Father" and "Mother" rather than the more familiar "Dad" and "Mom" was a pointless thing, not to say a kind of affectation, and I had taken to slipping every now and then into the simpler expressions. His attitude about these "slips" on my part was pained (it wasn't until I saw his reaction to Mother's calling Grandfather Tinan "Daddy" that I understood where it had all come from), and then it was simply unreasonable: he made demands; he insisted; he issued ultimatums and withheld privileges until the battle was won. He had been home from the war more than three years, and for such a long time after his return he'd seemed glad of us, appreciative, in fact, almost supernally grateful about everything — like someone freshly awakened from horrible nightmares — and so this change in him was puzzling. Over the years I have come to believe that the sense he must've had that his trouble was growing unmanageable could have undermined him, along with the memory of what he'd been through in Vietnam and the growing perception, nearly inescapable by 1967, that all of it counted for nothing. I'm certain he saw manifestations in me of a process he'd wanted to stop, of the old understandable world getting away from him, and perhaps this had

brought him to the point of some half-conscious effort to fend everything off: if he could just be a good enough sergeant, and a strong
enough father, maybe his troubles would stand still a while, and maybe
the authorities would let him alone.

They didn't.

One night in May, only hours after he'd hocked the typewriter at a
pawnshop off base, they came to our house at the end of a row of
officers' houses just inside the main gate, and with the dispassionate,
purposeful demeanor of people who know they have their man, hand-
cuffed him and took him away. It took less than a minute to accom-
plish, and to me it seemed terrifyingly like one of those awful historical
spasms I had been reading about in school — visits in the middle of the
night from minions of the Reich, Stalin's purges — as if the country in
whose freedoms and under whose protection we had so complacently
lived all these years had gone suddenly berserk.

As you might've guessed, the men who did the arresting — three
MPs in shiny white helmets, dress blues, and boots — were not very
expressive or careful of our feelings. It was as though we were all
guilty. They knocked on the door, and when my father opened it, they
grabbed him and put the cuffs on him.

"What in God's name," my mother cried. "What do you think
you're doing?"

"He's under arrest," the first MP, the one with the cuffs, said. "Back
off."

"You can't do this," she said. "Who do you think we are."

"Wait a minute," said my father. "Can't you let me get some things
to take with me? We're just going to have to pick them up later."

But they were already walking him out to the street, where they had
parked the dark blue van with the screened back windows, that polished and now appallingly serviceable vehicle I had seen cruising along
the base perimeter like a part of the scenery of my life. It was dusk. The
twilight was beyond them, so they were one struggling shadow. People
in the neighborhood were beginning to turn lights on. The van was
partway up on the curb along the front of the house, as if in their sense
of mission the MPs had nearly crashed it. My father went peaceably
enough, without saying any more, and even so they half carried him as
if he were one of those sad, dignified, and incongruously docile civil
rights protesters we had been seeing on the television news.

"Mommie," my sister cried, standing in the middle of that elegant, high-ceilinged living room, wailing, helpless, and in the throes of a tantrum, since that was the only way she could get the attention she needed at such a time. I watched out the big picture window as they all climbed into the van, and Mother ranted and shouted at them from the yard. They seemed bent on ignoring her. Or no, it was really as if they simply didn't hear her. They closed the back of the van on my father, then got into the front and drove away, and she remained where she was, at the edge of the lawn, her hands on her hips — a woman waiting for an explanation she has demanded of someone. Then she turned and came inside and, scooping Lisa up, carried her into the bedroom. "Thomas," she said to me, "please make a sandwich for yourself." There were tears in her voice. She closed the door. "Hush," I heard her say to my sister, who kept up a shrill keening. "Hush."

"Dad-eee," Lisa cried.

I went into the kitchen and sat at the table, thinking about Russia and the enslaved countries of the East, those films of the pathetic little villages of Europe when the Nazis marched through them. Our house had been violated. I sat there, alone in the light, hearing sirens far off, Lisa's cries from the other room, and all my outraged meditations gradually shifted to an idle, unbidden reverie about writing a protest song and becoming a rock star at my young age, the same age as the dark-eyed, eccentric Janis Ian, with her weepy lyric about a white girl in love with a Negro.

To be entertaining fantasies about rock stardom at such a time says something about what sort of boy I was, I suppose: without being quite ready for the feeling, I found that I was partly glad of the situation, relieved to have trouble that would put him at a distance from me. Life had been difficult; because I just didn't have it in me to, I couldn't please him. Because he didn't have it in *him* to, he couldn't accept me as I was, and again this is all quite ordinary and easily explained. Now. But I don't mean it to sound glib, because it is important that you understand something else: unlike so many of the people in the stories of conflict between fathers and sons, we happened to like each other, very much.

Oh, we had the family devotion, the love — that blood-simple feeling of connection that everyone has, even when there is great pain and anger — but we had been friendly, too. I had always looked forward to being with him, not just because he was my father and I looked up to him, but because he was fun to be with, and clearly enjoyed being with me. He had got himself in deep with credit cards and loans, buying clothes and jewelry for Mother, buying the fast little red Corvette they drove, taking all of us to the wilderness near Anchorage and to the Grand Canyon, and taking Mother to the Caribbean, and out of the wonderful times we enjoyed together had come this period of our lives during which he began coming down hard on me for what seemed the smallest reasons.

One instance of this seems important enough to set down here, given that it happened within a couple of months of the arrest, and it may also serve to illustrate something of my own attitude at the time. As I've said, I had been playing music with two of the young airmen who worked in my father's shop, but I hadn't told him about it — indeed, I'd worried about what he might say when he did find out, as of course he inevitably would. There had already been some tension over the music I was listening to. I'd built up a collection of records, some of them suggested by the two airmen (exactly what you'd expect, too: Beatles, Stones, Dylan, Lovin' Spoonful), and I had just come home with several new ones. I was putting them among the others, rearranging things, setting them alphabetically, side by side on a shelf in my room, having been, from babyhood, the sort who needed to have things ordered, manageable. It was just past dark. Mother had treated us to hamburgers at the local Burger Chef, and then she had taken Lisa with her and driven to the PX to get cigarettes and beer. Father came into the house and along the hallway to the entrance of my room, still carrying his satchel from work. When I saw this, I knew there was trouble.

"I'd like to know why I have to find out from *them* that you're fooling around with guys that work for me when you go to the band hall in the evenings."

I had half expected this confrontation for weeks, and even so I was caught off guard. I tried a lie. "Didn't I tell you about it?" I said.

He took a step toward me. "Don't insult me with that — that —"

"Okay," I said. "I'm sorry." And now I felt ashamed. I had one of those sudden moments of revelatory clarity: something had changed between us, something so profound as to make me feel that I had to act to protect his feelings. I felt weirdly sorry for him.

"Why, son?"

"I don't know," I told him. And the truth was I didn't know, beyond the fact that lately I had been finding it hard to tell him anything at all.

"What's that?" he asked, stepping toward me a little, looking at the record I was holding in my hands.

"It's a record."

He glared not at me but at it. "I can see that. Who's the longhair on the cover?"

"What's the difference," I said.

He looked at the room, at the pictures I'd hung up along with the ones for which he and I had posed over the years — glossy magazine photographs of Ginsberg and Kerouac; of Marilyn Monroe and Bob Dylan, Gandhi and Robert Kennedy and the Beatles. In the center of the wall was a big drugstore poster I had bought, a print from a painting: a series of letters made up of flowers, spelling out the phrase FLOWER POWER. "What the hell do you think you're doing, anyway?" my father said. "Who do you think you are? This is an Air Force base. That big noise you hear every night is fighter planes and bombers going over. Those are B-52s heading off into the sunrise every morning. You know what they have in them?"

I said nothing.

"Do you hear me?" he said, putting the satchel on my dresser. "Don't just stand there."

"What do you want me to do?" I said.

"Don't take that tone of voice with me," he said.

I was silent.

"Who do you think you are, talking to me like that?"

"I didn't mean anything," I said.

"Flower power. Jesus. What is this — what're you supposed to be, some kind of hippie or something? You gonna protest the war? Is that it? I was in this war, and I'll probably wind up in it again. There's men dying in those rice paddies, boy. And flower power isn't what's going on over there, you know? It doesn't have anything to do with what's going on over there."

"It's what's going on over here," I told him.

He took a breath. It was almost as if I'd struck him.

"I want to write music," I said, feeling that I had got through to him — and it seems worth the risk of repeating myself to say that, even in his bad time, as his troubles were catching up to him, even then, and even when his temper was up, this was often the sense you had when you were with him: that you could get through to him, you could make him see what you felt.

"Music," he said. "You call this stuff music?"

"It's music," I said.

"It's noise."

"To some people."

"I don't like that tone of voice," he said. "That superior tone of voice. You sound like *them*."

"Them." I honestly didn't understand him.

"The boys in the shop — that you've been hanging around with behind my goddam back."

"No," I said. But it was true. It was exactly true.

"What did you think I'd say when I found out?" he asked.

I took a moment to answer, and when I did it was in a voice I realized was sullen, and wished I could've controlled better. "I knew you wouldn't understand."

"Maybe I'll take the guitar away." He seemed actually to be considering this, thinking aloud.

"Why," I said. "Just because I don't want to play baseball? Just because I'm not the stereotype of an Air Force kid?" I was now mouthing the words I had heard from the two airmen, who had praised me shamelessly to my face, telling me how unique, how original and intellectually insightful I was for someone my age. They were both twenty-two. Grown men in my mind, and I looked up to them the way I now know my father must have been hurt to think I no longer looked up to him.

"A stereotype," he said. And then he shouted. "A goddam stereotype!"

"I just mean I'm not gung ho," I told him.

"Not gung ho. Suppose you tell me with your long hair and your beads just what the hell you think gung ho is. I'm standing here with more than twenty years in the Air Force, and I want to hear you say it."

"I'm not in the Air Force," I said. "I don't see why I have to live like I am."

"Christ, listen to you." He took the record from me, then moved to the shelf, and with a dismissive sound in the back of his throat let it drop to the floor. He was looking at the other records now, muttering the titles, the names. "Jesus. What is this? What in the hell is going on, anyway?" Then he reached in and gathered a bunch of them and turned, not looking at me, starting out of the room.

"What did I do?" I said.

"I'm not going to stand for this kind of thing," he said.

I followed him out to the living room.

"Open the door," he said. He was standing there with an armful of my music, and some of the disks were showing, about to drop from the sleeves. "Come on, open it."

"What're you doing?"

"Watch," he said, and let everything drop. It all clattered at his feet.

"Those are mine," I said to him, beginning to cry, despising myself for showing this weakness. "It's not fair."

"Get out," he said. "Get out of here." His lips were white. I think now that he must have hated the sight of me in that moment, standing there before him, crying like a baby. "Go on," he said. "Get out."

I went past him, and his hand came up against the back of my head, a cuffing motion, no rougher than his play had been in the easier times between us, but it might as well have been a blunt instrument. I was humiliated, and I stood out in the moist grass that warm, humid night, hating him with all my soul, watching as he sailed my records into the dark.

"This is what I think of the goddam music," he said, and *Revolver* made its saucerlike journey toward the stars. I stood watching him, the tears burning in my eyes. Even if they guaranteed me a plaque in the baseball Hall of Fame next to the beloved and recently inducted Ted Williams, I would never pick up a baseball again.

My mother stopped the whole thing by arriving from the PX with Lisa. She parked the car along the curb, shut it off, got out, and helped Lisa out. My father and I watched them, waited while they started up the walk, slowing a little as they saw us and all the records lying around, gleaming under the moon like perfectly round puddles of oil in the dim yard.

"What's this?" Mother said.

Lisa said, "Records."

I stood straight, with the eloquent silence of the persecuted. I may have even extended my arms slightly.

"It's nothing," my father said. "Go on inside."

"What're you doing, Daniel?"

"I told you to go on inside. This is between me and the boy."

"This one's broken," said Lisa, bending to look at it. Mother pulled her arm to straighten her. "The grass is wet, too."

"Will you get her inside?" my father said.

Mother was quiet a moment, and I could feel her eyes on me. "Are these Thomas's records?"

Silence.

"Daniel, will you answer me?"

"This is between me and the boy," my father said.

She said, "What is." There was no question in it, but she was clearly waiting for an answer.

"Connie, I said it's between me and the boy."

I turned and walked away.

"Thomas, where are you going?"

"Let him go," my father said. Then he went inside and slammed the door.

"Tommy?" my mother called.

"I hate him," I called back. I wanted to be far away from them both, knowing that she would demand to know what he had been thinking of, knowing that he would defend himself and yet knowing, too — because I had heard the unmistakable note of it in his voice — that he was already sorry.

I stayed away a couple of hours, wandering around the base, which was really like walking the streets of a small town except that the monuments and public art were all martial and imposing: sleek fighter jets on pedestals, in bold attitudes of flight, and the gargantuan B-29 with its crane-supported wings and its silver plaque explaining that this was a prototype of the plane which had dropped the atom bombs on Japan, the whole thing occupying a field nearly the size of a baseball diamond. I went past all this — it was the kind of scenery I had grown up with — and wound up at the Airmen's Club, a low-to-the-ground, institutional-looking brick building with bright wings painted on the façade above the doors and the odor about it, no matter the season or the weather, of cooking meat. I suppose I wanted to see if I could run into the two young men whose friendship was the cause of all my trouble. But they weren't there. The place was almost empty. Two shave-heads (our name for new airmen fresh from basic training) sat in the gloom of the bar, swilling beer and talking about home. I made my unpremeditated way over to the grounds beyond the physical plant, where one could lie down in the grass and watch the fighters that periodically lifted off the flight line, making their roaring ascent into the moonlit clouds. When I got home, the record albums were gone from the yard, and my mother was sitting in the kitchen drinking coffee. "He's gone to sleep," she said. "I'm afraid your records were all kind of wrecked. I have them in the garage, so you can go through them if you want."

"No." I felt sick. There was something so matter-of-fact about the way she dealt with such trouble.

"So," she said after a moment.

"I didn't go anywhere," I said.

"All right."

"I'm going to bed."

"You have to try and understand your father," she said. "He's a person, too. He can be hurt, like anybody else."

I was silent. My expression spoke for me.

"Well," she said, rising, "there's no kindness in expecting perfection." Then she kissed me on the cheek and left me there.

I went to my room and lay on my bed in the dark, hearing their muffled talk on the other side of the wall. I could tell she was using her low, soothing voice, and then I heard Lisa, too. Lisa laughed. They were in there with her, and it seemed that my troubles had been forgotten in the charms of the little girl. I looked at my decimated shelves, and then decided to make a point of my own. I put on the one Beatles album I had left, just loud enough for them to hear the drums and the bass — I admit I lacked the courage to put it any higher than that. I was sure they could hear it, and I was sure it would remind my father of what he had done.

The following afternoon, I came home to find that the damaged records had been replaced, doubtless through the spending of more money my father didn't have, though I hadn't the slightest notion of such things then. I never questioned it at all, in fact. And my father and I spoke of it only once.

Or, rather, we spoke around it. This couldn't have been more than a couple of weeks after our argument. I was lying on my bed reading a magazine, having just got home from school, when he walked in, opening the door as he knocked. He was wearing his uniform. His hair was cut short, shorter than he ever wore it. He had no sideburns at all. He sat on the edge of my bed and put his rough brown hand on my knee. "What're you reading?" he said.

I held the magazine up — one of those cheap comic songbooks with lyrics; it had a lead article about the new *Sgt. Pepper's* album. The article asserted that there were secret codes and messages in the design of the album front: government forces were being marshaled against the young. He took the magazine and flipped the pages, like someone looking for an insert, then he put it back on the bed at my side. "Listen," he said. "When you — when the boys and you have these music — these sessions. Do they ever mention me?"

I told him the truth. "Once," I said.

He waited.

"They said they think you're not like the other lifers."

"Lifers."

I nodded.

"Well," he said, looking down.

"I think they admire you," I had the perception, and the presence of mind, to say. It was, I knew, the truth — a sort of truth, since all of the younger airmen's opinions were colored by their inability to understand why anyone would want to remain in the military for a lifetime.

He was shrewd enough to take it that way. "Right," he said. "I'm an exception to the general rule that all lifers are messed up."

I didn't say anything.

He picked up the magazine and looked at the cover, the *Sgt. Pepper's* album front. "You have this record, don't you."

I nodded.

"I mean you have it *again*," he said, and smiled.

Then my mother's voice came to us — she was talking to my sister about something. He looked at the door of the room, as if expecting her to come through it, and I saw something dreamy and boyish in his face. It was a familiar expression, yet I had never quite seen it this way before. I knew he wanted to say something to me, that he couldn't find the way to begin, and in that expression there was something faintly demoralized. I can't explain this any more precisely, though I suppose I can add that in retrospect I saw something profoundly lonely about it, too. Abruptly I felt sorry for him again, and I tried to break the spell by pretending to cough into my hands.

"Okay," he said. "Well." And he stood.

"It's just a dumb magazine," I said.

He smiled a little. "It's probably got some interesting stuff in it."

"Not really." I dropped it on the bed.

"Well." He turned.

"Thanks, Dad," I told him.

He shook his head, rubbed the bare back of his scalp. "No need for that," he said. Then he opened the door and was gone.

And so I hid from myself the sense of relief that he was out of the stream of my life. I shook off the daydreams about rock stardom and set about trying to make things easier for my mother. Over the next few days, as the magnitude of the trouble became known to us, I learned to repeat her complaints about the unfairness of treating a man that way, for one mistake and after almost two decades of dedicated service. (But of course it was more than one mistake, for the bad checks and the theft made a pattern he had fallen into over many months. It was more like a failing, said the lawyer in his request for the court to show mercy on a proven hero of the strife in Vietnam.)

But the war wasn't quite as unpopular in 1967 — at least in the military — as it was about to become, soon enough. The men in charge had yet to reach that point of needing to highlight the smallest glimmer of heroics: Tet was still a year away. And questions of public relations regarding the war notwithstanding, in the minds of the presiding court-martial officers, the good feeling between the base and the town — where several of my father's bad checks had come to rest — was more at issue.

The trial took less than a week. My father was found guilty and then fell silent, sitting upright in his chair like someone at perpetual atten-tion while the proceedings went on around him. I couldn't bear to see the hurt, attentive expression on his face, and I spent much of that time in my room at the house — the nice officers' quarters we would all have to leave soon. I would spend hours sitting up in the middle of my bed, staring at the other pictures on my walls, the ones of him and me in various poses of recreation and comradeship: father and son with fish; father and son with basketball; father and son in the uniform shirts of Little League baseball; father and son with trophies, with gear, in boats, on horseback, or standing at the entrance of a camp tent. I gazed at this record of my life with him, wondering at myself, at the strange emptiness I felt.

It was now impossible to keep playing music with the fellows in the parachute shop, and yet I missed it, and wished for some pretext through which I might be allowed to continue. I would catch myself meditating over the possibilities, thinking of leaving the family and going off alone to be a stranger somewhere. Entertaining this vague daydream, I would sit with the guitar across my leg and stare into the sound hole, playing two chords over and over, E major and A minor, in the same drumlike rhythm.

"What're you doing?" my mother said. "How can you stand that. Don't you feel anything? How can you play guitar now, anyway?"

"I wasn't playing," I said.

"Please stop. Please try to think of someone other than yourself."

"I wasn't thinking of myself."

"Okay, well shut up. Try that."

"I was just answering you," I said.

The fact was I didn't feel much of anything very cleanly or purely, if that makes any sense. It was as if I had been churned up inside, so that all my emotions were colored with one another and had become one muddy shade. None of it was quite real. Yet I knew what I was supposed to be feeling, and the difference had made me sulky.

"I need you to help out here," my mother said. "I can't go through this by myself. I need you to help me with Lisa and pull out of yourself a little."

"I don't understand what you mean," I told her. "I'm helping."

I did understand, though. It was just that a part of me I couldn't master wanted to resist.

2

AS I SAID, the trial took less than a week. Father was pronounced guilty as charged, and sentenced, and there was a little flurry about the severity of two years at hard labor, some vague talk of an appeal. But nothing came of it, and within a month of the arrest he was on his way to Wyoming.

We said goodbye to him at the base's Flight Line Grill, which was where everyone waited for rides, or "hops" as we called them, to other bases. Pilots stopped in there for a greasy sandwich before putting in flying time. Mechanics sat around drinking coffee and smoking. Airmen from the tech training school ordered pitchers of beer. It was a small room not much bigger than a diner. A bank of windows on the other side of the counter showed the hangars and the runway, a bright blue sky with puffy little detonations of cloud in it. My father was seated with two MPs — not the same ones who had arrested him — and as we came in he waved to us, like someone waiting for people he would have lunch with. He smiled. We made our way through the crowd of tables to where he sat. He hugged Lisa and kissed the top of her head, and he looked almost happy. When he offered his hand to me, he glanced at my hair and then looked quickly away. I had put a bandanna on, the way I'd seen Dylan wear one in the magazine pictures, and even now, thinking about it, I'm appalled at the childish cruelty of the indulgence. Surely I must've known how it would make him feel.

"Thomas," he said.

My mother knelt, sniffling, and put her arms around him, and I saw the two MPs regarding her.

"Connie," he said. "Sweetheart." It seemed to me then that I had always felt a kind of blood thrill when he spoke the name. Whatever else was commanding their attention, and no matter what else happened to be unfolding around them, they had always had a way of engendering the sense that their particular intimacy was somehow different from that of anyone else. Now it made an obliterating little space around us. The MPs and the others in the room were all backdrop, and they appeared to know it; they were as still as furniture. "It'll be all right," my father said, and he looked at me over her shoulder. "You take care of them for me," he said from the back of his throat. "Do we have a deal?"

"Yes, sir," I said.

Then the spell was broken, and we watched as he and the MPs walked along the counter and out the back door into the air-rushing and engine-whirring sound of the C-47 which had pulled up to the windows. It was windy, and the spinning props made it windier, blowing the pant legs of the two men who stood gesturing to the pilot about where to turn and stop. Almost immediately four men wheeled a portable staircase to the silver fuselage with its thousand bolts and its ovoid black line of a door. For a short time the MPs and my father were obscured by the side of the building we were in, so we watched the plane. The door opened, looking as if that section of the fuselage had collapsed momentarily inward, and then several airmen emerged carrying suitcases and duffel bags. They went down the stairs and made their way toward us, and finally my father appeared from the shadow of the building, walking between the two men. He kept his eyes straight ahead, passing through the knot of airmen, who all watched him go past. He climbed the ladder, where he turned once, not quite seeing us, then was gone. We looked for him in the little row of windows, but couldn't see anything. Lisa said she saw him wave as the plane pulled away, but I doubted it. My mother wept soundlessly into a handkerchief she had crushed in one white-knuckled fist. The props made that deep whining sound of the engines cranking up, and the portable stair was pulled away. Refueling was finished. The men walked out to the other end of that concrete space and began performing their semaphoric task. The plane taxied slowly, turning, then droned on down the runway, lifting off into the blue.

One of the other airmen in the place had seen my mother's tears, and he approached us now. "Is there anything —" he began.

"You can keep away from us," Connie Tinan Boudreaux said. "The Air Force can just go to hell along with the whole goddam government of the United States."

"Yes, ma'am," he said, all umbrage and injured dignity. "Sorry." He moved off.

We had to go home and pack. The Air Force was going to pay for our move, which really meant that they chose the movers, and the days and times, and what should be boxed and what should not. My mother, talking to Aunt Elaine on the phone, said that they had sent us two mental defectives and a psychopath. She said this while the men struggled by her with boxes and furniture, sweating and cursing under their breath. One wore his hair long, with a red bandanna, and I spoke to him for a few minutes. He was standing in the yard, drinking a cold Nehi and watching the other two heft the living room sofa.

"Your mother don't like us a bit."

"She's mad at the Air Force," I said, and felt that I had given too much of us away somehow. There was in me then an infuriating need to ingratiate myself with people, especially strangers, and perhaps it had something to do with what I had been through in school during the trial.

"She's a sharp-tongued woman."

"Well," I said.

He said, "Hey. I don't mean it in no rude way."

"No," I said.

"Never mean nothing in no rude way."

"Me either," I said to him.

He looked me over. "You're a head. Right?"

"Right," I said.

He said, "Oh, wow."

"You know anything about Virginia?" I asked him.

"The person or the state?"

"Person?"

"Well, I got me a girlfriend name of Virginia. You know what to do with a girlfriend, right?" He smiled out of one side of his mouth.

"I meant the state," I said.

"Oh." He seemed almost disappointed.

"So," I said, "do you know anything about it?"

"I been there."

I waited while he drank.

"Guy picked up a hitchhiker in Virginia last week. They found him dead as a doornail by the side of the road a few miles from the Carolina border. Shot in the back of the head, man. There's a lot of rednecks in Virginia."

"I've been all over the country," I said.

He smiled. "You get to travel in the Air Force, right? Wild blue yonder and all that shit."

"I've never been to Virginia," I said.

"Lot of rednecks, man. They'll kill you quick as look at you."

I left him there, and though I had felt him to be badly exaggerating everything, I was filled with a new sense of dread regarding our move. Demera, Virginia, was a town that had just been in the newspapers for a racial conflict involving its one lake. And there was indeed also a story about an execution-style slaying, probably committed by a hitchhiker. But it was the home of a woman that Mother had gone to school with, and this person — whose name we never heard and whom we never saw, since Mother and she argued shortly after our arrival — helped get Mother a job with a savings and loan company. Of course, before we moved, there were several phone calls from Grandfather Tinan, each of which he began by adamantly insisting that he merely wanted to say hello and see how we were all doing, and each of which he ended by just as adamantly petitioning Mother to bring us back to North Dakota.

"Daddy," she'd tell him, and then her face would show her frustration at having called him that. "Look, I'll say it again, okay? This just doesn't have anything to do with my feelings about you or about Daniel or about anything that happened twenty years ago, when I was someone else and so were you. You know how I feel about you. But I have to do this alone — the children and me. Good Lord, I'm thirty-eight years old, and I think I can take care of myself. Don't be silly,"

she'd say. "You know I love you." The conversation always seemed to
circle upon itself in that way, and to be punctuated with sighs of
exasperation and fatigue, with many repetitions, with muttered apologies and tears. And then when Aunt Elaine got on the phone to talk
about coming to visit us, she would make her own attempt. "Elaine,
I've just finished going through this with Daddy. Can we please talk
about your visit? Well, that's the only way you're going to see me right
now, Elaine, by coming to Virginia."

I heard all this like background noise, sitting on a box, wrapping
dishes in newspaper or lounging among unpacked clothes on the sofa,
and I marveled at how well she kept her temper through such apparent
badgering. Sometimes she would go into her room and close the door
after these phone calls, and even Lisa knew enough not to bother her
then.

The new house was in Demera, on Mission Street, just above the
North Carolina line and only a block away from the volunteer fire
department. I'm fairly certain it was her resolve to get through the two
years on her own that made her ask for a lease that would run that
long. The property manager, a jaundiced, stooped, skeletal old man
with a lacquered-looking bald pate and dark, flat, vicious little wol-
verine's eyes, would not hear of it. "One year only," he said, offering
no explanation. Mother signed the lease and then made a gesture as of
someone swatting at an insect in the air around her face. "I do not wish
to be bothered once during the term of this agreement," she said.

"That is correct," he said.

"And I shall expect to have the chance to renew the damn lease in
one year."

"The owner may wish to sell the house."

"Then maybe I'll *buy* the damn house," she said through her teeth.

"Yes," he said, already forgetting about her. "Maybe."

For a while we were all too busy with the move to think much about
what had happened to us. We settled into a pattern of getting through
the change. Mother didn't seem willing to talk about any of it, and she
showed no anxiousness to count time down or mark off weeks on a
calendar. We got into the house and she started her job, and for weeks
we lived amid boxes, in the debris of pictures that weren't hung, of

books for which there were no shelves. She talked about the need to conserve everything, the lack of money; and she contended with us. Sometimes in that first week and a half, it seemed as though she were a widow. She was tremendously unhappy, and there wasn't any time for her to grow light of heart, even for a moment: the world had provided her with too much to worry about. We spent many nights in the sound of the television. Even during the time Aunt Elaine was with us, we kept it on — the situation comedies with their canned laughter and studied absurdity, the imbecilic game shows, and the news, with its pictures of the fighting in Vietnam and of what looked like civil war in the city streets of home. Aunt Elaine and my mother would sit in the kitchen, arguing in low voices, and between commercials Lisa and I would glare at each other almost as though in imitation.

I'm afraid we were not very pleasant people a lot of the time.

The house was a rambler, nestled in a thicket of shrubs, with a dirt-patch back yard bordered by a falling-down wood fence on three sides and a boxwood hedge on the remaining one. Two metal clothesline poles stood in the yard, the cords between them tattered and drooping, the skinny poles themselves rusted to brittleness like the bones of fossils. In one patchy corner near the back gate, there was an old sandbox with weeds growing up out of it that Lisa liked to play in. The rooms of the house were small and badly in need of paint — other people's fingerprints made dark patterns around the light switches and along the narrow corridor leading to the bedrooms — and the one bathroom was no larger than a closet. The sink in there was stained rusty, and when you turned the water on, it came in a copper trickle.

The night we moved in, I wandered from room to room looking for a door opening into something more than these tiny cratelike spaces with their warped closet doors and their smudged windows. The men hauled in the furniture while we watched, and when they brought boxes in they simply stacked them. Out in the yard, I sat on a lawn chair and tried to play guitar. The other houses were all quiet, deeply shaded by greenery, with awninged windows and closed blinds. Four teenage boys went by in a souped-up Ford; they honked at me and shouted epithets about my hair. I thought of men shot in the back of the head, and looked at the sloping green hills beyond the end of the street as if they were the terrain of another planet. Presently Mother came out and asked me to go inside and help her with some of the boxes. I stepped into the house as if ducking into a cave to hide. For all the traveling I had done in my life, I was unprepared for this feeling of having entered an alien landscape.

In the house, Lisa was playing on what would be the living room floor. I joined her there, sitting with the guitar in my lap. Clearly Lisa liked the novelty of it all and she liked the echoing sound her voice made in the rooms. She kept shouting names: Mother's, Aunt Elaine's, her own, and listening to the hollow reverberations in the walls.

"Keep it down," I said to her. "Jesus."

"I'll tell Mom you said that."

"Oh, shut up, Lisa."

I was suddenly so irritated with her that I came very close to striking her. The impulse blew through me like a storm, and it surprised and upset me. I thought of saying something to her, some soft thing, as if she had been privy to my thoughts and there were a need to reassure her, but then she smirked at me, and I left her, made my way through the men walking in and out of the place, to the hallway and the small bathroom.

There I saw my mother standing in the dim light, running the coppery water and crying. I couldn't say anything to soothe her, since I felt like crying myself. And when she saw me she shook her head as if to deny some request I had made, and closed the door.

The room I had to share with Lisa was gray, the color of an early night sky, and there were holes in the walls, bordered by lighter squares where pictures had hung; the light fixture had been removed, leaving a bare bulb, and one pane of the window was broken. A musty smell hung about the house. Now and again we would encounter the breath-stealing odor of heating oil from the rusty tank out the window. Standing in the doorway of the room, you saw part of this tank above the peeling white sill. It looked like the back end of some elephantine creature, and it partially blocked the view, not that the view was much: packed dirt and miles of marshland and sawgrass.

We had lived in small places; we had lived in places that were backed up to fetid swamps or were facing rundown streets; we had lived in row houses crowded one upon another, with dirt lawns and with windows looking out on ugly vistas of smoke and steel; we had lived in rooms with peeling paint and with faded areas on the walls and cracks in all the seams and cornices. But we had never felt the pressure of misfortune in those places, nor had we ever been faced with the sense of having been reduced to living there. I hated the house, the cramped feeling of the bedrooms, the dry, brittle leaves of the shrubbery that blocked all light from the living room windows, the tiny kitchen with its rucked linoleum and its water stains — the whole sad ramshackle place. Though I would not have expressed it in such terms, it seemed the precise picture of the misfortune that had befallen us, and when, in the evenings, after running some errand for Mother, I would see it from up the block, tucked among the other houses and lawns on that side of the street, it was not with much sense of refuge or shelter. My heart ached with the loss of my old life.

I should say something about my present circumstances. I'm in my early forties, and I live alone in a beach house toward the southern end of Asquahawk, Virginia, which is a finger-shaped island a few miles beyond the mouth of the Chesapeake Bay. The large window in my living room looks out over a sandy crescent of shoreline and a tropical-looking, palm-lined cove, with angles and edges and roofs of other houses showing through the drooping palm fronds and spiny shadows. In the summer, on cool sunny days when the breezes blow in from Newport News, the walls of the white cottages and the narrow gravel walking lanes which connect them are splashed with blue shade, and the trellises are decked with brilliant bursts of yellow and violet and lavender from the flowers the islanders cultivate at this time of year. It's a lovely place, and it would be exceedingly beautiful if the distant horizon was not perpetually serrated with the outlines of oil tankers lining up to head north, toward Annapolis and Baltimore.

I run a used bookshop in Asquahawk called Island Books. For a long time I worked as an administrator in a large public library in New York. I was married, but that has been over for some time now, and while I keep fairly regular company with a wonderful woman who lives on the other end of the island, I'll probably continue living alone. She prefers it that way, too, since she has her own business. She rents boats and bicycles to the tourists who congregate on that end of the island, where the surfing is best, and there's a boardwalk of sorts: three surf shops, a few game arcades, a bar, a palmist, and a pizza joint. Around the Fourth of July every year a carnival comes to town. For a few days the night sky is aglow beyond the trees, as if a city had sprung up in the course of a single day. And when the breezes are right, there's the fragrance of cotton candy and popcorn, and one hears the hopelessly jaunty sound of a carousel, the gear-grinding whine of a ferris wheel.

My wife, who is also a perfectly wonderful person, stayed behind in New York when I moved here, and now she lives in Boston. I hear from her occasionally, and it's always friendly. She teaches math at a college near Brockton, Massachusetts. We were married eleven years, and we had no children, which was a decision we reached by mutual consent, though my sister, who lives in Illinois now with her husband and three children, will never believe it was not something imposed on me by my wife's career aspirations: Sophie wants above all things to be a college dean.

I see Lisa every year or so, and predictably enough, her memory of the events I describe here is somewhat different. To begin with, what she does remember is sketchy and fragmentary (she was so young), and while she certainly saw enough to provide her own account of things, she has become a person whose past must necessarily conform to the notions she has embraced in the present — which is a polite way of saying that my sister has developed a capacity for self-deception in order to live her life as she thinks it ought to be lived. "Let's talk about something else," she'll say with an impatient little frown. "I never liked ancient history."

The fact is, her attitude about everything concerning her growing up, and the story I've set out to tell, is one of simple avoidance, not to say scorn. For her, it is all so far away. She's thirty-two now. When she got married, almost ten years ago, she converted to Mormonism. Her husband, Ted, is very devout — an amiable, soft-spoken man whose ability with computers is in demand, and while I have never received anything but quiet attention and kindness at his hands, I still sometimes feel as though he has taken my sister from me.

I should say something more about myself here. It must be abundantly clear by now that although I sell books, I am not even remotely comfortable with literary matters. I have never had the cheek to consider myself a writer, and I never wanted to teach, though I have always kept a journal, from which I will most likely be taking some things before I'm much further into this — whatever this is that I'm presently doing. You will doubtless be tempted to say it's a memoir, and perhaps you would be right. We don't bother to tell the stories that haven't changed us in some way, because those stories are not worth telling. But while I am not the protagonist here, I nevertheless feel the pressure to continue; the feeling is only a shade this side of desperation, in fact, because the true subject is love, at which it has always been so easy to fail. And in the telling, I am bound to go at my own pace and in my own way, since I cannot do otherwise. Even as the written sentences, one upon another, only seem to confuse me further.

Another home movie: we see a bright day on a green lawn and there are palms in the background, so this is probably southern California. He's in uniform, and she's walking around him with the camera. We know this because we can see her in certain angles of the picture window to his left, the entrance to our quarters. Curtains hang there — an odd, striped pattern, probably a holdover from previous tenants. We can be fairly confident of this because "holdovers" have been a joke in the family as long as we can remember and because in the next instant the smooth, tan slenderness of her free arm comes into the picture, points at the drapes, and makes a thumbs-down gesture. Then someone vaguely resembling me, a boy thirteen or fourteen years old, parts the curtains and looks out. His face is bunched in a frown, and he appears to be striving for a sort of sullen indolence. Then he smiles — clearly he's been told to — and the camera moves, leaves him, focusing on my father again. He's staring. His face is full of something complicated and serious. He doesn't smile. The camera keeps him framed there, and when he lifts his hand and waves, it's almost forlorn. They're talking. He shakes his head. He moves to the entrance of the place and tosses the drapes aside, obviously looking for the boy, who comes out with a wooden plaque on which ribbons and medals are fixed. The boy holds them up and now she moves the camera, trying for a closeup: boy and plaque. But then everything blurs, shifts abruptly to outside shots of the house and grounds: the palms and the beach through the blades of palm leaf, the sunny clefts and swells of sand, the front porch with its potted plants and easy chairs. Mother stands there with me, one hand on my bony shoulders and the other up to shade her eyes. Again I've got the plaque in my tight fists, and I hold it toward the camera, which seems to turn itself away precisely as a human eye might look away in embarrassment.

The plaque is something my mother put together, a collection of my father's medals for valor, for bravery, for exceeding the call of duty.

The least of his decorations, the one he would tell you he earned by accident, was the Purple Heart, which, as even I knew then, goes to everyone who suffers any injury related to duty during time of war. My father had told me that his was for a thigh wound he got while defending a Saigon restaurant from a group of attacking hoodlums. As he told it, the hoodlums were not VC, but were using the war as cover for a vendetta against the restaurant owner. "Thugs," my father said, "looking for a fight."

It had always seemed to me that at least in *his* mind the whole thing was a farce, though he had come home in a wheelchair and had spent three months in physical therapy, too, working to strengthen the damaged tendons of the leg. Anyway, he never took any of the medals very seriously. "The real worst thing that happened, even worse than my leg," he said once, "was that I got in the way of a right cross in that bar fight with the thugs. I lost a tooth on the left side, here." And he pulled at the flesh of his cheek to show me. "See? That hurt much more than the leg because that's permanent damage, and it was a punch I should've ducked. There's guys over there going through a lot more than I did, let me tell you."

I never had reason to doubt him about any of this, even after the court-martial. Yet very little of what he told me about his experience of the war was true.

In fact, the wound in the thigh would have killed him if the bullet had hit him a fraction of an inch higher, and the truth of the matter was that in Vietnam he had endured several weeks of mistreatment at the hands of a VC unit that had set upon him and the surviving members of a South Vietnamese air crew he'd been flying with as an adviser. They had developed mechanical trouble and gone down in a meadow, and they were trying to wend their way through a hellish little bend of the Ayun River. Two of their party had died in the crash, and one was badly injured. The VC came out of the woods shouting and brandishing their weapons; they shot the injured man and took the others prisoner. My father was forced to watch the execution by rifle fire of the two remaining members of the crew, and then he was the subject of several cruel experiments: he was put in a bamboo crate in the blazing sun and left there for hours on end, and he was forced to hop on his good leg until the tendons gave way. When they were not busy watching him suffer, they left him suspended in the river up to his neck, where he was fed upon by leeches and tormented by insects; and through it all he was repeatedly abused and beaten. He had received his wound while trying to run away one hot, terrible afternoon, and in fact his eventual escape had come about because his captors abandoned him, evidently deciding he was not important enough to keep. Perhaps they thought the wound would kill him before they could transport him anywhere. But, wounded, bleeding, confused, and sick, he had somehow managed to march seven miles across rough, wild terrain to get help for himself. The business about the fight in the restaurant he'd mostly made up for Lisa and me, no doubt out of the wish to protect us from the knowledge of what he had gone through (he'd lost the tooth in a fight, all right, but the opponent was a longshoreman he'd run into in a bar in San Francisco, before he ever shipped overseas).

At any rate, my mother decided we should know the truth, because it was important that we understand what kind of man he really was and what he had suffered for his country. It would make a lot of things we would have to endure less difficult to bear.

By now Lisa and I knew something of what those things were: we'd had to continue at the base schools over the roughly three weeks of Father's arrest and arraignment and court-martial, and our lives had not been easy. I suppose it's superfluous to mention that children are inclined to seize upon the differences between themselves. I learned it that spring, in spades. We'd had to endure countless jokes and taunts about being the jailbird's children, the children of a criminal, a paperhanger, a thief — the man with the shiny red car and the shiny fake checkbook. There was also the problem of the dishonorable discharge, one barren advantage of which was that we had to change schools. We had no money to speak of, and nobody Mother felt she could turn to for help. (For a while after we'd left Maryland, her sister Elaine lived with us, but she had come with a purpose, really, motives we understood without subscribing to, and in any case we were — or I should say Lisa was — far too much for Aunt Elaine, who was frightened of insects and certain amphibious creatures that Lisa had an unchecked fascination for, along with her curiosity about the gradations of fear she could cause in people much bigger than herself, simply by picking up a frog or a garden snake or a giant mantis and offering it to the subject of her experiment.) But most of what we went through in those months we went through alone, and my mother wanted us armed with the truth.

It was as hard for me to take the information that my father was a hero — a hero officially, with news clippings and a letter from the generals — as it had been difficult for me to believe the reality of the trouble when it first came to us. As it was nearly impossible now to think of him at a place like Wilson Creek, Wyoming. I saw him in stripes, in all the various poses and attitudes of convicts as I had observed them in the movies: standing in the exercise yard or working in the laundry, pacing his cell and smoking a cigarette (though my father never smoked). I couldn't make any of it quite vivid enough in my mind, couldn't make myself believe it, exactly.

But it was all true enough.

3

WE CARRY a version of our lives with us, a ghost of who we used to be, and most of the time we think we know. As I indicated earlier, I keep a journal. Indeed, from the time I was capable of the most rudimentary script, I have been an inveterate scribbler in notebooks and diaries — a facet, no doubt, of my old acquisitive habit of hanging on to mementos and keepsakes, including, among other things, ticket stubs from the movies, out-of-circulation soda pop bottles, and beer cans from defunct breweries, but that isn't exactly what I'm talking about. The truth is, I keep everything. I'm the sort of person who can't discard the scraps he may find in his pockets when he gets ready to hang his trousers up at night, the sort who's always hedging against that day when he might need something he has no present imaginable use for.

The journals I have kept, when they are not the notes of a diarist, are often in the form of plain entries — what I paid for something, or what I was given for a birthday, for Christmas — and sometimes lists of what I intend for myself in the way of self-improvement, or possessions, or schoolwork, or the spending of a summer afternoon. I have also, on occasion, come upon entries the significance or meaning of which has escaped back into the fog of old contexts.

> *Needed to get in, so used key. Left pennies in the pouch on the hook next to the door. Were there when I returned.*

The first two sentences appear to be a note to someone else (except that I know it could not have been any such thing, for I would never have showed these journals to anyone back then, and the entry is in the middle of a page of entries, dated around the time of our arrival at the Mission Street house); and even if there was any doubt about this, clearly the last sentence is a note to myself. I cannot recover even the insinuation of an idea as to what in the world I could have been talking about.

Here is another entry:

Things to work on:
  1. *Drawing*
  2. *Painting*
  3. *Dad's hat.*

The drawing and painting are self-explanatory, though I don't recall ever being much interested in either. The hat, however, what it might've been or meant, I can't begin to remember. My father wore only his uniform cap, and he hated wearing it.

But there are things the journals do call up, and many of the entries are not at all mysterious. One, dated June 1967, seems worth including here, since, looking over what I have already written, I see that so far I have concentrated almost exclusively on the arrest with its immediate aftermath, and on the trouble my father and I were having at that time. Yet for all the talk of epic quarrels and tempers, it must be clear by now that we had always been, without being particularly aware of it, quite happy together in our various houses. Here's the entry:

Aunt Elaine leaves today after two long weeks. Lisa knew what she was doing, too, no matter what she ever says. I know the little fiend. She's worse since Father left, and yet she doesn't even seem to notice he's gone. Four years ago today we went to the flight line at Andrews to meet him coming home from the war (entry for June '63). That seems like a week ago. I was so proud for not crying in front of him and so happy when he asked for a hug like always before, and how he said not to worry about the chair, that the chair wasn't permanent. It was very weird watching that stewardess bring him along the ramp, and then being asked to push him through the airport. I was surprised how heavy the chair was, and scared of it getting away from me. When we went so long without news I never thought it was anything, and couldn't imagine it, but the chair made it all real, and I felt scared, like we might lose him again. I looked at his neck and saw a little mark I never knew was there. He was holding her hand, and Lisa was riding in his lap.

Oddly enough, the entry of June '63 — the one for the day four years earlier which I described in such detail in 1967 — reads simply, *June 23, 1963. Picked Dad up at Airport. Home safe, with injuries.*

Well, he was gone again, and we were living on the outskirts of a little town in southern Virginia, far from the Air Force. The quality of our existence had changed so radically that before long we were not unlike three strangers who were forced into association with one another. And while we stayed only a matter of a month, the sort of life we lived there has some bearing on what happened later. For it's clear enough to me now that the troubles I was to be privy to, and was to make my contribution to in the months to come, were all somehow born in the solitude and loneliness we suffered during the time my mother tried to make a go of it in Virginia.

Now and again we received letters from Father, and there was also the occasional phone call they allowed him, so that at first his absence might've seemed like one of his tours of duty, except that I could hear my mother crying in the night. And the whole thing had shifted, too: I had begun to ache for him, to wish him back, to realize — or so I thought — something of the magnitude of the changes we were faced with.

It was in the first week of our being there that Aunt Elaine came to stay with us. She arrived before many of the boxes were unpacked. I was out trimming the grass that had grown over the edges of the sidewalk when she came driving up in her old green Pontiac, with its refurbished engine and its metal stripes down the middle of the trunk. She got out and looked over the roof of the car at me.

"Well?" she said.

I said, "Hello, Aunt Elaine."

"You just going to stand there?"

I put the clippers down and walked over to her.

"That's more like it," she said, putting her arms around me and crushing me to her. She smelled of talcum powder, and faintly of alcohol. Aunt Elaine drank wine with every meal but breakfast (if breakfast was late enough, she had it then, too), and I'm certain that people must have wondered about her. But I never saw her drunk, never sensed that she had in any way impaired herself. She seemed, in fact, always the same: rather abrupt and sharp, as if everything were the subject of a joke she was refraining, through good taste and discipline, from telling. Yet she was loving, and she took such huge delight in doing things for people. She was a tall woman with a boxy, square-shouldered appearance and large, round, heavy-lidded eyes which were an opaque shade of blue. When the light was wrong these pelagic-colored eyes of hers looked disturbingly like buttons, which must have upset any number of possible antagonists she had encountered in her life.

She said, "Help me get my things out of the trunk."

We stepped to the back of the car and she struggled for a moment with the key. "Moved in?" she said.

"Right," I said, with all the sarcasm I could muster.

"Are you?"

"We still have a ton of boxes and stuff."

"Well," she said, "unpack this." And she let the trunk swing open, standing back slightly. Lying across her suitcases and the pillows, sheets, and blankets she'd brought (she never traveled anywhere, not even on vacation, without her own fluffy pillows and clean cotton sheets and woolen blankets) was a new rod and reel, already assembled, and a shiny new tackle box.

I stood gazing at it all.

"Well, go ahead," she said. "Unpack it. I'm sweltering in this heat."

"Aunt Elaine —"

"Be grateful later, okay?" She reached in and lifted the rod and handed it to me. "Where's Lisa?"

"In the house," I said.

She turned then and took the house in with a look of pure dismay.

"I hate it," I muttered.

And she stirred, as if I'd startled her out of some daydream. "It's a perfectly nice little house. Go inside and tell Lisa to come out here. And hurry. I've been on the road four days. I want to get inside and wash the dust off me." Aunt Elaine was full of commands, and people were compelled to do as she asked most of the time. She had a way of calmly expecting you to follow her lead; it was almost as though she were paying you the compliment of putting her confidence in you.

I walked into the house and found Lisa picking through a box of old family photographs. Mother was sitting in the kitchen with a crossword puzzle book open before her.

"Aunt Elaine's here," I said, "and Lisa's got all the pictures out."

"Elaine?" She seemed surprised, though we had been expecting Aunt Elaine for several days now.

"Lisa's making a mess in the living room."

"Well, stop her," Mother said, rising, looking out the window. "What in the world? Go help Aunt Elaine with her things."

"I can't do two things at once," I said. I hadn't meant to sound petulant, but I heard the note of it in my own voice as she brushed past me.

"All right. Don't do anything, then."

In the living room she scolded Lisa, then walked with her outside. Aunt Elaine was standing, hands on hips, by the open trunk of the Pontiac, looking impatient and hot and somehow regretful, too, as if she were already beginning to wish she hadn't come.

"I took two weeks paid and one week without pay," she told Mother. Then she reached for Lisa and actually lifted her. "Look at this big girl. My goodness, how old are you now?"

"Eight," Lisa said.

"Seven," I said.

"But she's almost eight," said Aunt Elaine. And Lisa smirked at me from her comfortable height.

"Yeah," I said. "Next year."

"Thomas," Mother said.

We all went into the house, lugging presents and Aunt Elaine's suitcases and bed things. For the few minutes it took to get her settled in the little sitting room off the dining area, we had a feeling of novelty and interest, a bustling sense of preparation, like people getting ready for some sort of holiday. But very quickly Elaine was just part of the daily helping of strain we were all going through. She wanted Mother to quit this absurd posturing (her word), and pack everything and come home. "I'll help you pack," she said. "We can be in Minot in three days."

They sat facing each other across the dining room table, in almost identical poses, elbows resting on the glossy surface, steaming cups of coffee between their hands.

"I'm not going anywhere right now," Mother said.

I was standing in the doorway, having come to report some minor infraction of Lisa's — probably more photograph unpacking, since her feeling about our new house was that the lack of pictures in all the rooms was somehow threatening.

"Thomas," said Aunt Elaine. "Tell your mother what you told me."

I was at a loss.

"Come on, when we were outside. Don't play dumb."

"Aunt Elaine, I don't want to go to North Dakota," I said.

She looked at Mother. "He said he hates this" — she made a gesture to include everything around her — "place."

"Well, he'll just have to get used to it."

"I don't want to go to North Dakota," I repeated.

"Nobody's talking to you now," my mother said, and took a sip of her coffee.

"Don't *you* hate this?" I said to her, and now I, too, was gesturing to indicate the whole surrounding array of bricks and boards and windows and sun-bleached yard.

"That's enough. Go watch your sister."

I went back into the living room, and then out into the yard, where I found Lisa squatting to watch the slow progress of a tiny, crawling bug, the bottom of her dress taking on the clayey color of the dirt. At the end of the block an ice cream truck went jingling by and she stood, ran to the curb and then into the street. I watched her go, feeling peevish and persecuted. There wasn't any traffic. And then there was. That same car with the teenagers in it came roaring around the corner — I had an image of some immense, winding track they were fixed to, a circuit they were perpetually making — and when Lisa saw them coming she froze.

"Lisa!" I screamed.

The car breaks squealed, though they swerved in plenty of time and missed her by at least the length of the car. I went out and pulled Lisa back to the curb, and behind me I heard Mother shout something. She came running across the lawn. Aunt Elaine stood in the doorway, holding the screen open and leaning out. "Is she all right?"

Mother reached us, knelt down and put her arms around Lisa, beginning to cry. "You never go out in the street. You know better."

But of course Lisa didn't know any better, since the only streets she had lived and played on in her young life had been the narrow, shaded, often abandoned-feeling avenues of Air Force base housing, with their strategically placed speed bumps and frequent police patrols.

Now Mother was looking at me. "You have to do better," she said. "You have to watch her."

I refrained from saying that I *had* been watching her. Instead, I turned and started walking back up to the house.

"Everybody's all right," Aunt Elaine said from the door. "It's okay."

"Those guys that went by in the car," I said, "they yelled at me before."

She simply returned my look.

"I have to start school with them in September." The idea had struck me, as I spoke, like a blow to the stomach.

"You'll do fine," she said.

One thing we hadn't thought about during the period of the trial and the time we spent going through the move was what we would do once my father was restored to us. For twenty-one years, not counting the short six-month period in Alaska when he had made that one stab at civilian life, he'd served the Air Force as a survival technician and instructor, which meant he was responsible for performing maintenance on and training others in the operation of equipment used within seconds after it becomes impossible to fly, or to effectively land, an airplane — in most instances a warplane. He'd worked with the ejection seat, the survival kit the pilot wore as part of the seat, the parachute, the life rafts, the exposure suits and G suits and the helmets, the visor of which, he showed me once, was designed to burn with a bright white flame, visible for miles in the dark, like a beacon. My father taught pilots how to treat wounds and broken bones while floating in a life raft; how to climb into that raft in choppy seas; how to use shark repellant; how to kill and render fish and gulls for food with just the crude tools of the survival kit. It was a very specific kind of training, the civilian possibilities of which were almost nonexistent.

"What's he going to do," Aunt Elaine wanted to know, "be a lifeguard?"

"Stop it," Mother said, "please. It's enough to deal with having him in that place."

"Well, you have to think about it."

They were sitting on Mother's bed, in her room, which was the smallest one in the house, and which looked out on the street. It got the sunlight in the early mornings, and she had always liked to get up with the sun. I was standing in the hall, having just come in from outside, and they'd both looked at me, so they knew I was there. But neither of them seemed to take any further notice. In our own little room, Lisa snored like a heavy man trying to sleep off whiskey.

"We had a friend named Jack Wilcox," Mother said. "He left the Air Force at exactly Daniel's age, and he's managing a pizza restaurant and doing fine."

"Does he have a dishonorable discharge?"

"Of course not. Not everybody cares about that, Elaine."

"I'm just saying you have to start right now, thinking about what you're going to do."

"I'm going to get from today to tomorrow, right now."

"Walt Disney had a dishonorable discharge," I said. I had heard it from the two airmen with whom I'd been playing guitar; they had talked about it as if it were a sign of Disney's true genius: a man not made for regulations and orders.

"That's interesting," said Aunt Elaine. "Was it for stealing and paperhanging?"

"What do you want us to do," Mother said to her.

"I want you to come back to North Dakota with me. Daniel can come there when he gets out and he'll have a job. You know Daddy will get him a job of some kind."

My mother looked at me, then seemed to diminish somehow, her shoulders sagging. "I don't want to think about this."

"Connie, why won't you come home?" Aunt Elaine said.

"I *am* home."

"This isn't home. You hate it here. Tommy hates it here. Lisa's miserable."

"I don't want to go to North Dakota," I said. I hadn't wanted to leave Maryland, and I almost said that, too.

"Be quiet," my mother said. "Go see what Lisa's doing."

"Lisa's asleep."

"Is it Daddy?" Aunt Elaine asked her.

"Elaine, I have an almost grown child. I'm not moving into my old bedroom again. Come on."

"That's not what I'm talking about. You can get a place in town. You can get a job on base, even. I mean, *you* didn't steal anything."

"I'm never living near another Air Force base again."

"Well, what will you do? You're going to have an unemployable husband."

My mother was looking at me now. "Thomas, please go see what Lisa's up to."

"She's asleep," I said.

Aunt Elaine said, "Your mother wants some privacy."

"I have a right to hear this," I told them. I was thinking of my father's asking me to take care of Lisa and my mother, and while I'm sure I was acting out of that peculiar and always awkward eagerness of the near-adult to take on the comportment of adults, I also felt that Aunt Elaine was assuming more authority than she had a right to.

"Get off to yourself," my mother said through her teeth.

I went into the room where Lisa was still sleeping and took my guitar out. Lisa rolled over in her thick blankets and made a gasping sound, then slapped her pillow and buried her face in it. I sat on my bed with the guitar across my lap. The thing was badly out of tune, and though I could hear that it was off, I couldn't get it right, couldn't concentrate hard enough to mark the alignment of the notes. They all sounded wrong to me. I kept trying, and my mother and Aunt Elaine went on talking in the next room.

"Wake up," I said to Lisa finally.

"No."

I reached across and pushed her shoulder. "Up."

"Stop it."

I felt petulant and mean, but I also wanted company. Suddenly it seemed that she was purposely hiding from me in her stuffy pillow. There are moments in unhappiness when one is capable of almost anything: I leaned forward and pulled her hair, and she gave forth a blistering shout. "Stop it," I said. "I didn't mean it. Be quiet — it was an accident."

She was sitting up in the bed now, crying, looking at me as if to say that this noise she was making was just what I deserved.

"Will you quit it?" I said.

And then Mother was there, with Aunt Elaine looking over her shoulder. "What happened?" Mother said.

Through her crying, Lisa described how I had hurt her.

"It was an accident," I said.

"From where you're sitting?"

I remember being appalled that she didn't believe me, even in my guilty knowledge of how accurate Lisa's description was. I sat straight, still holding the guitar in my lap, and was silent.

"Well?" Mother said. But then she was busy with Lisa. "Oh, hush. He couldn't've hurt you that bad. Be quiet. Give us some peace, will you?"

Lisa buried her face in the pillow, and now her cries were muffled.

"For God's sake," Mother said to me. "You ought to be ashamed of yourself."

I answered with exaggerated indignation, still feeling myself unjustly accused. "I didn't do anything."

"Just shut up. Both of you shut up. You can stay in here all day if that's the way you want it." She slammed the door.

Lisa kept crying. "They're gone now," I said to her, "so you can stop."

"I'm not going to stop."

"Okay, don't stop," I said. And then I had the urge to say more; I did nothing to resist the urge. "You might as well keep crying, because we're going to North Dakota."

"No we're not."

She was sniffling now, curious. She came out of the pillow and looked at me with her mostly dry eyes.

"You little fake," I said.

"Shut up."

It occurred to me that I was not being much of an adult, and perhaps this contributed to my sense of frustration and anger. I was sitting there hating Aunt Elaine for having come into the house and asking all those unpleasant questions, and in the next instant she knocked on the door and then opened it as if summoned by my thinking about her.

"Look," she said, "I'm sorry."

I didn't say anything.

"Honey, you have to help me make her see."

Now I was flattered. I had been included in a way I couldn't have expected. Also, there was a pleading note in her voice that I had never heard before.

"You understand, don't you?" she went on. "This bad thing has happened to all of us. It's time for us to pull together a little. There's nothing for any of us here. You don't even have any friends here now."

"No," I said.

"See?"

"I don't have any friends *there*, either, Aunt Elaine."

"Be serious," she said. "This is nothing to be a child about. This is important. You have to stop being a smart aleck."

I hadn't meant to be, didn't think I had been. I was silent.

"Well?"

"Okay," I said. "What do you want me to do?"

"Just don't keep saying that about not wanting to go to North Dakota. You don't know that, for certain, do you? You might love North Dakota."

"I don't think so," I said.

"But how do you know that? You've never lived there before."

No, but I had visited twice with my mother and Lisa, during periods when Father was on temporary duty elsewhere, and those times Grandfather Tinan had frightened me with his irascible temper and his big voice, his concern for quiet when he wanted to concentrate, and his tirades at the dinner table when he wanted conversation: The whole world was falling apart. Everything was going to hell. "You wait," he'd say, chewing, not even looking up from his food, "I won't live to see it. But they'll be riding up and down the streets with guns, shooting people at random. With automatic weapons, you just wait. And you'll remember me saying this, too. You'll remember that I predicted it."

I never asked, and to my knowledge nor did anyone else, who it was that would be doing the shooting; and perhaps the object of the prophecy changed according to whoever happened to be in the news on a given night — the hippies, the Negroes (it was still offensive to call them blacks then), the peaceniks, and of course the commies (though several of these groups could be lumped under a single sociological heading, to which I'm sure my father had been added long ago: all the uncivilized rabble were getting out of control). Mother had said the real truth was that at this stage of his long life my retired grandfather tended to feel threatened by almost everything that was happening in the world, and so I believed I knew what would take place when he saw my long hair.

"Well?" Aunt Elaine said.

"I'm sorry, Aunt Elaine. I just don't want to go to North Dakota."

"This isn't about what you want. I'm asking you to see that."

"Is it about what *you* want?" I said.

"Don't be impertinent with me."

"Well?" I said.

"That's impertinent, too."

"All right," I said. "What is this about?"

"It's about what I want, all right? I'll admit it. But I want it for good reasons. You don't know anybody here — it's crazy to stay. You have no family here. No one."

"We don't want to move again."

"You haven't finished this move. You could make it all part of the same move."

"Aunt Elaine, it's not my decision."

"But you have a say."

"No," I said.

"Oh, of course you do. Don't be an idiot, for God's sake. You're old enough to have a say and you know it."

"You don't have to call names," I said.

She seemed genuinely contrite, and had already begun to speak. "I'm sorry for that. All right? I mean, I really didn't mean it. It's just that, well, I'm in the middle here and I can see so clearly what the best thing would be, and I don't understand why you all can't."

I was silent, though for a little space it looked as though she expected me to make some answer, and I felt the pressure of not having a response.

"Remember those boys who yelled at you from the car? Wouldn't it be better if you were back where at least you have some family around you?"

I had no answer for this, so I just returned her gaze.

"Oh," she said, "you're all batty. I haven't understood a single thing any of you have done since 1952."

She didn't mention North Dakota again that I recall, though she may have spoken about it with Mother when we weren't around. She didn't stay the planned three weeks, either.

Another journal entry:

> *June 14, 1967*
> *Tonight Lisa came in from the yard and put a little tree frog in Aunt Elaine's lap. Aunt Elaine made a sound like squealing brakes, and Mother sent Lisa to her room. Lisa looked so hurt and surprised that Aunt Elaine didn't love the little froggy. But last night she whispered to me when we were going to sleep that she wished Aunt Elaine would leave. Doesn't understand why Daddy can't come home and why he can't call us every night. Later: Heard Mother talking in the kitchen with AE. AE's proud of me I've grown so tall. M says Things weren't all that wonderful before, you know. Exact words. Then they don't say anything for a few seconds and then AE says In what way and M waits a little and then says Sometimes I'm not so sure he'll want to come home when it's all over. AE says Wait a minute, you mean Thomas? No, M says. Thomas, good Lord, Elaine. Have you been listening to me? Then what, Elaine says. And M says Who do you think? Okay, E says, suppose that's the case. Well, M says, I'm not sure I want him to come here, either, now do you see. Exact words. Now do you see.*

The handwriting here is tight, feverish, and hurried, the pencil point digging into the fiber of the paper, the letters running into each other as though I were making one long, distressed word; and even now I can feel something of the strain under which it was written. I have a painfully clear image of myself lying in bed with the blanket over my head and a small flashlight in my hand, scribbling away while Lisa sleeps. I had experienced those unwanted feelings of being relieved and glad my father was out of my life, and now, under the steady pressure of Aunt Elaine's wish that Mother return to North Dakota, Mother had, to my surprise and horror, echoed my own guilty secret — a secret that I had half kept from myself. I remember lying there under the little tent I'd made out of my blankets, in the pool of illumination the flashlight made, hearing Lisa's sleep, their voices in the other rooms, and coming to the conclusion that I had understood nothing at all about what had happened to us. The world was dividing up into unfathomable fragments, a confusion of parts. Mother had been so eager to tell us about the brave things he had done in the war, and had spoken so bitterly about all those who accused him, and I had heard her crying alone in her room at night. She had been in every instance his loyal and loving and grieving wife; she had even punished Lisa once for not paying attention when she was talking to us about him. I couldn't sort any of this out in my mind, couldn't really do anything but write it down in the journal, in the confused hope that one day I might be able to decipher some truth about it, although it wasn't quite as intentional as all that. Like anyone who feels compelled to keep a journal, I had always entertained the notion that some future version of myself would read it, and briefly I imagined that when, in whatever unexpected incarnation, that person came upon this scrawl, he would know enough of the workings of the world to feel tenderhearted toward the boy who had produced it in such pain and bewilderment all the years before.

A second later, I was assailed by the unshakable conviction that nothing could be further from the truth: that whatever was to be understood was to be understood now or not at all.

Finally I was too agitated and upset to think. I turned the flashlight off and lay in the dark, thinking of my father so many miles away, somewhere out on the vast midwestern plains, a man who must surely believe his family missed him. Well, *I* missed him now, and I felt all the more guilty for my earlier sense of liberation that he was gone.

In the bed beside mine, Lisa took in air and breathed out with a contented, snorting little sound. She had adjusted to everything with the same busy attitude; she was occupied. Every hour of the day she was occupied — even in her sleep, it was as if she were still one more level removed from what was happening around her. She had blithely drawn pictures in her sketchbook and on every scrap of paper in the house — pictures of houses, of skinny, elongated ladies wearing fantastic, beribboned, jeweled gowns of her own styling, with faces askew, with overdrawn noses and bug eyes and lips looking like enormous ruby plantains. She had played with her Barbies, dressing them and walking them into each other; she'd got into and out of a hundred variations of clothing every day, and when talk of my father started, she found other things on which to concentrate. The room we were in didn't bother her particularly, except that I was in it, too — and even that was sometimes a comfort for her, since on occasion she did have nightmares, and when she woke from these she would crawl into bed with me and shiver. The nightmares were always about the television she had watched, except the one nightmare no one could explain. She had begun to have it even before all the trouble started. In this dream, she's lying in her bed in a small white room, and, to use her exact words, "The green folk come from the windows." That is how she described them, and she held to that version of it through many inquisitions from us. Apparently she could say no more about them: they were green and they were the folk. The first time she had the dream, she shrieked like nothing human we had ever heard before — a blood-freezing, ear-piercing sound above the highest registers of anyone's musical notation. But as the dream repeated itself, she became rather accustomed to it, and sometimes would calmly report in the morning that she'd dreamed about the folk again. Even so, there were nights when I would be drowsing through some lovely fantasy or tossing in a nightmare of my own, only to discover her compact body trembling against me, her face buried in the pillow at my ear.

That night, the night I lay awake with the new knowledge about my mother's feelings, I thought of Lisa's recurring dream about the folk coming into the room to watch her. It seemed to me then that I had understood something whenever she talked about the dream — that something in what she spoke of had recognized me, if you'll allow the conceit. I wondered if perhaps I hadn't dreamed the same thing when I was small. And at the risk of making myself sound a degree more knowledgeable than I could have been, I'll say that I had a wordless thought about how the dream might be an unconscious reflection of just how strange the feeling in our family was. That is, I felt, without being able to express it, something of our strangeness as being all of a piece.

I couldn't sleep. My heart was beating in my face and neck. Lisa snored and sighed and made small smacking sounds with her lips. The rest of the house was quiet. Light moved on the walls when traffic went by in the street, and I must have drifted slightly, because for a time I thought I was in the officers' quarters on the air base. I might even have dreamed the sound of fighter planes lifting off.

Then I was awake and someone was standing next to my bed, a

long, liquid shape in white. I blinked, and when it moved I let out a small cry of alarm.

"No," she said. It was my mother. She reached over and put her arms around me.

"Oh," I murmured.

"You sounded like you were crying," she said. "Thomas?"

"What."

"Are you awake now?"

"Yes," I said, though I wasn't sure now whether or not I was dreaming.

"I took Lisa in with me."

"Okay," I said.

"Everybody's having dreams tonight."

"Did Lisa have her green-folk dream?"

"She said she dreamed about your father."

I gazed at the dim oval of her face.

"Does she talk to you about him, son?"

"No," I said.

"Nothing at all?"

I said, "It's like she doesn't even know he's gone."

"Poor thing," my mother said.

"Poor thing." I was incredulous.

"I don't think she grasps what it means."

"She doesn't miss him," I said, feeling almost as though I were pressing it, trying to get a response. I nearly went on to guess aloud that Lisa wouldn't mind if he stayed away for good.

"She doesn't know she misses him."

I didn't say anything.

"Are *you* all right."

"Oh," I said, "fine."

"We won't go to North Dakota." She touched my forehead, the lightest caress with just the tips of her fingers. "Can you sleep?"

"I guess."

"Do you want to talk?"

"If you want to."

"Do *you* want to."

"All right," I said.

"Well," she said, "I don't want to force you to."

"No, you're not," I told her.

"I feel like there's a wall between us sometimes. Like I can't ever know what you're thinking."

I didn't know what to say to this.

"You know?" she said.

And I couldn't resist the chance to confront her with what I knew — or, rather, I couldn't keep from offering her an opening through which she might step if she wanted to. I said, "I really miss Dad, and I want him to come home."

She didn't even wait to breathe. "Oh, I know, honey — me too."

I was silent.

"I miss him too," she said. I could think of nothing whatever to say to her. "We just have to get through this," she murmured. Then she leaned over and kissed me on the forehead. "Remember — Lisa's with me."

"Yes," I said.

"Good night, honey."

"Good night." I watched her move through the dark in her gown, like a ghost, and when for a second she was silhouetted in the doorway, the contours of her slender body showed through the translucent folds of cloth. For perhaps the first time in my life I was aware of her as a sexual being, and I felt an immediate wave of remorse, as though I had violated some primal law by allowing the idea into my consciousness at all. I suppose this is exactly as Freudian as it sounds, but I don't really mean it that way. I am talking instead about the separation of a person out of the abstraction one has lived with through years of habit and expectation; that first instance when Mother or Father steps out of being Mother or Father, clothed in your necessarily egocentric notions, and becomes just a person — a living, breathing, separate someone standing in the light of a different circumstance, newborn, in a way. It's possible that I am alone in this, but it seems to me that we never imagine that our parents have private lives, apart from us and having nothing whatever to do with us.

4

THE NEXT MORNING Aunt Elaine gave forth a small scream from the kitchen: Lisa had brought in a cricket with antennae the size of cat whiskers.

"See?" Lisa was saying to her. "See where its legs rub together?"

"Please, honey. Take it outside."

I heard all this but stayed where I was, lying on the sofa in the living room. I had put the Saturday morning cartoons on. Looney Tunes, most of which I'd seen before, though they always diverted me, and I watched them anyway. My mother hadn't emerged from her bedroom yet. Aunt Elaine was preparing breakfast amid the welter of still unpacked boxes in the kitchen. We had put everything away but those objects and utensils which never seem to fit anywhere: containers of various never used tools and accessories, rolls of duct tape, twenty different pairs of scissors, unmatched cups and saucers, pencils, cracked bowls and tarnished silverware of some sentimental value, tins of poker chips and playing cards, all the old home movie reels, and a little horde of knickknacks and porcelain figurines.

"Please, Lisa," Aunt Elaine said in the voice of the nearly damned.

"I won't let it get away."

"Put it outside."

"Mom lets me bring them in to show her."

"Will you please take it outside."

"Want to see the snake I found?"

Another little cry of alarm.

"I don't have him here, Aunt Elaine."

"Where do you have him?"

"Outside."

"Leave him there."

"I'm not sure it's a him."

"Out, young lady."

The door slapped-to twice. I turned into the back cushions of the sofa and tried to go to sleep. But then Aunt Elaine came into the room behind me. I heard her turn the TV off. She sighed, picked up something from the magazine rack. "Tom?" she said.

"I'm awake," I told her.

"Answer the phone if it rings, will you? I have to use the powder room."

Then she was gone. I listened to the house for a few minutes, beginning to feel the old sense of getting accustomed to a place. It wasn't home yet, but I was starting to know the sounds: the peculiar groans and creakings of the joists and floorboards, the way the wind moved in the trees out the screen door, the birds and insects making their daily racket, and Lisa's feet on the little wooden stoop in back. She was playing with one of her dolls now, or perhaps it was another of the crawling things she liked to experiment with.

Before, during my father's absences, time seemed charged somehow, and perhaps it was just that we lived in the bright anticipation of his return. We wrote letters to him, and planned what we would do when he did return (there was always the next tour of duty to think about, the next set of quarters, with its rooms that were like the rooms we had left, but different too, altered by the stresses of other climates and the faint traces of other lives — marks on the walls, exotic light fixtures, abandoned toys and tools, and the infinite variations in the configurations of the lawn, the placement of flowers and shrubs — and often when he returned, it was with orders for us to move again). But we had also spent whole days without thinking about him at all, and perhaps this was because, then, we had the luxury of doing so: we were busy with life at home, as Mother called it when she spoke to him long distance, and there was a kind of benediction in knowing he was doing his work, teaching men how to save their own lives. We were an Air Force family, and aside from Father's one bad tour of duty in Vietnam, we — Lisa and I, anyway — had little to keep us from believing that the basic tenor of our lives would go on undisturbed. It would be what it had always been, a series of goings and returnings, a pattern of happy reunions.

This new absence, with its aura of disgrace and ruin, had engendered something else entirely. Now it seemed to me that, excepting Lisa, we were obsessed with my father — he was more in our thoughts than he had ever been during any of the normal absences. Yet for me this had happened not in the way you might expect: there was something cruelly imprecise about the way he stood in my mind, and I had begun to discover an inability to call up a clear image of his face, or to recollect the sound of his voice. What I was left with was the need to do so, and it was while I lay on the couch and listened to Lisa playing outside that I realized, with an oppressive little jolt of the muscles of my chest, how desperate our situation really was. Is it superfluous to mention that I was feeling sorry for myself again? I had a moment of almost homicidal bitterness, thinking of the two airmen — Todd and Link were their names — and the music I would now never make with them, all my dashed dreams of being a musician.

I had started thinking of them in the context of the trial, because I remembered being surprised by the gravity with which they treated the situation. They had been sympathetic through the whole ordeal, and I had felt a bond with them, while also trying to put aside a sense that I was capitalizing on something, that their sympathy was misplaced, even as I basked in it. As nearly as I was able to gather, they truly did look up to my father. Todd talked about being impressed that Father had read Hemingway (a fact of which I was complacently aware: hadn't every adult?), and he went on about the drawing of Proust on our living room wall (I had attached no significance whatever to the picture, except its origin, which was that it had been a gift from my mother to my father during one of the Christmases he was always filming). "Sarge isn't any hanger-on lifer," Todd said. "I mean, he always considered the Air Force as one of the things that's provided him with adventure in life." This was in the days just after the court-martial began, when they had come by our quarters to see if they could be of any help. My mother answered the door, and was unable to say much to them, so I stepped out and led them away from her, off into the shade of the yard.

"Man," Todd said. "Bummer." He was the older of the two and

much less accomplished as a guitarist; he considered himself a poet and wrote florid lyrics to the few songs we'd tried to write. It was he who had loaned me the little City Lights paperbacks of Ginsberg's and Gregory Corso's poems, which I had read with the avidity of the newly initiated. When I remember Todd now I see someone skinny, ruddy, burnished-looking, freckled, a boy really, with already thinning hair and a permanent cough that sounded tubercular. I liked him. He had a southern accent and a way of looking off when he talked, as if he'd just thought of something else to say and was amusing himself with it. In this instance he was very regretful and quiet; it felt entirely unnatural. Everyone seemed so worried about *us*. "Man, your poor mother."

"I don't know," I said. "It's my father who's being court-martialed."

"A beautiful lady like that."

"We have to move," I said. And I began to cry. I hadn't known I would.

"God," Link, the one with the real talent as a musician, said. "The sarge was the best." I thought he might begin to cry, too. He was fair-skinned and blond, with a small, feminine mouth and very dark green eyes which had always made me feel uneasy. It had seemed that he kept some part of himself in reserve, for a kind of cold appraisal. But his eyes were full of pity now. He muttered, "Poor Sarge," and it occurred to me that they were both acting as though my father had died.

"I guess I have to go," I said to them, moving toward the front door again.

"Keep in touch," Link said.

Well, I knew we would not be in touch. I knew that was the last time I would ever see either of them.

And those weeks afterward, lying on the couch in the cramped living room of the house in Virginia, with the morning sounds wafting to me on the summer air, and the knowledge that I was beginning to get accustomed to the place, I had a stark, sudden, desolating realization of just that: I was getting used to this sort of privation.

Aunt Elaine came sighing down the hall, returning from the bathroom.

"What," she said.

I didn't move. "Nothing."

"You groaned. Are you sick?"

"No."

"Where's Lisa." She was looking around herself like someone half expecting ambush.

"Outside," I said.

"I want to let your mother sleep."

"We can't stay here," I said. "I hate it here."

"We can all live in Minot."

"I hate it there, too. And so does Mother."

"You're all crazy."

"He told me to look out for them both, you know."

"Your father."

"Before he left," I said.

"Yes, well, that's to be expected."

"It's true."

"I know it's true. And I know you take it seriously."

I left a pause.

"Do you think it's good for them that you keep saying you don't want to go home?"

"It's not home."

"You know what I mean, Thomas."

"Well," I said. "It's not home."

"You're just being difficult."

"It's the truth," I said.

"It's a child's truth. You're not a child anymore."

I sat up and felt momentarily dizzy. She stood with her legs slightly apart in the middle of the room, her hands on her hips; it was the pose of someone ready for whatever might be next. There was something almost too solid about her, as if her bones were heavier than a normal person's. I have pictures (and film) of her at about this time in her life, and I know that for her stockiness and the square cut of her shoulders she was not by any means an unattractive woman. To me, then, she might as well have been one of the hags in *Macbeth*. Except that I liked her, and I was suddenly glad of the fact that she had come to stay with us. Indeed, in those few seconds I felt as though her presence were the only hedge against the possibility that we might settle in the house for good.

"What if we go to North Dakota?" I said.

She seemed to brighten a little. "It would make everything so much simpler."

But it was not my decision and wasn't going to be, and nothing I said would have any real bearing on anything, and never mind the manly injunction my father had left me with before he climbed on the plane that took him from us. Aunt Elaine and I both seemed to acknowledge this in the same wordless instant.

"Just stop carrying on about how you don't want to go to North Dakota," she said, turning away.

Later we were all in the kitchen, making what we would eat for lunch — tuna sandwiches for Aunt Elaine and Lisa, peanut butter and jelly on white bread for Mother and me. Aunt Elaine was talking about how Grandfather Tinan had called the other day and said he might come to Virginia to stay for a while, around the Fourth of July. He had always loved Washington, which he apparently assumed was closer to us than it actually was (in fact, it was almost two hundred fifty miles north on the interstate), and he missed the children. Aunt Elaine said his voice on the phone had sounded so lonesome.

"Oh, stop it, Elaine."

"Well, it's true."

"So then is that a threat? He'll come here if we don't go there?"

"That's not fair. I haven't said anything else about that, have I?"

"All right," Mother said.

"Don't you want to see him, Connie?"

"He's welcome to come for a visit. Will he sleep on the sofa, do you think?"

"Grandfather Tinan?" I said.

Everyone smiled.

"I'll sleep on the sofa," Aunt Elaine said.

"If he's coming to visit and maybe drive up to Washington to see the sights, that's fine," said my mother. "But if it's to play Daddy for the injured daughter, the answer is no. The money I borrowed from him I'll pay back. He has not bought himself into the position of being my guardian again."

"When was he or anybody ever your guardian."

"Just so you know," Mother said.

At this, Aunt Elaine seemed to stiffen. "You know, I wonder if I'm welcome here myself."

"Now don't get offended."

The phone rang, and Lisa, who was sitting on the table next to it, picked up the handset. "Hello," she said. Then: "Hi," and "No."

"Who is it, Lisa?" Mother said. "Is it Grandfather Tinan? Tell him we were just talking about him."

Lisa thrust the handset at her. "It's Daddy."

"Oh," Mother said, rising. There was a quality of alarm in her voice. "I'll take it in the other room. Hang it up when I get in there, Elaine."

Aunt Elaine took the handset from Lisa, who got down from the table and sauntered out the back door in the slanting sun, letting the screen slap in the jamb and then standing there with her hands clasped on top of her head, looking out at the yard, seeming a little bored, then stirring slightly, strolling to the edge of the small porch, and folding her arms idly across her chest, exactly like someone under normal circumstances. Certainly nothing in her demeanor would compel an onlooker to believe that she was a girl who had been orphaned by the law, or that her father was just now calling long distance from a federal prison.

"Hello, Daniel," Aunt Elaine said into the telephone. "I'm staying with Connie and the kids a few days."

Then she was listening to whatever my father said.

"Well, you take care of yourself."

I watched Lisa go down the stairs and out onto the dusty lawn.

"They're fine. Everybody's fine, aren't we Connie?"

I went to the door. "Lisa," I said.

"What." She didn't even turn.

"He'll want to talk to us."

"I already talked to him." This was said in the tone of someone refusing another helping of food.

"Lisa, come here."

And now Aunt Elaine put the handset back in the cradle. "He'll want to talk to you in a minute. He said he couldn't talk long."

I moved to the table and sat down. There were still boxes on the cabinet, the open one full of old canned goods and spices and knickknacks. Aunt Elaine busied herself with this while I ate my sandwich. We could both hear the murmur of Mother's voice in the other room, and now and again Aunt Elaine paused, as if she had heard something of what was being said.

"God," she muttered.

"What?" I asked.

"It just hits me once in a while — what the situation is."

My mother opened the bedroom door and called to me. "Pick the phone up."

I did. I said, "Hello?"

Through the crackle of a bad connection, I heard my father's voice. "Hello." There was an awful, pained, fake heartiness in the tone.

"Hey," I said.

And then the connection came clear. I heard him breathe. "You doing okay, Thomas?"

"Fine," I said. I was searching my mind frantically for something to say, and there was nothing — a barren, empty waste of memory and whatever I knew about anything. Pure nothing, and the breathing on the other end became the smallest sigh. "We're still unpacking," I said, "all the little orphaned stuff." It was what we had always called it. "Aunt Elaine's here," I went on quickly.

"Right," he said. And I remembered with a sinking heart that he had just spoken to her.

"Are you okay?" I asked, feeling wrong.

"Well as can be expected," he said. "I miss you."

"We miss you, too," I managed.

"It's not so bad, son."

And I was crying, holding the phone tight and trying not to have him hear me. Bitterly, I recalled that other time when I had tried, without success, to keep tears back while talking with him.

"Your mother says you're helping out."

"Yes."

"I know it's tough."

"I watch Lisa when Mother goes to work."

"Your mother said you were doing that. Good."

"What's it like there?" I said.

"Sunny. Hot."

Of course I hadn't meant the weather. "It's hot here, too," I managed.

"You been over to the new school yet?"

"We haven't had a chance," I said. Always before, when we moved into a new town, one of the rituals we performed was a trip to the school I would be attending. We'd pick a time when school was not in session and drive over to the grounds, get out of the car, and explore the place for ourselves, looking in the windows at the rows of desks and the blackboards, staring through the wired glass of the doors at polished halls and metal lockers, just getting the feel of the new surroundings — or, as my father would say, making it ours.

"You don't want to go over there cold on the first day, do you?"

"No, sir."

"That's good," he said, and I heard his voice change. I had a sharp, breath-stealing pang, realizing that he was trying not to cry, too — this man who had been through war and had suffered the privations and torments of a cruel foreign captivity. Well, he was in another kind of captivity now, and someone was telling him it was time to hang up.

"Can you put Lisa on?" he said.

"I'll get her."

"She's not right there?"

"I just have to call her."

"I don't think I've got time."

"I'm playing baseball again," I told him. I hadn't realized I would do so.

"Glad to hear it," he said in a voice that was unmistakably dubious. I thought of what Mother must have told him about me, how I was staying close to the house and had deflected all her attempts to make me begin the process of assimilation.

"I haven't even told Mother yet," I managed to get out.

And his voice brightened a little. At least I thought I heard this. He said, "I'm really glad to hear it, son."

"I'll get Lisa."

"I'm afraid I have to hang up. Can I talk to your mother again?"

"I'm here," Mother said from the other phone.

I hadn't realized she was on. I said, "Oh."

"Go get your sister, Thomas."

As I hung up, I heard him telling Mother that the others wouldn't let him wait for Lisa to come to the phone. I went past Aunt Elaine, who seemed to want to embrace me, and on out to the back stoop, looking for Lisa. She was all the way at the other end of the yard, sitting on an overturned box, peering through the leaves of the hedge. The sun caught glints of copper light in her hair, a pretty little girl sitting in the sun, perfectly innocent of any cruelty. When I was near she turned quickly, with a guilty toss of her head.

"What're you doing, Lisa? I mean, for God's sake."

"Nothing," she said. "What."

Beyond the leaves of the hedge something moved — a man, sitting up on a blanket — and when I leaned close I saw, through the tiny interstices of leaves, that a woman lay beside him. They were sunning themselves, the woman with her bathing suit top unstrapped; she was stretched out on her stomach. He touched her back, ran his hand along her spine to the place where it curved into her bottom.

"What're *you* looking at," Lisa said.

I had looked, and had stopped still, I admit. And now I stood and reached for my sister's arm, all the more angry for having hesitated. "You're in a lot of trouble."

"I am not either," she said.

"Come with me."

"I don't have to."

"Mother told me to come get you, Lisa."

She stared at me as if trying to gauge whether or not I was telling the truth, then she got to her feet, brushed the dust from the front of her shorts. "I didn't do anything."

Inside, Aunt Elaine was putting things away in the cabinets, and Mother was in the bedroom with the door closed.

"He couldn't wait," said Aunt Elaine, giving Lisa a look.

"I already talked to him," Lisa said.

"Little girl, what is it with you, anyway?" Aunt Elaine said.

Lisa stood there with her hands at her sides, her head lowered. "I don't know." And then she was crying.

"Oh, Lord," Aunt Elaine said, lifting her. "Can you finish in here, Thomas?"

I muttered that I would, and she carried Lisa into the living room, murmuring to her and trying to apologize for upsetting her. I moved to the counter with the debris lying on it, the open cabinet doors with the shelves half full. Out the kitchen window the yard was in shade, almost the washed-out green of dusk. I could hear Lisa sniffling and sobbing, and Aunt Elaine's murmured placations, and then Mother came out of her bedroom.

"What's this," she said. It was not a question.

"She's upset," said Aunt Elaine.

"She should be. Why didn't you want to talk to your father, Lisa? What's the matter with you?"

"Connie, don't."

Lisa was now wailing. "Take her into her room, I don't want to listen to it," Mother said. Then she called my name.

"I'm in here," I said, and picked up a box of swizzle sticks to put in the cabinet.

She came to the entrance of the kitchen and then looked back at Aunt Elaine. "Take her into your room, will you, Elaine?"

"She doesn't understand any of this," Aunt Elaine said over the cries of my sister.

"Well, I can't help that now," said Mother. "Will you just take her somewhere away from me."

When it was quiet, and Lisa was safely in Aunt Elaine's room, Mother walked to the back door and looked out the screen, the relative brightness there making a lithe shadow out of her. I waited a moment, then began putting things into the cabinet, not paying much attention to what they were.

"God," she said.

I waited.

"Are you going to be okay?" she asked, without turning around.

It was strange, a very odd moment. This was not the kind of thing she had ever been inclined to inquire about in a general way, and there had been little time for any sort of solicitation in the determined, mostly self-contained manner with which she had approached our present difficulty. In fact, when I think of it now, it seems to me that Lisa and I were mostly expected to keep a straight, proud, stoic silence about the whole distressing business, as if we were soldiers in a circumstance allowing for no show of weakness at all.

"Well?" she said, almost impatiently, turning to look at me.

"Okay," I said. "I'm okay."

Again she was gazing out at the shade and sun on the lawn. "I don't know anyone here."

"No," I said.

"I've never done any of this alone before."

I waited for her to go on.

"Do you understand?"

"Yes," I said, though I didn't think I really did at all.

"Lisa's too young to understand."

"She knew what she was doing," I said.

"No, that's just what she *doesn't* know."

I let my silence concede for me.

"Are you playing baseball again?"

"I was thinking I might," I said.

She turned and regarded me. "You said you were."

"Well, I was thinking about it."

"Just thinking about it."

I said nothing.

"You told your father you were playing again."

"Well, I meant I was thinking about it."

"We can't be like other people, Thomas. We can't give in."

"I don't know what you mean," I said.

"We have to be straight and angry and stronger than anything for a while."

"I just said I was thinking of playing baseball —"

She interrupted me. "I understand what you were feeling and I'm sorry for all of it, but you volunteered a lie and he knew it right away. He knew it and it hurt him."

This had the effect of some static charge entering my blood. I felt the heat at the back of my neck, climbing up both sides of my skull.

"Don't you think he deserves the truth?" she said.

And now I tried to challenge her with a look: I can think of no other way to express it; I meant for her to see the challenge in my eyes. "Yes," I said.

"Well?"

"I don't know what you want me to say."

"Don't say anything. Don't volunteer lies, it's patronizing. It means you feel sorry for him, and he doesn't want your pity. It hurts him to think we feel sorry for him."

"Well, we do," I said. "Don't you? *I* do." I had nearly shouted at her, and in my own surprise at myself I took a step back, bumping against the counter.

"No," she said. "That's not it. You don't understand." She seemed to be muttering the words to herself, her head down, one hand combing through her hair. "This isn't right. We're not characters in your story, Thomas."

I wanted to say something about what I knew, then — what I had heard, and what I more than suspected. But I did not. I walked over to her and said I was sorry, and she kissed my cheek, putting her small hands on my arms above the elbow, saying she was sorry, too. It was hard for each of us, she said. It was all so new. We would just have to make everything up as we went along, until we found the way through.

I had the distinct feeling that we were on the verge of something, that all I had to do was ask her directly about her feelings and she would say it out. I deliberately held back because I found I lacked the courage, just then, to have what I thought I knew confirmed.

"We're not characters in your story, Thomas," she had said. She didn't know it, and probably wouldn't have conceded it, but these are some of the truest words she ever spoke to me, in spite of the contradictory and melancholy fact that by all appearances she is presently occupying that exact place here. The old cliché, as most old clichés do, contains more than a kernel of the truth: appearances are deceiving, and in a way she is not a character in my story; I am a character in hers.

These days in Asquahawk, where for a long time there was a lot of agitation about the rapaciousness of developers and the encroachment of a mercantile crassness, a species of swaggering satisfaction obtains: whereas certain opportunistic people along the south shore had been selling their fine old houses to a huge corporate conglomerate whose interest was entirely material and commercial and whose bumbling, landlocked representatives in most cases had never even set foot on the island, that particular conglomerate, for all the talk of its public relations men about the march of progress, has been stopped dead in its money-slick tracks by the decline of the real estate market. And while on other parts of the island two shopping malls have gone up within the last three years, most of the construction and the furious activity one might have observed here only eighteen months ago has halted. New homes sit empty, and the FOR SALE signs in front of unsold houses have taken on the patina of the old humble yard ornaments — the lawn jockeys and the birdbaths, the garden gnomes, the occasional grazing stone deer. At the tip of the south shore, far out on that lonely spur of rock and sand, the skinny steel frame of an unfinished hotel stands, its completion indefinitely delayed, all its financing in doubt, tied up in legal wrangling and bankruptcy. In its barren, solitary aspect it looks like a preposterous piece of abstract sculpture. Stairs make their alternating westward- and eastward-facing way up into the borderless blue, and when the wind blows it whistles in the angles of the landings and the useless steps. About halfway up the structure there's a harp-shaped twisting of the girders, like the appalling signature of the powers that erected it and then were rendered helpless to carry the project forward to its conclusion.

Lately I have found this a comfortable place to spend my evenings. The sky here grows dark before the light is quite gone from the tidelands behind me, and the ocean goes through every deep shade of blue. The water licks at the shoreline, which is in the rickety-looking, sticklike shadows the hotel frame makes. All the trucks and all the piles of stone and girder and brick are gone. At one end of the beach, a stack of heavy pine boards bends and warps in the sun and rain and wind, whitening with weather, all the luster and the piney fragrance leaching out of the cracked wood. I sit here and gaze out at the sea, remembering how it was all those years ago, with the war growing wider and lightning striking in the cities of home — all of it played out on the television like one fantastic show — and how none of it quite touched us anymore, or even seemed to apply to us. It was history happening, and it couldn't have mattered less. Do you understand me? We lived in our rundown little house on a quiet street in Virginia, and Lisa put another something natural and startling in Aunt Elaine's lap, sending the poor woman on her way back to her own life in Grandfather Tinan's big white house, and nothing in the newspapers or on the television had anything to do with the way we went through the days. It wasn't even backdrop, since we paid no attention to it at all. Mother went to work in the mornings and I contended with Lisa, who resisted me at every turn, as if it were her assigned place in the scheme of things — and just maybe it was.

In the evenings Mother came home tired and irritable, with a demoralizing number of tasks she wanted done, none of which had been done in her absence: picking up in the rooms, running the vacuum, dusting, emptying the garbage, doing the day's dishes. Outside, the patchy grass needed cutting, and there was trimming to do. I couldn't remember how we had handled all these things before; it seemed that they had somehow multiplied a hundredfold. While we worked on our chores, Mother put something together for dinner. We'd eat without much talk. Then she would put the television on, and it would play into the hours of the night whether anyone watched it or not, just for the sound of other voices. Sometimes I walked in the dusky light of evening down to the end of the block, through a stand of tall old sycamores and across a little clearing near the interstate, to a shallow, clear-running creek, the water gurgling over the stones with the same steady rush, and when I put my hands down to cup some of it into my mouth, it was as cool as if refrigerated. In that lovely little spot, known only to me it seemed, I cast a line and sat waiting for the fish to bite. It was really more for the sound of the water and the solitary peace than for any sport; whatever I caught I threw back. When I returned, well after dark, the house would be all lighted up, every window, and the sound of the television would be clearer and stronger as I approached. Lisa would be in bed, and Mother would be sitting alone on the sofa, drowsing through the *Tonight Show*.

Now and again we heard from Father, usually by mail now — plain, spare, carefully worded missives in a uniformly slanted, barely readable script, with precise reports of weather where he was and very mild admonitions for Lisa and me to help out and be good. Now and again he talked about what he was doing: they had put him to work in the laundry, and he hated the odor of detergent; he had played softball all one Saturday afternoon; there were basketball teams and intramural leagues, and he could spend some time in the evenings reading; they had a pretty good library. Mother read these letters aloud to us, and then we would pass them back and forth, to read and savor them ourselves.

One night, Mother said, "You don't play your guitar anymore, Thomas."

"I haven't," I said.

We were sitting in the living room with the TV on. Lisa lay asleep on the floor at our feet, having drifted off while watching a movie.

"Are you giving it up?" Mother said.

"I don't know," I said. "There's nobody to play with around here."

"Then why don't you get your hair cut?"

I'm sure my look of hopeless incomprehension set her off.

"Don't sit there staring at me. I asked you something."

"We were talking about my guitar."

"It's all part of the uniform, isn't it?"

Now I thought she was talking about the Air Force.

"The hair," she said. "The long hair. It's all part of the rock 'n' roll uniform."

"Oh," I said. "No."

"Sure it is."

Well, she could have it her way, I thought. I shrugged, as if to indicate that I was tired of the subject.

"I think we'll get your hair cut," she said.

I stood.

"Where're you going?"

"To bed."

"Did you hear me?"

"Yes," I said.

"I'll tell you why, Thomas."

"You don't need a reason."

"I think we're going to move again."

I stood there looking at her.

"That's right," she said. "The only reason to stay here was the job, and I hate it. I hate it more every day."

My own experience inscribed an arc that was the precise opposite of hers, for I had discovered the little creek. And now in the sudden heat of realizing that she was serious, I felt threatened. To my own astonishment, I realized how much that meager little sluice of water under the long shadow of the interstate overpass had come to mean to me.

I didn't want to move again. At least I didn't want to move from Virginia.

"You're kidding," I said to her.

"No."

Lately we had begun to speak back and forth to each other on an equal footing — mostly about Lisa, who was proving to be too much for me. But about other things, too. I had started to sense that I could argue with her when the occasion called for it; I could make my own feelings known, not just about the day-to-day things I was going through, but about the way we ran the household and what we would eat and how the money was to be spent. I did not want to move again, and not a little for the thought of how much trouble it would be, so close upon the heels of what I could rightly call the present move (it had been only a little less than a month, and we weren't even completely unpacked yet), but mostly, in some odd, nearly atavistic way, for what I had begun to feel while fishing the stream under the overpass. I'm certain that I can't explain this any more directly without sounding sentimental, though there was nothing at all sentimental about it.

Anyway, I was aware, with an acute ache, that I did not want to move again, and I said so.

"Well, you'd better get used to the idea," she said. "I've already started making the arrangements."

"You're not serious."

She nodded slightly, but her answer was in the steady way she returned my look.

"I've been using my lunch hour at work. I've already got us a place to live."

"In North Dakota?" I said.

"No, not there."

"Okay," I said impatiently, "then where."

Perhaps three or four times in my life I have felt cast up onto cold currents of air, adrift on swirling gusts, as though experience were centrifugal and each new shock hurled me farther and farther from the center. I might well have sailed up to the ceiling before her eyes as she answered. And yet I had the feeling that I knew, too, for all my confusion about what I'd heard her say. I had the sense that somehow I knew all along it would come.

"We're moving to Wilson Creek, Wyoming," she said.

PART TWO

5

I WENT THROUGH a curious stage shortly after Lisa was born, in which I spent many lonely hours wondering what it felt like to be someone else. This was not, as far as I can tell, a reaction to unusual stress of any kind — I mean that I don't remember feeling deprived in any way — but I would watch the other children of the neighborhood where we lived, or stare at my father and mother with the baby, and almost invariably I would begin to experience the sensation of having been checked or obstructed at the limit of my eyes. Often, possessed of a sort of visceral, unformed discontent at the obvious facts of the matter, I would add to my own growing frustration by trying to imagine myself inside those other bodies, looking out. Doubtless this is nothing more than a normal stage of the development of identity in childhood, and is well documented by those whose business it is to study such things. The only reason I mention it now is to emphasize the level of my bewilderment concerning my mother as, during the course of the next few days, all her preparations for our move to Wyoming began to be revealed to me: for I had exactly that old childhood feeling of being stopped at myself, of having reached borders to my experience that I could never cross. I wanted, with something like a physical pang, to look through her eyes, to *know*. Even as I began to grow excited about the prospect of being where I could see my father again.

Somehow, without my knowing it, without my receiving even a hint of it, she had sought and found another job ("There's always somebody who needs a secretary, right?"), had worked out a way to sublet the house, had committed us to another lease in Wilson Creek — three rooms in a three-story house on Jewett Street, just above the widest part of the creek itself and almost within sight of the town's biggest nonagricultural industry, the federal prison. She had also borrowed more money from Grandfather Tinan (on the promise that we would take the northerly route, through Bismarck, North Dakota, where Aunt Elaine could pick us up and drive us to Minot for a visit — this plan necessitating a long journey across much of Montana, to Billings, and then back south and east to Wilson Creek — all of which she had arranged), and she had set up appointments for three different moving companies to come and give estimates. This while I went on in the belief that she was losing herself in television and in the long hours of the weekends spent polishing and repolishing the furniture, or nagging Lisa and me about our assigned chores.

The events of the days following her revelation about the move to Wilson Creek are mostly gone. I know from my journal that she sold the car and much of the furniture (all the moving estimates were higher than she liked, and we were not going to need it anyway, our rooms in the Jewett Street house being, she told me with what I thought was a strange mirthless smile, furnished), and I know that she shipped many of our things to Minot, where Aunt Elaine and Grandfather Tinan had apparently agreed it could be stored. According to the journal, twenty-five days after the car was sold we headed out by cab to the train station, yet I have no sequential memory of the wait, the time spent between her announcement to me that night in the living room and our standing on the platform at the station. In a way, it seems that we headed out the morning after she said we would move, and if I didn't have the journal as evidence to the contrary, I might swear to it. Yet I know I chafed and worried about it, and perhaps this failure of recollection has more to do with what happened later than with anything else. I do have an image of Lisa standing alone at the center of the empty living room, her small, solid shadow looking printed on the hardwood floor. But I can't be certain that this isn't a scene from our first days in the house, since in this image she's also trying out the sound of her voice against the echoing walls.

The train station in Demera was in the historic part of the town. Though the smoke-darkened red brick façade was still preserved much as it had been a hundred twenty years before — with its tall windows, like the windows of an antique train car, and its ornate scroll patterns in the wood of the doors — inside, the floors and walls had been modernized, and the ticket counters were all aluminum and glass. Above the entrance was a steel-gray plaque whose inscription read that this was one of the depots from which thousands of captured Union troops were shipped south to the dreadful Andersonville prison, in Georgia. I stood in the gray light and read this, thinking of prisons, and of the fact that we were going to Wyoming.

Wyoming.

I'd imagined big rolling hills backed up to snowy mountains with great craggy bluffs, and huge blue pockets of distance and ice, treeless rocky wastes. "There's nothing but grass out here," my father had said over the telephone, his voice sounding full and somehow confident, almost happy, I thought, attributing this to the fact that he knew we were coming west.

I stood there in the terminal and tried to imagine miles of open grassy country with a prison standing up in the middle of it.

"Stop daydreaming," Mother said, lightly pushing my shoulder. "Come on."

There were only a few people waiting on the benches under the windows. She had already got our tickets and checked the bags, and now she ushered us out onto the station platform in the sun. Lisa had insisted on carrying her teddy with her, but the heat had begun to oppress her, and she wanted me to hold it for her.

"You wanted it," I said.

"Please," she begged in a familiar, high-pitched whine which was always a source of piercing aggravation to me.

Mother looked down the track, then took something from her purse and swallowed it.

"I want one," Lisa said.

"It's a stomach pill," I told her with all the exasperation of the better-informed older brother.

"I don't care, I want one."

"Be quiet, Lisa," I said.

We waited for the train. I felt weirdly dissociated from them both, as if I had come here alone and had been forced into their proximity by the conditions of the place, by the fact that I was waiting for the same train. There were other people on the platform, most of whom had something to read and all of whom were clearly not going much farther than Union Station in Washington, D.C. I was looking at the faces, all the bland, concentrating expressions, the gazes that just brushed past us or glided politely over us, when quite suddenly, with an involuntary shudder of mortification, I wondered how we must appear to these others. A moment later, it began to seem that they were watching us. I imagined I saw the signs of curiosity and interest, the glances beginning to linger and become something more, so that by the time the train rolled in, I was unable to convince myself that all our misfortune was not plainly evident in our clothes and in the way we stood so close together. I caught myself scowling at people who had not even looked up from their newspapers.

The train rumbled along the edge of the platform — a sound like huge electricity, a whirring — kicking up dust and dragging the rough winds of the Shenandoah Valley into the station with it. Blue dust swirled up between the ties and around the iron wheels, and something — a mote, a piece of cinder, a particle of glass — caught under my eyelid. It stung beyond the telling, and I screamed, turning, trying to fend off the sudden confusion of hands around my face, and then my mother was trying to make me hold still, reaching up, trying to get me to open the eye. I thought I might go blind, that I had already been rendered so in that eye.

"Hold still," Mother said. "Honey, hold still and let me see." Her voice seemed to come from a long, long way off, somewhere far on the other side of my own howling. It felt as though something were tearing the surface of my eye every time I moved the lid, but I couldn't help moving it. She'd got me over to a water fountain, and stood with her hands tight on my head (I remember being surprised at the strength of her grip, even in my increasing pain). I had never felt anything nearly so urgent or searching; it felt like a live thing, something that was reaching for an opening, a place to burrow into my skull. I kept yelling, kept struggling to get free of my mother's strong grip, and then we were bending over the fountain, running the water across that part of my face and dousing my neck and chest in the process. I had no idea how we had got there, or even how long we had been running the water — the whole front of me was soaked — but now it was time to board the train. The train was leaving, the high, calm female voice in the walls saying, "Last call for boarding," that watery echo of the soft voice in the speakers. We had to run, impeded by our carry-on bags and my blindness, and after we were in our compartment, sitting down, Mother worked on me again. My eye wouldn't stop watering, but by this time the pain had subsided a little, and I could begin to believe it would quit altogether soon. I looked at Lisa, whose face was both terrified and curious, and even as I felt the immaturity of the impulse, I wanted to stick out my tongue.

"Better?" Mother said.

"I never felt anything so awful," I told her.

"But it's better now."

And just then a man appeared in the door of the compartment. "Need help?" he said.

My mother looked at him, but did not answer.

"I'm sorry," he said. "I saw you out the window. I wished there was something I could do, but I was already on the train and I couldn't get the window open. I'm a couple of cars down." He smiled.

My mother said, "Everything's fine now."

"Well, that's good then." He looked at me. "That sort of thing smarts, I know."

I nodded. I was still holding one hand over the eye.

"The stinging stop?"

"Mostly."

"Takes a while." He looked at Mother. "My name's Terpin."

"Well," Mother said, "thanks for your concern, Mr. Terpin."

"Don't mention it," he said, smiling again, and I thought I saw a touch of irony in the smile, as if he were about to add a joke or a teasing line, perhaps even a flirtation — or had at least entertained the thought and then decided against it. He was lean and rather sharp-featured, with a small pointed chin and close-cropped black hair, and there was something held-in about him. He might be using only a fraction of the energy he possessed. Perhaps it was just that the seersucker suit jacket he wore was too tight in the upper arms and shoulders. Now he turned toward the corridor, but he paused to look back in at us. He was obviously waiting for Mother to say her name.

"Is there something else?" she said.

"No," he said. "Well, nice journey."

And he was gone.

We watched the door for a moment. The compartment was a sleeper, and there were three fold-out cots. Two of them doubled as seats, and below these were small storage spaces, for baggage. I thought there would be a bathroom, but the little space in the wall next to the windows yielded up only another storage space. "Where's the bathroom?" I said.

"I guess it must be outside, at the end of the corridor maybe."

"You're kidding."

"Close the door," Mother said to Lisa.

The door wouldn't move for Lisa, so I had to do it. When we were all sitting down again, with me facing the two of them, Lisa drew the muscles of her face together and tried a scornful imitation of the man's voice. "Well, nice journey."

"Lisa, there's no reason to make fun of people all the time," Mother told her. "I don't like that in you."

"Nice," Lisa said under her breath. "*Nice.*"

Aunt Elaine had said once that Lisa was too precocious for her own good. I didn't think much about it back then, though I was occasionally impressed by her outsized vocabulary, and had been brought fairly often to the point of rage when subjected to her ability, if the mood was on her — that is, if she was unhappy about something and solutions were not promptly forthcoming — for finding evil combinations of things to say or do. In any case, the beginning of our journey furnished her with several choice opportunities, none of which she ignored. Our compartment was supposedly air-conditioned — the result of Grandfather Tinan's efforts to provide us with the comforts of first class — but it was equipped with only one small vent, which gave forth a feeble sigh of coolness that was almost immediately overruled by the stifling air. We suffered the heat for an hour or so without saying much, and when the porter came Mother mentioned the lack of ventilation. He shook his head, frowning — this was clearly not the first time he had heard about it — and then he went on to say that the train's air-conditioning unit was operating at maximum capacity, and there was nothing to do but close the curtains and try not to move around very much.

"Oh," Lisa said, smiling brightly at him. "You mean, we have to pretend we're deceased."

He seemed for a few seconds to doubt that he could have heard her correctly. "Pardon?" he said.

But now Mother had spoken, too. "Lisa, be quiet."

The man smiled at us, then, and I must say he did look a little absurd, with his cap pulled down to the top of his ears, bending them slightly, and his one front tooth that jutted out from the others as though something had forced it from the inside of his mouth.

"Deceased means dead," Lisa told him in that bright, fake cheerfulness.

"Lisa."

He stared at her now, as if intending to remember the face; he was a man who knew when he had been insulted, even if the one delivering the insult happened also to be a seven-year-old girl.

"Where is a bathroom we can use?" Mother asked him.

"There's one at the end of every car," he said. "Even these."

"Do any of the compartments have bathrooms?"

"Not many lately, ma'am."

"Why?"

He shrugged. "Railroad's run up on hard times. Maintenance is one of the things they cut around here."

"But there's no trouble with keeping the train tracks working right," said my sister. "And we're not all going to go flying off the first bridge we come to."

"We've been over some bridges already, miss." He smiled; he had been trying for a joking tone.

"We made it," said Lisa.

It was as if Mother and I had decided to let her speak for us.

"Will there be anything else?" the porter said to Mother.

"It says 'air-conditioned,' " Lisa said. "Maybe you should change it."

"I don't make the ads," he said simply.

"Lisa, that's enough," Mother said.

"Well," said the porter almost grudgingly, looking at Mother, then at me, and then at Mother again. "You folks have a nice trip." And he shut the door.

I got up to close the curtains.

"Don't," Mother said. "I can't stand to be closed in. I have to be able to see out."

"I'm sorry," I said.

"And stop apologizing all the time."

"I'm not apologizing all the time," I told her.

"Hush," she said.

Lisa scowled at me and then lifted her chin, a smile of childish satisfaction on her face. I tried to dismiss her from my thoughts altogether, gazing out the window at the walls of the station platform with their ads for whiskey and cigarettes, and for the fall season at some theater in New York. The train started moving, and the whole car pitched and yawed, as though it might jump the track before it left the station.

We were quiet. In some way, I think we were all aware of what this moment signified: we were heading for a new and undreamed-of fate. Mother gathered Lisa a little closer to her side, and the train picked up momentum, swaying and clanking and groaning. The countryside grew briefly less suburban: we saw a wide field of tobacco, a fallow acre of weeds and rocks and wildflowers, and then a creek winding away from us in a glassy replica of the willows that dipped their branches at its edge. Beyond this, we rumbled past a smooth open lawn and a farmhouse tucked amid soft green maples, adjacent to a country road. It was a beautiful scene, and I knew people lived in that house; it was a place for them to come to and be safe together. The road wound sharply away from it and ran alongside the tracks for a mile or so, and at a crossing it ended in a small gas station and market, with twenty or thirty empty husks of automobiles in the wild grass of the yard. Three black men lounged in cane chairs on the porch in front, their dark faces not much darker than the shade they sat in, their work clothes faded, salt white. One of them lifted a thin black arm and waved at me as we went by. I waved back. He stared after me, and we did not look away from each other until he had been screened by the long, rocking motion of the rearward cars. If I could have stuck my head out the window I would have, for I had discovered a curious sense of bereavement in myself, as if some vein of grief had been opened near my heart at the moment the black man disappeared from view. It was a strange few minutes. My mother and sister had settled themselves, had seen nothing, and yet I felt that something important had transpired.

"What," Mother said when she caught me looking at her.

"Nothing," I said.

The heat was almost unbearable. We were nearing the central counties now — Roanoke and Amherst. In Roanoke there were narrow streets with houses on either side of them, and at one point we passed through a busy shopping area. Now and then the sun poured in the window. Everything was too bright. I closed my eyes for a moment, then opened them again. Lisa was staring at me. "Don't breathe toward me," she said. "It makes me hotter."

I made an effort to ignore her.

"Turn your head," she demanded.

"Lisa, just shut up," I said.

"Mother, he won't stop."

"Please leave her alone," Mother said, staring at a magazine she had opened in her lap.

"I'm not doing anything to her," I said. "Can't a person breathe?"

Lisa leaned forward, obviously feeling confident that she had Mother's tacit allegiance. "Stop looking at me," she said.

I said, "I don't believe this."

"Both of you hush," said Mother. "Thomas, leave her alone."

"Nobody would believe this in a million years," I said.

"Just the both of you stop it."

I looked out the window, and then felt Lisa staring at me. Now it seemed that both my eyes were stinging. I had a headache. I could feel the blood rushing to my face and neck.

"Now who's breathing toward who?" I said.

"Mommy."

Mother looked at us as though we were some careless stranger's children, and said, "I can't bear this another minute. I swear I'm going out to the club car. You can sit here and bicker all the way to North Dakota if you want to, I've had it."

We quieted down, and for a few minutes she sat there biting the cuticle of her thumb, staring at the empty space next to me as though it were something to read. In the next moment, I realized that I was staring at her again. I know now that my mother was beautiful in a strange, dark way. Back then, I had no opinion of her looks at all except to say that they were familiar to me; I recognized them. So I stared at her, with my old sensation of wondering what it was like to look out of someone else's eyes, idly guessing at her level of discomfort in the heat. She looked almost cool, in fact. Her pale skin was dry; her small hands flew to her hair and back down to her lap. Her dark, dark eyes were restless. Outside the window, a river shone brightly with reflected sun, and we were crossing it, within a few sunny yards of the shade trees flanking its winding edge. I thought my mother seemed scared, sitting there watching everything trail past the window. Then she was looking at me.

"What," she said again.

"Nothing," I said.

"Lisa's right. Don't stare."

"I'm not staring."

"Yes, you are," Lisa said.

I said, "Shut up, Lisa."

Without saying anything further to us, Mother gathered her purse and went out of the compartment.

"Now look what you did," Lisa said.

I have always been tempted to believe that in a way this bickering of ours led to everything else we were to go through. By this I mean that when I think back on it, it has the feel of one of those emotional tripwires by which a susceptibility is irritated into action, and a weakness of character is exposed to the wrong stress at the right time. Of course nothing could be further from the truth; the idea is patently ridiculous. Our bickering led to nothing, and my feeling about it is atavistic, like that sense the doomed man has that his medical exam has brought about the catastrophe he faces, and if only he hadn't gone to see the doctor, he might still be in the bloom of health.

Since all this happened more than twenty years ago, there are elements of the story I'll have to make up, trying to fit all the pieces together, and so I want to be as honest and careful as I can with what I *do* know. Moreover, I think it's important that you not be misled by anything I say, and perhaps it's best to leave it at that.

You'll see.

After Mother was gone, I got up to look out the door of the compartment, feeling contrite and wanting to go bring her back. Behind me in the room, Lisa said, "I wouldn't open the door like that if I were you."

I said, "Shut up."

But she had already forgotten me, and was ranged on all fours across the part of the seat where Mother had been, her face as close to the vent as she could get it, breathing deeply, basking in the comfort born of relief. I turned from her and looked up and down the thin corridor. It was clear. Through the window of the vestibule I could see the next car swaying back and forth, people standing in a line in that window. I walked down there, rocking with the motion of the train, and when I got to the end of our car I peered through the glass, saw that the next car was the dining car and that Mother was standing in the line. She had lighted a cigarette, and she didn't see me. The woman in front of her was also smoking. They both seemed to be mulling over something one of them had said.

Once I'd satisfied myself that I was not missing anything by remaining in our compartment, I returned to find Lisa with her face still pressed against the air-conditioning vent. The train was passing through a town — a station platform glided by the window, an old red brick building, and then a row of buildings with cars parked in front of them, and people walking along a sidewalk. It was late in the forenoon. There were sharp shadows in the street, and dust was kicking up in the wind. I watched all this for a time, and then the train stopped. "We're there," Lisa said.

I explained to her, quite gently I thought, and with a great deal of mature patience, that we had a long way to go yet.

"I'm talking about Washington — we have to change trains."

"It's not Washington yet," I told her. I hadn't seen any signs, hadn't bothered to read them.

"People are getting off," she said.

I wondered if we weren't in fact supposed to be getting off: I knew we had to change trains at least twice, because I'd heard Mother talking to Aunt Elaine about it. Feeling a stir of panic, I went back out into the corridor and almost ran headlong into the conductor, who took my arms above the elbow as if to steady me. I looked into his eyes, his vaguely clownish face.

"Whoa, there," he said.

"Is this Washington?" I asked.

"Roanoke," he said, and moved on past me.

I turned back into the compartment. "Did you hear?" I said to Lisa.

"If you know so much," she said, "how come you didn't know this was Roanoke and not Washington?"

I sat down across from her and looked out the window. Two men in Army uniforms stood in the sun, trying to read a piece of paper one of them held open in both hands. The wind blew their tan shirt fronts and pulled the folds of their sleeves back. I thought of Father.

"Close the door," Lisa said. "The hot air's getting in."

"You've got the vent," I said. "If you want the door closed, you close it."

"Where's Mother?"

I closed the door and stood over her. "I swear, Lisa."

"I want a Coke," she said.

"Get away from the vent and sit down."

"I don't have to listen to you."

I reached down and pulled her away from the vent. "Now sit there and be quiet."

She waited a moment, staring at me out of a deep frown, and then she screamed her scream, that long, piercing racket that felt as though it might shatter my eardrums.

I sat still, pretended that it wasn't anything. But she kept on, and finally I stood over her again. She let it wind down, still looking at me, half smiling now, her mouth open on the end of the shout, so that it was nothing more than a kind of singing.

"Are you finished?" I said.

"No."

I sat down again.

"Where's Mother?"

"Just be quiet — she'll be back in a minute."

We sat there. The train had begun to move again, and soon the land was gliding by us, opening out into a view of the backs of shopping malls, the littered alleys and rows of dumpsters, and the occasional glimpse of a street with houses.

"It's too hot," Lisa said.

"Be quiet," I told her.

We glared at each other. It was clear that there wasn't much affection between us. She sighed, and when she saw by the expression on my face that this irritated me, she sighed again. I ignored her and looked out the window. She sighed deeply this time, breathing it out with a small throaty whine that went along my nerves like the sting of a nettle on the skin.

"You're not bothering me," I said, barely able to control my voice. She sighed again.

I took one of the magazines from Mother's overnight bag and sat with it open in front of my face, blocking my view of her, and of course she kept it up. I fixed my gaze on a photograph of five people standing on a sunny pier beside a stupendous marlin which was strung up on a winch or cable, the sharp mouth open, the great silver length of it gleaming in the light. The people held up cans of beer, and their faces were lined and brown and healthy; they were all smiling, confident, calm, delighted to be where they were. I stared at this picture, at these people with their money and their leisure under the sun of some tropical midday, squinting into the brightness that bathed them, no loved ones languishing in prison, each of them with homes to go to, the immaculate blue ocean shimmering and sparkling beyond their burnished shoulders as if patiently waiting for them to turn around and appreciate it — and for a second I had a sense of the happiness, the hard, narrow carelessness of this pause in their lives. It filled me with a longing so deep that I must've sighed, too.

"You're not bothering me," Lisa said, "so you can just quit it."

I tore the page out of the magazine, folded it, and put it in my shirt pocket.

"I'm telling."

I said nothing.

Once more we were quiet. Apparently I must've sighed again, because she said, "You might as well quit it." Then she moved on the seat to put her face against the vent.

"Get away from it," I said.

When she didn't answer or move, I leaned across and kicked at her hip. I barely made contact, but she wailed as though I'd broken the bone. "Come on," I said. "I didn't hurt you."

She sat there with the tears streaming down her cheeks, waiting for Mother to come and find her like that.

"Lisa," I said. "All right. I'm sorry." And this seemed to placate her a little. She sniffled, looked out the window.

"How do they do it when you visit somebody in prison?"

I didn't know. I knew what I had seen in movies. I said, "You talk through a screen, maybe."

"Like in a window?"

"Maybe."

"Well is it?"

I didn't answer.

"Tell me."

"It could be a window or it could be a table."

"Well, which is it, do you think?"

"I don't know, all right? I've never been in a prison."

"I bets it's bars. Like jail."

We were quiet. She'd said so little about what had happened to us, and now she seemed anxious, tentative, as though afraid of what she wanted to ask next. But then she sat back and looked away from me. "I have to go to the bathroom."

I observed her without answering: a miserable little girl in a wrinkled, light blue dress, hot and sticky, her hair matted to her forehead, her face red and smudged and tear-streaked. I thought about how she was not much more than a baby, and how it wasn't her fault that she was cranky and irritable. Perhaps she was old enough to know that what we were doing was unusual, and perhaps she could divine that it was tinted with embarrassment and shame, but she had nothing, really, with which to face up to it all: in a sense she was quite alone, encapsulated by her own innocence. At least *I* was partially in Mother's confidence.

"Come on," I said, and reached for her hand.

We went out into the corridor and stood for a moment, leaning against the closed door. The car swayed, and there was the sound of the wheels under us. Through the windows of the opposite compartment we saw the houses of Roanoke, and the back yards. In one yard a woman in a white dress stood at the entrance of a gazebo, holding a drink. No part of her moved as we went by, not even her head, though

I was certain that she looked through the shadows of the corridor at me. Briefly I felt pinned where I was, an object of curious attention in the mind of a goddess. But then she was gone, and Lisa was leaning into the window, trying to see her. "Rich people," she said. "You can tell because they have a little house outside their regular house."

The bathroom was at the other end of the car from the vestibule leading to the dining car with its snack bar. I took her there.

"You're not supposed to come in with me," she said.

I said, without much patience now, "Lisa, just go in and take care of it, will you?"

"Nobody's around," she said. "Please?"

And it came to me that she *wanted* me to go in there with her. "It's all right," I told her, feeling a little sick of myself. I hadn't been much of a big brother, and the fear in her eyes made me wish I had at least tried a little harder. "Really, honey. I'll wait right here."

"Suppose somebody's in there lurking about or something?"

It struck me that this was a line Mother or Father might have laughed at in other times. "I'll be right here," I said.

She gave me a doubtful look, but then pushed the door open and went in. A second later she pulled it back. "Don't go anywhere."

"I won't," I said.

"Promise."

I held my hand up. "Promise. Lisa, do you have to go or not?"

"I'm afraid you'll leave me." She seemed about to cry, and looking at her pale, distraught features I received an impression, fleeting but quite clear, of having continually to be reminded that I was unhappy — that we were in the middle of what anyone would say was serious misfortune. The daily flow of our lives had kept lulling me into an accustomed lassitude, a kind of weary trance. This was what constituted our lives together now, this unexpected journey, this time cooped up in a swaying, clattering, oppressive train car. For the fact was that there were appetites to satisfy and comforts to seek, and the small momentary reliefs were providing a more general pattern of alleviation than I could understand. And perhaps it isn't even necessary to say that there exists a moment in human unhappiness which is so much itself, so much its own reference point, that one loses the sensation of life ever having been otherwise: one goes on, suffers indignity and shame, and finally begins to grow at home in it.

When Lisa had been gone a minute, I walked to the other end of the car to look for Mother. There wasn't any line at the snack bar now, and I saw no one. I wanted to see Mother because I had remembered our extremity, our aloneness. And then Lisa came from the restroom, hurrying along the wall of windows, whining about how I'd left her.

"I didn't go anywhere," I told her, irritated again.

"I couldn't do it," she said. "There's no toilet paper. Everything smells in there."

I took her into the men's room, which was closetlike and urinous and badly neglected. But there was toilet paper. I stood outside the metal stall and waited for her, and when she took longer than I thought she should, I said, "Are you finished yet?"

"A minute," she said in a tearful rush.

"Take your time," I said, feeling another spasm of guilt.

"Please don't leave me, Thomas."

"I won't leave you." I had spoken evenly, without any trace of irritation, I thought.

"Well, you left me before," she said.

Finally she came out, taking my hand quickly, as though uncertain of my presence there. We held tight. I wanted her with me now, and was afraid of losing her in the bigness of the world outside the door. We went into the corridor and along the shining metallic wall of closed doors to the open entrance of our compartment. Mother wasn't there. Inside, we sat side by side and watched the country change out the windows. The train had picked up speed. We were flying now, and when you looked close, the ground was a red blur.

For the next half hour or so we entertained ourselves, looking through the magazine and talking. We got close to the air-conditioning vent and breathed, and Mother startled us, having come to get us for lunch. We went to the dining car and sat in a booth. The train food was almost inedible, and anyway I didn't have much appetite.

"Come on, Thomas," Mother said. "Eat."

"I am." The ham I'd ordered was ribboned with gristle, and after a while I wiped my mouth and sat back. Out of the crowd moving through the car, Mr. Terpin appeared. "Good lunch?" he said.

Mother smiled politely. "Not too," she said.

"The pictures on the menus look so appetizing."

I watched him move on to another table, and thought about how there seemed a difference in his demeanor toward her, a new familiarity.

"Well?" Mother said. "Are you finished?"

"Yes," I said.

She led us back to our compartment, carrying a tray of iced Cokes. And then when we were situated, and she had sat watching us drink, she got out of her seat. "I'll be back."

Lisa and I waited.

"Goddammit," Lisa said.

"Don't cuss," I told her.

Mother came back and took her seat, and we rode in silence, not even attending to each other, really. At length, she fidgeted and sat forward a little. "Do you mind if I go up to the dining car again?" she said to me.

"No," I said.

"Will you watch Lisa?"

I nodded.

"I can trust you?"

"Are you going to see Mr. Terpin?" I said. I hadn't known I would say it.

She gave me a look. "I'm going to get a drink and talk to any other adult."

"Mr. Terpin?"

"Yes, if he's there. He's a nice young man."

I said nothing. But I had heard what she said to Aunt Elaine, and I'm sure that what I was thinking must've been all over my face.

She stood, put her purse over her shoulder, and stared down at me. "Would both of you like to come along?"

"No," I said.

"I'll be back in a few minutes."

When she was gone, Lisa and I looked at each other. "I'm going to take off my dress," Lisa said.

I watched her do this, then curl the dress up and use it as a pillow on the seat. Out the window there were mountains, and wildflowers looking like spilled colors in the hills. I fell asleep without wanting to, and when I came to, my neck was stiff and sore. Mother was standing in the entrance looking at us. "How long has she been asleep?"

"I don't know," I said groggily.

"We'll be in Washington in a couple of hours," she said. "You've both missed Charlottesville."

"I didn't sleep," I said, and she smiled at me.

The next thing I knew, Lisa was pulling on my arm. She had to go to the bathroom again.

"Thomas, come on."

"Okay," I said.

She struggled into her dress and I took her to the men's room, where I waited for her, lurching with the motion of the train slowing down. She hurried out.

"Where's Mother?"

"She was just here," I said.

We went back to the compartment. Through the windows I saw what I knew was the Potomac River, its weed-choked banks and its cherry trees standing in their lovely pools of shade. Beyond the trees stood the scrubbed-looking marble façade of the Lincoln Memorial. We were coming into Washington.

"Look at it," I said to Lisa, feeling in some dim proprietary way that I ought to point these sights out to her. She wasn't interested.

"Where *is* Mother?" she said. "She's been gone all this time. We have to get off the train now."

"Not for a while," I told her. "It'll be a few minutes."

I went to the window and watched the river glide on out of view, the trees and buildings and grassy banks reflected in it as though lovingly and exactingly painted onto the placid surface. For perhaps the first time I had something like a sense of adventure about this trek we were making. Andrews Air Force Base was only a few miles away from the city, and so I had seen Washington — I had walked its streets — but this was a different vision of it, and under different circumstances. From here we would begin the long passage west.

We slowed and entered a narrow place, like a rut in concrete, between the backs of gray, featureless office buildings. I thought of the worried face of the President, who just the evening before had been on television talking about the war I now knew my father would not go to again. For some reason it hadn't occurred to me until that moment, but the fact that we would never have to worry about his having to return there was a positive thing, and I decided I would try and remember to tell Mother about it.

"Look," Lisa said to me.

We had come out into open space, into a panorama of streets, along one of which there was a big crowd of demonstrators, many of them carrying signs. They were chanting something, shouting it really, but I couldn't make out what it was. Policemen stood in close ranks on either side of the road where the demonstrators marched. They wore helmets and held nightsticks in their fists, and yet, as I recall, their faces were faintly amused. It was as though they knew something, some surprise they were holding back. Everyone, including the demonstrators, seemed to be having a fine time. There were also tourists crossing the yellow gravel paths and grassy places between streets, wearing bright summer colors and carrying cameras. The whole tableau made it appear that three distinct groups of people had decided to occupy the same city block at the same time — and no one knew quite how to behave. The train had stopped momentarily, but then we moved again, gathering some speed, leaving all of it behind. As we went over a narrow bridge near a wharf, we could see a row of houses with dirt yards, in one of which a dark woman in a faded checked dress was hanging wash on a line. A baby played on a blanket in the dust behind her. All around were other clotheslines, some with wash on them. I saw flowers blooming in partly open windows, and then the railroad bed sank between two thick concrete walls splattered over every inch with paint: a jumble of graffiti — exhortations, names, symbols, cartoon faces and shapes. The train was slowing to a stop. "I'm scared," Lisa said.

"We're not staying in Washington," I told her.

"Where's Mother?" She was getting ready to cry now, and I gathered her to myself.

"We'll be getting off in a minute," I said, patting her shoulder, trying to soothe her, though I was beginning to wonder if something hadn't happened to prevent Mother from rejoining us. I was resolved to wait at least until the train had come to a complete stop before we went searching. The truth was that I had discovered how frightened I was, too.

6

I MENTIONED EARLIER that I would have to reconstruct some elements of the story, and we have now arrived at one of those passes where conjuring becomes necessary (though even for what follows I have the considerable authority of my mother's testimony, because we did eventually talk about these and other events of that year, and she told me a lot).

So, for now, let us leave Lisa and me in that hot compartment, gazing out at the freight yards west of Washington's dilapidated old Union Station. Moving along the narrow, polished train corridor, through the vestibule of the neighboring car with its meager snack bar and its skinny, bored, discouraged-looking attendant — its clutch of jostling people waiting for the sorry approximations of food offered at exorbitant prices — let us pass on into the adjoining dining area, where Mother sits fidgeting in a booth with Mr. Terpin and a young blond woman, Penny Holt, from Wise, Virginia. Ms. Holt is small and yet somehow voluptuous-looking, as if she were more full-figured than she is (it's a quality of her flesh, a softness coupled with something else, not quite definable). She's possessed of a clean, washed lightness of hair and skin. There's a natural vividness about her, and she is truly beautiful — except for one rather unnerving flaw, which Mother has just discovered with chilly astonishment: the woman's left eye is false, is made of milk-colored glass with an off-blue, intricately foliate iris which does not exactly match the color of her lovely good right eye. Penny Holt gazes with the one eye at Mother and then at the table and then at Mother again while Terpin talks about serendipity, the mysteries of coincidence. After having discovered that they are all three bound for the same connecting train out of Washington, they have gone on to the surprising, and for Mr. Terpin the almost occult, revelation that Mother is also traveling to visit someone in prison: Mr. Terpin's younger brother Buddy is serving time at Leavenworth, in Kansas, for refusing to be inducted into the Army. Terpin describes his brother's pride and anger, and hatred of the war, talking on with a complacent and confident fluidity as if there could be no doubt of Mother's sympathy with the incarcerated brother — and it has become clear that he assumes Father's imprisonment is also political.

Indeed, he seems now to be making so much more of the coincidence than seems reasonable, and Mother wishes she hadn't said anything at all about where she is headed: she had blurted it out, to her own amazement, as he began telling her about his brother. She knows that it's because she did so as he was describing the political nature of his brother's trouble that he has come to this embarrassing conclusion about her husband. And now Terpin is rattling on in his fascination, going so far as to wonder how many others on the train are on their way to government prisons. Mother knows he'll have some questions that will be difficult to evade, since under the circumstances her very reluctance to answer them will give something away.

Imagine her in this odd situation, sitting in the booth with Mr. Terpin at her side, between her and the aisle, and the blond woman opposite them both, gazing quietly at her with that weirdly beautiful face, saying nothing. Having come here to find someone other than Lisa and me to talk to, having wanted just the space and the air and a few minutes to be herself, she had sat alone in the booth, trying not to cry and thinking about going home, about being in her father's house again, and the unspoken pressures to stay which she knew would be brought to bear immediately upon her arrival — thinking about the old steady pull of those ties she'd thought she had broken years ago by traveling the world with her Air Force husband. All of this, and wanting some relief from having to worry about any of it, had made her nod at Terpin as he approached and began to talk. There was no flirtation; Penny Holt was with him. The three of them chatted idly about the discomfort of trains, the green hills and mountains out the windows, the dark red color of the earth in the bare patches of passing fields. It was refreshing to speak of these things and to say, truthfully, without thinking about it quite, that she was heading west to visit family. The time flew by. At Charlottesville, she went to check on Thomas and Lisa, and looking at them asleep, felt instantly beset and sad again. She shook Thomas awake, and was in that moment guilty, too, for the stricken look on his face, coming out of sleep. And she had made her way back here because she simply couldn't stand the stifled air of the compartment with her sleeping, unhappy children in it.

Now she smiles and nods and makes all the gestures of attention and appreciation, but she feels hemmed in. Time seems to have disintegrated somehow, and she has to remind herself where she is, sitting here with these people while the train slows down. She's seen the river, the day-moon color of the Lincoln Memorial in its circle of traffic. There's a sweating glass of iced tea before her, which she hasn't touched. Terpin goes on. "The whole damn government's implicated, you see, and it's time people took matters into their own hands. It's what democracy cries out for, really. But I mean, you know, my brother is the one. He went out and did something. Challenged the powers, and I admire him for it. I look up to him for it. He's had the bravery to live at the edge. It's people like him that'll bring the whole thing to a stop. And then everybody will see that guys like that are the real heroes. Not the ones like me that just talk about it and make theories about it, even if the theories are true, which I think they are. It's coming down that there'll be a whole new way of seeing the world. People will learn to stop killing each other and robbing stores and all — all that sort of thing. Because that's all it is — it's the killing. Everything else comes from that."

Connie Boudreaux says, "Is the train stopping?"

Terpin brushes this aside. "It takes them a while to get into the station. Anyway, see, everybody on an individual basis just has to refuse to do any more killing —"

But now Penny Holt interrupts him. "I think we might be stopping now." Her voice is a kind of luxurious whisper, and yet there's nothing sultry or sensual about it; it seems more an aspect of some slight trouble or condition than anything else. Terpin has explained that she's the incarcerated brother's fiancée, and how if only they had stayed together none of this would have happened.

"Buddy is going to freak when he sees Penny," he says now. "It's a surprise, you know. But there I was in Demera, no other family, out of work and having trouble trying to pay the rent and Penny all alone in another town, and with Buddy gone all the way to Kansas. She was living in Tennessee, you know. And it just seemed like the thing to do. Look her up and head out. And I had some money from a settlement out of court and so here we are."

"I was in school when I met Buddy," Penny adds, seeming eager for clarification. "We went together in high school."

"So," Terpin says, "tell us about your husband."

"He's at Wilson Creek, Wyoming."

"That's right," Terpin says with an encouraging nod. It has of course already been established that Connie is on the way to Wilson Creek, Wyoming.

"He — he was in the Air Force," she goes on, and discovers to her great chagrin that she's about to cry. I have a mental picture of her in the light of the window, trying desperately to master herself, to keep the tears back and show nothing of what she's feeling, caught there under the stupidly expectant gaze of Mr. Terpin, who assumes that her emotion is a reaction to the huge injustice of the Johnson government, which is misguided if not corrupt — Mr. Terpin being all good nature and wanting to believe the best about everybody. That is how he presents himself.

"They gave him orders and he wouldn't go," he says, trying to help Mother along.

"Chummy," Penny Holt says to Terpin, "maybe she doesn't want to tell about it."

"Is the train stopping?" Connie says. "I think I have to get back to my compartment."

"We have to go past the Capitol," says Terpin. "It's a ways yet."

The train stops, then lurches forward, picks up a little speed. Mother looks out the window at a weedy open place with other tracks running through it on which several cars sit, their undersides obscured by tall stalks of knife grass. Beyond this, the ornate marble towers of a cathedral are visible, bathed in sun.

"So was it Vietnam they ordered him to?"

"Yes," Connie tells him. "I mean — he — he went to Vietnam. He was wounded there."

"Jesus, and they sent him to prison?"

"Vietnam was before. Four years ago."

"A veteran. God. So what did he do — he refuse to go back? They can throw you in prison for talking out of turn if you're in the military. You know, they were going to draft me but I had asthma real bad. I mean, I still do."

Connie says nothing. There's an odd sort of light in his eyes now, and she has the feeling that he's toying with her.

"It must be really hard if you're in the military and you're against the war and all," he says.

"I'm afraid I can't talk about this. Please."

"How could they do that to someone? After he served, for God's sake. With everything — everything they go through."

Connie glances out at the shadows on the tracks, of phone lines, the leafy shade of trees. There's a pressure now, coming from both these people, about which she is unable to decide. It's as if she were someone they had fixed upon as a sort of test of their own reality. The young woman is now staring at her, so she smiles and nods slightly.

"I hope we're not bothering you," Penny Holt says.

"Well, we won't talk about the war anymore," Terpin says. "We understand everything."

"You talk too much, Chummy." Penny says.

"I'm excitable," says Mr. Terpin. "I know. That's why people call me Chummy."

"But that's what everyone loves about you."

"I don't know."

Penny reaches across the table and takes his hand. "We're good friends."

Terpin says to Connie, "I love her like a brother."

Penny says, "Dear old Chummy."

"My real name is John," he says.

"John," Connie says, merely repeating the name.

"A lot of people don't even know that, you know — people who have known me all my life."

Connie wonders if this is meant as it seems to be meant: he has given her something rare.

"I notice you kind of taking an extra look at my soon-to-be sister-in-law," Terpin says suddenly. "You figured out anything different about her?"

Appalled by the bluntness of the question, Connie can only stammer that she wasn't taking any extra looks at anyone.

"It's perfectly all right," Terpin says. "Isn't it, Penny?"

Penny murmurs that people have been giving her extra looks all her life.

"You know she lost an eye," Terpin says. "See here?"

Connie Boudreaux nods hurriedly and feels her face grow hot.

"You know how it happened?" he asks, and then waits for an answer.

She's now convinced that something pathological has begun, that she has stumbled into a trap. "Please," she manages, "I have to get back to my compartment now."

"Buddy put her eye out accidentally with a stick when they were both five years old. Little babies, and they've known each other all their lives, haven't you, Penny? Since they were babies, and now they're engaged. They're going to be married." He says all this with a brightness that makes Connie recoil, like a reflex against something flying at her.

"I have to go now," she says, a little louder than she has intended to. "Please," she adds more calmly.

Terpin appears not to understand. Then he seems startled. "Oh, I'm in your way. Jesus." And he lunges out of the booth, stands there with an expression of great mortification and sorrow on his face. "I'm such an idiot," he says.

Connie slides out, and when he offers his hand she takes it. "Please forgive me," he says.

"Nothing to forgive," she answers, forcing a smile, and feeling a sudden surge of affection for him too, now, in his deep embarrassment and agitation. She looks at the other woman, whose expression is one of almost dreamy noninterest.

"Well, of course there's something to forgive," he says. "I mean, I've done it again. I've made a perfect fool of myself."

And Penny Holt says, "Oh, stop it."

"Well," Connie says, meaning to excuse herself. Inwardly she's deciding that all her unease is unwarranted.

"Lord," says Terpin. "I wish you'd please try to excuse me." And he hurries away from them both, through the dining car and on. Connie stares after him.

"Believe it or not, he has a little trouble just being with people sometimes," Penny Holt says in that whisper, standing out of the booth and running her hands over the front of her skirt to smooth the cloth. "Really, he's kind of lost sometimes."

"I'm sorry," says Connie, because that seems to be the only possible response. She feels only curiosity now.

The train is swaying slowly, rolling through a series of obliquely intersecting tracks, curving toward a massive stone bridge. There are deep shadows and dimnesses beyond it. The battered-looking main building of Union Station rises in the brightness on the other side.

"Well," Connie says, "it was nice meeting you."

"It's been a very pleasant trip, yes."

"I hope you'll tell Chummy there's no offense."

"He has this idea about the way life is supposed to be," Penny Holt says to her. "He had his mind made up that you'd be friends, because your son got that cinder in his eye and he spoke to you about it. He's very generous and sweet, but when he gets things in his head it's hard to shake him loose from them. He had a whole story made up about how you'd be lifelong friends and how years from now you'd remember the moment on the train when he spoke to you about the cinder in the young man's eye. He's — he's a little eccentric, I guess."

Connie says, "I'm sorry," and this time she means it.

"Don't be. He's happy most of the time, you know."

Again, Connie has the sensation that this is meant as a way of testing something against her reactions.

"Well," she says, "it was nice talking to you."

"You must have a special marriage."

"I'm going to see him, just like you're going to see Buddy."

"Actually," Penny Holt says, "to tell you the truth, we're just sort of drifting."

"I know what you mean," says Connie.

The other woman stares at her. "Sometimes you feel like everything's falling apart."

"Yes."

Penny moves with her through the dining car and into the vestibule. "What did your husband do?"

"He was in the Air Force."

"Right, you told us that. Did he refuse to serve?"

"No."

"Something else. Something bad?"

"No," Connie says, opening the door to the next car.

"You don't want to talk about it."

"I really have to get back to my children."

"I've never been to Kansas."

"Well."

At the door to our compartment, the other woman actually grasps Connie's upper arm to stop her. "Can I write you in Wilson Creek?"

My mother looks at the face, and wonders. There has been an eerily invasive feeling about the whole episode with this woman and her friend. Penny gazes back at her with the one deep blue eye, repeating the question, this time in an almost supplicating tone — which I hear, because the door to the compartment is open now.

"Can I write you, please?"

7

I WAS SITTING across from Lisa, with the magazine open on my lap, when the door opened, and I saw Penny Holt for the first time. I didn't notice the glass eye, and even so I was struck deep down by her face, the lucid, strange glory of it: perfect skin, full lips, thick dark lashes and deep-set eyes, a faintly skewed shape to the bridge of the nose which somehow contributed to the effect of the whole, and an odd, broken something in the expression, as if she had been molded by or had lived through catastrophe.

I don't mean to give an impression of the glass eye as being the cause of our particular responses to her. It wasn't really the bad eye that one reacted to, finally, so much as the astonishing creamy beauty of the face and the way she herself seemed — with each gesture and with the agitated, vaguely injured murmur of her voice — to be harboring something mysterious and infinitely delicate, already damaged. One might indeed notice the glass eye with a shock because it was set into that beauty, that dreamy animation, like the very principle of stillness; and yet there was something about her own attitude concerning herself that expressed an expectation of harm coming from the world.

It's probably superfluous to point out that I'm speaking from more fulsome knowledge of her features than could be discerned in a single glance, even knowing that I missed the eye. And yet I would swear I had some sense of all of it in that first instant, looking through the narrow opening of the doorway and hearing her ask in that voice if she could write Mother.

"Write me?" Mother said. She had opened the door all the way, and had stepped into the compartment. This dazzling girl stood in the opening and pouted, or seemed to pout.

"I don't understand," Mother said.

"The truth is, I'm afraid I won't like Kansas."

"Well, I don't know what to tell you," said Mother.

The girl looked at me and then at Lisa. "These are your children?"

"That's Thomas and this is Lisa."

"Hello. I'm Penny Holt."

I said, "Hello."

Lisa's lips curled in a bored smile. She nodded.

"Wonderful children. You're so lucky. You're such a lucky woman."

"Thank you," Mother said.

"Please don't mind Chummy."

"No."

"I liked you. I mean, you know, I just thought we might correspond."

Mother seemed confused. But there was a certain agitation in her motions that I had seen before, whenever she was pleased and embarrassed at the same time — the way she always took praise of any kind.

"I know I'm a bit forward."

"No," Mother said. "Really."

"I bet a person could just disappear from the face of the earth in Wyoming."

The train was stopping now. We were coming alongside a concrete platform, where clutches of people stood waiting.

"I've gotta go get Chummy. Maybe we'll see you on the next train."

"Goodbye," Mother said, and closed the door.

"Who was that?" Lisa wanted to know.

"Come on," Mother said. "Let's get our stuff together."

"Kind of pretty."

"Will you get going?" Mother said to me.

We gathered our few things without saying any more, and, in what I thought was a surprising departure from character, Lisa kept silent about our earlier altercation.

The corridor was jammed with people waiting to get off the train. We stood packed together in that confining corridor, and someone in front of us coughed, muttered "Shoot," then coughed again. Mother was holding my hand so tight it actually began to hurt, and as I started to tell her about it, Lisa spoke up from the other side.

"You're hurting me."

"I'm sorry."

The crowd moved, and we moved with it. When we got to the vestibule, Terpin was there, coming from the next car. Penny was with him.

"Hey," Penny said, "here we are."

And I saw that the one eye was lightless. I stared. She had turned, her arm locked in Terpin's. "Poor Chummy, thought he stepped over the line."

"I did not, Penny. Stop that."

I had no idea what this meant, and my confusion irritated me. It was as if I were automatically being put on the level of a child Lisa's age. "Who stepped over what line?" I said.

"Thomas, be quiet," said Mother.

Terpin stared at me with the expression of a man who has been shamed into silence.

We all filed out of the opening, stepping down to the platform. The crowd hurried to our left, toward the main terminal, and from beyond the platform came the shrill tumult of another train arriving. Through all this, a voice spoke behind a distorting echo in the walls. It sounded like words in a foreign language. We moved with the others, Mother holding on tight, and then at one point she stopped suddenly to talk to a porter.

"Will our bags go through to Bismarck? We don't have to recheck them here or in Chicago?"

"Did you check the bags?" the porter said.

"We checked them. Of course we checked them."

"All right, then. The ticket agent would've checked them through to your final destination."

"Come on," Penny said. "We'll miss the Chicago train." Her tone was exasperated and impatient, and had a quality of the familiar about it. I watched Mother's face as we all picked up speed. Nothing registered there — certainly not the resistance I thought I might see.

"This way," Terpin said, taking Lisa's hand.

"What the hell," I said.

"Be quiet." Mother squeezed my hand.

We went along a corridor of plasterboard and metal, out onto another platform and a wide, arched entrance. There, the main terminal opened out before us like the far reaches of a stadium or coliseum, the high, scalloped buttresses and the many-paned windows full of sunlight and dust. The floor was marble, and everything — every sound — echoed, mixing with the garbled ring of the voice speaking in the stratospheric spaces so far above us. I stood for a moment and stared.

"Thomas."

Mother was a few feet away, flanked by Terpin and Penny Holt and Lisa. They looked like a family.

"Hurry."

I went over to them, and together we made our way to the ticket counters, where we discovered that our train was already boarding. A porter led us to the platform, and we all climbed on, still together. Our compartment was exactly like the one we had just left. Terpin and Penny Holt hovered near the doorway while we got in and settled ourselves.

"Well," Mother said, "thanks for all your help."

"Nothing of it," Terpin mumbled.

"I think we're in the next car up," Penny said. "We'll come back and let you know."

"I'm going to try and take a nap," Mother told her.

There was a brief pause. "You must be exhausted."

"Maybe we can have something to eat together later on," Terpin said.

"Yes, maybe we can."

"Well, so long." He leaned in and looked at Lisa and me. "See you," he said.

Mother closed the door and breathed.

A moment later, Lisa said, "Jeez . . ."

"Be quiet," Mother said.

"I hate this," said Lisa.

We sat facing each other as before, while Mother stood leaning on the door.

Lisa was staring at me.

"What," I said to her.

"This car is hotter than the last one was."

Mother shook her head, then sat next to Lisa. "Be quiet, please. Both of you."

"Who are those people, anyway?" I demanded.

"They're going to Kansas," Mother told me. "They're just people on the train."

"If you ask me, I think they're odd," Lisa put in.

"Well, we didn't ask you."

"They were being awful familiar with us," I said.

"I don't know what the etiquette is on trains — what's polite. They seem very nice."

"One of that blond lady's eyes doesn't move when the rest of her face moves," said Lisa. "I saw it right away, and I know there's something wrong."

I decided to let Mother explain. We were already moving again, lurching back and forth over the complaints of the wheels, that iron-screeching sound. She told us what she knew. Her voice was clear and rather toneless, and she didn't really say much. She might have been describing some task she wanted us to perform.

"Why didn't they send Father to this prison in Kansas?" I asked when she had finished.

"How would I know that?" she said. "I don't know."

"I'm sorry," I said.

"Those people think your father —" she began, then hesitated. "Never mind. We probably won't see them anymore now, anyway." The darkness outside the windows gave way to light, and we saw the back end of row houses again, beyond shining tracks, each with its own ribbon of sparse grass down the center.

"Doesn't it hurt having a glass eye?" Lisa asked.

"I guess not."

"Can she take it out?"

This thought had the effect of upsetting my stomach. I said, "Come on, Lisa."

"I just asked a question," she said.

"Both of you be quiet," said Mother.

"Well, I didn't do anything and Thomas kicked me before."

"Lisa, be still."

"He did. And it hurt."

The ghost of the seven-year-old in me couldn't resist: "And you said 'Goddammit,'" I said to Lisa.

"I did not," she said. It was almost a shout.

Mother squeezed Lisa's arm. "Young lady, the next time you open your mouth I'm going to smack it."

Lisa hunched down in the seat, her arms folded tight, and even at a mature seventeen I made no effort to refrain from giving her a smug little gratified smile of triumph. She glared out the window, and Mother opened the magazine that I had been reading. The train was picking up some speed and was now moving through the neighborhoods — there was even open country in the distance. We wouldn't have to change trains again until we reached Chicago. I felt that everything up to now had been a sort of preliminary, and that at last we were on our way. I had an image of Father sitting in his cell, staring at a barred window and waiting for us. Perhaps the sky was blue outside his window, and perhaps a bird sang in the branches of a tree. He had said it was sunny where he was. He had said the weather was warm. I pictured him sunbathing in a yard surrounded by high walls. I saw a man pacing on top of the walls with a rifle, and another man in a booth, sitting at a machine gun. It was momentarily all very clear in my mind, and it made me angry with myself, as if I had shown him some disrespect. Something in my boy's heart was excited about the prospect of seeing the prison, actually entering its walls and looking around. There was an element of drama about our situation which was somehow separate from what we felt, but which colored our actions nonetheless. Or I should say it colored our thoughts. At least it did mine, and I was conscious enough of it to try and shake it off, to try thinking about anything else.

I watched the countryside change from urban to rural again, the tenement houses and tight neighborhoods and old schoolyards north of Washington giving way to littered, grassy hills and empty fields, and the small Maryland towns gliding by with their quiet streets, their rows of shops with cars parked face-in along the curbs. Outside a restaurant a group of men, blacks and whites, were arguing, but we had gone by them before I could see enough to guess what might be at issue between them. And I was only vaguely curious, anyway. You have to understand the feeling then. I was going to live in the faraway town where my father was imprisoned, and I did not care about anything else. I had no hopes for the future, no opinion as to the great upheavals we saw on television in the evenings. As I said before, the war was going on across the world and the enemy body counts were being announced on the news, and none of it had anything to do with us. Nothing seemed to change about the news from day to day: the fire-fights and bombings were always there, and every newscast had some chaos in the streets to report, but it was all just the same as white noise. I was one year away from an unrefusable invitation to serve in the armed forces, the President had doubled and tripled his calls for more troops — yet even now, riding toward Chicago on the train, I gave very little thought to any of it. I had experienced that moment of being glad that at least my father couldn't go to the war anymore, and it didn't even occur to me that I was only months away from being eligible to go there myself.

We were an Air Force family. The war was something the Air Force had been ordered to prosecute, and it was in the process of doing that. If it was true enough that the Air Force had recently treated us badly, we were nevertheless imbued with the attitudes of all our years as a part of it. Then, too, we had believed the history books and the movies and television shows — we had the evidence of the other wars we had fought and won, and in those days we all believed, didn't we, in the advance of our causes through those means. For a long time we never questioned what the outcome of this particular war would be. But I offer this only as an item of curiosity, for even if we had known it was a dreadful, blood-soaked mistake, we would probably not have given it more than a passing thought.

We *could* not have, given our circumstances. Its effects seemed too far away.

I'll say here, too, that if in that week I had gone to the war, if I had been drafted into it, I would probably have tried to put down the natural urge in myself toward resistance, would probably have swallowed the universal fear and stepped into line precisely because the war did not truly concern me. (Eventually, without any draft, that is what I did. But I'm getting ahead of myself.) Going to war, a man leaves behind the personal tangle of the life he is leading, and escapes from the complications which for a young lifetime have confronted him as himself.

I ask forgiveness for including this sort of comment. I do so only to be as clear as possible about the way we actually were — what we thought and felt about things — in our specific circumstances: part of a broken family riding in a compartment on a train, crossing a country which was at war with itself, in the summer of 1967.

8

_____

THERE WAS a twenty-minute stop in Pittsburgh and another, longer one, lasting almost an hour, in Cleveland, but we didn't get off the train. And then we were riding on toward Chicago. At some point near evening Mother left us again, this time to go bring us dinner. I waited a minute and then followed her, leaving Lisa asleep, head lolling on the seat back and blocking the useless air-conditioning vent, her hair slicked down with perspiration along the gleaming, feverish-looking sides of her face, her mouth open in an expression of humid exhaustion. I crossed through to the next car, a coach filled with people in all the attitudes of discomfort, many of them sleeping, their arms and legs thrown over armrests and propped on seat backs. They looked as though they had been dropped into that cramped space from above, dolls in the bottom of a closet. I moved past them, barely noticed by anyone, and out to the ovenlike vestibule, where I paused and watched Mother, who stood in a line of people at another snack bar, talking to Chummy Terpin. He was turned away from me, but I could tell from the movement of his shoulders that he was laughing at something and trying to talk. Mother smiled, then seemed to shift herself away from him. I don't know what I thought I might see in that moment. I only know that I hesitated there, and perhaps it was just the interest anyone might have upon seeing either of his parents in such a candid way, as themselves. When she turned and saw me she seemed concerned, and I entered the car, starting toward her.

"Thomas," she said. "Where's your sister?"

"She's asleep, and her head is blocking the air-conditioning vent." This was not what I had meant to say. I had meant to seem grown-up and casual, merely wondering if she needed help carrying the food. And instead those words had come, with all the juvenile sourness of a bored, unhappy child. I had no means to describe this at the time, but I knew it as surely as I knew that she would order me back where I belonged.

When she did so, Terpin gave me what I later decided must have been intended as a sympathetic look. There was such benignity and attempted understanding in it. I glared back at him and saw that he was now embarrassed. He looked down at the floor. I noticed that he was balding at the top of his forehead.

"I'll bet your boy wanted to help carry the food back," he said to Mother.

"Well, I would've asked for his help if I thought I'd need it. I need him to stay with his sister."

"Oh, certainly."

"Lisa's asleep," I said.

"There," said Terpin, and smiled at me. His eyes in this light were the color of a hot summer sky in midday. Indeed, they were not far from the color of Penny Holt's glass eye. He folded his hands and leaned toward me.

"No more trouble with the eye?" he said.

This stunned me.

Mother said, "He's fine now."

"Those cinders can really smart."

"I'm fine now," I said, understanding at last.

"You shouldn't leave Lisa alone," Mother said.

"Sometimes I wonder what in the world is going on," said Terpin, apparently referring to whatever they had been talking about before I arrived.

Mother laughed at this, but it was an automatic, ungenuine laugh, a kind of aural punctuation. Then she looked at me and took my wrist, as if to hold me there. "Go sit with your sister and be patient with her. I'll be back in a minute with something to eat."

"I'm thirsty," I said, now actually feeling the thickness in my throat of wanting to cry.

"Get," she said, pointing at me. "Act your age."

I went back through the two cars, nursing my wrath, hearing the wheels whining beneath me as though my own feeling were a sound. The train rocked and swayed, and twice I almost lost my balance. In the vestibules the air went over my face like the breath of someone gasping in the heat. And here was poor Lisa, standing out in the corridor, wringing her hands and looking like all those magazine pictures of children in the midst of disaster. When she saw me coming through the sliding door she ran to me, put her arms around my waist, burying her small, wet face in my abdomen.

"It's all right," I said. "It's okay."

"Where did you go," she said, crying.

I took her back into the compartment and sat with her by the vent. Out the window there were trees now, and then the trees gave way to a high trestle overlooking a winding, shimmering river. "Look," I said. "Look how the water shines."

But I realized quickly enough that this couldn't possibly soothe her, since she had always been terrified of heights. She was too bleary-eyed and upset to see it, though, for she gave no response but crying. I put my arm around her and pulled her close. "Mother's coming with dinner," I said. "Hungry?"

"Not really."

She stared at the floor, sniffling, and the distressed look on her face, the tears running down her cheeks, made me sorry for everything I had ever done to annoy or thwart her. "I'll bet the food's lousy anyway," I told her, gently dabbing her cheeks with the front of my shirt.

We had gone over the trestle and were among trees again. The trees blotted out what was left of the light for a few minutes. Lisa was shaking. We waited for perhaps another ten minutes, saying nothing but just watching the window as the shapes of leafy branches glided past and the rails made a long, lazy curve between two steep, grassy banks. When Mother came back she had Terpin with her. He sat down at her side, and now there were four of us in the compartment. He had helped carry the food — sandwiches and plastic cups of Coke. He rattled the wax paper of one wrapped sandwich, then held it up and parted the slices of bread. "Ham," he said. "Who wants ham?"

"They're all ham," said Mother.

"That's right." He handed the sandwich to me.

"I'm not hungry," Lisa said.

"Try to eat some of it," Mother told her.

Terpin put a sandwich on Lisa's lap.

"Come on, honey," Mother said.

Lisa took a bite, and was quiet.

"You know," Terpin said, "I heard they're going to march on the Pentagon. Not just peaceniks, either. Regular people. I think they're going to demand that the government stop the war. Maybe my brother and your husband can get out before too long."

I caught Mother looking at me, and knew that I should say nothing about our situation. Clearly, she had already said some things, and I had a fleeting awareness of the nervousness she felt about it. Somehow I knew she would not have told him the *exact* truth, and in knowing this I felt the sense of humiliation all over again for what had happened to us. I cleared my throat, aware of myself as taking part in a deception, a ruse born of shame. Staring out the window with what I hoped was the blank expression of calm, unthreatened self-possession, I saw farms and fences and silos, green and black expanses of ground rolling on into the hazy, ragged line of the horizon, where people went on blithely with their calm, settled lives. It was a huge, still landscape, and there seemed nothing at all to talk about anymore.

Lisa began to fidget next to me, interested now only in her discomfort.

Terpin said, "I guess I better get back to Penny."

Mother said nothing.

"If you can't sleep tonight, I usually can't sleep either."

"I'm exhausted," Mother told him.

"It's so uncomfortably warm."

My very advanced sister spoke up. "Mostly because the compartments are so *crowded*."

Mother actually gave forth a small laugh at this, covering her mouth with her slender fingers.

"Good evening then," said Terpin, who had managed to smile at the remark, as if appreciating Lisa's adult demeanor. "I — I hope I haven't intruded."

"That's fine," Mother told him. "Thank you."

When he was gone, I said, "What does he want, anyway?"

She said, "Oh, be quiet."

"He keeps hanging around."

"He's just a nice young man who wants to talk."

"I'm thirsty," Lisa said. "I hate Coke. It leaves a film on my teeth."

"They don't have anything else, Lisa."

"Can I just have some water?"

Mother looked at me. "Go get her some, will you?"

I didn't want to move. It was just too sweltering to stir from where we were.

"Will you?" she said.

I rose and went out, feeling childish again, almost ready to pout or cry. It was astonishing, and really very depressing to me, how quickly these infantile urges, feelings I was supposed to have outgrown long ago, could burrow up out of the dark of myself and begin clamoring for release. Out in the vestibule there was a small pocket of cooler air, and I paused to breathe it in, watching a farmhouse as we moved by it. The windows were open, white-curtained, but no one and nothing moved in its vicinity.

When I entered the dining car, I found Chummy Terpin waiting while the man behind the counter opened him a beer.

"Hello," he said to me.

I made a gesture which I hoped he took for politeness, but I didn't really feel like talking to him. I didn't know what he expected of me.

"Your daddy must be proud of you," he said.

I felt vaguely patronized, though I don't recall that I knew the word. I was tremendously uneasy. I asked the man behind the counter for Lisa's ice water, and then decided I wanted one myself. "Two of them," I said.

"My brother doesn't really have any family to worry about," he said. He took a long swallow of the beer. I didn't know why I felt that there was something to be wary of in him. He looked at me with his bright, uncommonly clear eyes and seemed ready to be interested in anything I might choose to tell him. It appeared to be friendly interest, and perhaps he was just a lonesome man — he was in fact not far into his twenties — on his way to Kansas to see his imprisoned brother.

"All this must be hard on a kid your age."

"I'm not that much younger than you," I said.

"Six or seven years, maybe." His voice was matter-of-fact. "It's not a lot, I guess."

The man behind the counter gave me the two glasses of water, and I moved toward the door.

"Here," Terpin said, "I'll get it for you." He held the door open, then stepped into the vestibule and pushed the door to the next car. "Can you make it the rest of the way?"

"I can hit the doors with my foot," I said.

"Heck," he said, and went on ahead of me.

When we reached the door to our compartment he knocked, and Mother opened it. "Thank you," she said to him, smiling. "You keep getting stuck, it seems, helping us."

"My pleasure," he said. Then he turned and was gone.

That night I had a dream about my father in prison. I woke, tried to sit up, and bumped my head on the low ceiling of the cramped, drawerlike space in the wall from which my bunk was suspended. Lisa was below me, curled to the wall and snoring. I found that Mother was also awake, lying on her stomach with her chin resting on her folded arms, staring out the dark window. I couldn't remember the dream I'd had, only that it contained a prison and that Father was in it. She looked at me. "Have you been awake?" she said.

"Just now," I said.

"Did you have a dream?"

"I can't remember it."

"You were moaning."

I lay there for a moment, and the bell of another train came by and faded somewhere beyond us in the night. "Where are we?"

"I think Indiana."

"It's so slow, isn't it?"

"I have always liked the flatness of the plains," she said. It might have been the preamble to some larger speech, and I understood that in a way she was speaking beyond me. She wasn't even aware of me now.

I leaned down and looked at the dim horizon, the far-off shadows of houses, their small lights amid tall stands of trees. Power lines ran with the moonlight along the track, and the land was as straight as these, seemed somehow a part of their evenness, as though someone had used the horizon to measure the height of the line. "I dreamed about a prison," I told her.

She said nothing. Presently she sat up, pulling the blanket around her shoulders, rocking slightly, still gazing out the window.

The train whistle went off somewhere ahead, a sound that all my life had invited sleep. But I wasn't sleepy now. I thought about the prison in my dream — there had been something dank and brooding about it, as though it were alive — and I realized that I didn't want to see my father in a place like that, didn't want to see him in prison at all. That would be a memory I could never wipe away.

"Are we going in with you?" I said.

This seemed to startle her. "Go to sleep, son."

"Are we going in with you?"

"What're you talking about?"

"You know. The prison."

She took a long time to answer. "I don't know. We'll see. Probably not at first." I sometimes wonder if the prospect of the prison, its reality, was not growing all too real for her, as well. It must have been, though any number of things about her situation could have had her sitting there rocking slowly, nervously, in the lunar dark.

"Maybe they won't allow it," I said.

"Of course they will."

"Where will we stay?"

"Thomas, you know where we're staying."

But I didn't mean the house on Jewett Street. I said, "When you're talking to him."

"You'll be with me, of course."

"Do you think we'll be able to touch him?"

She sighed. "He said we'd sit on either side of a table. We'll be able to reach across and take his hands."

Now the silvery light of the window showed me that her eyes were swimming. "Mother?" I said.

"Stop talking so much. Go to sleep." She looked out at the glimmer of some body of water in the distance. "I know you can't help being curious, son."

I lay back down. "I'm scared."

"You don't know."

I thought I did know. And just then I couldn't stand the quiet — though this quiet was bordered by the incessant clacking sound of the wheels on the track, the distant clamor of the engine.

"Have you ever been to Wyoming?"

"No."

"When we get to Bismarck, Aunt Elaine'll try and talk us into staying there."

"Yes." She sighed again.

I squeezed over onto my stomach and rested my chin on my arms. Outside, far off in the moonlit sky, the shadows of clouds looked like mountains suspended a thousand feet above the plains. I don't know how long we went without speaking. Drowsily comfortable, almost, in that little space, I seemed to settle slowly as if into a deep fold of cotton, and yet I was somehow aware of time gliding and halting with me as I drifted off and came back.

Then I was wide awake, out of breath and somehow unnerved. The compartment light was on; Mother had closed the curtains. And she was just entering, returning from somewhere, moving stealthily. Lisa coughed below me and said, "I'm scared."

"Be quiet," Mother said.

"What is it?" I said.

"Nothing, go to sleep."

"Why was she crying like that?" Lisa said.

I said, "Who was crying?"

"Both of you go to sleep."

A moment later, there was a startling rap on the door. Mother leaned into it. "Yes?"

I heard the muffled sound of another woman's voice.

Mother opened the door and Penny Holt rushed in, wringing her slender hands and looking behind her as though she were being chased. Mother closed the door and locked it, then turned and pressed her shoulders against it. All the color had left her face. "For God's sake," she said.

"I can't," said Penny. "I just can't."

In the next instant I understood what I was looking at: she was in her nightclothes, shimmering white pajamas with wide long sleeves and black slippers showing a sprinkle of silver sequins. She might have been someone out of those elegant movie comedies of the thirties and forties, though I could not have made such a connection then.

"I can't tell anybody, please," she said.

"Oh, come on," Mother said, turning with her in the center of the compartment. "I have a seven-year-old child with me." They looked like people confused about the seating arrangement, and then Penny put her arms around Mother.

"What's going on," I said, loud enough to be heard.

"But I can't go back there," Penny was saying. "I woke up and he was touching me."

"The conductor will know what to do," Mother said. "There isn't anything I can do."

And the other woman looked at me. "I feel sick."

I scrambled out of the bunk, holding the blanket around my middle, and now there was a general commotion — more rapping at the door, Mother's raised voice telling Lisa to get back into bed, and Penny Holt saying, "That's him. I won't talk to him. I don't want anything to do with him anymore. Tell him to go away."

Mother pushed past me and stood at the door again. She ran one hand through her hair, looked back at us once, then turned and spoke. "Who is it?"

The voice came: "Please, I only want to talk to Penny."

Mother's tone was gentle, the tone one uses when addressing a child. "Mr. Terpin, why don't you go on back to sleep and we'll straighten everything out in the morning."

"Tell her I'm sorry," he said.

Mother gave Penny a helpless look, then leaned into the door again. "I will."

"Is she all right?"

"She's fine."

"I don't know what happened," he said. "I guess I was sleep-walking."

"Sleepwalking," Penny said. "Right."

"I'm so sorry" came from the other side of the door. The voice was almost tearful.

"Good night, Mr. Terpin."

"Good night, yes," he said.

A moment later, we knew he had gone away.

"Sleepwalking," Penny said. She was sitting on Mother's bunk, trembling. "He had his hand in my pajamas."

Something leapt in my blood. I couldn't take my eyes from the shimmering creases of the white pajamas. The place where they came together, several inches below her neck, showed the beginning of what I knew to be her breast, and I looked away, feeling as though I had been disrespectful somehow.

"He was feeling around between my legs."

"Please," Mother said.

"I can stay," Penny said, "right? I'll sleep on the floor, if you have an extra blanket."

"You can sleep in my berth," I said. Her reaction, a kind of jerking backward, embarrassed me into silence. I watched my sister arrange herself in her own bunk so she could stare.

Penny was talking. "We decided to make this trip, and he's been so nice and so anxious to please, you know. And really, he's not a bad man or anything. It's only that he hurts so much all the time. I swear you can smell it on a guy — you can tell when he's like that."

"Can we please talk about something else now?" Mother said.

"You don't think he'd hurt himself or anything, do you?"

Mother stood back and seemed about to say something sharp. But then she just sighed and eased herself down on her bed. "I don't know him. I mean, how would I know a thing like that?"

"I guess not," Penny said. Then: "Maybe I better go check on him."

No one said anything for a few seconds.

"It's just that he's had episodes. I know for a fact that he's had episodes."

"Doesn't anybody ever sleep around here?" Lisa said.

Penny moved to the door. "What do you think I should do?"

"I don't know what to tell you," Mother said.

"You think I should stay here?"

"I think you should do what you feel you have to do."

"I'm sorry," Penny Holt said.

"We're going to sleep now, Penny. Please don't wake us."

"No."

There was another pause.

"You're welcome to stay, if you want."

Penny opened the door and began backing out. "Let me just go make sure he's not going to do anything to hurt himself."

"Two minutes," Mother said.

"I won't even take a second."

When the door closed, Lisa said, "God."

"Be quiet, Lisa," said Mother. "Go back to sleep."

"Who can sleep?"

We waited. Perhaps ten minutes went by. Finally Mother went out into the corridor and looked up and down, then shook her head and came back inside, locked the door and turned out the light.

"Shouldn't we go check on *her* now?" I said.

"Go to sleep."

"Maybe he's got her or something," Lisa said.

"Both of you go to sleep. It's none of our business."

Then we were all lying there in the moving glow of lights passing at the window. I turned in my small space and breathed the odor of what I thought must be Penny's pajamas, and I heard Mother cough once, then clear her throat. Another train bell went off in the distance, and a brief shining on the other side of the closed curtains showed me the bare closet door. The bell came near, as if seeking entry somehow, and then faded into nothing again.

"Hey?" I whispered. It seemed that a presence was stirring in the dark around me, close by. I thought I had seen the dark move. I lay absolutely still.

The wheels clacked and sang beneath us.

Just as I had arrived at the conviction that the shadows and gleams of the night were playing tricks on my eyes, I began to imagine someone standing outside the compartment, waiting at the door. I listened, even as I knew that I would hear nothing through the roar and whoosh of the train. After a long while my curiosity got the better of me, and I climbed down out of the bunk, crept to the door, and put my ear against the cold surface, which gave forth nothing but the roar of motion, metal on metal.

I turned the latch as soundlessly as I could, feeling my heart pounding in my ears and expecting to find her huddled against the wall in that pearly, flimsy garment. When the light of the corridor poured into the room, Mother awakened.

"What?" she said. "What is it, Thomas?"

I leaned out. The corridor was empty. "Nothing," I said. "I thought I heard something."

"Please, son."

I closed the door and climbed back into the bunk.

"Go to sleep," she said. And I had the curious sensation that she was about to tell me she was sorry, as though she had trespassed somehow on my privacy. It was an odd moment, and I was obscurely embarrassed about it.

"Good night," I said.

"Did you lock the door?"

I had, and I told her so. But she got up and checked it anyway. Then she took what seemed like a furtive glance out the window, as if she were looking for spies out there in the dark, shadows following us, the enemy. I thought of movies, and a thrill went through me.

"Let's not talk to anybody on the next train," she said.

"I didn't say anything to them," I told her.

"Don't take everything so personally, Thomas."

I watched her get back into her bunk.

"I can't sleep," I said.

"Try to get a little, you'll need it."

We lay there without saying anything for several minutes.

"Thomas?" she said.

"Yes?"

"I love you."

"Me too, you," I said. It was an exchange we'd had many times, one of our small family's best habits. Now, we might have been saying it to each other for the first time. In the next moment, I heard her make a small sobbing sound in the dark.

"Mother?"

"Try not to worry so much," she said.

"Are you all right?"

"Sleep," she said.

I said, "Yes, ma'am."

We were quiet again. I don't know which of us fell asleep first.

9

IN THE MORNING Lisa said her stomach was bothering her, and she had a slight fever. During the course of the long night, I had surfaced once or twice from dreams of jails and windowless dark rooms to hear her moaning softly, and, given the accustomed pattern whenever she had nightmares, I had drifted back to sleep half expecting her to crawl into my bunk.

Now I woke to Mother's troubled questioning of her. "Do you think you're going to be sick?"

"No."

"Can you eat anything?"

"I'm afraid to."

"Do you have a headache, too?"

"A little."

"You're probably just tired."

"I'm sore where Thomas kicked me."

"Thomas kicked you?"

"I did no such thing," I said with the false outrage of a guilty man.

"Oh, please," Mother said. "Can't we get along?"

The backs of buildings were gliding by, an incredible assortment of broken-windowed factory walls and metal doors, flanked by grain silos and mountainous piles of wood, of sawdust and coal. We were nearing Chicago. In the distance I could see a row of towering buildings in white sunlight.

"Well, come on," Mother said to me. "Get dressed. We have to change trains again."

Lisa groaned. She was sitting on Mother's bunk with her hands folded in her lap. "I have to go to the bathroom again."

"Thomas, will you?" Mother said, closing my bunk.

I got into my clothes, and helped Lisa into hers. Outside, we went along to the end of the bright corridor, and she walked right on into the restroom, turning to push the door shut behind her. From the other end, I saw Mr. Terpin enter the vestibule, hesitate, then make his tottering way through. He glanced at me and, recognizing me, approached.

"Your mother awake?"

"No," I said. I felt a little scared, I confess.

"I need to apologize," he said.

"No need to apologize," I told him.

The train lurched and we were almost pitched toward each other.

"Everything's fine," I said.

"Strange to think I might never see you all again." He seemed about to cry. I have never felt more strange with anyone. I nearly touched his arm.

"Well," he said, "we have to head to Leavenworth, you know."

"Yes," I answered.

"Are you waiting for your sister?"

I nodded.

"It was all a misunderstanding," he said. "Last night."

I was silent.

"I guess you were there for it when Penny came over here —"

"I don't know what you're talking about," I said. And I remember associating, for some reason, his troubles with those of my father. That is to say, in his specific circumstance — standing there mortified and hurting over something he had done, that he now wished fervently he had not done — he put me in mind of Father; and the least I could do was provide him with some alleviation of his discomfort. He did not appear to me to be a bad or dangerous man, but only someone a little sad, someone I myself would never be, if I could help it. And indeed there have been moments in my life since then, doubtful or uneasy passages when, perhaps half seriously but with that small unsettling grain of belief nevertheless, I have felt the arid suspicion that every book I've ever read, every poem I've ever memorized, every painting and work of sculpture I've studied, all the arts of grace and peace that

I've worked so diligently to cultivate in myself, may be seen in the light of a nearly atavistic commitment never to be remotely like that lone and lonely man, so cloddish, so pathetic in his bungled, vulgar attempt at loving. This image of him has remained with me all these years, still gives me pause: poor Terpin standing in the corridor of that moving train, with his sad love written on his face and his meager ability to express it having caused him such humiliation and regret, his discomfort compelling him to blurt out a frantic confession of the whole chastening business to a seventeen-year-old boy.

"I wasn't really awake, see," he told me. "I'd had this dream we were together. I was partly awake, you know. I mean anybody can understand that, can't they? A person is half asleep and — I mean, I can't really explain it. It was like a caress, that's all. Like a sleepy caress, sort of. She was lying there and the one pajama leg was pulled up, like. She — she has such — beautiful skin. You know. I mean — did you ever dream about somebody and dream about somebody every night, and then you wake up and feel like you were closer to them than you really were? A person can have a dream like that about a stranger, you know. It happens all the time."

I said nothing. I think I must have nodded at him — that at least. I couldn't decipher what was expected of me, but I felt sorry for him, and sensed that this was not something he would be glad of, either.

"Well," he said with a forlorn bowing of his head. And now I was angry with him. I had not expected this sudden antipathy, yet in the next instant I wanted to get as far away from him as I could, and any uneasiness or pity I had felt for him was gone. It was as though I'd realized some natural superiority to him.

When Lisa came out of the restroom, I took her hand and we walked back to our compartment, both of us working studiously to ignore him. "Do you think your mother will let me explain?" he asked, following along.

"Man," I said, "I don't know. I don't think it matters much now, do you?"

"Sure it matters. How can you say it doesn't matter?"

"I don't know," I said. "I guess it matters to you."

"I would like to have her good opinion," he said, standing straighter, tilting his head back a bit, as I had seen my father do in the presence of the arresting officers. Except that now he put both hands to the sides of his head and smoothed back his hair. "If you have a person's good opinion —" he said, and then stopped.

It was almost too absurd to respond to. "We're going on to Wyoming," I told him. "It's not like whatever she thinks about you will change anything."

"Will you ask her to let me apologize?"

"Jesus," I said.

Lisa was too concerned with her sour stomach and her headache to do much but stare at him through this exchange, but then she said, "Where's Penny?"

The look on his face was quite pitiful. I thought he might cry. With obvious effort, he straightened again and his whole demeanor changed, grew faintly irritable, almost affronted. He turned to me. "It was Penny's idea that I come and apologize, you know. It's not as if she's breaking up with me or anything. I mean, I'm supposed to be her brother-in-law, for God's sake."

I opened the compartment door and found Mother packing up our things. She saw Terpin and moved back a step. "Yes?" she said. A strand of hair had slipped down across her face, and her expression had something of what she had shown the airman that day at the Flight Line Grill, when they put Father on the plane.

"I just wanted to apologize for any trouble I might've caused," Terpin said in a voice that fairly trembled.

The train was rolling to a stop. "Where's Penny?" Mother demanded.

"Penny sent me." Apparently it was all right for Mother to ask this. "Is she all right?"

"Yes," he said. "We're like brother and sister, you know."

"Well," Mother said, "I wish you both good luck."

"Thank you," said Terpin, backing out.

The train had stopped, and people were crowding into the corridor, filing out of the coaches, hurrying along in front of our windows. Mother gathered the few bags, and we headed into the hubbub. On the platform, Penny Holt emerged from the confusion and put her arms around Mother.

"Thanks for everything."

"I didn't do anything," Mother said.

The other woman took a small note pad and pencil from her purse. "Let me have your address in Wyoming," she said. "I'll write you."

Mother gave it to her, watching her small, white-knuckled hands as she wrote the numbers and the street name, and glancing at her face.

"Great," Penny said, closing the note pad and putting it back into her purse. She hugged Mother again, and I thought of the separations when our family moved to another of Father's duty tours: Mother's goodbyes to friends. We had been through so many moves.

The sound roared around us, and Penny stammered out something about trying not to cry. There was an almost comical element about the way the two of them wobbled there, holding on to each other, and then Penny backed off, gripping her scarf at her neck, lifting her purse by its strap, shouldering it, and turning to make her way, hurrying, toward the next platform. She did not look back, and we watched her go.

"Jeez," Lisa said.

And Mother said something, too, though I lost it in the sound of the amplified and echoing male voice announcing the arrivals and departures, the destinations. We headed into the main terminal, where I caught a glimpse of Terpin and Penny moving through a group of people at the ticket counter.

The train for Bismarck wouldn't leave for an hour, and so we went into the restaurant, which was crowded and smoky, too well lighted and not very clean. We waited, sitting at a table with food scraps on the polished surface and an ashtray with one black cigar crushed in it. The train for Leavenworth and points west and south was announced, and a few moments later we heard the final boarding call.

I felt abruptly marooned and alone, and I watched Mother's face. She gazed at the people in the terminal, the travelers walking by.

"Do you think Penny'll actually write you?" I asked.

"Oh," Mother said, "I'm too tired to talk, son."

Lisa had leaned her head on my shoulder and was holding her stomach. "This place smells," she said.

Mother took the ashtray and put it on the next table. "I guess we should eat something."

"Not me," Lisa said.

I wasn't hungry either.

We boarded the train to Bismarck a little more than an hour later, and then sat in our compartment for the better part of another hour. Lisa's fever had gone up, and she was growing more nauseated by the minute. This compartment did have a small workable toilet, and before long Lisa had to stand over it, with Mother holding her hand and trying to soothe her. Nothing would come. It was just travel sickness, Mother said. The jostling and the wakefulness and the bad food.

"Oh, I hate trains," said Lisa.

We had begun to move again.

I pulled my bunk down and climbed in, turning to the wall, away from whatever the outcome would be with Lisa. And in a little while I was asleep, the deep, dream-haunted sleep of the exhausted. My dreams were vivid, and they were all of Father. I was talking to him, trying to calm him, to ease his regret over what he had done. When I came to, Lisa was worse. Mother wanted to go see about getting a doctor to look at her. But then the fever broke, and she said she felt better. We were speeding across the plains, late in the morning, and we knew that in Bismarck Aunt Elaine would be waiting. As the time neared, we seemed to be given a new increment of energy, and of good feeling, too. There would be the trip to Minot in Aunt Elaine's car, and then we would be in the big family house with all its comforts and its places to get off to and be alone. What we were finally headed for, the house in Wilson Creek, would be far different, and I suppose we knew this in our own way, each of us. In any case, we grew more excited as the miles rolled by on the other side of the window glass, and the last few hours were almost pleasant.

It wasn't Aunt Elaine who greeted us at the station in Bismarck, but Grandfather Tinan. A chilly wind was blowing when we got off, and leaves were already beginning to show faint color in the trees. Grandfather Tinan stood waiting at the baggage carousel in blue jeans, a white shirt, and red hunting cap. He had taken to wearing his hair longer, and it lay in curls on his shirt collar. It had gone from gray to white; he had grown a beard.

"You look like Santa Claus," Lisa said to him. "I've been sick."

"Little ticket," he said. It was his pet name for her. "Look how tall you are."

Mother kissed him on the cheek, and he reached for me to shake hands. His grip was firm, a test. I stood my ground.

"Well, boy?" he said.

I said, "Yes, sir."

"You're at least four inches taller. Are you four inches stronger?"

"I don't know," I said.

"A man is definite," he told me. We were standing there gripping each other. I thought the bones in my hand might break. "How long's it been since you were here?"

"A man is definite," I said, and he smiled and let go.

"Are you satisfied?" Mother said to him.

"Quite," he said, and rubbed the back of my neck. His hands were rough, the texture of unsanded wood.

"Where's Aunt Elaine?" Lisa wanted to know.

He turned, looking for Lisa, then lifted her. "Aunt Elaine is waiting for us at home."

"Is everything all right?" Mother asked.

"Now, why wouldn't everything be all right?"

"She was going to meet us."

"I decided I wanted to."

"Well," Mother said.

I didn't know how to read this. I looked at his face, with its lines of the upper midwestern winters and its dark tan. He looked like those old photographs of fierce Plains Indians, whose blood, he was fond of pointing out, came down to him from two generations back on the distaff side.

"What's this?" Mother said, lifting a curl at his neck.

"What about it?"

"I think it's longer than Thomas's."

"Wouldn't want to be outdone by young Thomas."

The bags arrived, and he insisted on carrying most of them. It was a long walk out to the car — the green Pontiac Aunt Elaine drove all those miles to see us when we were in Virginia — and then we had the trouble of trying to get everything into it. Grandfather Tinan and I worked together, without saying much, and I knew this quiet would have obtained no matter who was standing there.

William Tinan had never been an outgoing sort, and perhaps because in his work he had grown used to being listened to, he was not very adept at simple polite talk. He would say he had worked his way to the federal bench without apologies and without catering to anyone. And if one explained the stridency of this assertion by calling up the considerable vanity he possessed, one also had to admit that the assertion was almost exactly true. Having entered the Army in 1917 at nearly the precise age of the century, he had seen the bloody mess at Belleau Wood, and had come home with a case of influenza that came close to killing him. His people were mostly farmers and tradesmen — no doubt some of them must have feared and resented the Oglala Sioux woman who had married his great-grandfather — and his father's farm was waiting for him when he returned, along with several cousins, nieces, and nephews who had gravitated to the place in the wake of the great flu epidemic, a calamity that had ended up claiming the lives of more people in the vicinity than had gone and died in the war. Having come from the farm, he was expected to carry on with his father's work, but he was not interested in farming. He had in truth always hated it, and so with the admittedly quixotic sense of himself as being a sort of spiritual or temperamental heir to both Lincoln and Crazy Horse, he sold the place to a cousin at the rock-bottom price the cousin could then afford, and moved himself into town, where at the age of nineteen he began the pursuit of the law. It took him more than twenty years and was the ruin of two marriages, but he persisted, in the face of his family's disapproval. He had worked, he would proudly say, thirty different jobs, paying his way through the courses of study, then hanging his shingle and riding the farm roads, going after selection to the bench, getting no help from any quarter — though he would occasionally acknowledge that Elaine and Connie's mother, his third wife, had at least tolerated the quest.

But she died unexpectedly of pneumonia while the girls were still small, and when at last he had reached his goal, the world was at war again and he found himself laboring under the chronic suspicion that somehow in his single-mindedness he had spent all the value of himself. Increasingly the accomplishment of his lifelong ambition felt like some peculiarly cruel aspect of failure. Moreover, his almost grown daughters, whom he had been forced by circumstances occasionally to neglect, were beginning to show interest in the soldiers who were streaming into Minot.

Enter my father.

About most of what he had been through, Grandfather Tinan was quite forthcoming, since it made a story with himself as the towering central figure, and it was a story he liked telling. Sometimes he told it as a cautionary tale; sometimes as a tale of inspiration, of the worth of diligence and hard work and stubbornness.

All the way to Minot in the car, he managed to bring this history into the conversation, as if there were something valedictory about the trip and things needed saying. Anyway, that was his tone. He talked about his struggles as though they made a paradigm, it seemed to me. His recounting of old hardships became more than simple reminiscence: he reminded Mother of funny things she had said and done during times when they had been in contention with each other — but in particular, and in some detail, he talked of that period when she was deciding not to go back to college. And while he never crossed the line into talking directly of her marriage, I sensed the unnamed third party in this equation they made.

Lisa and I were in the back seat. She had put her head in my lap. I felt that I ought to bring up my father, the apparent forbidden subject.

"Don't worry," Lisa said, "I'm not sick anymore." Her eyes were a dark, glassy blur.

I looked at the countryside — all distances and the far shadows of hills. The old man talked about stubbornness.

"It's a quality I've always admired, Connie. And I have my share of it, too. It's a survivor's trait, as your mother used to say when she'd try to explain me to myself. But I guess she'd be impressed with you even more, if that's poss —"

"Oh, Daddy," Mother interrupted him, "please stop."

"It's true."

"Well, thank you."

"Of course, sometimes stubbornness keeps people from what's best for them. It cost me two marriages."

Mother was silent.

"I have too many regrets, and they all come from what I thought I wanted. I could've spared others some pain."

"What are we leading up to here?" Mother said.

"Nothing."

"We're going on to Wilson Creek."

"Well, I'm goddamned if I said anything different."

"Let's not fight."

He looked back at me. "Boy, did I say anything different?"

I said, "Leave me out of this."

Now he almost turned in his seat to look at me.

"Watch the road," Mother said.

We went on in silence for a time. He held the wheel with both hands, staring out. The road was a two-lane highway north, but it had wound westward for a mile or so, and the sun shone in our eyes.

"You let him talk to adults that way?" Grandfather Tinan said.

"Please," said Mother. "He's had one or two things happen that make it hard to treat him like a child anymore."

Again, we were quiet.

"Thomas?" he said.

I leaned forward, being careful of Lisa. "Sir?"

"Do you want to drive the car?"

"He doesn't have his license yet," Mother said.

"Why not?"

"Daniel was withholding it until his grades in school were better."

"Really."

Mother said nothing.

"No kidding," said Grandfather Tinan.

"That's right," Mother said. "No kidding."

"That seems like a good plan."

"Well, it was a plan."

"And in your opinion, has it worked?"

"I wouldn't want to say."

"Well, have the grades improved?"

"Not appreciably."

"So, then it hasn't worked."

"Look," I said. "What is this, anyway?"

"Be quiet," Mother said. "This is your grandfather making a point."

"All right," Grandfather Tinan said. "And what point is that?"

"Please," Mother said. "Are we just going to argue all the way there? If I'd known that, I'd have gone straight to Wyoming."

"I wasn't under the impression we were arguing," he said.

"Okay."

"I just asked my grandson if he'd like to drive the goddam car."

"I said *okay*," Mother told him.

"It's okay, then?"

"He doesn't have a license. I meant okay. As in, whatever you say. I was agreeing with you. But if he wants to drive a little, that's okay too, I guess. Okay?"

He said, "Then we're agreed."

"Right," Mother said. "Agreed."

He said, "And what exactly have we agreed to?"

"Let's say we've agreed not to discuss anything but Thomas driving the car, all right? And we're of one mind on that, so let's look at the scenery."

We did so for a few moments.

Then he said, "It just struck me that it's a bit ironic, that's all. Holding the privileges back in order to extract better behavior."

"Why is it ironic?"

He said nothing.

"Is there something else you want to say?" she asked him in a voice which was brittle, yet somehow pleasant, too.

"I think I just said it."

"Ironic," Mother said. "God."

"You can't blame me for the impression."

"I have no idea what you're talking about."

"I think I'm talking about felony."

"Stop this car and let us out," Mother said.

"Connie, for Christ's sake. I haven't even started."

"I didn't come here to listen to this kind of talk."

"Lisa's asleep," I said.

"Be quiet, Thomas."

"I wish everybody would stop shouting," I said.

"No one's shouting," Mother said at the top of her voice.

Grandfather Tinan said, "I'm supposed to say nothing at all about anything, is that it? I can have no opinion on the matter whatsoever?"

"You can please keep your opinion to yourself."

We said nothing for a mile or so. I read the signs for motels and gas stations, looked at the occasional farmhouse in its clutch of trees, set into the right angles of intersecting roads that were straight as

ruled lines. Lisa stirred and said my name irritably, then went back to
sleep.

"I just wanted to talk about your situation," the old man said. "I
didn't mean for it to be a war."

"But you don't really want to talk about it, Daddy. You've never
wanted to talk about it. You want to give a lecture. I'm not going to sit
here and listen to it."

"I'm old," he said. "I don't have the smoothness to say things like I
used to."

"Oh, and when was this, that you were so smooth?"

"All right," he said.

Mother glanced back at me and the corner of her mouth turned up in
a rueful little knowing smile. Then she looked at her father again. "You
mean to say you were once silver-tongued?"

"Well, I could talk to my children without having everything I said
tossed back in my goddam face, yes."

"I was just teasing, Daddy."

Again, they were quiet.

"Thomas," Grandfather Tinan said abruptly. "Do you want to drive
the car or not?"

I did, but my little sister's head was in my lap, and I could feel so
much tension now that taking him up on it seemed all too complicated
a proposition. "Maybe I'll drive it some other time," I said.

Mother gave me a quick, evaluative look, without quite making eye
contact, then turned in her seat, smoothing the front of her blouse.

A moment later, she said, "I told Daniel to write me in Minot."

"We haven't heard from him," the old man said.

"Well."

"I didn't check the mail before I left."

She said nothing.

"I don't suppose I'm allowed to wonder what you'll all do when
Daniel gets out."

"Elaine has already brought that up."

"And?"

"I'm sure she told you what I had to say about it."

"No, Elaine doesn't tell me much of anything these days."

"What's the matter with you and Elaine?"

"Not a thing. She just won't talk about you."

"Oh, you poor man. What will you ever find to talk about?"

"Forgive me, please. I'm goddamned if I know where I get the idea I have the right to worry about my family."

"I didn't know it was a right," said Mother. "I've always felt it as an affliction."

"Yes, I know that."

"And I wasn't talking about your worrying, Daddy. I was talking about mine."

"If you say so."

"Well, you'll just have to take my word."

His knuckles were white on the steering wheel. I thought we were going a little fast.

"I'm all grown up now," Mother said. "Christ, I'm middle-aged. I have a grown child of my own."

This reference to me felt dimly unnerving. I said, "Could we please stop arguing?"

"There," Mother said. "See? He's old enough to ask for some peace and quiet."

"I don't suppose it's crossed your mind that you could buy a car here and drive to Wilson Creek," said her father.

"I don't want to drive to Wilson Creek."

"What'll you drive when you get there?"

"I'll buy a car there."

"Do you have the money to do that?"

"I have a job lined up."

Grandfather Tinan made a sound like a stifled laugh. "As a secretary, right?"

"That's right."

"Did Daniel leave you with anything?"

"God," Mother said. "You make it sound like he's — look, I've worked everything out, all right?"

"How long will you go without a car, and what sort of car will you be able to get on what they'll be paying you?"

"I'll get something. I still have some of the money you sent us, and I saved up some over the spring and summer."

"He was writing bad checks. You couldn't have started with much."

"I'm not going to discuss this now," she said.

"Well, if you'd quit being defensive for five seconds you might see that I'm trying to ascertain what I can do to help out some more."

"We don't need any more help."

"That's just pride speaking, isn't it."

"No. You've done enough. Dan and I are very grateful —"

"I wasn't doing it for gratitude."

"All right."

"I didn't have any motives."

"No one said you did."

"It's what family members do for each other."

"Well," Mother said. "Thank you anyway."

He gave forth a sigh, like someone quitting on a long effort, and stared straight ahead. "This house you're going to stay in, is it far from the prison?"

"The lady said it wasn't too far."

"Well, how far?"

"I don't know. A mile or so, maybe."

"More than walking distance."

"I suppose."

"Look, I'm just offering you the money to buy a goddam car if you want it. No obligations attached. Not even a smidgeon of simple politeness or affection for me. You can kick me and still take the money."

"Listen to you. For God's sake, will you just listen."

"Well? I'm offering the money. I'd like to help. I don't mean it as an insult, though you seem determined to take it as one. I just don't know how to make it any clearer than that."

"Okay, I'm sorry," she said. "It's clear."

"You'll take the money?"

"I'll accept it as a loan."

"I wasn't offering it as a loan."

She said nothing.

"Goddammit, I'd like to help. I'm not interested in doing any banking with you, you know? I think it's my position to try and help any way I can."

"All *right*," she said, and she sounded as she had many times when talking to Lisa and me, trying to get us to be quiet, to stop arguing or bickering over something.

Grandfather Tinan put the radio on loud, some country music station. He stared straight ahead at the road, and Mother leaned back in the seat, her head turned away from him, gazing at the landscape we were heading through.

"I can't sleep," Lisa said, sitting up, blinking, heavy-eyed. "Are we there yet?"

"We have a long way to go," the old man said.

I do not remember that another word passed between any of us, all the way to the house in Minot.

IO

OF THE TIME we spent in Minot I remember somewhat less than I'd like. I recall feeling more at home there than I could have imagined, and I found to my surprise that I enjoyed the old man's company, for all his fierceness and his stern midwestern ways. But the fact remains that much of the two weeks is blurry and rather confused in my mind. My journals are scanty at best for that short period, and perhaps it's just that we didn't do a lot when we were there. Aside from an occasional ride into the country, I don't recall that we did much with the days but lie around the house, with the morning's newspapers and with the television on. I've even questioned Lisa about this time, without much luck. When she'll talk about it at all, she claims to remember only that she was afraid to be alone in that big drafty old house, with its leaded glass windows and its attic rooms, where the wind blew and whistled under the eaves, and one always had the feeling that presences lurked in the shadowed corners. She would look out the topmost windows, she says, and her knees would shake as she stared at Aunt Elaine's Pontiac and the Ford pickup that Grandfather Tinan drove out on the country roads — his "personality," as my aunt liked to call it. Everything looked reduced at that height. The attic windows were a vantage point from which to watch all the comings and goings along the street. It was a thrill Lisa gave herself, watching for any movement in the yard below, flirting with what she was convinced was mortal danger, a kind of bravado I'm afraid she hasn't shown as an adult.

In the upstairs bathroom a claw-footed bathtub seemed crouched on the dull linoleum floor, and it terrified her. She could imagine it stalking through the dim rooms of the upstairs, and the sounds the house made were all the sort that might be made by a walking something. She had her nightmare several times while we were in Minot — once in the middle of a brief afternoon nap, with sun pouring in everywhere and people talking all around her.

I don't recall feeling any great tension in that pause we made. And the odd thing is my journals, sparse as they are, do record that the old man used those few days to try making his way toward Mother through me. By this I mean that although he never allowed himself the luxury of direct speech about our situation again, at least not while Mother was there, the journals record several attempts with me.

On the surface, anyway — that is, when we were all together, not spread about the house in various closed rooms, when we were at meals, and during the long evenings when the television was on — he seemed to have grown used to everything and to have accepted it. He talked about taking us places and showing us things in and around town, but he seemed quite content to have us for the visit, and his interest in showing us things seemed finally to be confined to me.

Here's a journal entry for that summer:

Grandfather T. took me with him to a range where people stand in cages and try to hit baseballs shot toward them from machines. A bunch of batting cages side by side. He wanted me to stand in and hit a few. I've never really seen you play, he said. Go on. I stood in and the thing shot a ball at me sixty miles an hour. I missed. He was leaning on the screen watching me like a coach, like Father used to. Good cut, he says. He said it every time I missed, and the one time I made any contact at all it was a foul ball and stung all the way to the shoulders. Something, he says, those machines. And I said, I pitch. I'm a pitcher. And he told me, Well, you have to learn to hit it, too. I'm faster than this machine, I said. He said, You couldn't hit yourself, then. I said, You couldn't, either. I said, You hit some. And he paid and stepped in and cracked the first one on the ground. It would've been back to the pitcher and he would've been out at first but it was contact and he was proud. He stood there holding the bat waiting for the next pitch. It came and he missed. I almost yelled I was so glad. But then he popped the next one up, and hit two more ground balls. Terrific reflexes for a guy his age. I'm beginning to like him, and then when we're getting back in the car he says, Your mother trusts you like a man now. And I said I guess so. And he says, Have you offered an opinion about all this? And I said, Sure. He says, And? And I said, I wish it hadn't happened.

And him: That's all?

And me: I guess so.

Him: A man is definite.

Okay.

Okay what?

Okay, that's all.

Do you want to go to Wyoming?

Sure.

Your father could come here when he gets out. He could be out in a matter of months. You know that, don't you?

I couldn't say anything or look at him. I think he'd say almost anything.

He says, You didn't know that, did you. Exact words.

And I tell him I don't know much.

So you're all going to move to this little prison town in the middle of nowhere and be maybe halfway through a school year when he gets out, and then what? No job, nothing to do. What's there to do in Wilson Creek?

I don't know, I said.

And he says, You're going to have to think about these things. You're the man of the house now. Someone's got to take the responsibility.

He went on that way. Qualities of this and qualities of that. Leadership and stubbornness, what I have from him by inherited strength. I can't get what he thinks I can do or should do if he can't do it himself. I almost told him, too.

And another entry, much shorter, from two days later:

A lot of questions about Father and me. You and your father get along? What sort of things did you do together? Why did you quit the baseball, anyway? I haven't said much. Mostly that I don't know, or I haven't given it much thought. And he seems a little frustrated by it, but he never really says anything.

Here's another:

Short letter from Father. She took it up to her room and read it. There's only say hello for us. Tell us he loves us. He called once, too. We heard Mother talking to him in the other room. Talking low, not quite a whisper, and we're all trying not to listen. When we got to talk to him it was just to say hi. I couldn't tell what was in his voice. It didn't really sound like him. Nobody says anything, but Grandfather Tinan keeps looking at me when we're all together. He's waiting for me to do something. He was going to go get ice cream. I'll take Junior there, if he wants to go. Exact words. I said I didn't want to. Oh, come on, Junior. And Mother said, Don't call him that. And he said, It's what I always called him.

He was a little boy, Daddy.

I always called him that.

Daniel doesn't really like the name Junior, and he never has.

But I always called this boy Junior. Why didn't Daniel say something to me?

And yet another:

Tonight, G.T. looked at Mother and then took her hands. I knew all his questions to me and what he really thinks. He said, Well, Connie, if we didn't have the rough where would we find the smooth? Exact words.

In the evenings, when we all sat down to dinner, he teased with Lisa or talked in his usual way about the depredations of Lyndon Johnson, the failures of discipline and law, and occasionally he allowed himself a small remembrance of when his daughters were small and their mother was alive. He was presently seeing someone, a woman he said reminded him of the girls' mother, though this someone had yet to make an appearance in the house, and even Aunt Elaine was skeptical.

"He goes out and is gone for stretches," she said. "But I don't have any idea where he goes or what he does. And he's very close-mouthed about it. And I've stopped asking."

"Good," Mother said. "Then I can be close-mouthed, too."

But she didn't have to be.

One of the clearest memories I have from then is of the day I took my little trip with him, the one to get ice cream, which is mentioned in the journal. It was not even the first trip we took together that day.

This was the Sunday before we left for Wilson Creek. Early in the morning he came to the room where I slept — it was my grandmother's old sewing room — and, standing in the doorway, knocked on the frame: three peremptory raps of his fist on the wood, as though he would not really wait for an answer. But he was there when I opened my eyes. "Your mother says you should go to church with me."

"I'm asleep," I told him.

"Come on, son." There was something almost grudging in it. One might've thought I had been bothering him for weeks about going with him, and there didn't seem to be any graceful way of bowing out.

So we drove into the country to a little white clapboard chapel crowded with farmers and their families, and pastored by a priest whose rough features and five o'clock shadow gave him the appearance of a man with dark associations. We sat in the very back, the last pew, and no one looked at us or seemed to notice us at all. When the collection plate was passed, the old man fished a dollar out of his pocket and dropped it in. There was something pinched about his motions in that place, as though his age had suddenly caught up to him. When he looked into the plate he put his head back, attending to the amount, I suppose, through his bifocals. When the mass ended he turned to me.

"You've been to church with me before," he said. "Why all the fuss about it this morning?"

"Fuss?" I said.

"You didn't even mention church last week."

"No, sir."

"I decided to wait and see if anybody mentioned it, and no one did." I kept silent.

"Ever been without me?"

"Here?" I said.

He simply stared, and of course I understood.

"No," I said.

"Your mother ever go?"

I said, "I don't know."

"A man is definite," he said, rising.

I had grown tired of this particular prod, if that was what he meant it to be, though it could just as easily have been a kind of nervous tic. "I definitely don't know," I told him.

He smiled. I followed him out to the sidewalk, where the priest stood talking to a group of women.

"William Tinan," one of them said, "is this your boy?"

"My grandson," the old man said.

"My, I am impressed. He looks just like Constance. He has her eyes."

"Yes, he does."

"And how is Constance?"

"Connie's visiting for a few days."

"How wonderful. There's nothing like it, having your family around you. And how's — is it Daniel?"

"Constance is here alone with the children."

"Oh, just the children."

"That's right."

"Isn't Connie's husband an Air Force man?"

"Air Force, yes."

"They do travel the world, don't they?"

"Yes, they do."

The woman looked at me — a pretty face, a strikingly classic countenance, with sculpted features and very light blue eyes, surrounded by skin so covered with wrinkles it seemed somehow artificial, like a young face made up to look old. "You must have seen a lot of the country, being an Air Force child."

I nodded.

"I was an Army brat myself, so I know," she said.

I said, "Yes, ma'am."

"Do you like to travel and see new things?"

"Yes," I told her.

"Well, that's fine. You give your mother my best. Tell her Jane McKissick says hello."

"We'll do that," Grandfather Tinan said.

"Maybe we'll try and stop by," she said.

"Well, we'll be moving around quite a bit."

"Bill Tinan, are you saying you plan to avoid us?"

"Now, Jane."

"I know. I know how it is."

The old man nodded at the priest, and we moved on.

"Who was that?" I said when we were out of earshot.

"That," he said, "was your mother's twelfth-grade teacher. The one who told me that your mother was too flighty to finish college. She was goddam right, too."

We got into the car, and I thought he slammed the door a little hard. I didn't say anything.

"People are too curious," he said when we'd got under way. "Always fishing."

I could do no better than to make the observation that she had an odd sort of face.

"What does your mother tell people?" he said suddenly.

I knew what he meant. I said, "She just says we're on our way to rejoin Father."

"I have the damnedest time trying to decide what to tell people."

"Why do you have to tell them anything?"

His answer came quickly — he'd been thinking about it all for a long time. "Because if it doesn't come from me and they find out, the whole thing is a goddam humiliation."

I watched the countryside go by. I couldn't look at him.

"It's a goddam humiliation anyway," he said in a furious, tight little voice.

The trip to the ice cream parlor, later that day, was awkward because I had the feeling that he wanted me along for a reason — that he had decided upon something concerning me. I had spent the day avoiding him, keeping my face burrowed into a book about the sea, sitting on the sofa in the warm light of the living room while everyone else, even Lisa, played gin rummy at the dining room table. When, later in the evening, I wrote that scant entry in my journal, I was too distracted to say much of anything.

He had requested that I come along, calling me Junior, and we had climbed into the cab of the old pickup.

"You want to drive?" he said.

I said, "No."

"Definite," he said, turning the key in the ignition. The engine roared, and then sputtered, and he tried again. "What kind of ice cream should we get?"

"Chocolate," I said.

The engine caught. We pulled out of the drive and headed down the tree-lined street.

"Why don't you want to drive?" he said.

"I've never driven a straight stick."

"Jesus," he said, "what the hell are they teaching you, Junior?"

"Don't call me that," I said.

He looked at me. Since the morning, there had been some slippage between us. I sensed that he had given up on me, that in his estimation I could be of no use to him after all in getting through to his daughter. Except that I don't believe this was a conscious thing with him, any more than I would assert that I understood it quite so clearly as I have stated it here.

"A man has responsibility," he said, concentrating on the road.

I said nothing.

"He can't escape it."

I remained silent.

"Do you understand me?"

"Yes," I said.

"No, I don't think you do."

"I do," I said.

"No matter where he goes and no matter what he tries to do, he can't get away from it. If he tries to, he ruins his own life and he can ruin the life of everyone around him, too."

"My life isn't ruined," I said.

And he fairly shouted at me. "I wasn't *talking* about you."

We said nothing then. Perhaps a minute went by. The ice cream parlor came into view and he drove past it, down to the end of the street, where he slowed, inched up to a stop sign and waited, seeming to gather himself inwardly. "I wasn't talking about your father, either. Do you understand?"

I waited.

We inched out into the intersection and went on.

"The ice cream parlor's back there," I said.

"You never really cared much for being here, did you?" he said.

"It's all right," I said. "I like to visit."

"That's not what your aunt Elaine tells me."

I gave no answer to this; I wasn't sure one was expected.

"I know I'm a bit gruff," he said.

"Where are we going?" I asked.

"We'll get to the ice cream parlor," he said. "Just be patient."

I sat back and stared out the window. The porches along the street were sagging a little, and some of the houses needed paint. I saw the interiors through curtain-lined windows, certain angles of hallway, hutches, paintings in frames, sconces, shelves of bric-a-brac, lamps, bookcases, wall clocks. I might have well been gazing into the exhibits of a museum, for there were no people about, no shapes moving in the rooms. The yards were generally fenced in, overgrown and patchy, and everything looked neglected, though these were rather large places and obviously this had once been a prosperous section of town, the sort of midwestern street where, as Fitzgerald once said, houses were known for generations by a family's name. Now, my grandfather explained, a lot of the well-to-do had moved on, or run into hard times, and some of them rented the houses out, room by room, to Air Force people — the overflow of married servicemen from Minot, whose tech training school, he said, had recently begun operating shifts around the clock, seven days a week: the war. There were thousands of airmen on the street in town on any given day.

We rode along the quiet street, and I knew we were both thinking of Father now. But we said nothing. The houses looked like what they had all become: dilapidated old clapboard shells containing the various belongings of transient strangers, people passing through, as Mother and Lisa and I were passing through. All the eaves were rucked with peeling paint, and the porches showed elaborate attempts at personalization: gimcrack plaster saints and fake Roman statuary, painted hexes and potted plants, tall plastic trellises tangled with sparse ivy.

"Are you going to start college next year?" Grandfather said.

"I don't know."

"Well, have you given it any thought?"

"No," I said.

"Don't you think you should?"

"I guess so."

"Did your father talk about it at all with you?"

"Yes," I said. "He wants us to go to college."

"But you haven't made any plans or anything?"

"We didn't know where we'd be living."

"Son, you go *away* to college. You don't bring your parents with you."

I didn't say anything.

"Well?" he said.

"I haven't decided yet," I said. "I don't want to talk about it now."

"Sit up straight," he said. "You've lived with the military all these years and you still slouch like that?"

"Sir, are we going to the ice cream parlor or not?"

"We're going to the ice cream parlor. Just listen to me a minute. You're going to be eligible for the draft in a few months, son, and if you end up getting drafted, you won't have any choice about college, or much of anything for that matter."

The draft seemed too far away, too remote to think about. I waited for him to continue, but he didn't say more. He was concentrating hard on the road before us, the houses on either side, which were smaller now and less uniformly rundown-looking. Finally he pulled to the left, into a narrow, grass-sprung driveway, under the drooping frondlike branches of a willow. He turned the motor off and seemed to pause, as if trying to decide upon something.

"Wait here," he said, getting out.

The house was a squarish, two-story building with a small side porch attached. There were wicker chairs on the lawn, near the cracked sidewalk. I watched him go up onto the front stoop and knock on the door, standing with all his weight on one foot, gazing off down the street. A woman came to the door, a dark-haired someone I couldn't see much of, who spoke to him for a moment, then pushed open the screen door and let him in. She held the door, hesitated just long enough to glance my way before moving out of sight. The inside door remained open. I waited. The street was quiet. Only the chirping of birds, the rustle of leaves blowing out of the willow. In the side yard of the house was a tire on a rope hung from the lowest fork of a big oak. I thought of being young enough to swing on the tire, and suddenly the very air seemed heavy with portent: something was about to happen. Children were playing in another yard, and a woman's voice called a name. "Warren. Warren, come eat." A soft voice, full of the languid peace of an afternoon in summer; and I had an image of the street in other times — these small houses with families in them, where children grew up and where people expected to remain, and did remain. The idea filled me with a longing so powerful that it was like a touch on my skin, the feeling of invisible life hovering near. I almost got out of the truck. And then, to my complete astonishment, I was crying. I can't really explain this, even now — why all that we had been through should have struck me just then. I sat there staring at the tire swing on its rope, trying to keep from losing control entirely, wondering if perhaps I was coming down with a fever. For a few hard minutes it was as though everything inside me had turned to water.

Then Grandfather Tinan came out, walked slowly around to the driver's side, and got in. At the door of the house, through the screen, the woman watched us with a blank expression — someone merely taking in the sights of her street. Grandfather Tinan turned the key in the ignition and hesitated a moment. I knew he was looking at me.

"I'd introduce you," he said, "but she's a bit nervous about it."

I could not imagine what sort of response was expected, and in any case I was too busy trying to compose myself.

"We've been friends a long time," he said, backing out. The truck bounced, rolling back, then picking up momentum. We coasted out into the street, where the sun was bright, and the old man paused, grinding the gear, turning to wave at where the woman had stood in the door. His hand came down on the wheel as if out of a kind of weariness, and we headed back toward the ice cream parlor. "She has a slight speech impediment. Doesn't like to be in crowds, you know."

I said nothing.

"Has kids of her own." He concentrated on the road again, both hands resting on the wheel, and I tried to think of something to say to him. I felt the pressure of the effort like a weight on my chest. In the next instant I understood that he was being careful of me, keeping his old eyes averted — this big, gruff, proud, blunt-speaking man — and I remembered that he was my grandfather after all, and loved me. It struck me that in my whole life I had never once quite thought of him in terms of love.

He said, "I just thought I'd see if *they* wanted ice cream, you know. Her kids."

"Did they?" I managed.

"She'd just come from the ice cream place, no kidding."

"Is she your friend?" I could hear the forced sound of my voice, and I tried to breathe out. "You know, the one you're — seeing."

"How about you?" he said, nodding. "You leaving any lady friends behind?"

"No."

"A handsome fellow like you?"

"No," I said. "Not yet."

He reached over and touched my shoulder. "Well, that won't take so long once you get settled."

I told him I wasn't worried about it, because that seemed the polite thing to say. (The truth was I had lacked the nerve to seek the company of the girls I knew. I saw them in my sleep, I ran with them there, and I spent a lot of daylight hours conversing with them in my head, but when I spoke to any of them my voice cracked, a tremor seized my hands. I had lately been having dreams about Penny Holt, but those were really dreams of women, of the idea of women.) Presently I said, "I'm not so interested in mere girls anymore, sir."

This delighted him. He laughed and slapped my knee. We were past the embarrassment of my crying, and everything was back on the old level.

Or, rather, we were rapidly approaching a new level, a new rapport, something like camaraderie, where we could say things to each other that were not freighted with our difficulties.

We pulled into the ice cream parlor parking lot and he suggested, with a wink, that we should have a little to eat at the counter before ordering what we would take back to the others. "You know," he said, "just sample it a little."

"Okay," I said.

"You can't imagine how silly it felt," he told me, "walking in there with my idea about the ice cream parlor and there they are, sitting there with the stuff on their faces."

"How many children does she have?" I asked.

"Three boys. But there were neighborhood kids, too. I swear the woman was born to have children around her. She understands them in some way that other people just don't. At least I don't."

We had never talked like this. I could have been someone he had worked with in town. I felt ten feet tall.

"They flock to her," he went on. "I mean she could be the pied piper of the town if she wanted to, and I've told her she ought to be a teacher.

But you can't make her listen. She's a very stubborn woman. Of course, she's a lot younger than I am."

The ice cream parlor was a small white room with a lazily turning ceiling fan and the constant noise of the freezer; it smelled heavily of candy. We sat at the counter, through the streaked glass of which we could see two rows of open cylinder-shaped containers of ice cream, the various flavors written out by hand on index cards that were taped to each one. The boy behind the counter looked about my age, but his hair was cut short, and he wore a T-shirt with a bright blue hawk emblazoned across the chest. He gave me a derisive glance, wiping the countertop with a wet rag. No one else was in the place, and yet he took a while getting to us. The old man didn't notice this because he was still talking to me.

"Your grandmother was always stubborn, too, you know. Even more so than your mother. To tell you the truth, I never quite understood any of the women in my life. My own mother wouldn't speak to me for a solid year after I decided I wasn't interested in farming, and I still don't understand that, since she was always the one pushing me to go study law. There's no puzzle in this world like another person."

It occurred to me to mention my own confusion concerning what I had overheard Mother saying to Aunt Elaine that night in the house in Virginia; it was in my mind as I nodded, agreeing with him.

"Especially a female person," he said, and smiled.

Somehow I knew to keep silent. To have spoken about any of our recent complications would have broken the spell of simple kindness between us, because it would have scraped across wounds he was at that moment taking some trouble to ignore. On impulse, I started to tell him about Penny Holt.

I said, "There was this woman we met on the train," and he sat forward, leaning his elbow on the counter, nodding. I had the suspicion that he knew some of the story from Mother, or even from Lisa. It stopped me.

"Go ahead," he said.

But now the boy was standing before us with his pencil and pad, waiting to write down our orders, and when we'd got through all that, the moment had passed. Grandfather Tinan and the boy talked about the Hawks, which was the name of the local high school football team.

They had won the county championship the previous fall, and were expected to repeat.

"My grandson here is quite a baseball player," the old man said, licking his double-scoop chocolate cone. I felt dimly sorry for him, for what I knew was his pride in me.

The boy glanced my way. "Really," he said without interest.

"Yes, he's quite good." Grandfather Tinan had never seen me pitch a game.

"I'm on the baseball team, too," the boy said, pointing to the hawk on his shirt.

"You pitch?"

"Some."

"Tom's a pitcher."

The boy looked at me, and I returned the look. We were not being friendly, but the old man either hadn't noticed this or was choosing to ignore it.

"Tom's visiting — on his way to Wyoming. If he was staying, he'd be a Hawk."

"Would he."

"I guess he would."

"I don't really play anymore," I said in what I recall now, with no small embarrassment, as the tone of a grizzled retired pro.

"You don't look like you do," the boy said, obviously referring to my hair.

"No," I said. "I've gone on to other things."

The boy went about his business, using the same damp rag to clean the nozzle of the frozen custard machine, and we ate our cones, not speaking now.

"We'll want a gallon of Neapolitan to go," the old man said.

The boy got it for us. Grandfather Tinan paid him, saying nothing. Outside, he paused and looked at the red sky. "Everybody's so touchy these days," he said.

"Yes, sir."

He turned his attention to me. "It's our hair."

His smile made me sorry for every hard thought I'd ever had about him. "Guess so," I said, trying for exactly the tone I'd have used with my best friend.

We got into the truck and drove back to the house. "I've had my ice cream," he said. "I don't want anymore."

Although I did want more, I said, "Me either."

"Let me take this inside, and then you and I will go for another little ride."

"Sure," I said.

He got out and crossed the lawn, and I saw Mother in the open door, watching his approach. She looked beyond him and waved at me. I felt good now. The truck idled, and the old man disappeared into the house. Splashes of sun poured down on the shady street, and up the way a dog lazed in the gold-hued grass, rolling and writhing, propelling himself with quick stretching motions of his back legs, sliding along on his back and shaking his long nose as if with the pleasure of his own ability to breathe, his front paws curled tight, his white chest jutting out, showing ribs. Grandfather Tinan came from the house and walked around the truck and climbed in, shifting the gears with something like emphasis. "Women," he said.

I said, "What."

"They thought I should've taken Lisa with us."

"Oh," I said, hoping I'd struck the right note of agreement with him, along with the sense that I was not surprised.

"Well," he said as we pulled away, "Lisa's a little too young for this, I think."

We went to a bar near the Air Force base and he bought me a glass of beer. I drank it slowly. We sat in a corner booth in the dim light and quiet. Some men were shooting pool in the farthest reaches of the back, standing around in a smoky, fan-shaped plash of light. I didn't much like the beer, but I drank it all the way down and then he paid for it, and we walked out into the bright sun, where he belched and slapped his chest. "Now," he said, "let's go."

In the truck we didn't talk. He drove away from the town, into the miles of open farmland, the wide black expanses of ground and the small clusters of white buildings far off, past the signposts for smaller towns, and on until we reached the edge of a long, descending hill, beyond which one white church stood, its tall, skinny spire gleaming in the sun. "We used to ride this hill when I was a boy about your age," he said. Then he pointed at the surrounding fields. "All that, as far as you can see. That was Tinan farmland. My father and his two brothers — a couple of uncles. A lot of land, all owned by the same family and fenced off in parcels. Big parcels. Mine would've been right over there on the other side of that church."

We started down the hill, and he let the truck coast. "Weeee," he said. I put my hand out the window in the cool force of the air.

"It's hard to believe a hill like this could be anywhere around," I said.

"We used to have to get out and push the cars, coming up this thing," he said. "All of us. The cars back then just wouldn't make it."

At the bottom of the hill, perhaps a half mile from where we'd started, we climbed the rise beyond to the little church, and there he pulled in and stopped by a low stone fence bordering the church lawn. "Come on," he said, getting out.

It was growing chillier, and a wind blew across the far spaces. I followed him along the stone wall, around to the back of the church, my arms wrapped about myself for warmth. We came to a cemetery, a scattering of graves on another low hill beyond a stand of trees. The white headstones in their uneven ranks looked stained with ash or coal dust, and the names on some had been effaced by weather, so that only the faintest shadow remained, an insinuation in the smoothed marble. Grandfather Tinan strode among these graves with the purposefulness of someone who knows what he has come for. We made our way to the farthest edge of the grounds, where the grass was tallest, and there he stooped down, pulling the weeds from a flat marker. "Here," he said. "We start right here."

The stone said WILFORD. I stood over him and read the name.

"My mother's people," he said. "Sam and Eva. They came from New Haven in 1875. They met in a saloon in the town of New Haven in 1871. She was from Luxembourg. Couldn't speak a word of English. I remember her when I was a little boy — you couldn't understand her. At least *I* couldn't."

"My great-great-grandmother," I said, wanting to return to him something of the reverence he obviously felt, and, I'm afraid, not feeling much else but the pressure to do so.

"She'd been gone a long time when you were born. Him too."

"What were they like?"

"Oh," he said. "Stolid. Quiet. Farm people. They didn't know much but work and the King James Bible. But they knew those two things, all right." He didn't move for a few seconds. He remained crouched there, staring at the mossy green stone. "They valued work differently. They believed it kept them from the devil." He stood. Three stones over was a smaller one, tilted forward as if about to topple to the ground. "Now this one," he said, "my mother's sister, Constance. Your mother's named after her."

I looked at the name.

"She was a wild one."

"How?" I said, half expecting to hear that she had run away to get married to an airman.

"Oh," Grandfather Tinan said, "she just couldn't take things the way they were. Died of TB when she was thirty-six. Or they said it was TB. Consumption, they called it then. But it was drink. Too much of everything, really. I remember once I helped carry her from a car into the living room of our house. She was all bones by then. I was fifteen, maybe. She'd taken a bottle of aspirin, and they'd had to do all sorts of things to purge her. My father kept talking to her, the way you would — the way a person talks to a child who has misbehaved — and she looked at me. She was really awfully beautiful. And she said, 'I guess this will teach me a lesson.' She seemed about to laugh. And I never saw another pair of human eyes with a light like that in them, not ever. Positively ghostly, just shining terribly — with something terrible. I think she knew where she was headed, and in fact she didn't live longer than another month or so. The whole family came out here the day we buried her, and it was like we were all to blame somehow. Of course, nobody said as much. But we all felt it, I'm sure — that we'd all done it to her by being the type of people we were. We just didn't know what she needed. None of us. And that's one reason I let your mother run off when she did. I thought it was my aunt Constance again, happening in her namesake. I didn't want to compound the mistakes I'd already made preventing her . . ." He stopped, ran his rough hands through his hair. I knew we were now thinking about my father. "She's right," he went on, in the tone of someone changing the subject. "She *is* a grown woman now, and what she does is her business."

"Yes, sir," I said.

He looked at me. "This is all pretty dull, isn't it."

I hadn't felt that it was. "Are all these stones our family?"

"Most of them," he said, bending to pull the weeds from another one. "This one here," he said, "this is your great-aunt Pat. She was only three months old when she died."

The years of birth and death were inscribed below the words *Gone among the Angels to prepare a place for us.*

"Little Pat," Grandfather Tinan said. "The quietest little thing. Big soft eyes. She just didn't have the strength to keep on breathing, and she seemed almost sad to be causing all that — that grief. She went with the smallest — just the faintest sighing sound. I still hear it in my sleep sometimes, and think it's her. All the time since then, all those years, they just collapse, you know, and I'm back there. Back — just a boy. My father used to say that we didn't deserve her because she was an angel, and sometimes I wonder if he wasn't right about it. Anyway, I wish I could believe it the way he did. He never questioned it for a second, and I'll tell you, boy, it made him strong." He cleared his throat, and I thought his voice had quavered. Now we were both standing. The wind blew, and was colder. "Well," he said, "I thought you might want to see some of these."

I walked over to the next row. All the names were Wilford. Several of them were children, and one marker contained an explanation that a cholera outbreak in 1877 had taken twenty-three lives, mostly those of children. One stone, larger than most, was for someone named Dalton, whose life had been long. The years were 1820–1924.

"Look," I said.

"Right," Grandfather Tinan said. "He was a colonel in the Civil War. Fought with Lee, believe it or not. And on Fourth of Julys he'd wear that damn confederate gray right down the middle of Main Street. Old Eldrich Dalton. A great-uncle by marriage, on my mother's side, and old enough to be her grandfather. Had the gruffest voice I ever heard on a man. He'd yell at you out of these big white whiskers he wore, and you'd jump just from the sound of it. Like thunder. He wore those whiskers over his lips and on up over his ears, and he was as bald as a billiard ball on top. Still had all his faculties when he died, too. Died in an automobile accident — one of the first really bad ones in the area."

I was beginning to shiver now. And though I wanted to stay, the demands of my body were making themselves apparent.

"We better get on back," he said.

"A hundred and four years," I said.

"Makes two years seem kind of short, doesn't it."

I was at a loss.

"Your father's sentence."

"Oh," I said, and heat rose to my cheeks.

"I mean by comparison."

"I guess so."

He put his hand on my shoulder as we walked back to the truck. "It'll go by fast enough, son. It just won't seem to."

"Yes, sir," I said.

We climbed into the truck. He ground the gears, looking back, concentrating on getting us out of the lot. I looked at the markers in the tall, waving grass. Everything seemed so accomplished and peaceful, and for a moment I felt a kind of exhaustion, except it wasn't quite that, either: I was in the beginning, really, of my grown-up life, and the years ahead seemed daunting, the agitation and confusion I was already in, already subject to, seemed more than anyone should be asked to bear for long. And yet I was coming to see that I would have to bear it all the time, all the years, simply by being an adult. I looked out at the wide country, and then we were climbing the hill, heading back.

"I'm glad we did that," my grandfather said.

"I am, too," I said. "Thank you."

He smiled. "It's sort of my job."

We rode back in silence. We had become friends, it seemed to me, and I liked the new relation.

"I'd love to show all that to Lisa," I said.

"When she's old enough," he told me, and strangely his voice had taken on the old gruffness.

"Oh, of course," I said.

"You all belong here," he said.

I nodded automatically, but he hadn't looked my way.

"It's a shame," he said, "you know? It's a goddam shame."

This didn't seem to require an answer, and in any case I had none to give him.

*　　*　　*

Aunt Elaine drove us the hundred miles south to the train. Over the last days we were in Minot, Grandfather Tinan returned to his choleric taciturnity, and when we were ready to leave he took himself upstairs to his room. Mother stood in the foyer and called to him. And then Aunt Elaine went up and spent a few minutes in a low, murmurous quarrel with him. But he would not relent. He told her to tell us goodbye.

"Childish old fool," Aunt Elaine said, and looked on the verge of tears.

Mother shouted up to him. "We'll call you."

We all stood in the doorway and listened to the silence.

"I'm not going up there," Mother said. "I thanked him for the money, and I even said I'd accept it as a gift. But I'm not going up there now."

"I'm sure he doesn't expect you to do anything."

"Granddaddy," Lisa said. It was almost a dismissal, but there was a question in it, too.

"Granddaddy is acting your age," Mother said to her.

This offended Lisa. "Not me," she said with some force.

"I don't mean you. Don't take it personally."

We went out to the car and got in, and I looked at the house, at his curtained window. Aunt Elaine and Mother were talking about him, arranging themselves in the front seat.

". . . supposed to be a judge and he's an emotional infant and always has been, too," Aunt Elaine said. "I feel like I'm babysitting a lot of the time."

"Well, why do you put up with it? You should've moved out long ago."

"Stop it," I said to them. "Just lay off him."

Mother looked back at me, and Lisa said, "God."

"We're just talking," Aunt Elaine said to me. "We love him dearly."

"Well," said Mother, "not quite dearly."

They both laughed.

I huddled against the back seat and sulked, and Mother reached over to touch my knee. "Hey," she said.

"What," I said.

"Don't sulk."

We headed out of town, onto the interstate, south. I watched the signs glide by the window.

"Hear me?"

"I'm not sulking," I said. But my throat constricted, and I could barely keep the tears back; it was all a combination of what they had said and of sensing that I might not see the old man again for a long time. I felt certain that he knew this, too, and that this was why he couldn't face us, couldn't have us see him break down. When I turned and looked through the back window of the car, I couldn't make out the house among the other houses of Minot drifting off to the north. Beyond the roofs the sky was bright and vivid, striated with long folds of sunny clouds, white waves in a preposterously blue sea.

The ride south was fairly quiet. There didn't seem much else to say. Aunt Elaine muttered something to Mother about the old man's woman friend, glancing back at me as if to monitor my reaction, but I said nothing. It was all their business, grown-up business, and I was tired of worrying about it — our painful journey westward had resumed, and already I felt depleted and depressed. To be uprooted again, hurtling through space toward that unknown prison town, disheartened me in some primal way — this in spite of the knowledge that soon I would be seeing my father. And I think something of what I felt must've been working in each of us. For the longest time no one spoke. Aunt Elaine contended with the truck traffic on the interstate; Mother lay her head on the seatback and took in the passing fields; Lisa sat with a book of puzzles on her lap, turning the pages and then concentrating: and I kept a watch on them all. Finally Mother went to sleep, and I noticed that Aunt Elaine's gaze in the rearview mirror kept settling on me.

"Hot for this time of year here," she said at last.

I nodded.

She opened her window. "Is that too much air on you all back there?"

"It's fun," Lisa said, letting her windblown hair cover her face. "It feels good."

"Tom?"

"It's fine," I said.

"Are you mad at something?"

"What?" Mother said, and sat forward to look at each of us in turn. Her eyes were glazed over with sleep. When she had satisfied herself that nothing was amiss, she rested her head on the seatback and drifted off once more.

"Are you mad at me?" Aunt Elaine said.

I said, "No."

"You wanted to stay, didn't you?"

I leaned forward so that I wouldn't have to raise my voice. "I don't know."

"But you liked it this time."

"I liked being with Grandfather Tinan this time."

"I could tell."

"He makes me nervous," Lisa said.

"It's just his way, honey," Aunt Elaine said.

"He was nice," I said.

"I didn't say he wasn't nice," said Lisa.

"Nobody said you did," I told her.

"Well, I didn't."

A moment later, Aunt Elaine glanced back at me. "He didn't want you to see him — how upset he was."

I stared through the windshield at the road ahead.

"He wasn't angry."

"He sounds angry all the time," Lisa said.

"Well, he wasn't angry."

"Who are we talking about?" Mother said, sitting forward again. "As if I didn't know."

"I was just telling the children —" Aunt Elaine began.

Mother interrupted her. "I heard you."

We rode on in silence, and during one hot stretch of the highway I dozed off, too.

At the station Aunt Elaine cried, hugging each of us, and helped with the luggage. She kept admonishing us about the perils ahead — not just inattentive porters and bad food, but thugs riding the cars looking for helpless women and children: drunks, con men, criminals, deserters and draft dodgers, not to mention the whole angry population of the dispossessed and the unfortunate, people with grievances who could conceivably see us as belonging to something they hated. As she went on talking about these hazards, her voice took on some of the heat and stridency of one of Grandfather Tinan's tirades, except that I could hear a frantic note in it, too, as if poor Aunt Elaine were more frightened than certain. We were to let her know the minute we arrived, and we should call her if we needed anything at all.

"You know we will," Mother said. "Tell Daddy I love him."

"He knows you do," Aunt Elaine said, crying. She put her arms around me and sobbed. "Take care of them."

"Don't worry," I told her.

"I don't want to go," Lisa said. "I'm tired." I lifted her up onto the first step. "Put me down. I can do it myself."

"Stand up for yourselves," Aunt Elaine said, trying to laugh through her tears. "All of you."

We climbed up into the vestibule and almost immediately the train began to move.

"Goodbye," Lisa called.

Aunt Elaine stood on the platform alone, crying, making no effort to wipe her face, one hand lifted in farewell. She looked broken.

"We'll call," Mother shouted before losing her own voice. I saw her put her hand to her mouth as she turned and moved through the car. She led us to our seats — we were to have no compartment for this leg of the trip — and she spent much of the next couple of hours silently brushing tears from the corners of her eyes. Lisa and I talked a little, both of us keeping quiet. We were drawing near our destination, and it made us more considerate of each other somehow. Lisa's eyes were wide with what looked like fright. She trembled some. When I took her hand, she squeezed. "We're almost there," she said. "Aren't we?"

"In a while," I said, low, putting my arm around her. Across from us, in her own seat, Mother seemed to be looking for something in the distant green hills, in the mountains, with their snow-capped heights and ribbed outcroppings of stone.

"I don't want to get there," Lisa said. "I want to go back."

But we were not going back, and she knew it. I held her close, feeling the little tremors in her body like the shivering under my own heart.

"Why am I so scared?" she said.

I told her to be quiet, speaking gently, pulling her even closer to me.

"It'll be fine," I said. "It's just another move." We had moved so many times; we had been through plenty in the way of picking up and starting over again. We had made it this far together. I wanted to say this to her, yet I couldn't find the way to begin, couldn't bring the words out of myself — and even if I could have, I don't know that she would have been able to hear or understand. Outside, the land rolled by, the country changed to open spaces, miles and miles of grassy hills without the first sign of a town or a farmhouse. Across the aisle from us a big pale man with a crown of false-looking black hair unfurled a newspaper on whose front page, under the headline NEW RIOTING CLAIMS 15, was a large photograph of a littered and burning street, broken glass and pools of dark liquid reflecting flames, automobiles engulfed in fire.

"Look at that," Lisa said, shivering against me.

"It's far away," I told her. "Don't worry about it." But then, looking out the window at the vast openness of the plains, I had a moment of dumbfounded incredulity. I thought of the war, with its litany of Oriental names and its smoking villages in the nightly films on television news, and in the next harrowing instant everything came home to me, the whole furious, falling-apart system, like a revelation of death, and it was all mixed in somehow with Father's arrest and incarceration and this strange westward journey we were making. It was all one, all a function of the same collapsing reality, and I felt as though I were a visitor from some distant, alien place, an invisible observer, watching in abject horror as a man calmly turned the pages of pictures showing flames licking up the sides of buildings, showing the maimed and wounded, bodies lying in the rubble of destruction — the man sitting quietly, gazing at everything with the same stolid, accepting expression while the train in which he was a passenger hurtled across the face of that very country, his own appalling country.

I had no words for this at the time, not really. But I remember the moment, with its strands of panic, and the faintly vertiginous sensation of seeing it all at a remove. I felt the sense of horror, of things disintegrating around us, like a shock to my spine.

"Stop it," Lisa said. "You're squeezing me too tight."

"I'm sorry," I said.

"What's the matter? You look white as a sheet."

"Nothing," I told her. "Stop worrying about everything." I might well have been talking to myself.

"You can hold me," Lisa said. "Just not too tight."

"Please," Mother said without quite looking at either of us. "Don't squabble. We'll be there soon enough."

Then we were all watching the land glide by the windows, as if waiting for something to begin moving toward us from those endless fields of grass.

PART THREE

PART THREE

11

WE ARRIVED in Wilson Creek in the middle of the night, and we were the only family to get off the train. Two girls also got off. They were greeted by other girls, and they all went along the platform talking excitedly. We were behind them, and behind us was a group of four men who didn't appear to be together at first. One of them wore handcuffs. He looked too young to be wearing them, and I saw the frightened expression on his face. He kept turning his blond head — a mass of tight curls. His demeanor was that of someone expecting to be hit from behind at any moment.

"Wait," Mother said.

We watched the men go by us and along the platform in the harsh glare of the station lights. The train was already grinding toward motion again, and I looked down the track in the direction of where we had come. The twin rails went curving off into the darkness, with the thinnest thread of silver moonlight on them. The moon shone brightly in a circle of moving clouds above the roof of the station.

It was chilly now, and the smell of ash and coal grit hung in the air. I remembered the pain of getting the cinder in my eye, and out of reflex held my hand up to cover my face.

"What is it?" Mother said. I heard such unhappiness in her voice that I looked around us for some other obstacle.

"No," I said. "I'm okay."

"Don't do that," she said.

"I didn't mean to scare you," I told her.

"We'll have to take a cab," she said. And then, half to herself, "Everything scares me."

There were the bags to carry. I shouldered one and picked up two more, and Mother got the last two. Lisa walked between us, carrying a book that she'd fished from Mother's handbag.

Inside the station three of the men, including the one in handcuffs, were sitting on a bench while the fourth stood at a telephone, leaning against the wall and smoking a cigarette. He was waiting for someone to answer, or finish talking. Behind the ticket counter, a man in a white shirt sat paging through a ledger book.

"Excuse me," I said, meaning to take charge, to take some of Mother's worry away. "We need a cab."

"Phone's right there," the man at the counter said without looking up.

"That's the only phone?"

"Only one, yeah." Now he glanced at us, and I saw him sit back, concentrating on Mother. "I guess the phone's being used now."

"Yes, it is," she said.

"He won't be long, ma'am. Men from the prison were supposed to be waiting here for them. Did you say you need a cab?"

"Yes."

He looked at me and then at Lisa. "We don't usually get nice ladies with kids in the middle of the night out here, you know. I'll call a cab for you."

Mother thanked him, and we moved toward the bench where the men were sitting.

The station lobby was not much more than a tall room, with narrow windows and oak wainscoting all around. It smelled of old wood and cigarette smoke and something else I couldn't place, but which, for some reason, reminded me of the ice cream parlor in Minot. The light was too bright, and made the men's lips look bruised. We sat at the other end of the bench, Lisa clinging to us both, peering over and around us at the others. The one on the phone shifted his weight and smoked and seemed impatient, then said a name. "All right," he went on, "I know it's one-thirty in the morning and I'm telling you to wake him up. Christ's sakes, *I'm* up."

The young man in handcuffs made a small choked sound, then

cleared his throat. "Hey," he said to Lisa. His voice was high-pitched and breathless. "You ever see anything ugly as me?"

Lisa gave him a little smirking laugh.

"Me either," he said.

"Be quiet," one of the other men said.

And Mother turned to them. "Are you coming from far away?" She was clearly addressing the young prisoner, who shrugged as if to indicate that he wasn't allowed to answer.

The man who had told him to be quiet glanced angrily at her, then crossed his legs and glared in the direction of the wall clock across the way. The time was wrong by hours, and he shook his head, glanced at his watch. His cheeks were pitted and dark. His hair was cut so short it revealed a scar above the curve of his ear.

"What are you going to the prison for?" Lisa said.

Mother pulled her closer but didn't try to shush her.

"I ran away from the Army," said the boy. "Didn't want to get shot for democracy."

"Be quiet," the man said.

And the one sitting on the other side of the prisoner said, "Aw, Smitty. Let them talk."

"The prisoner is not allowed to talk to passengers."

"Nobody's a passenger now. Jesus."

"You know the rule, goddammit."

"Hey," the prisoner said, "watch your language in front of the pretty lady."

"Just shut up, Oliver."

"I'm not talking to no passenger now. I'm talking to you, man."

"And I'm telling you to shut up."

"What're you gonna do, Smitty? Throw me in jail?"

"Just keep pushing it, boy."

We were all quiet. The man on the telephone dropped his cigarette and stepped on it. A moment later he lit another. Then he cussed into the phone. "Bullshit. You heard me. I said bullshit. Well, where the hell is it, then? We've been here fifteen minutes. We shouldn't have to sit here in the goddam train station."

"They can't find a way to get me over there," said the young prisoner. "Guess they'll have to let me go."

"All right," Lisa said to the others, almost singing it. "Let him go."

"Thank you, sweetness."

"You better be quiet, boy, if you know what's good for you."

"Life's bad here," the boy said. "Man, I know that." His voice sounded almost tearful.

The doors opened then, and a small, wiry-looking man in a visored cap stepped in. "Cab?"

"Yes," the man named Smitty said.

"That's *our* cab," said Mother.

"Yeah, well, the government needs it, lady."

"You can shove the government," she said, already starting for the doors.

"Yay, lady," the boy said.

"Just hold it there," Smitty said.

And the other man said, "Let her go, Smitty. For Christ's sake, stop being a Nazi for five minutes."

"Woman talking that shit. Whole goddam country's coming apart."

"Take the cab, miss. Never mind old Smitty, here."

"It's my cab," Mother said, "and I *am* taking it."

We moved through the doors and out into the street in front of the station. The cab was idling at the curb. "Here," the cabbie said to Mother, "let me help you with that."

I had hauled most of the baggage, and I was burdened down now, but he took the one bag from Mother and threw it in the trunk, then stepped back and let me put the rest in.

"Where to?" he said.

"Twenty-six Jewett Street," Mother said. It was, I believe, the first time I had ever heard it spoken. I looked up and down the road we were on, with its closed shops and open concrete spaces, and to this day the mention of 26 Jewett Street makes me think of the view outside the station in Wilson Creek, the middle of the night on the plains. There was a lumberyard adjacent to the building, and beyond that a huge mound of coal or gravel, I couldn't tell which. We climbed into the cab, all three of us in the back seat.

"Is Jewett Street far?" Mother asked the cabbie as he set the meter on and pulled out.

"Not too."

"I don't have a lot of cash."

"You got four dollars?"

"Good. Yes," she said.

He was turning the wheel with an exaggerated swing of his arms. "Won't be much more than that."

We drove through the town, the dilapidated appearance of which made me sick to my stomach. I saw boarded-up shop windows and empty buildings and vacant lots with debris in them, the litter of places left untended. In one lot, the burned remains of a building lay like a huge dead hulk.

"Old folks' home," the cabbie said. "Everybody got out, believe it or not."

The street divided, and we took the right fork past a big triangular structure, a pawnshop, and used car lot. Now there were lawns and old houses, and we crossed a bridge over a wide, moon-haunted stream, then went over a pair of railroad tracks, the car rocking with the rucks in the asphalt.

"Should be right here," the cabbie said, leaning to his right and peering at the addresses.

Mother sighed and held my hand. "They're expecting us," she said.

"There it is." The cabbie slowed to a stop and put the meter handle down. It read $3.90.

She gave him a five dollar bill from her purse, and her hand trembled. "There don't seem to be any lights on."

I had opened the door on my side, the street side. The cabbie got out. Mother began talking to me, holding back tears, and there wasn't anything I could give her. My sense of utter helplessness in that moment contained all the hard, spasmodic pain of a slashed nerve.

"It's all dark," Lisa said. "I don't like it."

The cabbie had already put all the bags on the curb. "Okay," he said, almost hurrying, "bye, now." He ducked back into the idling car, and it was as though the sounds of the night had stopped save that of the cab and its driver. He closed the door with a muffled clunk, then pulled away, the engine whining into its higher gears, the tires popping gravel. When the twin red lights disappeared past the next block, I felt marooned. The silence surrounding us now felt like another presence, some listening thing. I looked at Lisa, and at Mother. Their skin shone pale blue in the glow of the streetlamp. The wind had picked up. It moaned and gusted at us, a gesture the night made, offering a touch of the coming winter chill. We saw the darkened house and the lawn, the shapes of the five fir trees flanking the porch, and the one big shape of the twisted oak in the yard, the ends of whose branches reached across the white front of the house.

"Well?" I said, and put my arm around Mother's waist. I felt her shivering.

"I'm cold," Lisa said.

Mother made a sobbing sound that was more like a laugh. "Come on, honey," she said, stepping out of my grasp and picking up two of the bags. "We'll get to see your father soon."

As we bumped and lurched up the walk, a light went on in the house, a dim glow beyond the oval window of the front door. Then the whole front of the house was illumined, and the door opened. In it, a big woman stood in a flannel robe, her heavy arms folded tight. "Welcome," she said. "Welcome to Wilson Creek."

"Hi," Mother answered.

"You look worn out."

"Yes."

We had come up onto the porch, which was wide and spacious and showed signs of work — someone had been sanding it. Unopened cans of paint were stacked against the railing to our left. Part of the bare wood of the porch floor had been exposed, a dark swath. Mother introduced us to the woman, Mabel Wilson, who shook my hand and hurried to say that the town was not named after her, or anyone in her family. "Nobody on my husband's side of the family, up to and including my husband, was the sort of person you name a town after," she said, vigorously shaking my hand and smiling. There was something deep-throated and musical about her voice, as though she had just come down to us from an evening of operatic flourishes. She turned to Lisa. "Look at those big dark eyes," she said.

Lisa immediately looked down.

"Shy, huh," said Mrs. Wilson.

"Well," Mother said, "no. Not really."

"She just has to get to know us," Mrs. Wilson said. "We're just ordinary people. Nobody in our family is on any statues or anything, that's certain."

"I guess nobody in our family is, either," Mother told her.

I wondered how much the other woman knew about our reasons for coming to be her tenants in the first place. I could not imagine Mother telling her about Father, but I knew she must've told her something: it's possible that Mrs. Wilson's talk — all that business about no one in her family meriting the honor of a town's name or a statue — came from her knowledge of our situation, of where Father was out in the dark beyond the street.

"You'll have to forgive me," Mrs. Wilson rattled on as we struggled inside with the bags, "We have a situation here. I've just thrown out one of my other tenants."

Mother didn't seem to understand this. She paused, and Lisa took her hand, holding tight, her scared gaze darting from place to place in the room. I thought she would probably have one of her bad dreams tonight.

"We still have our rooms?" Mother said.

"Oh, of course. No, I mean I'm going to have to rent the top-floor room out, after five years. This horrible little filthy man who was a tenant here for God knows how long brought a — Lord, he brought something dirty into the house and I just won't have that sort of thing."

"No," Mother said, clearly trying to reassure her. But I heard curiosity in her voice, too.

I wondered what the item in question could've been. Mrs. Wilson had used the word "filthy," and so I thought of books or pictures. In the last school I'd attended — the Andrews Air Base High School, a century ago, it seemed — a boy named Harley Meyer had brought in photographs of men and women having sex. He had set about charging other boys five dollars a day to keep them overnight, and because I was Harley's partner in art class, he showed them to me. I had stood in the darkroom in back of the art studio, looking at them under the red glow of the lamps while Harley guarded the entrance. He had chosen me as his first prospective customer, and it was with a sense of nervous anxiety, as though in response to some unspoken peril, that I eventually turned him down. In saying this I don't mean I had any worry about being caught with the pictures. No, that never even entered my mind. This feeling had instead to do with my profound apprehensions about the thing itself, as though by merely looking at these images I might open gates in myself through which forces I didn't understand would pass. Something shivered in my soul, and I began rifling through that pathetic little pile of photographs like someone counting cards in a deck, trying to look at all of the images in the same trembling instant. They were graphic beyond my wildest imaginings, but in a coldly biological way. The whole enterprise had the look of some preposterous anthropological display. The faces, male and female, were almost cadaverous in their total lack of expression, of any passion, or even of the slightest sign of pleasure. The men had elaborate bruise-colored tattoos on their arms, and the women generally kept their colorless eyes on the camera, staring at it. In one, a blond woman lay back in what seemed a bizarre position, legs up and spread wide, the man ranged between them, supporting himself on the backs of her thighs, her black high-heeled shoes giving the whole thing a weirdly transactional feeling, an aspect of an acrobatic sales demonstration. But the place where his body entered hers was the central thing in the photograph, as indeed it was in all of them, except the one where a couple in the background were performing oral sex on each other. That one, Harley said, would rent for ten dollars a day. I can still see those photographs under that hot light, the carnal-feeling glow of the school darkroom. I felt heat in my face and neck; my heart pounded. I couldn't breathe. The sound of Harley's voice startled me.

"You gonna stand there forever?"

Other boys were waiting.

"I've got money, Harley," one of them said.

"Five dollars, Harley," said another.

"Ten. I'll give you ten. I'll steal it from my mother's house money."

I could almost hear those whispering, urgent, excitedly contending voices now, two thousand miles and more than a year away, as Mrs. Wilson went on talking. "You wouldn't want somebody like that living here, would you? With this beautiful little girl, and your son, in his young manhood."

"Of course not."

I had closed the front door, and the realization that the phrase "young manhood" applied to me — that I was the subject of this odd woman's plainspoken estimation — sent a small tremor of unbidden excitement through me. The idea of the photographs, and the fact of my nearness to the experience they depicted, made my heartbeat change. I thought of Penny Holt in her shiny white sleep clothes, but then I saw Mother's pallid, uncertain features in the light and was ashamed of myself.

"Where should I put the bags?" I said.

No one heard me. Mrs. Wilson nervously wrung her hands, talking. "You think you can trust a person to exercise some judgment in life, and you think he's a nice person, someone who shares your values, and you can depend on him, you understand his character."

We had moved slowly to the base of a stairway going up into the dimness. To our left was a big room crowded with furniture — three stuffed chairs, a long plush sofa, a pair of ottomans, a heavy glass coffee table — and a fireplace. Beyond all this was a tall, arched opening, through which you could see the shadow-haunted shapes of a dark oak table and chairs, and a great black hutch full of curios and china. A door in the far wall opened onto a scene of disarray, clothes strewn on chairs, glasses on tabletops. I realized I was seeing into the rooms where this woman did her living from day to day. A boy there lounged in pajamas in an easy chair, reading a comic book. He looked at me, then rose and pushed the door shut.

Mrs. Wilson went on talking: "And — just, can you imagine — my other tenant, Mr. Egan, was watching the thing with him. The most outrageous and shocking thing — like two people looking at home movies, you know, only it's this — this — this film. I heard the projector, you understand, and I — I wouldn't've walked in on them except that I thought something was rattling around in there and I didn't know anyone was home — and, see, I don't know for sure what I'll do about Mr. Egan. He's — he's painting the porch, and I do need that done."

Mother said nothing. The three of us just waited for Mrs. Wilson to continue. So the offending thing was a movie! The idea of it made my mouth dry: an actual film of people doing the sort of thing I had seen in Harley Meyer's creased, much-handled, brutally graphic little photographs.

"Would you like something to eat or drink?" Mrs. Wilson said.

Mother looked at me.

"I just want to sleep," I told them. But my secret excitement had exacerbated the disturbance in my stomach; I was feeling sicker by the minute.

"Are you all right?" Mother said.

"He's white as a sheet," said Mrs. Wilson.

Lisa pulled Mother's coat and murmured, "Maybe it's travel sickness."

"Well," said Mrs. Wilson, giving me a doubtful glance, "let me show you your rooms."

We all clattered up the stairs to the second level of the house, a long hallway with a room at one end and the small landing which contained the entrance to our apartment at the other. Stairs led down at either end of the hall, one set going to the kitchen, Mrs. Wilson told us, and the other, just past our landing, to the front hall of the house and continuing to the top floor. Our apartment was accessible through a small, foyerlike space of linoleum tile and bookcases: a person coming downstairs, or walking up from the first level, would have to cross this space and climb a little four-step entry to see into the second-floor apartment. Our new place, doorless though it was, consisted of two bedrooms and a small sitting room, a tall-ceilinged bathroom, and a little storage closet under the stairs leading up to the third level. The stairs were sectioned off from our rooms by a paneled partition, but it was clear enough to me that when someone came down from the third floor we would know it; we would hear the creaking protest of the wooden steps (the steps had made their rickety complaint under our feet as we had climbed this far), and the whole idea of strangers going and coming past the opening to our rooms made me more nauseous somehow.

I asked to be excused. The bathroom, which had none of our things in it and therefore felt quite unfamiliar, was a musty-smelling room with stained dull porcelain and uncurtained, leaded windows looking out into the ghostly, moving shadows of trees. I leaned against the closed door, trying to breathe, and when I saw that the bathtub was on claw feet, like Grandfather Tinan's — almost exactly identical to his, in fact, down to the tiny metal scales imitating fur above the bony, leonine talons — I felt a tiny increment of relief.

In the next moment, though, everything went hazy and I was very sick indeed, leaning down to brace myself, trying to make less noise than I knew I was making.

"Are you all right?" Mother said through the door.

"No."

"Let me in."

"No," I said. "Please." And I was sick again. The whole room spun. Outside the dark windows, in the near distance, I knew, was my father; and this thought, which ought to have felt soothing to me, only made me more ill. It seemed that whatever I thought about in those seconds aggravated the nerves of my stomach, and I ended up trying not to allow any image to pass through my mind at all.

"Thomas."

"Leave me alone," I said.

The two women talked quietly outside the door, no doubt debating what they ought to do. I flushed the toilet and washed my face, then knelt over the bowl again, breathing slowly, taking in air, trying to keep my mind empty. "Do you want help, Thomas."

"No," I said.

"Honey, please let me in."

"No, will you go away?"

I wanted to ask if Mrs. Wilson had gone downstairs, but then I heard her voice. She was talking to Lisa. I felt crowded. I wanted to get over to the prison, into the imaginary place where my father might reach across a table and shake my hand. But the room was unsteady, seemed to be rocking like a small boat on a stormy sea. I sat on the edge of the claw-footed tub and held my hands tight over my eyes, everything roiling inside. Gradually it passed.

"Thomas, can you let me in?"

"I think I'm better," I said.

"Let me in," Mother said.

I told her I was sorry and opened the door. She studied me a moment, looked into my eyes. "You just got too tired."

"I'm cold," I said.

"Maybe it's a touch of something."

"You'll feel better in the morning," Lisa said with the confidence of a veteran sufferer.

I went to my room and saw that she had begun unpacking for both of us. Our clothes lay across the red plush chair in the corner. The bunk beds were made, the sheets turned back. "Like a hotel," she said.

I got out of my clothes and climbed into the top bunk.

"Don't worry about anything," Lisa said. "I'll pick it all up."

I had just dropped my coat, walked out of my trousers and shirt, pulled my socks off, and tossed them atop the pile of unpacked clothes.

"Don't throw dirties on top of the clean," she said kindly, and touched my hip. "I'm sorry you feel bad."

Then Mother was in the doorway. "It's just all the strain of the trip. I don't feel very good either. Just think about being near your father again."

"Can we see him every day?" Lisa asked.

"Almost," Mother told her.

"Won't that be good, Thomas?" Lisa was being as kind and brave as a much older, much stronger girl. I understood from the faintly apologetic look she gave me that she was thinking of her bad dreams, and that she would probably be crawling into bed with me before the night was over. My heart went out to her, and I said, "Listen, if you get worried or anything tonight, you know. You don't want to catch this — but we could talk or something." Her sharp gaze wandered the room. Then she smiled, showing some softness in her eyes, a very tentative gratitude.

"Don't worry about waking me up," I said.

"Oh, I won't wake you."

Mother came into the room and put her arms around Lisa, holding her very tight. "We've actually made it here," she said, looking at me. "We're here."

"Hard to believe," I said, starting to feel sick again. I could hear the wind blowing in the eaves of the house, and I saw that Lisa was hearing it, too.

"I'm right in the other room," Mother said. "Okay?"

When she was gone Lisa said, "Why are we all so sad?"

"I'm sick," I said.

"But — you know what I mean?"

"I want to go home," I said. It came from me like a whimper.

She got into her bed. "The lady said it was against the county ordinances for you and me to sleep in the same room. She said she wouldn't pay any attention to it because Mother started to look like she might start crying."

"Try to go to sleep," I said.

She was quiet. We heard stirrings in the house. At my side was a window. I parted the curtains and looked out through more tree branches at the configurations of light and dark. I didn't know which part of the house we were in, really, and I couldn't tell if the part of a road I saw was the street we'd stood on only minutes before. Then I was sure it wasn't a road at all, for it ended in a series of white stakes, and beyond it a glimmer of water traveled away from me, a shallow trickle over a sandy creek bed. I saw a gleam of shifting light on the surface, moonlight or lamplight I couldn't tell. A spar of dry earth went down the winding middle of it like the spine of a half-submerged whale, and an iron bridge shimmered with facets of the same source-less light in the distance: a railroad trestle. Presently, as if the sight of that black iron fretwork had produced it, I heard the big, far-echoing moan of a train. I closed the curtain; I'd had all I wanted of that sound.

"Thomas?" Lisa said not much later. "I'm cold."

"I'm afraid I'll give you this — whatever this is that I have," I said.

"It's travel sickness," she said. Her voice quavered with fear.

"Come on," I told her.

She climbed up, and I made room for her on the other side of me, by the window, leaving myself free to get down, as I feared I would have to, soon.

"Comfy?" I said.

"Thanks." She was crying, keeping it to herself. I thought about how much she'd grown over the course of the trip, and I stroked her hair.

"We'll be all right," I murmured.

"This house makes noises."

We listened.

Someone moved in the hall outside the apartment, and then water went rushing through pipes in our wall. We heard Mother say some-thing, apparently to Mrs. Wilson, and the stairs creaked. Somewhere in the boards and joists a faint tapping sounded. I thought of a mouse worrying his morsel of stolen food from the kitchen.

"What is it?" Lisa said.

"Nothing." I stroked her hair again. "Go to sleep."

"I'll never sleep."

But in a while she drifted off, and I realized that I was alone. The house moaned and settled. The heater kicked on with a dull clank under us, and I was beginning to feel ill again. I lay there. Lisa stirred, then lay still. Her breathing eased. Outside, the wind raced through the treetops and made the shadows move. Then Mother stood in the doorway. I'd seen something change in the composition of the darkness and realized with a little shock that she was standing there.

"Mother?" I whispered.

And she seemed startled. "Is Lisa in with you?"

"On the other side of me, yes."

"Go to sleep, honey."

I heard tears in her voice.

"Is it okay?" I said.

She said, "It's never what you expect it to be."

"No."

"I thought the rooms would be a little bigger."

"It's okay," I said.

"We'll go look at things in the morning."

"Right," I said.

She came to me, put her arms around me again. "I'm proud of you both," she whispered.

I kissed her cheek.

"Are you feeling better?"

"Yes," I lied.

She reached across me, coming up on her toes to do it, and touched Lisa's shoulder. "We better not wake her."

"No," I said.

"If you need me," she said. "That's what I wanted to say to you. Don't go through it alone."

I nodded, then understood that she couldn't really see me very well. "I'll be okay," I said.

"I know," she told me. "But wake me."

"Okay."

When she was gone I turned in the bed and held Lisa close, breathing her hair and trying not to think about what my stomach was doing. Perhaps I was feverish, for I drifted off, and was visited with an image of many people, all unrecognizable and all naked, in a tangled array of sexual poses, a vision of flesh sliding on flesh like a lot of fish in a barrel, except that it was all bathed in a garish, blood-engorged light. I woke with a start and lay trembling, thinking of my father in prison, trying to imagine what he might be doing at that very minute, and feeling the nausea start again.

12

THE NIGHT wore on that way, and I didn't think I could have slept more than a fitful minute or two. Sometime just before dawn, Lisa had her dream, and I calmed her, whispering that it was all right, not to wake Mother, it would be morning soon. You could already see the bureau across the room, and the big oak armoire in the corner. Someone was moving around downstairs. We heard water running.

"See?" I said to her.

She trembled, snuggling tight against me. "It's like we're visiting again. I hate it."

"We'll get used to it. Maybe we'll see Father today."

"I'm scared."

"It's okay."

The darkness was changing to light at the window. Mrs. Wilson had taken pictures off the walls so we could put up our own. The little square patches of wall reminded me of the house in Virginia. Our stay there had been so brief, and yet something about it felt, now, more like home than any of the various and far-flung other places we had lived in before. I couldn't explain that to myself then, and I'm not quite certain about it now. Perhaps it was just that all the other history of us had been altered for the worse by how it ended: the arrest and the court-martial, our eviction from what we had learned to take for granted. Anyway, as I lay there watching the early dawn light come to that strange room, the fact that I missed the Virginia house more than any other seemed important enough to mention to Lisa.

"Yes," she said, almost tearfully. "I wish we didn't have to leave there."

"You didn't seem to mind it when we left."

"I did, though. I don't ever want to leave anywhere again." She buried her face in the blanket at my shoulder.

"You just had your dream," I said.

"Don't talk about it."

"I'm sorry."

Then she seemed restless. "It's hot."

"You were shivering a minute ago."

"Don't argue with me."

"Well, you were."

"Just quit it," she said, "will you?"

We were returning to our old ways. I removed myself from her, rolling on my side to face the room.

"Where're you going?"

"Nowhere."

I felt her move, heard the curtain being pulled aside. The room was now suffused in pale light. "Look," she said. "I bet that's Wilson Creek."

Leaning over her thin shoulder, I looked out through the mostly bare branches of a tree at the lawn — a gray, shadowless expanse, leaf-littered and overgrown, the field beyond it dotted with a strange weed, black stalks topped by big round yellow flowers that were blackened at the edges, as if scorched in some conflagration. It wasn't even September yet, and the leaves were all burnished and dropping from the black branches. The sky was one cloud, one smooth cover, with dim light behind it. I remembered what I'd heard of the great West's violent thunderstorms, high winds and hail and lightning, and the threat of tornadoes.

"Don't," Lisa said.

"What," I demanded.

"You're leaning on me and you're shaking."

The field sank to the spar of asphalt that I had thought last night was the street, a small cul-de-sac ending in seven white posts, the weedy ground beyond them descending steeply to the creek bed. Down the length of the creek, the banks receded, the surface of water widened

and showed rivulets of current. Beyond the railroad trestle I could see
a factory building of some kind, with tiny square windows and signs
painted onto the bricks. Looking up the other way, I saw a tremendous
concrete block jutting out into the creek from the opposite bank. This,
I soon learned, was the supporting foundation of a bridge that no
longer existed. Someone — many people — had painted words and
names and dates, and drawn hearts on the concrete. One word, in dull
red, was quite clear, even from that distance: PLAINS. I had an image
of myself on winter mornings, looking for the one word among all the
others in the snow and ice: PLAINS. The word was like a totem,
addressed to me from the world where I now found myself. And I
remembered that one of my brief dreams of the night just past had me
standing alone in the middle of a great black field, with nothing but
space opening out all around; I seemed in this nightmare to have
arrived at some pole of myself, some axis from which I might travel in
any direction and be wrong, find nothing and no one.

"I don't like the look of it," Lisa said. "It's all so — there's no
colors."

"It's just the light," I told her, though I didn't quite believe it myself.

Finally we closed the curtain and lay still a while, side by side in the
changing dimness. Perhaps Lisa drifted back to sleep for a few minutes. I held her, beginning to feel the chill in the room.

"I'm hungry," she said. "Are you still sick?"

"I'd rather not think about food."

"Do you think Mr. Terpin will follow us here?"

"What gave you that idea?" I demanded.

"I thought I heard him say something about it."

"When?"

"I don't know."

"Oh, come on, Lisa."

"Well, I did. I guess it was when we were all getting off the train."

"Why would he want to do that?" I said.

"I don't know."

I climbed down from the bunk and got into my clothes.

"Shouldn't you unpack some clean clothes?"

"Shhhh," I said, and moved to the door.

"Where're you going?"

"Be quiet," I said.

Mother's door was closed. The little sitting room looked wrecked with our things: she had begun the process of unpacking, and boxes she had sent from Virginia before we set out were stacked along one wall. Clothes lay strewn across the sofa. I moved to the entrance, and on an impulse stepped out onto the landing. In the relative brightness of the hall light, I stood squinting, trying to get my eyes adjusted. Facing the long hallway to my right, I saw a man framed in the open doorway of the room at that end. He was perhaps fifty years old, and he stood with his spindly white legs spread wide to keep a pair of pants up while tucking in his shirt. What I was seeing was a mirror on the open door, and now the man looked into the mirror head-on at me, showing me for that instant a wildly deranged and color-streaked face. He moved as if startled, disappeared from the mirror, and leaned out the doorway of the room, glaring at me. He had a perfectly round head ringed with very curly white whiskers, and bulbous blue close-set eyes on either side of a golf-ball-sized red nose, like a clown's. An instant later I saw that it *was* a clown nose, that the face was painted across the cheeks and around the mouth. He had the nose on, but the eyes were not yet done, nor the forehead and hair, which was ruffled and sparse.

He looked me up and down. "Well?" he said in a hoarse voice.

I was at a loss.

"Who are you?"

"We just moved in," I told him.

"Damn," he said. Then he looked past me and shouted. "Mabel! You could at least say when you're taking people in, couldn't you?" He slammed the door.

The noise brought Mrs. Wilson to the narrow stairwell from the kitchen. She came halfway up the steps so that her head was visible above the line of the polished wood floor. She stared at me, not quite smiling, holding a plate of hot biscuits with a padded glove. "That's Mr. Egan," she said in a matter-of-fact tone. "Please don't pay him any mind."

The door opened again, and he leaned out and around to confront her. "This is my punishment?"

She regarded him for a moment. "You just wait and see what that might be."

"Go ahead and evict me. You won't get your house painted."

"Maybe I'll just live with that."

"No, you need the slave labor."

"What labor? The slaves *worked*."

He looked at me. "This is a house," he said, "not a home."

"Mr. Egan cries at certain songs," she said. "And he likes to quote them. His heart is one big pile of mush, you see."

He stepped back and slammed the door again, then opened it almost on the instant and looked at me. Mrs. Wilson had turned and stepped out of sight down into the kitchen. "I don't mean to seem rude, lad."

"No," I said.

He looked down the stairwell there, but Mrs. Wilson had gone. Then he turned his attention once more to me. "How old are you?"

I told him.

"Don't look at me like that. You never saw a clown before?"

I hadn't been aware that I was looking at him in any unusual way, and now I ran one hand over my eyes out of reflex, as if to wipe sleep from them.

"Well?"

"I've seen clowns before."

"Well, you're looking at one." He said this with a kind of bluster, and perhaps he thought I might challenge him about it all. "And, I don't mind saying, a damn good one, too."

I tried to indicate with a nod of my head that I found this a perfectly agreeable statement.

"Not all of them are with the circus, you know."

"I knew that," I said.

"Well, then. You might stop staring at me." Again he slammed the door.

"What's going on?" Lisa said from the entrance behind me.

"Nothing," I told her. "A clown."

"Where?"

She still wore her nightgown. "Lisa, go back and get dressed."

"I can't wake Mother," she said, starting to cry. "It's scaring me."

One of Lisa's dominant traits, then and now, has been a tendency toward alarm, a hectic willingness to believe the worst possibility first.

She was and is like that about almost everything, and one can see it in the careful demeanor of her children: they have learned, even at their young age, that every situation is shaded by or contains some possibility of harm, however remote, which must be attended to. At least Lisa's worries must be attended to, and her three girls, I've noticed, are very conscientious about it.

Now I followed her back into our badly cluttered apartment, across the space of the sitting room to Mother's small bedroom, where Mother lay with her back to the door, one arm thrown over her tousled head, the blankets sliding off her hip.

"Mother?" I said.

Nothing. She was breathing, I could see that — long, sighing, troubled exhalations. I touched her shoulder. "Mother?"

And she stirred, sat up, gasping, holding tight to my hand. "Oh, I didn't know I was asleep."

"Lisa was scared," I said.

"Scared of what?" she said in a voice heavy with exhaustion. "I was up most of the night, Thomas. I kept waiting for you to get sick again."

"I was up all night, too," I said.

"You snored," she told me.

"Not much."

"All night," she said, rising. She was still in her clothes. "I did some unpacking and you slept right through it."

Lisa moved to her side and began to cry.

"What's this?"

"I'm scared," Lisa said. "I don't like it here."

Mother patted her shoulder. "It's going to be fine, you'll see, honey."

But Lisa persisted. "I want to go back to Grandfather Tinan's."

"Shhhh," Mother said.

We waited for her to use the bathroom. We sat on her bed, not speaking, while she showered and changed clothes and then came out and sat at the small dresser in one corner of the room to put some makeup on. The room looked like any of several that had been Lisa's in Air Force housing: a little girl's room, not a woman's room at all, with its small dressing table and mirror, its cedar chest and bureau. There was a small canopy over the bed. In one corner was a tall white metal cabinet which looked out of place. Lisa was sizing up everything, sniffling. You could see the resignation in her face, that her mother had been reduced to this.

We heard Mrs. Wilson call us to breakfast.

"Jeez," Lisa said, "is it going to be this way every morning?"

"Mr. Egan's a clown," I said.

"Thomas," said Mother, "don't."

"No, I mean a real clown. You'll see — if he comes to breakfast."

Mrs. Wilson called again. And Mr. Egan's door opened and slammed out in the hall. They were contending with each other about something, only we couldn't distinguish the words.

"God," Mother said, low, "how I dread this."

We were the last ones to come in for breakfast. Mrs. Wilson sat at the head of a large banquet table in the middle of a room crowded with tall, imposing pieces of dark oak furniture: a dry sink with small shelves built across its top, backed by a mirror; two big hutches, a grandfather clock, and a big double-doored cabinet, like an armoire, containing a portable television on a little ivory stand. The doors of the cabinet were open, and the television was on. She liked to catch the news in the mornings. We took three of the four empty chairs, all in a file on one side of the table, and Mrs. Wilson introduced us to the others; Mr. Egan, in full clown regalia now, who stood and placed his napkin on the table and reached across to shake Mother's hand; and her son, Russell, whose elongated, ruddy face looked as though it might have been constructed as a backdrop for the very wide, down-turning mouth he had, the violet lips of which made a kind of kissing noise when he opened them to smile. This smile was rather cryptic; it might even have been faintly disdainful, for his small green eyes gave forth no greeting, but were purely curious. He trained them on me as his mother spoke.

"I think Russell's just a year behind your boy, there."

"You'll be a senior?" he said to me.

I nodded.

"Yeah," he said. "I saw you last night when you came in."

Mrs. Wilson had passed me a bowl full of scrambled eggs. I put a few spoonfuls on my plate — my appetite was still not what it should have been. I passed the bowl to Lisa, who, not liking scrambled eggs, passed it on to Mother.

"The beautiful little girl doesn't like eggs?" Mr. Egan said.

"You never mind that little girl," said Mrs. Wilson.

"Well, for heaven's sake." In the clown outfit with its high collar and its streaks of primary colors, his displeasure seemed staged somehow, and vaguely amateurish. He shook his multicolored head slowly, drooped the big red nose in the direction of his plate. "I was just making what I thought was a perfectly harmless observation."

"Well, keep it to yourself."

"I'll be back at noon to work on the porch," he said. "This clowning is just to make a little extra money. We don't have Mr. Falmon's rent now, you know. You may need a little help with the income."

"I'm sure that's very thoughtful of you." Mrs. Wilson passed the biscuits and a plate of very brown sausage patties. She'd also prepared a bowl of fruit — oranges, apples, grapes, strawberries. Lisa took an apple and a few strawberries, and asked for some milk. Mrs. Wilson was already passing the pitcher of orange juice around the table. "Coming right up, dear."

"Lisa, wait your turn," Mother whispered.

Mr. Egan chewed avidly, staring off. His jaw worked in an odd, almost circular pattern, suggesting the motion of a horse eating grass. Beside him, Russell gulped orange juice, and I noticed that his fingernails were dirty. My stomach was still a little sour, so I had taken little of the food.

"What's the matter?" Russell said.

I said, "Nothing."

"You were staring at us."

"No," I said.

"Russell, that's enough of that."

We were all quiet. There was just the sound of forks against plates, and Mr. Egan's steady chewing. He had got a speck of egg on the side of his lip, and it adhered to the makeup there. I couldn't eat anything more.

"I've got a little girl's birthday party," he said to Lisa. "Girl about your age." He moved his tongue over his teeth, and sat back in his chair. "Just down the street."

Lisa lowered her eyes, half nodding. She hadn't eaten much, either.

"So," Mr. Egan said, "you folks have come to be near the prison."

Mother looked at Mrs. Wilson.

"I didn't think you wanted that held back," Mrs. Wilson said to her. "See, it would be hard to do in any case."

"No," Mother said.

"It's your husband, is it?" Mr. Egan said.

"You know it is," Mrs. Wilson said.

"I'm just making conversation, Mabel. What's wrong with you this morning?"

"I'd rather not talk about my husband," Mother put in, "if you don't mind."

Mr. Egan finally wiped his mouth. "Well, it's up to you, of course."

"They've had escapes from there before," Russell said.

"Russell, be quiet," Mrs. Wilson said.

"They have."

Mrs. Wilson looked at Mother. "Some years ago. A couple boys ran away from a work detail — on the road. There was a lot of shooting and hollering and sirens went up, you'd have thought World War Three started. But nothing came of it, really. Both boys gave up, and the only person hurt was one of the police chasing them. He got nicked in the leg by a ricochet from one of his own bullets. And that was that."

"They toughened things up in there after that episode," said Mr. Egan. "Doubled the guards — that sort of thing."

Mother was staring at her hands. "Are they —" She stopped. I believe she'd realized she couldn't get the answers she wanted here.

"Hard labor," said Mr. Egan. "That's what it is in that place. A lot of hard labor."

"Mr. Egan was a guard for a few years."

"Three," he said. "I worked in the administrative offices for almost fifteen years, and they moved me into being a guard. So I retired two years ago last spring. I said I wanted to get a thousand miles away from it, and I'm still nine hundred ninety-nine air miles short of my goal." He stood, arranged his chair, then bowed politely at Mrs. Wilson. "I'll be back shortly after lunch, so you needn't put anything on for me."

Mrs. Wilson said nothing.

"Russell," he said, "behave yourself, my lad." Then he bowed at us. "Madams, lad."

When he was gone, Mrs. Wilson said, "I don't know what to do about him. I actually liked him at one point, you know."

"Hey," Russell said to me, "you finished?"

I nodded.

"Can we go out?" he said to his mother.

"I think we're going over to the prison," I said. But I faltered on the last of it, seeing Mother's unhappy expression.

"I have to go alone this morning," she said. "There are some things I have to take care of. And you'll have to watch Lisa."

"She can come, too," Russell said. "I just want to show them the creek."

"Is the water very deep?"

"Oh, no. My land," Mrs. Wilson said. "It's only ankle deep when it's not a trickle at this end."

Mother looked at me. "If you want to."

"We can't come with you?" I asked.

"Not this morning. I have too much to do."

"Are you going to see Father?"

"'Father,'" Russell said. "Jesus."

"Russell, mind your manners," his mother scolded.

"I don't mean anything." He looked at me. "Is that what you call him?"

"What's wrong with that?" I said.

"It's funny."

"We think *you* sound funny," Lisa put in.

"All right, all right," said Mrs. Wilson. "Russell, help me with these dishes if you want your allowance."

"Are you going to see him?" I said to Mother.

"You know I am. Will you just do as I ask, son?"

I took Lisa by the hand and we started for the stairs.

"You guys coming or not?" Russell said.

"I don't want to," said Lisa.

"Okay," he said. "It's your decision." When he went out, we felt a small gust of the chilly air outside. It smelled of coal.

Upstairs, Lisa and I set about putting our clothes away and organizing the room. Mother came to the door and smiled at us. "We've gotten pretty good at all this," she said. "Haven't we?"

"I want to go see Father," I told her.

She said, "You can call him Dad, if it'll make things easier."

I knew then I would never use that word to describe him as long as I lived, and it was more than simply the wish to hold on to an old family habit in the middle of unfamiliarity and confusion; it was like a moral choice somehow, because it seemed that to speak of him in that harmless diminutive would have helped strip away the meager dignity that remained to us. I said, "Can't we come with you?"

"In a day or two," she said. "Maybe tomorrow."

I remembered what I had overheard her say to Aunt Elaine, and before I could check myself I said, "Aren't you going to see him today?"

Her response was a bemused frown, as though she hadn't been quite able to distinguish my words. "Of course I'm — look," she went on, "will you please just cooperate with me on this, for Lisa's sake?"

"I'm sorry."

"I know you want to see him. I know you both want to see him."

Lisa was sitting on the edge of the small couch, running a scarf through her slender fingers.

"You just have to be patient," Mother said. She reached over and took the scarf. "All right?"

Lisa nodded at her.

"Now Mrs. Wilson's agreed to take me to the auto dealership this morning."

"Can't I help with that?" I said.

"Thomas, please."

"*Okay.*" I gave her what I intended to be an impatient and frustrated look, but it was apparently lost on her.

She had turned her attention to Lisa. "You mind Thomas, now, do you hear?"

"Yes, ma'am."

Then she put her coat on and left. We went to the window of her room and looked out at the street. Russell was in the front yard, tossing a red ball in the air and catching it. The two women got into a big, dull red Buick. When Mother closed the door on the passenger side, she glanced at the house and then at the surrounding houses. Russell strolled over to the edge of the sidewalk and waved to them as they pulled away, then he turned and looked right at us in the window.

Lisa stepped away. "Is he coming?" she said.

He was.

We froze, hearing him on the stairs. In the few seconds it took for him to get to us, I realized what it was going to mean not having a door to our apartment. Lisa moved behind me just as he entered the room. It occurred to me that there was no reason I should be frightened.

"Hey," he said.

"This is a private apartment," I said.

"I know, I know." He frowned. "What's wrong, anyway?"

Lisa was holding on to my waist, peering at him from behind me. "Go away," she said.

"Jeez, what's the matter with you guys?"

"We have to finish unpacking," I told him.

"I don't bite," he said. "Maybe I'll help you." He reached into the pocket of his shirt and brought out a pack of Tareytons. "You smoke?"

"No."

"Nothing?"

I looked at him. Though he probably didn't weigh as much as I, he was perhaps two inches taller, and I recalled with chagrin that he was a year younger. I said, "Not anymore. I quit a while ago."

"You never," Lisa said to me.

I told her to be quiet.

Russell walked over to us with his cigarettes and held the pack out to me. "Know what's in there?"

I looked at it. "Sure."

"What?"

After a slight hesitation I said, "Cigarettes."

"Yeah," he said. "Maybe." Then he put the pack into his shirt pocket again. "Does your father let you wear your hair that long?"

"Sure," I said.

"My mother thinks it's queer."

"It's the style," I said, and felt the lameness of it. I made up my mind that I wouldn't answer any more questions.

"Hippies," Russell said. "Right?"

We were standing amid boxes and piled clothes, and he pushed a stack of coats aside to sit in the wing chair beside the couch. It was as if he were some mildly amused but very busy official before whom we had been brought to explain our case. Folding his hands under his chin, he smiled complacently. I saw something obscurely haughty in it. "So," he said, attending to his own fingernails, "why don't you tell me what the deal is about your father."

I said, "We're not allowed to talk about it."

"You mean it's a secret?"

I was silent. Lisa turned from us and climbed up onto the top of one pile of boxes, huffing and breathing like a runner. When she was perched there, she leaned her back against the wall and regarded us. Her eyes were wild. "Lisa?" I said.

"I don't care," she muttered. "Just leave me alone."

"You guys don't know anything?" Russell said.

"We know enough," I answered. "It's private."

"Look, I don't mean anything. I'll show you the house. You want to see the rest of the house?"

"Not now," I said.

"You read a lot?"

I stared at him.

"I saw this movie on television about a kid who lives in a boarding house, and his father makes gravestones. They said it was based on a book."

Lisa was crying, and trying to control it.

"Please," I said. "We have a lot to do."

"I think I'm sort of like that kid in the movie, except I don't read much. The funny papers. Comic books. You look like you read a lot."

"I read," I said. "I don't know."

"You want to go see the prison?"

I must've shown him something of my surprise, for he sat up a little, as if to draw me further into this newly hatched plan.

"It's not that far. There's a back way along the creek. We could go that way and nobody would see us."

"I can't go anywhere now."

"We can all go."

"I don't like it here," Lisa said from her perch. She was looking at the room, at the angles of doorway and window and wall, the dark wood of the crown molding, as though she were searching for another way out.

"Please leave us alone," I said to Russell.

"All right," he said. "Jeez."

When we were alone, we went to the window again and watched him go across the yard, heading down the street. He didn't look back.

"Ohhh," Lisa said, crying, "I hate this, I hate this."

"Let's just put some of these things away," I said. "Let's just get busy."

This is the moment which, all these years later, my sister remembers with particular clarity; and she has attached a kind of significance to it as an indicator of my character. No matter how many other examples of procrastination and hesitancy I've given her over the years, she sees me in the light of that single instance of practical will, and I've been present when she's actually boasted to people that I'm the sort of man who focuses on what *can* be done, the sort who takes charge, becomes pragmatic and clear-thinking, and who assumes command.

13

_____

THE TOWN of Wilson Creek came into being not long after the first encroachment of white men into the northern plains. Fur trappers, fugitives, hunters after gold or treasure — predators who went for months or years without any sort of utterance at all. Like a lot of plains towns, it was named after its first inhabitant, a man with shadowy antecedents (according to some stories, he had left Ireland in the winter of 1824 after murdering a man in a pub) who called himself Henri Wilson, apparently insisting on the French spelling, and who carried a small, pearl-handled pistol in his trousers. He staked a claim on the undulant and grassy area along the northern edge of the creek, and built a cabin there and a stable for the horses he had come with. He had a wife and four sons, and a half-brother whose name was Dolph Crasson, who built his own cabin on the other side of what they agreed they would call WilCrasson Creek — a branch, they would later know, of the Belle Fourche River. WilCrasson was the name they gave when they filed their claims, and that was what most people, including the United States Army, called it for a brief period during the early 1850s. Time and the weather shortened it to Wilson Creek — at least according to the town's lore. The winter in that northeastern corner of Wyoming is so fierce, the air so stingingly cold to breathe, that it was just simpler that way, easier to say in the subzero wind. But even before the name evolved into its final version, the half-brothers quarreled over the fact that Dolph had taken for his wife an Indian woman. And it was because of this that the two men went almost ten years without speaking, though the two cabins were within sight of each other and the two women happened to get along quite well, both recognizing far more similarities than differences in their mutually hardscrabble existence.

Over the next ten years, many new families came to the area — most of them having headed for new surroundings as a result of the ravages of the War of the Rebellion, as it was then called — and one result of the heavy influx of new settlers was increasing trouble with the Indians, who saw what was coming. In any case poor Dolph Crasson, with his Indian wife, became a bit of a pariah. People were more circumspect with him, they even took pains to avoid him, and they tended to watch him wherever he went, as they watched her. Even relations between her and Henri's wife had become strained, since the white woman had recognized what trouble she might cause herself if she seemed too friendly with Mrs. Crasson, who, for all the bad suspicions swirling around her, continued to wear her tribal dress, exactly as if nothing were happening at all. And Dolph became the most vociferous of those calling for revenge on the marauding Indians, who had burned several homesteads and were engaged in an ongoing battle with the Army. Finally the scare settled into a half-formed disquiet in the wide, unoccupied country around Wilson Creek, and poor Dolph seemed to everyone to be growing a little crazy. He had taken to painting his face like the Indians, and wearing feathers in his belt. He worked his land into the night and then seemed to lose track of where he was supposed to be. He might show up at a neighbor's door in the first gray light of dawn, decked out in Indian paint, and begin a tirade about how it was every man's duty to help rid the plains of the savages.

"Go home, Dolph," women would say. "It's all right."

"Go home," said the men. "Protect your own homestead."

The winter came, and there were massacres farther up the creek: the Army was clearing the Indians away. Mostly, then, it was the Indians doing the dying, and it had been that way for some time.

One dark, wind-howling blizzard of a night, Dolph shot his Indian wife, then set fire to his cabin and turned the rifle on himself. It took a while for the other people of the fledgling town to understand what had taken place; indeed, they thought the Indians had done it, and so they banded together and created a charter officially naming the town

Wilson Creek, and then they sent for the Army, which rode in at the end of the month, after everyone had come to understand what had really happened out at the Crasson place. In the summer of 1869, the Army built a stockade a few miles down the creek, and their presence in the vicinity became permanent. The stockade was enlarged several years later, and then abandoned for almost a decade as the soldiers moved their outpost to a more level and advantageous location, Fort Wyoming. For a very long time the old stockade sat empty, eroding, until in 1922 an ambitious young entrepreneur named George L. Jewett decided to make a museum out of it. He hired people to come in and put on a Wild West show, and he paid some half-starved, alcoholic Indians to dress up in their ceremonial raiment and walk around looking fierce and wild-eyed. He had signs erected along the byways leading into Wilson Creek, inviting travelers to come see the show at the old stockade. For a few years he did a fair amount of business, but he had it in mind to grow rich, and he eventually sold the stockade to a land developer and left the country, owing everyone who worked for him at least three weeks' pay. The man he sold it to was interested in it purely for the land, as an investment opportunity. He sold it to the state of Wyoming at more than twice what he paid for it. The state sent a group of engineers to look at the site, and within a year some men arrived to tear down the old stockade and build a penitentiary, as if the ground, having once been designated for the purpose of jailing human beings, could never really be anything else: I imagine that even when an ersatz museum and Wild West show went on inside the old wooden walls, the poor Indians walking around must have looked, to anyone who really saw them, like prisoners, the inmates of some deplorable confinement. Before the state was finished with construction, the panic of 1929 stopped everything, and the site, with its incomplete structure sitting upon it like a ruin, was sold at auction to the federal government. Toward the mid-thirties, the Army went on with the building, and they produced what was essentially another military stockade. Finally, in late 1945, it was named the Wilson Creek Federal Penitentiary, and the Army moved permanently to new quarters fifteen miles away, where preparations had already begun to construct what would eventually be a ballistic-missile complex.

Wilson Creek became, then, a town of government workers, whose two principal industries were the prison and the army base. The shops along its main street catered to soldiers, offering custom-made military uniforms and accessories, including barracks sandals and shoeshine kits, special field caps, brass insignia, even weapons. Prison-related items were offered, too — uniforms, guard caps, sleeve markers, night-sticks, and various types of handguns — for back in those days, though there were provisions in the prison budget for procuring these supplies from the federal government, all the guards were substantially responsible for clothing and arming themselves. In its first operational year, the penitentiary housed seventy-five prisoners of all kinds, mostly soldiers who had got into one sort of trouble or another, and one or two civilians, including an infamous gangster who had, to the aston-ishment of everyone, been successfully prosecuted for jury tampering. By 1967 the size of the prison had been increased from three to nine buildings; it held twenty-six hundred men, and included a library and furniture shop. And in the town of Wilson Creek, all the shops selling uniforms and small arms were gone.

Mother returned late that afternoon in a 1960 Ford sedan. It was in fairly good shape, a plain white car with no frills — not even a radio — but with low mileage, new tires, and a clean V-8 engine: its previous owner had taken care of it. Mother said all this, sounding like a salesman, while Lisa and I stood by and stared in the windows at the sky-blue interior.

"We can go to the prison now," I said.

"No," Mother said. "It's not like a hospital, you know. The visiting times are very specific."

I waited.

"Is Daddy sick?" Lisa said.

"Don't be silly, Lisa."

"When can *we* see him?" I said.

She said nothing for a moment, and in the way she looked at me I knew she had already seen him, and that she understood I knew it.

"Well?" I said.

"We'll talk about it tomorrow, Thomas."

"Tomorrow," Lisa said, making the assumption that we needed only to wait a day.

Mother turned. Mrs. Wilson had driven up in the Buick and now she emerged, already making appreciative noises about the new car. She hurried over to us, gripping her purse in both hands as if nervous about its contents. In her dark polka-dot dress and her crescent-shaped glasses she looked like someone trying to affect a kind of glamour that was in fact far from her, and I had a moment of feeling that I ought not to trust what she said. "My, you've got yourself a beautiful deal on this one, just wonderful."

Russell came over from the side yard carrying a stick, swinging it casually, like a cane. "Nice car," he said.

"Isn't it, honey?" said Mrs. Wison.

"Well," said Mother, "it'll get us around."

"In style."

"Not really."

"Oh, yes."

We went up the walk and into the house, and Mrs. Wilson followed us all the way to the entrance of our apartment. "If you don't mind," Mother said to her, "I'm really tired. I think I'll take a nap."

"Oh," said the other woman, obviously embarrassed. "I just thought, you know, if you wanted to talk about it. You know, we've had relatives of inmates staying here before — lots of times, in fact. Haven't we, Russell?" She turned on the stairs, but Russell had melted back into some other part of the house. "Now where did he get off to? I need him to do some work around here."

"Well," Mother said.

"Yes, of course. But listen — if you change your mind or anything comes up."

"Yes, thank you."

"Why don't we get a door," Lisa said.

But I don't think Mrs. Wilson heard this in the clatter and moan of the stairs as she descended, the close echo of her big voice talking about the benefits to be derived from confiding in people, the healing power of a sympathetic ear. Mother sighed, then made her way unsteadily to the sofa, removing her jacket, unbuttoning her sleeves, and rolling them up. Her demeanor was that of someone preparing to go to work, but she lay down on the sofa and put one arm over her face, sighing again.

"We put some stuff away," I said.

"Thanks."

For a small space, Lisa and I stood there waiting for her to speak. Then Lisa sat down at her feet and touched her knee.

"Mom?"

"Don't, I'm — I've got a terrible headache."

"Come on, Lisa," I said. "Let's go work on our room."

"I've been thinking," said Mother without taking her arm from her face. "Lisa can stay in my room with me."

The prospect of having the room to myself was attractive until I thought of the nights; I didn't want to be alone, and how much I dreaded the idea of it came down on me like the weight of a guilty conscience. I said, "No, that's all right."

Lisa had spoken in the same instant: "Can I sleep with you?"

"We could separate the bunks and move your bed in with mine."

Lisa went to the entrance of Mother's room and looked in, considering, knotting her fingers together under her chin. "No," she said finally. "It would be too crowded."

"I don't mind," said Mother.

"It's fine like it is," Lisa said.

Mother sighed. "Mrs. Wilson said we might have to make some sort of adjustment if the wrong person finds out that you two're sharing one room. I guess we ought to be ready."

"For God's sake," I said. This seemed utterly superfluous and insignificant to me. After a moment I said, "Did you go to the prison? Did you see Father?"

She removed her arm from her face and propped herself on one of the embroidered pillows. I thought she might begin to shout. It was as if she were seeing the room for the first time, and I understood somehow — I was as certain of this as I was of my own displacement — that its meagerness, its sheer distance from what we had been used to, after all her struggling to put the best face on things and to be strong and not to give in, was rushing in on her, closing down even the faintly emollient release of tears. I thought of the summer I had gone hunting with my father, and we had trapped a rabbit. The wide-open stare of the rabbit's eyes as it waited for us to open the cage and bring it to harm. My mother's eyes had that look. But I was wrong about why.

"Yes," she said, "I saw him."

"Can we see him?" I asked.

"Yes."

"When?"

"Tomorrow, I guess."

"Do we have to go into the prison?" Lisa said.

"They have a room for visiting."

"Is it in the prison?"

"I have a terrible headache," Mother said. "We'll go over all of this tomorrow, or later tonight. I know you're curious." She got to her feet and went to the doorway of her room, then turned to look at me. "I'm sorry, Thomas. Could you please stay with Lisa a little longer?"

"I don't need anybody to stay with me," Lisa said.

"Will you both just — find something quiet to do?"

"We will," I said. "Is Father all right?"

She answered through a sigh of frustration: "He's lost a little weight. He doesn't like where he is. Honey, what could you expect?"

"But he's all right."

"He's healthy."

She went in and shut her door.

In another room, Mr. Egan began singing along with some bright, bouncy tune he had found on his radio, but he was far off key and the total effect was almost numbing. Lisa put her hands over her ears and lay down on her bunk.

"I'm just going to sleep until we move away from here," she said. "Time goes really fast when you sleep. I'll just sleep as much as possible and it'll go fast. I'll wake up and we can start back home."

"Oh, home," I said, suddenly angry. "Right. Home."

"Well?" she said.

"Would you like to tell me where you think that is?" I demanded.

She shrugged. "I don't know."

"It's right here," I said. "Right where we are now."

In the far room, Mr. Egan broke into another song. His voice was comically without the slightest suggestion of melody or tunefulness.

"What's happening?" Lisa wanted to know.

"Don't you get it?" I said to her. "This is where we live now. This is home."

She sat up, clasped her skinny knees, and stared out the open entrance of our apartment, from which Mr. Egan's clamor seemed to come, and then she turned to me. "God, two years," she said, beginning to cry. "Two years. We have to go to school here."

"Don't talk about it," I said. "I don't want to think about it. I don't want to think about anything."

She lay back down, sniffling.

"Stop that," I said. I got into my own bed.

"I can't."

"Try to sleep some."

She was quiet. Mr. Egan's voice seemed to come caterwauling through the very boards of the house. It was as though we were lying there being quiet so that we could hear it, but then very quickly I was drowsy, and Mr. Egan's voice lost definition as a human sound.

A few moments later, when I stirred myself to look down at Lisa, I saw that she had fallen fast asleep, her distressed face streaked with tears, her hands folded across her chest.

I had the time, then, to imagine what my mother had seen and done that day, and if one considers accuracy of any import at all, I was not very successful. What I saw were the representations of the movies: the old image I'd conjured earlier about my father in prison — convicts in stripes milling around in an open area, surrounded by high, solid walls and four roofed towers, each manned by someone with a rifle. I tried to picture my mother in such a place, and then saw her in an enormous room in the shadows of barred windows, walking down a corridor between rows of cells with guards on either side of her.

Of course, it wasn't like that at all.

And again we are confronted with the necessity of moving away from Lisa and me — the one sleeping deeply and the other lying in rigid wakefulness — to make our ghostly passage through the cluttered central room, into the small cubicle to which Connie Boudreaux has consigned herself, so that we may see her troubled expression — the one she has tried so hard never to show us, or anyone else — her brimming eyes, her downturned mouth, the beaten, helpless expression of the rabbit in the trap, except that it is colored with bitterness, too. She lies there fearing that she has made a terrible mistake, hauling her children across all these miles to look upon the face of her husband — a man who has already changed beyond the worst expectations she might have had — after the months of worrying about him, and worrying too about her own still-changing feelings for him, wanting so desperately to keep her family together, to make it all work somehow in spite of everything.

It has been a bad afternoon indeed.

Imagine her driving in her freshly bought car that her stubborn father has paid for, over to the grounds of the Wilson Creek Federal Penitentiary, following Mrs. Wilson's scrawled, hard-to-read directions. She stops along the side of the road to look at the crumpled piece of paper, holding it against the steering wheel and trying to discern the odd, slanting letters. Is it *two* blocks past the turn to the railroad station and out Route 11, or *ten* blocks past it? She can't tell from the tiny script, and she hasn't seen Route 11. She turns around and heads back into town, then pulls over again; she thinks of asking someone, but then decides against it. She turns the car around once more, and a few blocks down (neither two nor ten, but somewhere in between) she finds Route 11. Gradually she figures out for herself that this road which will take her there is circuitous and orbits the town, running for a time with the winding creek. She comes over a rise, past a small, boarded-up cottage. (Who lived there, and where could they be now? She conjures a family, all gone, scattered to different parts of the world, buried in different cities, different climates, or living in other houses. She thinks of the last of them, the last person to leave the empty rooms, and she sees herself, some other woman, her attention lingering over the corner where a child took the first tottering steps, the place where a favorite picture might have hung, the angle of a hall where someone was kissed — oh, and it seems to Connie Boudreaux now that life is almost unbearably lonely!) Past this little tumbledown house and out of the trees which shade and obscure it is the prison, ranged across a distant green hill, all red brick and white cement, looking like a big clutch of school buildings, except that it happens to be surrounded by high, shining chain-link fences with rolled barbed wire on top. She drives right up to the gate, her heart beating in her throat. The guard steps out of a booth next to the gate and walks over to her. A black man whose youthful appearance vaguely reassures her. When he bends to peer into the car, she glances at the highly polished bill of his service hat and can see her own reflection in it, with that of the top of the car window, the cloud-studded blue sky beyond. He has small darker places on his cheeks.

"Yes ma'am," he says. "Can I help you?"

Somewhere she hears a bell, like a school bell, the old fire-alarm bells from her time in high school in Minot.

"What are visiting hours, please?"

"You here to see an inmate?"

She nods.

"You living in the area, ma'am?"

"Yes. We've only just arrived."

"Wait a minute." He walks back to the booth and enters it. Beyond the gate, some men in a small group walk between two buildings. They are perhaps two hundred yards away, and they look like soldiers, though they're without hats, and there's something ragged about them. They aren't marching. She looks for her husband, but these are other men, other prisoners.

The guard comes back. "You have to go to the administration building and fill out some forms," he says. He hands her a pamphlet. "This'll tell you some of what you need to know."

"Thank you," she says.

He gives a kind of salute and steps away.

"Sir?" she says.

He turns, but doesn't come back.

"Would it be possible to see my inmate now?"

He nods. "I think so. If he's available."

"I'd like to, if I could."

"You have to fill out one form for that. If you'll just take this drive to the right, the administration building is down about five hundred yards there to the left. You don't need to come into the gate to visit. This is mostly for deliveries."

"Thank you," she tells him, wanting to touch his face, he has been so kind. His voice so gentle and somehow sympathetic. She thinks of me, and then for some reason she thinks of Father when he was young — the person she had not known she was looking for.

In the administration building lot there are several dark blue military cars with police insignia on the doors. Two men in uniform stand at the tail of one, leaning against it and talking. One of them is smoking a cigarette.

"Hel*lo*," the other says as my mother crosses the lot. "The afternoon got nice."

The one smoking the cigarette tells him to shut up.

Inside the building there's a long row of desks behind a central counter, where a pair of women sit drinking coffee and talking about school starting for their children. The older of the two looks at Mother and says, "Good afternoon. May we help you?"

"I'd like to visit my husband."

"Is he an inmate here or a guard?"

"Inmate," Mother says, watching the other shuffle some papers on the counter.

"We allow twenty hours a month for visitation," says the woman. "Family only."

"Thank you," Connie says, and feels oddly reduced by the woman's rudely speculating glance at her.

"Fill this out, please. There're desks against the wall over there."

These are school desks. She sits in one and, under the whir of a ceiling fan, fills out her name and that of her husband and children, the address where she currently lives. The purpose of her visit, which she has trouble answering: to tell him we have arrived? to see if he's all right? to tell him she loves him, because she still does? no matter what has happened or how the feeling inside has changed, she still does? The pen shakes in her hand, and she's trying not to cry. When she returns to the counter, the older woman takes the form and asks her to wait a few moments. Connie stands there watching as the other reads over what she has written.

"All right," the woman says. "Now, you'll need to submit to a search. It's routine. Leave your purse here. And your coat."

"Yes, ma'am," says my mother.

The woman puts the purse inside the coat, then folds the coat and places it in a small locker in a row of lockers along the wall. She opens the counter and Connie steps through, stands still while the woman gingerly pats her down. "There we are," the woman says, as if they had just completed some ordinary medical procedure. "Right through here."

Connie follows her down a shiny hallway, with pictures in glass frames on either side: wardens and associate wardens and various employees, along with one of President Johnson, and of Kennedy, too. At the end of the hallway is a steel gate, the bars gleaming like aluminum. A man opens the gate and Connie steps through. The man is lantern-jawed, perhaps sixty years old, with a large belly and small white hands. He closes the gate and leads Connie into a large, open room. It looks like a cafeteria. Several sets of tables and chairs are arranged in rows, and vending machines stand along the walls.

"Have a seat," the man says, and closes her in.

She walks around the room. The windows are high up, but plenty of light comes through. The floor is polished. Some of the tables have ashtrays cut into the surface. The walls are painted a beige color, and the pictures on the walls consist of scenes of nature: mountains with snow on them, trees showing the burnished colors of the fall, streams and oceans, and the spectacular fire of a western sunset over a desert. The opposite wall contains only a heavy iron door with a wire-glass window in it, and this door opens now. A man leans in, wearing a uniform, the first one she's seen since the guard at the gate.

"You're here to see?" he says.

"Daniel Boudreaux," she tells him.

"Nothing's come through yet. Just a minute, please."

The door closes and she hears his muted voice through the metal; apparently he's talking on a telephone. He sounds irritable and impatient. The door opens again and he looks her over — a man taking in the charms of an attractive woman. "We have to locate your husband. He's out on one of the field details."

Connie simply stares back at him.

"We have a field camp," he says. "They get to be outside a little."

"Thank you," she says.

"It'll be a minute or two."

She nods.

He closes the door, looks through the window at her, then is gone. A moment later, the other door opens, and the heavy man leads in another woman, much younger than Connie. The younger woman doesn't seem to notice the room, and Connie realizes that she must be accustomed to it: this is not her first visit.

"Hello," she says.

Connie says, "Hi."

"It's usually more people," the young woman says. "My name's Delia. Nice to meet you." She offers her hand and Connie takes it, a rough, small paw with an energy, a quickness in it. The other woman sits at the next table. "I'm here to see my brother, Earl."

Connie tells her that she has met someone else going to visit a brother in prison.

"Here?" Delia says.

"No, on the train. Coming here."

"Where're you coming from?"

Connie tells her.

"All that way. Huh."

"Yes."

"Some life we got," says the girl.

Connie nods.

"I ride the bus here every week."

"We just moved here."

"Not much of a place." The young woman begins taking her hair down. "Wish they'd get some music or something in here. I hate waiting. I tell Earl to be here on time, and he's always late."

"Isn't he — doesn't he —"

"All they have to do is say they're expecting a visitor and make a request to be brought here. It's not hard to get through. Unless they do something, like get into trouble. I mean, it *is* a prison, after all. Earl's always complaining about how bad the food is. He's sort of a gourmet-type guy, I guess. He likes to have his food cooked just right, and that's a lot to ask in a place like this."

The heavy iron door opens, and the guard steps aside for a young, dark-haired man, who smiles and then moves almost drowsily into the room. The young woman named Delia gets up and strides to the farthest table, and the prisoner is led there by the guard, who holds the chair for him to sit down. He does so, his hands down in his lap, his face expectant. Delia sits across from him and begins to chatter. "I swear, can't you be on time once? And look at you — you look like something the cat dragged in. Here I come all this way in a crowded bus alone and in my condition and you could at least groom yourself a little to see me."

He mutters something Connie can't hear.

"Well, you sure don't look it," says Delia.

". . . so loud," Connie hears him say.

"Well?"

The two lean toward each other, and their talk now is only a series of low murmurings, like people whispering in a church. Connie folds her hands on the table, trying not to look at them or hear them, and finally the door opens and her husband walks through it. Daniel, thinner than she has seen him in years, his hair cut shorter than she ever liked it, his jaw showing a shadow-line of whiskers. He walks to her in green Army fatigues which are a size too big, and when she rises he puts his arms around her. She breathes the heavy odor of sweat on the clothes. "They got me out of a work detail," he says, stepping back to look at her. "Connie." His eyes brim. "Oh, baby." Again he embraces her. His arms feel so thin through the cloth.

"Are you all right?" she says, because she can't think of anything else to say.

He seems disappointed somehow, standing back again, nodding and looking away from her. "I'm okay," he says. "We have to —" He gestures for her to sit on the other side of the table. She does so, watches him settle in opposite her, sees him glance at the other two, sitting across the room. Then he sits back and looks around him. "Never actually seen this room," he says. "Can I get you a Coke or something from the machines?"

"I'm fine," she tells him.

"You didn't bring Thomas or Lisa?"

"Not this time."

"Yeah." He looks down. For a hard moment he seems to be struggling for breath, and then she sees that he's trying not to cry. "I don't think Lisa — at her age —"

"I thought we'd already settled that," Connie says.

He wipes his nose on his sleeve, takes a furtive look in the direction of the guard, who stands with his hands clasped behind his back, leaning against the frame of the door leading into the prison.

"Jesus," he says. "I mean, I went through it in Nam. I don't get this." She waits.

"It's worse. I can't explain it. But it's worse."

"Daniel, are they treating you all right?" The question sounds ridiculous to her. It's as if she is reciting bad lines from a B movie.

He looks at her across the table. "Oh," he says, "compared to Nam, this ought to seem like a hotel."

"It doesn't, though."

"I'm telling you it feels worse."

She reaches across the table for his hands. Slowly he brings them up from his lap, and now they are looking at each other as they might have over a picnic table in other times. Except that, then, in the ease and happiness, the confidence of their old love, they often hadn't particularly felt the need to talk. Now it's a stress which seems to be building with each passing second. He turns his head, then watches as another woman, this one with a teenage son, enters the visiting area and takes a seat to wait.

"Lisa wants to see you and so does Thomas," Connie says, low.

"Look at me, Connie." He has spoken too loud. They both shift in their chairs and wait for the others to go on with their own talk.

"We'll go slow," Connie says.

"How is it at Mrs. Wilson's?"

"Oh," she says, smiling, "like a hotel."

"You shouldn't have come here."

"Of course we should."

He shakes his head. "I can't make the days go by."

"They will."

"Your father gave you money?"

She nods.

"We'll pay him back."

She says nothing.

"I mean *I'll* pay him back."

"He doesn't expect it."

"I'm going to pay him back."

"We'll have enough to worry about."

"I said I'm going to pay him back." Again he has spoken too loud, and again they wait a minute. Another inmate comes in and walks over to the woman and the teenager. They all embrace; they all talk at once. Things have happened for the boy since the last visit — the talk is of track and field.

"Listen," Connie tells her husband. "The lady said they allow twenty hours a month for visitation. That's five hours a week. We can come see you for a little while every day. Every day, honey."

He says nothing to this. In fact, he appears not to have heard it.

"Daniel?"

"Okay," he says. "Right."

"Which do you prefer?"

"They have school. Or they will. They can't be coming here every day."

"We'll save up time on weekends, then."

"I don't want them sitting in here two hours on weekends."

"All right."

He looks at her. "I miss you. I miss you all so much."

"We miss you, too."

"I don't know that your coming here was such a good idea," he mutters.

"Well, you've been worried about that all along," Connie tells him.

"I'm scared," he says, pulling his hands away. "Jesus, honey. I'm terrified. I was never any more scared than this, ever."

"It's all right," she tells him. "We're here."

"I can't shake it," he says. "This feeling."

She waits for him to go on.

"It's like it's over, like I've ruined it and it's done."

"What?" she says. "What is?" But she thinks she knows.

"Us," he says after an awful pause. His eyes are fixed on the floor beyond her. He has brought one hand up on the table and is inscribing some invisible name on the surface with one too-long fingernail.

"Well," she manages, "don't be ridiculous."

"I can't help it," he says.

She watches him write the invisible word, over and over.

"Well," he says finally, "I guess I ought to get back."

"We have an hour."

"You don't want to sit here that long."

"This is like our phone conversations," she says.

"I can't help it," he tells her. "Things happen. I can't help anything anymore."

"I won't bring the children in to hear you talk like this."

"No," he says. "Right."

"Please, Daniel."

"You're right," he says.

They are quiet. The boy at the other table gets up and wanders past them to the vending machines. He puts a coin in, and a can clatters into the stall at the bottom. He pulls it out, opens it, then walks back to his table and sits down.

"I wish I could help it," Connie's husband says. "I wish there was something I could do about it."

"I'm coming back tomorrow," she says. "I'm bringing Thomas and Lisa with me. I wish you'd tell me now if you don't think you can do it."

"Do it?" he says. "Do what? Hey, I can do anything."

"Well, all right, then."

"I love you," he says in a broken voice. "I can't even begin to say."

She reaches across for his hands again. "We'll be all right," she tells him. But she can't find the belief anywhere inside herself. She looks for it, listens to her own voice say she loves him.

"Connie," he says, "I always wanted you to have the best."

"Don't," she says. "Not now. We've been through that so much. Please, Daniel."

After a pause, he nods. "They've put me to work in the wood shop. I'm learning a trade, believe it or not. I have a sort of talent for it. We make cabinets and hutches and things like that. I'm doing some carving."

"That's what you said."

"Right," he tells her. "What can I tell you that I haven't told you over the phone?"

"It's better in person," she says.

"They had me in the laundry."

"Yes."

"I didn't like that."

"Tell me what your day's been like."

"Oh, that," he says. "Well, it's been like a day — you know, a day in prison."

She says nothing.

"I had this dream, you know. A — a terrible nightmare — that I was in prison and that I had almost two years to go. I was walking around in this dream thinking about two years — and how terrible — in prison. And I woke up. I woke up, coming out of this dream, you know, and for half a second I had the relief of knowing it had been a nightmare, and then I remembered that I *am* in prison, and I have almost two years to go." He laughs, but it's like a mirthless, frantic tic.

"It won't be the full two years," she manages.

"Right," he says, almost laughing. "How long have I been here? I still can't believe it. Every day it gets harder to believe."

"I guess I believe it," she tells him, meaning it to sound less harsh than it does. "You know," she goes on, "we've all had a lot of time to think about it."

"Yeah," he says. "Me too. Time."

"And it can be just ten months, right?"

"No, right. I'm making points. I've been a good inmate, really."

"You could get out sooner," she says.

He nods, looks away from her.

"Will they let me bring you food? Cookies? Something like that?"

"No."

"Books?"

"Yeah, books. They have a library. I did a little time in the library, too." A moment later he says, "I lie awake at night and try to imagine that I haven't lost you."

"Well," she says, "you haven't lost me."

He's staring at her.

"Daniel," she says.

"All those other times I was gone," he says, "I just wanted to get back to you, and I could feel you wanting me back."

She returns his look, feels as though something annihilating is about to happen. And then she has the sense that it has already happened. She's in the middle of it, with him, and he's sitting there staring, the unhappiness showing in his eyes like another self. He's someone who has changed utterly. "Will you stop looking at me that way," she says. "What do you want? I'm here, aren't I?"

"I have to go now." He stands. "We're on a quota today. If I don't finish, I'll have to keep after it tomorrow."

"All right." She rises too.

He comes around the table and embraces her. "You're all I ever cared about," he murmurs. "You know? Nothing else mattered to me at all, honey."

"Your children." She smiles, patting the side of his face.

"You know what I mean," he says.

"I love you," she tells him, and her heart sinks.

Slowly he backs away.

"Daniel."

"Yes, I know," he says.

"Don't worry."

"Right. No."

"We'll be here tomorrow. Early afternoon."

"Please," he says, "I want to see them so bad it hurts me to breathe. But not like this. Not in this place."

"They'll be all right about it, you'll see."

"No. I mean it, Connie."

She stares at him. "What will I tell them?"

"Say they don't allow children — say anything. Tell them the truth if you want to."

"They won't understand."

"Make them. Please, Connie. You have to make them."

"Will you think about it, at least?"

"There's nothing to think about."

She sees the pain it is causing him, sees that there's nothing she can say or do to change his mind. "Don't worry about anything," she says, thinking that she is the one who'll have to do the worrying, already picturing the trouble her son will give her about not being able to see his father. "Okay?" she says. "Really. Don't worry."

His smile is brittle. "Wouldn't dare."

"Tomorrow," she says.

He turns, and the guard steps away from the wall, pats him down, then holds the door for him. He takes one last look at her from the narrow hallway leading back into the life he leads now, and my mother waves, watches him disappear, watches the iron door close. It makes a heavy chinking sound, and to her surprise the room reminds her of the barracks rooms of seventeen years ago, the Alaskan night outside, all that distance, when she was young and had a baby and the oil business wasn't panning out. It comes back to her with a strange stab of nostalgia, and she has to make an effort not to think of it. If she allows herself to think about any of it, she might go out of her mind.

Quietly she gathers herself and starts out of the room, past the others, who are talking as naturally as people do in a lunchroom. Outside, in the sunny chill, she makes her way to the car, gets in, sits staring out the windshield at the red brick buildings before her, the many glass panes reflecting sun, the angles of window and wire and barred doors. She thinks of how she decided to come here, how she resisted every attempt to convince her to do otherwise. Turning the key in the ignition, she has a brutal moment of feeling like a person bereft of every common earthly solace, and the possibility strikes inside her that all her exercise of will had been only an element of despair. She drives toward us, her children, uprooted and strange to contemplate in such a mood: for the present she's only an aggregate of nerves, a collection of momentary impressions moving along a street in a town whose existence depends on a prison. Her heart is empty, a small agitating muscle. She pulls up in front of the house, the cold pulse of fear spreading through her veins — that this journey she began all those days ago has not been a traveling toward anything so much as it has been a kind of desperate flight.

She knows this possibility. It's quite clear now, and it is terrible. Lisa and Thomas are coming across the sunny lawn, interested in the car and in whatever news she has for them. She sees them. There's no space, no time or place, to go through alone what she's going through now. She opens the door and somehow manages to put herself in motion — getting out of the car, standing in its open door, trying, though it feels as if the effort might kill her, to face her children with a smile.

14

THAT EVENING at dinner, Mr. Egan said that several bad things had taken place at the prison while he worked as a guard there. He hoped things were calmer now, and probably they were. Such troubles tended to run their course fairly quickly, like summer storms: a few claps of thunder, a little lightning, then calm. He said this last with an air of increasing consternation, apparently conscious — finally — of the effect he was having on his unhappy but attentive audience, and yet unable to stop talking. He reminded me a little of a man who has slipped on an embankment and whose efforts to right himself only make him slip further. Even in my anger at him for what he had begun telling us, I felt sorry for him, too, seeing the sweat break out on his upper lip, watching his eyes move from Mother to me to my sister and back again. If he had managed to find some way out of it — and he did hesitate three or four times, as if to leave the damage where it was — Mother would not have let him off the hook. During the hesitations, she pressed him: "Tell me," she said, or, "Go on." Or, "You're not finished."

And he went on. "It was — it —" he said, fumbling for speech. "Uh, it was just a period of time when I was there. A very specific time when they happened to be having some few occasional problems . . ." He trailed off.

"I want to know everything," Mother said.

"I'm sure it's all cleared up by now." He looked diminished without his clown makeup on. He took a handkerchief out of his shirt pocket and wiped his brow, as though to remove some small residue of grease-paint. "In fact, it *must* have been corrected by now, wouldn't you think, Mabel?"

"You may call me Mrs. Wilson." She had prepared roast beef and gravy, and she was spooning it onto her plate.

"Wouldn't you think, Mrs. Wilson?" he persisted.

"I don't know what goes on over there anymore, and I don't think you should speculate."

"I want you to tell me, please," Mother said to Mr. Egan. "You'll tell me, won't you?"

"It really isn't anything that goes on every day."

Mother waited, her eyes as fierce and darkly focused as those of a stalking cat.

"I bet they whip them with chains," Russell said from the other end of the table. "I bet they use stun guns and electric shock. I saw a movie based on true stuff and that's what they did. Torture and whippings and everything."

Mr. Egan said, "For God's sake, boy. You're letting your imagination run away with you."

"I bet they do."

"Nothing of the kind," Mr. Egan said to Mother. "Besides, your husband's probably on good behavior."

"Just tell me," she said to him. The two of them could have been alone in the room.

"Uh," he said. And then he halted, muttered, looked around the room, wiped the back of his neck. His tone was apologetic, as if he had been responsible for everything. "Mostly," he said, "it was when we had discipline problems."

"Go on," Mother said.

And he began to tell us, like a confession.

The events he described had to do with certain excesses of the guards, the forms of punishment that were used when inmates got out of line. Prisoners had been beaten with sticks and made to stand in tubs of ice water. They were occasionally forced to work into the hours of the night at some backbreaking task, digging a ditch or moving a pile of coal from one end of the generator yard to another. There were a lot of very tight rules and restrictions, and the inmates had to ask permission before doing absolutely anything; any prisoner who failed to remember these rules was punished, and for those whose problems remembering were more complicated or serious, there was a thing called the gauntlet: twenty men facing each other, five feet apart, each holding a belt, buckle-end down, and the poor prisoner had to run between the two lines. No one ever made it all the way, and when an inmate fell, Mr. Egan said, some of the men with the belts took the chance to step in and give him another whack. It was a kind of instinct, he said, like a pack of dogs worrying the body of a fox. But this sort of thing did not really happen all that often. And anyway, it was not sanctioned by the authorities who ran the prison, or by any governing body higher up, either. It was just how some men arrived at discipline in such a place. He himself had asked to be transferred because he had no taste for violence, though of course he knew men who did, who in fact got a charge out of watching other people being punished for their mistakes. There had been times, Mr. Egan told us, when it was hard to distinguish the inmates from the guards; moreover, there existed several kinds of hazing among the inmates themselves, mostly having to do with attitudes about the war: the mix of prisoners included men who felt strongly about winning the war, who were always interested in winning any fight, their troubles with the government having to do with other trespasses — usually resulting from excesses of appetite or extremes of temper, the aftermath of rage or pain, or their own obvious inability to obey authority — rather than the failure of their government to compel them to serve in Southeast Asia. But there were also young men who had been sent to Wilson Creek for refusing to go to the war, and these were held in a dangerous contempt by all the others.

"My husband was wounded in the war," Mother said to him with an urgency.

"Then he's in a special category," Mr. Egan said. "If he let it be known."

"How can it not be known? It's in his record. He was decorated."

"You never can say."

"Well, dear," Mrs. Wilson said, "how did your husband seem to you when you saw him?"

Mother stared at her plate. She hadn't eaten much. "He was fine, really. I don't want to talk about this anymore."

"Mr. Egan," I said, "what special category are you talking about?"

He dipped a piece of bread into his gravy, then looked at Mother. "Should I tell him?"

"Please," she said. "Go on."

"Well, you know, it's a funny thing. It's — it's like a scale or something. A ruler, let's say. And you can't be at either end of the ruler — draft evader or kidnapper at one end, or hero at the other. They seem to like everybody in the exact middle, see. If you could put it on a scale. Robbers, murderers, you know, they're all right. But guys who kidnap little children, guys who ran away from a fight, guys who stole money with paper — or guys who were big heroes — you know, it's different."

"What do you mean, 'stole money with paper'?" Mother wanted to know.

"You know — paperhangers. Embezzlers, bad-check guys. Bookkeepers and the like."

Mother glanced at me, then straightened suddenly in an attempt to cover her own lapse of attention to her reactions.

"Why?" Mr. Egan said. "That's not the kind of thing your husband did?"

"He was decorated," my mother said, beginning to cry.

No one said anything for a moment. Across from me, Russell was using his fingers to trim a thin strip of fat off a slice of beef. His concentration made him look cross-eyed. Lisa was watching him.

"What're you doing?" she said to him.

Mother said, "Be quite, Lisa, please." She sniffled.

"Russell," said Mrs. Wilson quietly, "put your food down."

"I didn't mean to cause anything," said Mr. Egan.

"You've been very kind," Mother told him, dabbing at her eyes with her napkin.

"There," Mrs. Wilson said. "You've been through a lot."

"I'm just so tired."

Mrs. Wilson was looking at me now, and I realized that she expected me to do something. I stood, put my hands on Mother's shoulders. I felt very strange for a moment, her tight muscles moving under my fingers.

"Please, I'm fine." She put her hands on top of my fingers and patted

them. I took my hands away and sat down again. They were all looking at me.

"You're red as a beet," said Russell.

"Russell," Mrs. Wilson said.

"Well, he is. Look at him."

Mother reached over and touched my cheek, smiling, her eyes brimming. "He's my shy, thoughtful young man."

I felt proud and mortified in the same instant. Russell was staring at
me with a look of pure juvenile malice. I decided to ignore him, and not
to glance Lisa's way, either, since I could hear her small snickering at
my side.

"You just have to settle in," Mr. Egan was saying. "This sort of
move can take it out of a person."

I shifted in my chair, attending to the adults, aligning myself with
them. I wanted to let Russell know by my attitude, and by the way I
listened to and spoke only to the adults, that I considered him to be at
Lisa's level: he was at least as rude as she was, and he didn't have
babyhood to excuse him.

"If you ask me," Mrs. Wilson said, "the whole country's just gone
crazy. See, when you got young families broken up like this because of
a person's political beliefs — it might just as well be communist Russia
or some other such place."

"Nazi Germany," said Mr. Egan.

"There you go."

"Imperial Japan."

"Right."

"Fascist Italy."

Mrs. Wilson just nodded this time.

"Red China."

"Right, China."

"Cuba."

Again, she nodded, staring at Mr. Egan.

"Several countries in Latin America," he said.

"That, too, yes."

"Spain."

Mrs. Wilson put her hands on either side of her plate, as if she were
about to get up.

"Most of Eastern Europe," he said. "Yugoslavia, Bulgaria, Albania. And my God, poor Hungary. Remember what the Russians did to them in 1956."

"All right, Mr. Egan."

"Well," he said, "I was trying to help."

"The point is made."

A moment later, he said, "Oh, I forgot to mention North Vietnam."

"Mr. Egan, please."

"What about North Korea?" I said.

"That, too," said Mr. Egan. "Thank you."

"Can we please talk about something else?" Mother said.

Then we were quiet. Perhaps a full minute passed. We were not even looking at each other. Finally Mrs. Wilson wondered aloud if the food was to everyone's liking, and Mr. Egan spoke about the fine cuisine, Mrs. Wilson's ability to make interesting and delectable meals on a small budget. It sounded to me like the baldest flattery, but she took it with a deprecating smile, choosing, I suppose, to believe that it was sincere.

When dinner was over Mother offered to help with the dishes, and Mrs. Wilson seemed insulted. "It's all included in your rent."

I went out on the porch with Lisa, and Russell followed us. "School in a week," he said. "Shit."

The trees that lined the street were bright with color, and leaves littered the ground, lifting with the gusts of wind in the chilly twilight.

"Gonna be colder than a pail of penguin shit pretty soon."

I looked out toward where I had been told the prison was. "How's it feel having a father who's a convict?" Russell said. His expression was one of harmless concern. He merely wanted to know, and didn't have the subtlety to understand how such a question might make us feel.

Lisa said, "How's it feel having no father, period."

"Never knew him, so I ain't got nothing to compare it to."

"It's cold," Lisa said. "I'm going back inside."

When she had gone, Russell said, "She's pretty smart, I guess."

"Plenty," I said, meaning it but half joking, too, now. I wanted to be friendly. I was certain that his bluntness was similar to what I had been self-conscious enough to recognize as my own reserve: it was the way he had of dealing with new people and new situations.

"I didn't mean nothing by that question about your father."

"It's okay," I told him.

We stood at the edge of the steps, and I looked at the place where Mr. Egan had been working to paint the porch. For some reason I began wondering about who the new boarder would be — all in relation to the prison. I had an image of myself telling someone else, the new boarder, about the horrors inside Wilson Creek Penitentiary, and then I dismissed the thought with a small, guilty shudder. In the next moment Russell spoke, and it was as if he had been privy to my thoughts.

"About now's the time when I wonder about who my mother'll dig up next for a boarder, you know?"

"Dig up," I said.

"I don't mean you guys. Man, you're all like exposed cuts or something. I just mean the next tenant she gets — to replace the guy she kicked out."

I nodded, staring at him, no doubt, with something of the mystified appreciation of a person in a magic show, the contents of whose wallet have just been revealed through hocus-pocus.

He went on. "I always like to imagine who it'll be and then see how far it is from what I imagined. Like, I didn't think your mother could be so beautiful — and I thought you'd be a tough guy. That I'd have to fight you or something."

"No," I said. "Not me."

"Hey," he said, "you want to walk over to the prison? Take a look at it?"

"Walk?" I said.

"I told you. Right along the creek and then across it, and then it's just a ten-minute walk from there."

The dark was coming early. I turned and glanced at the lighted windows, the shadows in the hallway.

"Come on," Russell said. "We can be back in an hour."

"Shouldn't we tell them?"

"Fuck, no."

Again I glanced back. He had already gone down off the porch and started across the lawn.

"Come on."

We went around in back of the house and through the heavy growth to the damp grass at the edge of the creek. I followed him, tramping down a swath through the tall weeds, hurrying away from the view of the high windows of the house. Our feet made a loud rustling as we walked, and somewhere inside the noise I thought I heard my name called. I stopped. An insect landed on my face and stung, and I swiped frantically at it, turning to look back at the house.

"What's the matter?" Russell said.

"I'm going back," I said. "Something stung me."

"They're sweat bees. They won't hurt you."

I followed him, expecting to be stung again any time. We crossed the creek, balancing on stones in the small trickle of the stream, and then climbed an embankment and went along a path. The trees had closed around us, and I heard an owl call, very near. I stopped again.

"Come on," he said, looking back. "It's not far now."

We went on. The path descended to the creek bed again. We crossed once more, then entered a field. I saw lights in the distance. Ahead of me, Russell had begun to pick up speed. He was pulling away, taking wide, leaping strides.

"What're you doing?" I called after him.

He stopped. "I'm always afraid of rattlers here."

I stopped, too. The tall grass was quiet all around me.

"Take big steps," Russell said.

"I can't do this," I told him.

"What the hell?"

"I don't want to see the prison now."

"Why not?"

"I changed my mind. A person can change his mind, you know."

"But why? There's probably no snakes."

"That's not it," I said.

"It's right there." He indicated the lights.

Beyond the glare, I thought I caught the shadow of a building.

"Come on," Russell said.

We went a few paces farther, and I could see the dark angles of roof and wall, the tall fence. It made me sick at the pit of my stomach.

"No," I said. "I can't do it. I'm not going any closer."

He came back toward me, shaking his head. "Hell, all right. I've seen the damn thing before. It's nothing to me. I was doing it for you. You can't get much closer than this anyway."

"I'm going to see it from the inside," I said, "soon enough."

"Yeah, I can't help that." He went past me, back toward the creek. "People can't make up their minds. Jesus."

I watched him go on, and suddenly realized that for all my juvenile curiosity about being inside prison walls, I did not want to see Wilson Creek prison at all — not then, not ever. The knowledge arrived like an unfortunate revelation about myself, some fact of my existence and makeup for which an apology to someone would be necessary — that all the slowly unscrolling miles of the trip had somehow stood between me and that time when I would have to walk into the institution knowing my father was an inmate there.

Back at the house, everyone had scattered to their separate rooms. I went upstairs into our apartment and found Mother sitting on the sofa, refolding clothes from a box at her feet. Lisa lay on her bunk in our room, looking through a magazine. I paused in the doorway and stared at her.

"What is it, Thomas?" Mother said behind me.

I turned. "Nothing."

"Something's the matter. Tell me." She went on folding the clothes.

I went over to the chair across from her and sat down.

"Don't slouch," she said. "Help me unpack some of these things."

"I've decided that I don't want to go over there," I said.

She halted, but did not look at me.

"I don't want to see it."

After a pause, she said, "He needs to see you. He doesn't know himself how badly."

"I know," I said. "I don't think I can, though."

"We'll talk about it later." She handed me a small stack of folded T-shirts. "These are yours. Put them in the bureau in your room." And when I didn't move: "Come on, son. It helps to get yourself busy doing something."

I took the shirts from her, a folded stack I steadied with my chin, and went into the other room, where Lisa now lay on her back, arms folded, staring at the bottom springs of the top bunk, the magazine open across her chest. Her relaxed air made me irritable; it got under my skin. "You could help, you know."

"I'm tired," she said. "Leave me alone."

"Lazy," I told her.

"Just shut up, Thomas."

When I returned to the sitting room, Mother, without taking her eyes from what she was doing, said, "You're too old for that, you know."

"Well," I said, "she's just laying there."

"It's almost time for her to go to bed."

"I mean it," I said. "I don't want to go out there."

"Well, you have to."

I didn't say anything.

"There are things we all have to do that we don't want to, and we do them anyway because it's a part of being grown-up, and you already know that, don't you?"

I can't explain it, but I was feeling sullen and darkly thwarted, and I had the urge to lash out. I remembered her firmness with Grandfather Tinan about not staying in Minot. Minot seemed almost perfect to me now: the place where I was treated like a man, where there was money for whatever I wanted, and we were still hundreds of miles from Wilson Creek. "I don't see why we had to come here, anyway," I muttered.

She said. "Now you're being a baby."

I turned and stared at her, and as she brought one of Lisa's blouses up to her face to assess its odor, to decide whether she would refold it or wash it, I said, "You're not even sure you want him back."

She brought the blouse down to her lap, crushing it in her two small white fists, and looked at me with a kind of frowning curiosity, as though I were someone unpleasant that she had known once, whose name had escaped her.

"All right," she said. "Why don't you tell me what you think you know."

I couldn't speak right away.

"Come on," she said — almost shouted.

"I heard you," I said. I had almost shouted back.

"Well?" she said. "Answer me, then."

"No, I mean I heard you and Aunt Elaine — you were talking, and I heard you say something."

She folded the blouse and set it aside. "You heard me say what." It was as if each word were a separate sentence.

"In the house in Virginia. After we were in bed."

She lifted another blouse out of the box. "I said a lot of things to Aunt Elaine in the house in Virginia."

"You said something I overheard."

"What?" Her tone was insistent, as it had been with Mr. Egan at dinner. "What did you overhear?"

"You said —" But I couldn't continue, couldn't meet her hard black stare.

"Go on," she said.

"Nothing," I said. "It's nothing."

"No. You think you know something. You tell me what you think you know."

"I didn't mean it, all right?"

"Oh, you meant it."

"I'm sorry," I said.

She put the blouse down and stood. "You're not going to get off that easy now, Thomas. You started this, you go on and finish it. Tell me. I want you to stand there and say out loud what you think you heard."

"It was nothing."

She had moved to confront me. We were face to face, and now Lisa appeared in the doorway of our bedroom. "Go back to bed, Lisa."

"Will you both please stop fighting."

"Do as I say."

When Lisa had stepped out of the doorway, Mother took the front of my shirt and smoothed it against my chest. Recalling that gesture now, it seems to me that there was something almost coquettish about it. I might as well have been a stranger she was trying to charm into giving her something. "Now," she said, "I want you to tell me what this is that you've been carrying around with you all this time."

I drew a breath, then stammered. "I — I — I heard you say that you didn't know if you wanted him back."

Her face didn't change. She watched her own hands moving over the cloth of my shirt. Then she took the collar and pulled at it gently, setting it right, swiping lightly at something on my shoulder, and, having apparently satisfied herself, let her hands drop to her sides. "Anything else?" she said.

"No."

"Well, you must've heard more."

"That's all I heard," I said. "You didn't want him back, and you didn't know if he'd come back." I couldn't read the expression in her face. Yet it was not impassive. I have come to believe I was not old enough to recognize the shade of feeling in it, whatever it was: sorrow and some measure of guilt mixed with confusion, mixed with anger, perhaps. But it was not the expression of someone who believes a mistake has been made; in a way, it admitted something to me, even as her words offered a denial.

"That's all I heard," I repeated.

"Well, I don't remember that," she said. Her hands fluttered near her face and she turned away. "That's ridiculous. I must've been talking about something else."

"All right," I said.

She had picked up the box of clothes, and set it down on the sofa. She had her back to me now. "I don't care what you think you heard, Thomas. You don't know what you're talking about and I don't have to listen to it."

This seemed queerly off the subject. I said, "Why wouldn't he want to come back?"

She whirled around to face me. "Back to where, Thomas? Maryland? Where this terrible trouble came down on him?"

"To us," I said.

"Get out of here," she said. "I'm not going to stand here and discuss my marriage with a seventeen-year-old snip."

"You wanted to know what I'd heard."

"All right. Now I know. You didn't hear anything *I* heard, though, and I can't be held responsible for what you imagine in that head of yours."

"I wrote it down in my journal."

She said nothing.

"I'm sorry," I said.

"Oh, Thomas," and now she seemed about to cry. "Will you please — just please leave me alone?"

I went into the bedroom, where Lisa lay crying quietly on her bunk.

"What're you crying about?" I said.

"Nothing."

"Well, stop it."

"I hate it here," she said.

"Keep it to yourself," I told her. "That's all you've had to say for the last ten days." I got out of my clothes and into bed.

Out the window, the creek shone in the soft twilight. The moon was already above the level of the trees on the far bank, brighter than I could believe. I lay on my stomach, listening to Lisa crying in the bed below me, and then I could hear a television playing in one of the other rooms: Mrs. Wilson's downstairs, probably. Mother was still putting things away. I turned from the window and looked at her shadow on the wall outside our room.

"Thomas," Lisa said, "can I come up with you?"

"No."

"Please?"

I didn't say anything, and in a little while she climbed up. When I looked out the window again, I saw Russell walking down the incline toward the path we had taken to look at the prison. I wondered what sort of household this could be, where a boy that age was routinely allowed out after dark. He went on into the shadows, and perhaps he was headed over to look at the big shape of the prison in its pools of light, its sharp, dark angles of wall and window.

Say that in this moment of my looking out the window of the house on Jewett Street, in one narrow opening atop the east-facing wall of the prison, my father stares out at the lights of town. He can see a neon sign blinking at slow intervals in the distance: PINKY'S PINKY'S PINKY'S. And the pink outline of a cocktail glass above the name, with a swizzle stick and an olive inside it, submerged in a drawn oval of bubbly liquid, also pink. The bubbles, a sequence of flashing bulbs, rise out of the rim of the glass. Next to this, jutting up out of one corner of the building, is a gas station light, ESSO, and past that he can see part of the highway. The sky is suffused with the electric glow of other lighted buildings, the city across the creek, beyond the dark, uneven line of trees in the distance. He never knows what day it is anymore, nor what hour. Each day goes on and on, and he can never get to the end of it. He's afraid he can't bear it any more. It feels like an extension of his earlier captivity, though he's fed three times a day here and he has a certain amount of leeway in his movements and the cruelties are certainly less serious than they ever were among the Vietcong. Even so, nothing he went through over there seems as harrowing — being the man everyone knows was a hero, the man his fellow inmates consider to have earned their quiet hatred just by being who he has been, in contrast to who he mostly is now: that man who of all things got his time for the botched theft of a typewriter. Moreover, there's the conviction, which he himself has reached, that he's come through all his life's struggles and been brave only to have it mean, finally, nothing.

And he has been brave: official records and citations exist to prove it.

But worse than any of this is the feeling, which he cannot shake, that he is the object of his wife's pity and that she's already leaving him, has been in the process of doing so for a long time in fact, even as she has so faithfully traveled such a great distance to be near him. Each day seems to teach him this lesson again. He sits in his small cell, with its one bunk bed and its toilet and sink, its thick walls the color of gray water, and because he believes he is without love anymore, his strength has begun to abandon him. Each long day is filled with the increasingly frantic effort to avoid being noticed and to get along. He moves among the other inmates with a nervous quickness, and the other inmates, having noticed this, are finding ways of getting to him and at him — they trip him up whenever they can, doubtless hoping to provoke him into some response. They tamper with his food, they jostle and elbow him in crowds, they soil his sheets, they pilfer his laundry. There have been several sexual advances, which he has managed to fight off. He's been buffeted and knocked around by the guards. His bones ache; he has bruises under his clothes.

On this particular evening, he thinks of his wife somewhere out in the soft, carmine glow of the town, and he thinks of his children there, too. He can't call up the shapes of their faces. He especially can't envision them waiting for him in the big open visiting room with its long tables and straight-backed chairs, its wired windows, its constant smell of disinfectant and spilled soft drinks and sickness — that room where, if he is to see them now, he will be led in to see them, and to have them see him.

No. It's not going to be possible. He can't do it, can't allow it. He doesn't even want Connie to see him like this. Perhaps he might recover something of what he knows is lost between them if he can find a way to simply walk out of this life and back into theirs, if he can keep his present life from them somehow. He should never have let her come here in the first place. Looking out at the pink dusk with its cottony ledges of smoldering cloud, he begins to weep quietly, holding his hands over his mouth. He worries that other inmates might hear him.

Not far away, in the oncoming darkness, the members of his family may be visible from the shadowy street, figures in the windows of a strange house. It's easy enough to suppose, isn't it, that while I lay at my window imagining him in his prison cell, he was imagining me in my small curtained room . . .

"Thomas?" Mother said, standing in the doorway. "Are you asleep yet?"

I didn't know how much time had gone by. Lisa answered for me. "No, we're not."

"I need your help, Thomas."

I climbed over Lisa and got down.

"Get dressed," Mother said.

"Are we going out?"

"I want to move something out into the foyer downstairs."

"Can't it wait?" I said.

She stirred, then seemed to hesitate. "All right."

"No, I'll do it," I told her.

Mrs. Wilson had agreed that Mother could remove the standing metal cabinet in her room. It was such a little room — not even enough space for a small TV or a nightstand. The tall cabinet stood in the corner opposite the window, like a big mute presence watching over everything. If you opened its door and let the door go, it would swing out, smacking against the side of Mother's bed with a clatter; and the shelves inside it were too widely placed to be of much use for the storage of anything Mother had to keep. In any case, she could think of nothing to store there, and Mrs. Wilson had reluctantly given permission for its removal. (We were to find, during the period of our sojourn in her house, that any change in the status quo could be a source of pained exasperation to Mrs. Wilson, who would throw her hands up and, sticking out her lower lip, blow the hair off her forehead as if to indicate that life was continually presenting her with the necessity of making these difficult concessions.)

"Well?" Mother said.

"Let's walk it," I said.

"We can't lift it?"

"There's nothing to grab on to."

"It's going to be noisy."

And for no reason, we laughed. We held our hands over our mouths, hearing the television in the walls and Mrs. Wilson walking back and forth downstairs. "I'm sorry," Mother said to me. "I feel like I'm in Minot."

"Me, too," I said.

We waited, listening. "Why should I feel that way?" she said, still trying to stifle her laughter. "I'm paying rent."

"Right," I said.

She said, "Come on. Here we go."

We walked the thing in a metallic clatter of empty echoes out onto the stairs, and then began lugging it down, the noise growing louder as we descended, with me backing up the whole way and with Lisa following us, not wanting to be left alone in the apartment. We worked slowly and uncertainly, stopping several times to rest, and it was Lisa — standing on the stairs halfway down, looking beyond us, beyond the dusty top of the slowly descending cabinet — who first saw the figure in the oval window of the front door. She saw the figure, and then she saw the face.

"Hey, you guys — look," she said, her voice filled with wonderment and surprise. "Look in the window. Isn't that — ?"

We had got almost to the bottom of the stairs, and at first what she was saying didn't register with me. Mother said, "Set it down a minute. Can you set it down?"

"Two more steps," I said.

Then we had reached the foyer and stood the cabinet up and turned, and the doorbell rang, that startling bell, and Mrs. Wilson came hustling through from the big living room.

And the window in the door showed me the face of Penny Holt.

15

MRS. WILSON opened the door. "Yes?"

"Is Mrs. Boudreaux in?" Penny said. She looked right at us.

"Why, yes." Mrs. Wilson stepped back. "Standing right here with a cabinet I don't know what I'll ever find to do with."

"Excuse me?" Penny leaned inside, tilted her head, and waved at us. "Hi." She wore a tattered gray coat, and you couldn't see her shape under its heavy folds. Her lovely blond hair was pinned back along the sides of her head, and some wispy strands of it had come loose. Seeing her, I felt my own heartbeat as though it had begun only a moment before.

"The lady from the train," Lisa said. "You remember." I didn't know whether she was talking to Mother or to me.

"Yes," Mother said. "Hello."

"Can I come in. Is it too late?"

"Please," Mrs. Wilson said. "We're heating the outside."

Penny said, "I have a bag."

"Well come on, come on."

She moved out of sight briefly, then reappeared holding a heavy suitcase. She hauled it over the threshold, and we stood back to make room for her. The metal cabinet was in the midst of us, like an absurd object of study.

"Are you a relative?" Mrs. Wilson said to Penny.

"Oh, no."

"This is — I'm sorry," Mother said. "I can't remember your name."

"Penny," I said.

She was pleased. She made a gesture, almost like a curtsy, and pushed the loose strands of hair back from her face. "Yes." Then she turned to Mrs. Wilson. "Holt."

"Holt," Mrs. Wilson said.

"Penny Holt," I said.

"Oh, all right." Mrs. Wilson offered her hand. "I see." Then she looked at Mother, who seemed for the moment at a loss as to what to do, how to proceed.

"I — couldn't stay in Kansas," said Penny, looking at Mother and then at me. "It just got worse."

"Worse," said Mrs. Wilson.

"It's a long story. The whole way there it got worse."

"I'm afraid we don't have any room," Mother said. "We were moving this cabinet out to make room for me."

"I won't stay a minute. I just — I didn't think of going anywhere else. Just came straight here. I was so relieved to get here and everything, and I guess I wasn't thinking. I have a little money."

"Let's just not stand here in the foyer all night," Mrs. Wilson said.

We went into the downstairs living room, with its dark pictures on the walls and its heavy furniture. It was as though we all made up a kind of delegation, and the next few moments were confusing. Mother explained that we had met Penny on the train coming west, that there had been some trouble with her traveling companion.

"You don't know the half of it," Penny said.

We were all seated now, the three women on the sofa, Lisa with me in one of the stuffed chairs across from it. She wouldn't let me go; she'd taken hold of my arm when we started into the room and was still clinging to me, staring at Penny as if she had materialized out of the dark woodwork of the hall.

"So you all don't really know each other," Mrs. Wilson said.

"Well, not really," said Mother. But then, upon seeing the look of confused sorrow on Penny's face, she tried to amend herself. "I mean, we made friends on the train. We — we were going to keep in touch."

"Will you vouch for her?" Mrs. Wilson wanted to know.

Mother merely repeated the phrase: "Vouch for her."

"Yes. Will you speak to her reliability."

This occasioned a silence. Mother's eyes wandered, as if the answer were elsewhere. "I . . . ," she began.

Mrs. Wilson looked at Penny. "Will you excuse us?"

It took a moment for Penny to understand. "Oh, you want me to leave." She stood and lifted her bag.

"You can set the bag here for the time being. Don't you want to freshen up?"

"Oh, if I could."

"There's a bathroom right through there." Mrs. Wilson pointed between the heavy shapes of the dining room, to the doorway leading into the kitchen and the back hall. We watched Penny until she was out of sight beyond the opening.

"Now," Mrs. Wilson said, "will you recommend her?"

"Yes," I said, "we will."

Mother said, "Be quiet, Thomas."

"Well?" Mrs. Wilson demanded.

"I . . . ," Mother began. "I can't be responsible for anyone but these children."

"All right."

"But — I mean — she seemed nice. She *seems* very nice. She was going to write us, you know. Keep in touch."

"I have this empty room," Mrs. Wilson said. "I thought if she was the right sort of person."

"Oh, I'm sure she's fine."

"You think she'd be steady and pay her rent?" Mrs. Wilson appeared eager to receive an answer she could use to persuade herself to go ahead with her idea.

"Oh, well," Mother said, "I don't have any reason to suppose she wouldn't pay her rent."

"There's something about her, though," Mrs. Wilson said. For some reason, she had descended precipitately into doubt.

"It's her eye," Lisa put in with an air of suspicion and awe.

Mother said, "Hush, Lisa."

"What about her eye?" Mrs. Wilson wanted to know. "Is there something I should know?"

"It's nothing. She has a glass eye."

"Well, I saw that. Is there something about it?"

We said nothing.

"Is there something I should know about it?"

"She lost the eye when she was small," Lisa said.

Mrs. Wilson looked at Lisa and seemed to consider. "A beautiful girl, really."

"Yes," Mother said.

"But I always say, pretty is as pretty does."

"I'm sure she'd be fine, Mrs. Wilson."

"Let me talk to her when she comes back. I do like to conduct an interview. I can usually tell what I need to from that, though I guess you could say Mr. Egan and his friend have proved me wrong. Would you all mind going back upstairs?"

"Where would you like Thomas to move the cabinet?"

"Oh," Mrs. Wilson said, "that. I'll have Mr. Egan put it out in the utility shed, if he doesn't want it himself."

"Come on," Mother said to us.

We went back through the foyer and on upstairs, and I had the strange feeling that we were the offspring of Mrs. Wilson — all children together in that big old house.

We had got upstairs, and Lisa began to ask the questions that were on our minds.

"What's she doing here? Where's that guy she was with? I mean, what happened? What does she want?"

"Hush," Mother told her. "She'll hear you."

"She scares me."

"Be quiet."

We all waited. We could hear Mrs. Wilson talking to Penny in the kitchen. Her voice sounded as though it were coming from the bottom of a well.

"Do you think she'll get the room?" Mother asked me.

I shook my head.

"No?"

"I don't know."

"A man is definite," she said, and smirked.

"I definitely don't know," I said.

She sighed. "I don't need another personality to contend with."

"I wasn't contending," I said.

"Stop interpreting everything I say to be about *you*," she said. "We'll get along much better."

We heard Mrs. Wilson come into the hallway, and then they were both ascending the stairs. Mother stepped to the entrance of our apartment and looked out.

I heard Mrs. Wilson's voice. "It's settled."

"Isn't it great?" Penny Holt said. "I'm so happy. The luckiest thing."

There was a bump, which I realized was the big suitcase being dropped, and now Penny Holt appeared in the entrance and threw her arms around Mother's neck. Mother staggered back a step, so that it looked almost as though the other woman had attacked her. "I'm happy for you," she said, clearly unable to maintain her reserve.

Now Penny let go of her and turned to Lisa. "Isn't it wonderful?" She reached to touch Lisa's shoulder and then looked at me. "I feel like I've come home." I returned her bright smile, though I must say this, too: although I had been deeply taken with her, and was therefore very glad she had shown up and been allowed to stay, the shadow of something unresolved and dark moved through me as well. I accepted her affectionate, happy gratitude and experienced a disquieting sense of this good feeling as an element of some obscurely worked-out stratagem that she'd decided upon before she ever walked up the ragged steps of the front porch. It made me self-conscious, and I looked away. After all, there was no reason for someone like her to latch on to us.

"It's Thomas, isn't it?" she said.

I nodded.

"See," she said, "I remembered your name, too."

I wondered if she had seen something of the doubt in my face, for her tone was almost sad. But then she turned and went back out into the hall and climbed the stairs with Mrs. Wilson, talking on about how small the world was, how strange time and distance were, and where life took a person.

"Well," Mother said, "I wish there was a door I could close."

"What's wrong?" I asked her, because I honestly wondered myself.

"Nothing."

We busied ourselves with what remained of our own unpacking. But then Mother wanted to rearrange the furniture in her room so her bed was nearer the window, and all three of us worked to get things where she wanted them. When we had finished, she lay face down at the foot of the unmade bed, her forehead resting on her folded arms. Lisa lay beside her and put one leg over her back.

"Nice, sweetie."

Downstairs, someone else arrived. Mr. Egan, I could tell from the cough.

And then Penny Holt came back down from her new apartment. She stood with her hands clasped at her waist in our cluttered sitting room. "I'm not intruding, am I?" She stepped to one side so that she could see into where we were.

"Not a bit," Mother said with a trace of irony.

"I'll come back another time."

"No," said Mother, rising, "it's all right." Then she looked at me. "Thomas, will you tuck Lisa in?"

"I don't want to go to bed," Lisa said.

"Thomas."

I took Lisa's hand, and she didn't resist. We went into our room, and the two women went down to sit in the kitchen with Mr. Egan and Mrs. Wilson. A few minutes later, Russell came home from wherever he had been, and when his mother sent him to bed, he strode to the apartment doorway and looked in. I saw him from the dark of our room, and waited until he had gone to his own part of the house before I stirred. Lisa had fallen asleep on my arm. I hadn't even felt the change. I got myself free of her, put the blanket over her shoulder, then crept out of the room. Our sitting room, for all the work we had done, was still at that stage of unpacking which suggests transience either way: we could have been coming or going; it would be difficult for a stranger to guess which. Out on the landing, I found one of Lisa's little camisole tops. I put it in my jeans pocket and started down the stairs, hearing Penny Holt's voice, that murmur with its hint of old pain, and the soft, alto lilt, the intimations of the South.

They were sitting at the kitchen table under the light — Mother, Mrs. Wilson, Penny Holt, and Mr. Egan, who turned toward me as I entered and said, "Well."

Now they all looked at me, and I received the impression that they had been talking about something I shouldn't hear. In fact, I had approached them with some stealth, no doubt at least partly to hear whatever they might not say if they knew I was near. But I'd heard nothing, and in the next few seconds their relaxed demeanor made me see that I had merely walked in on a pause. It felt good to know that my arrival hadn't changed anything. It made me feel quite grown-up.

"What else?" Mother said to Penny Holt, who evidently had been telling about her few weeks in Leavenworth, Kansas. Penny went on then, talking about the strain of spending days and nights with her would-be brother-in-law, who kept making moony eyes at her, trying to get her to fall in love — while her fiancé refused to see them.

"Sit down, if you want to," Mother said to me.

There was another chair and I took it.

Mr. Egan said, "I love to sit in a kitchen and talk."

"So, your husband wouldn't see you?" Mrs. Wilson said to Penny.

"Well, not my husband."

"But he didn't want to see you," said Mother.

"No," Penny said. She looked down at her hands. "It's — I think maybe it got him crazy, being in there. And really it wouldn't've worked out. He and I are really — I mean, I didn't really know him anymore, you know. I thought — I mean I didn't think —" She seemed to catch herself. Her lips closed tight as if to keep a word from escaping, and she looked up at the room light. I thought she might start crying.

"Well," Mother said.

"There's no way it would've worked out anyway," Penny said. "The only thing between us was Chummy, really. I can't explain."

Mother glanced at me, then at Penny again. "Why do you think he didn't want to see you."

"Maybe he's ashamed," Mrs. Wilson said.

"No," said Penny. "There's no reason for him to be ashamed. He was protesting the war. That's why they arrested him. I was working in this grill in Bristol, see, and Chummy walked in and I hadn't seen him or Buddy for a long time. I — I mean Buddy and me were supposed to get married, and he went into the Army and we sort of lost touch. He didn't write and I went with another boy, only that went bad. So I was in Bristol — it sounds awful, saying it out like this. It wasn't all that simple."

"Where's Bristol?" Mr. Egan asked.

"Tennessee," Penny said. "I moved back to Demera, though, and stayed with my mother a while. And then she passed away. I never saw my father. He died at Pearl Harbor —"

Mother said, "I thought Chummy said he looked you up in Bristol and you headed out together."

"No."

"I'm sorry — you were talking about your parents —"

"My mother was tired," Penny said. She paused and seemed to think about this a moment. "We lived in a trailer. Kind of rundown, but we kept it nice." She folded her hands tight in her lap.

For a moment no one spoke.

"Anyway," she sighed, "Chummy did look me up in Bristol. He said Buddy was in jail for resisting the war. And he knew I'd want to run to him." She laughed and touched the corner of her good eye.

"What did he do to get sent to Leavenworth?" Mr. Egan wanted to know. "If you don't mind my asking."

"Oh, no," she said. "I don't mind. I guess it must've all got started even before he went into the Army. He sort of had his mind made up he wasn't going to go. He tried to pretend he was crazy first. Pulled all kinds of dumb stunts to make them think he was crazy, but they didn't go for it, really. That was when I got engaged to him. It was funny, in a way. We had to go in together one day for some of those tests, like, interviews with the head doctors, especially with me, so they could ask me how he was in a normal day and all that, see if what I said matched everything, and this one doctor, this very sharp woman shrink, finally told him it wouldn't work, and then asked him what the hell he thought he was doing. And poor Buddy just couldn't help himself. He smiled and shook his head, like, and then leaned over to her and whispered, 'Well, Doc, I guess if I didn't know that, I'd really be fucked.' "

There was a silence. Mrs. Wilson sat back in her chair and looked at each of us.

"I'm sorry," Penny said. "That's what he told her, though."

"An understandable expression under the circumstances," said Mr. Egan.

"It's not allowed, I guess. I am sorry."

Mrs. Wilson adjusted herself in her chair, apparently having decided to let the moment pass.

"So when they drafted him," Penny went on, "he didn't go at first, and then he did go. And we wrote letters for a few weeks while he was in basic training. But I didn't hear and I didn't hear. And finally I met this — this other guy. I just thought Buddy had found someone else.

But Chummy — you know, his brother — said he got into trouble and was kicked out. And when he came back and found me gone, he sort of went off the deep end. That's what Chummy said. And he got going with these protests about the war. They were burning files in the draft office and the whole office sort of caught fire. They didn't mean for that to happen. Or that's what Chummy said, anyway, after he found me. Finally the FBI came and got him, I guess. They were both in trouble, it looked like, even though Chummy wasn't anywhere near the building and didn't know what was happening. He stayed out of it, mostly. So when they saw for sure he wasn't involved in any of it, they let him go. But it was serious with Buddy and a couple of his friends — I mean — well — they got some serious time."

"And Buddy's not at Wilson Creek," Mrs. Wilson said.

"No. Right."

"What was this train you all met on? Some sort of government transport train for prisoners' families?"

"We just happened to meet," Mother said. "A coincidence — there wasn't anything special about the train."

"That is really quite amazing," Mr. Egan said.

"We thought so," said Penny. "I think it was like fate, because now look, here we are." Her gaze went around the room, as though to gauge the reaction in our faces.

"Well," Mr. Egan said, "I've got to get an early start on the porch in the morning, while it's still cool." He stood with some effort. You could almost hear the bones creaking. "I've got a birthday out in the county, too." He turned to Penny and explained this remark, telling her of his work as a clown.

"I'd like to see you in your costume," she said. "I always loved the clowns when I was small."

"I make a good one," said Mr. Egan.

"When is this birthday party?" Mrs. Wilson wanted to know.

"Afternoon, afternoon. Two o'clock."

"You'll work right up to then?"

"If the weather holds."

"I've got to have this porch done before the cold weather gets here."

"It will be." He stretched and yawned, then shuffled past me into the hallway. "Watch a little TV," he said.

Briefly, I felt as though we were ending one of many nights in the house. I nearly felt at home. Penny Holt got to her feet and began putting coffee cups in the sink. I looked at the shape of her hips in the bright light, and shivered inside.

"I'll take care of all that," Mrs. Wilson said.

"I don't mind."

Mother helped, too. I made my way up to our apartment and into the room where Lisa lay sprawled on the top bunk, one arm dangling over the side. Quietly I undressed and got into the bottom bunk, reached over and turned the light out, then lay there wide awake, hearing Lisa's stertorous breathing, staring at the faint cross-haired patterns of the bottom springs with the small bulge of her weight on them. A few moments later, Mother came in. I heard her say good night to Penny Holt, and then Penny's footsteps sounded on the stairs going up into the top-floor room. The ceiling above me creaked faintly with her weight as she undressed. I thought of those shimmering white pajamas she had worn on the train, and in the next moment Mother walked into the room. She checked Lisa, pulled her blanket up, and when she leaned in to look at me, I said, "I'm awake."

Sitting down on the edge of the thin mattress, she took my hand. "I don't know what to do about tomorrow."

I waited.

"He doesn't want you to see him there."

"Then why did he let us come here?" I said.

She put her hand on my hip. "I know." I could see that she was about to cry.

"Mother?" I said.

"I don't know anything anymore. I wish we'd never done this."

I suppose it was my unreadiness for such an expression of doubt from her, who had with such strength of purpose led us here, but in any case I was filled with a cold dread, perhaps worse than at any time since all our trouble began. I couldn't bring myself to touch her, or say anything to her at all.

"Uprooting everybody," she said. She seemed to be talking to herself now.

"He doesn't want us to see him there and I don't want to see him there," I said.

"I don't even think he wants to see me," she murmured.

"Sure he does," I told her. I had no way of knowing this to be true, of course, except that I had grown up in places where they were in love.

"I don't know whether your sister ought to see him there, even if he decides he wants to see her."

We both listened to Lisa's breathing for a time.

"I think she's too young," I said.

"Maybe," said Mother. Her hands came up to her face and she sat there rubbing her eyes. "Oh. God."

I said, "What?"

She looked at me. "Nothing. Everything."

"I can get a job," I said.

She patted my hip. "Don't be silly."

"It's going to be all right," I told her.

"Go to sleep." She bent down to kiss me on the cheek. Then she stood and ran one hand over the soft strands of hair that had come down over her eye.

"Mother?" I said.

"Go to sleep," she managed, and I knew she was crying, knew it as certainly as I knew she didn't want my consolation, or my notice of the fact. I kept quiet, watching her switch the light off and move out of view. For a long time she was in that small sitting room, quietly unpacking our things, muffling her sobs in one fold of cloth or another among the many she had stuffed into boxes to send west, back there in Virginia, where she must have felt that she was at last taking charge of her own life. I got up and went in to her.

"Honey," she said, "what is it?"

"Let me help," I said.

She sobbed. "You know, he — he looks so sad."

I couldn't speak then.

"Beaten," she said. "Inside."

"He'll be okay." I sensed immediately the emptiness of this. But I couldn't stop myself. I said, "He's been through worse, right?"

"You don't understand," she murmured. Presently she said, "I start work tomorrow. Then I have to get you guys registered for school. I'll drop you two off here and go see him after that. But if he changes his mind, Thomas, I want you to change yours."

"I will," I said. I would've said anything.

PART FOUR

16

IN ASQUAHAWK NOW, my neighbors are having meetings about the Summer Festival, which will be held over the last week of July and the first week of August. Spring has arrived. Soon the sky above the trees beyond my back yard fence will be suffused in the glow of the carnival, and there'll be activity along the boardwalk again. We have had what will probably be our last snowstorm of the year, and the rainy chill of March is giving way at last. This winter has been hard, not a little because I've been laboring to make sense out of all this material from twenty-five years ago. Reading through it, I discover all too often the sort of reportage that might easily leave an impression of a dreadful concentration of misery; and though I have already re-marked upon the ways in which we had begun to grow accustomed to the trouble we were in, it would not be accurate for anyone to suppose that our days were solely made up of the difficulties I've described in such detail, hour by hour. Any more than it would be true to say that, here, in the early dark and brittle cold of winter, in this cottage by the snowing sea, I had spent every waking moment writing.

There are other things to do in Asquahawk. First, I have a bookstore to run, such as it is. When the weather warms up, the flow of traffic increases. My regular customers are more likely to spend part of the day visiting with me after they browse among the shelves, and I always prepare a little coffee and hot tea for the occasion. Most of them have known me since my first days on the island, when I was freshly di-vorced and fairly miserable. My personal history in this place provides some excellent testimony concerning the quiet, unqualified kindness of strangers, and of course many of these kind strangers have become good friends. Consequently, when they stroll into the store with a clearly announced intention not to buy anything but just to sit with me for a spell, I can never bring myself to the point of letting on that just for the time being I'd prefer some solitude. In the good weather, I know that for days at a stretch I'll have trouble acquiring the space and time to think clearly, and so I understand quite well the old complaint of the would-be literary man that he lacks adequate time to work.

This morning I was looking through my journal entries from those first weeks in Wilson Creek. They're strikingly devoid of direct references to what we had all been going through. For example, here is the one for August 29, 1967:

> There's a movie theater down the street. We saw "Father Goose." Lisa fidgeted and I wanted to take her out and leave her in the lobby.

And here's another, from several days later:

> Mrs. Wilson tells us about her husband, and shows us his picture. He was a bit of a cad, really, she says, and then she says she just never will understand the male point of view. It's exactly as if she's giving Mr. Egan hell. The same tone, only quieter. Every Sunday night, like the biggest event of the week around here, the Ed Sullivan Show.

And one more:

> The kids at school are strange. Everybody seems so anxious to make friends. It's embarrassing and I don't know what to tell anyone when they ask. I know I seem surly and not very friendly but can't help myself because when people come up to me like that offering everything too quick it puts me off. The front office people called me in today and told me I had to get my hair cut. Mother got on the phone with them: He has my permission to wear his hair long, and I don't like being dictated to about this sort of thing — it's not shoulder length or anything, and a lot of kids wear it this way. School wouldn't hear of it. Only military cuts. Mother: I'm not in the military and I don't like being forced to behave as though I am. She slammed down the phone. I felt bad for her, for involving her. You have to get a haircut. So now I look like a Nazi soldier. But to tell the real truth I don't mind it. Was getting a little tired of always having it to take care of.

Hardly the words of a young man suffering the alienating effects of a move across the country, though I do recall that everything was suffused in a kind of raw fearfulness much of the time. I simply tried not to let anyone see it, evidently even refraining from expressing it for myself in the journal — and maybe it's true that something essential in our lives is woven out of an awful solitude. The few pictures of Lisa and me that my mother took that fall show no hint of the strain we all were under; on the surface, we had each settled into the stream of things, once more.

The weather had turned cold. Lisa and I were duly registered at our respective schools — mine was the county high school, a sprawling flagstone building which looked like a medieval castle. The architect, we were told, had been a man from Pennsylvania who intended to form a commune in the place, but then decided to donate it to the town for whatever use they could find for it. He had discovered that he wanted to go back east.

I understood the feeling.

We went through the days, and I'm sure we were for long stretches fairly unremarkable, not discernible as being in any difficulty at all. We watched TV, or we read, or we took part in the talk that went on in the house. Whenever the sun was warm we went out into the neighborhood; I tossed the baseball around with Russell and some other boys, or we strolled into town and visited the music and record stores. In those days there were booths in the back of the stores where one could listen to a record before buying it. Russell wanted me to hear a group called the Fugs, who used obscenities in their songs. I listened to them without being much impressed, since the music really wasn't very interesting as music; it was just a pretext for the dirty words, and I told Russell that.

"You know what your problem is?" Russell said. "You think too much."

I was also responsible for Lisa, of course, though Penny Holt, who was paying her way by helping Mrs. Wilson with some of the household tasks and working temporary clerical jobs in the area, sometimes took charge of her, too. They got along wonderfully, better than anyone could've hoped. Mr. Egan — always either made up in his bright clown outfit or draped in his smeared coveralls and splattered with white paint — commented on how alike the two of them were, "Like two peas in a pod," he said. He had developed a teasing proprietary attitude toward Penny, as though she were not much older than Lisa.

One night not long after school began, I heard him making his careful way up the stairs to her room. There was the muffled rapping of his fist on her door, and then it opened. They were moving in the room; it was almost as though they were pacing. I got out of bed and crept to the partition at the opening onto the stairs, where it was just possible to hear that they were talking. Once or twice Mr. Egan laughed, and her voice was like a soft undercurrent to his own. He stayed up there a long time, and I grew sleepy waiting. When he headed down again, the protesting of the stairs startled me. I got back against the partition and listened to them whisper to each other as he descended.

Penny's voice: "Don't wake everybody up."

And Mr. Egan's: "These old steps."

"I think you woke someone up."

"Stop it. You're going to make me laugh."

"You're ripped."

"High comedy."

"Cute."

"Oh, and I am ancient. The Dead Sea was still alive when I was born. I gave Moses the idea for the burning — I gave Moses the — I gave — uh-huh, I —"

Penny (laughing): "Shhhh. Stop it."

Egan: "I'm an ancient old clown with Mexican Christmas in his pocket."

"Shhhhhhhh."

"Can I visit you again?"

"Maybe."

"Shhhhh. I can get more."

Penny (laughing): ". . . wake the whole house."

Egan: "I'm going to fall down."

"Don't fall loud."

"Jesus Christ, it's turning my head around."

"Shhhhhh."

"Good night, sweet princess." He was now right outside our entrance, and she had come partway down.

"The creepiest old stairs," she said. "Maybe the house is haunted."

Then he moved along the hall and stumbled into his room, and she turned and went back up to her own.

The next day I watched them both and could see no sign that anything had happened between them. Mr. Egan maintained the same avuncular, proprietary attitude toward her, which she ignored — or, rather, basked in, the way a child basks in the attention of an adult without seeming to notice it. And again, that night, after everyone was asleep and the house was still, I heard him come out and go up the stairs. This happened the following night as well.

I told no one about it, not even Lisa, and particularly not Russell, though I did grill him about Mr. Egan.

"Where did he come from?"

"I don't know. You think I listen to anything they say? He's just somebody who worked at the prison and doesn't anymore."

We were sitting on the steps in back of the house, in the warm sun there, out of the wind, whose every motion reminded us of the approach of winter.

"How old is he?" I said.

"He told Mom he was fifty-one when he got here, and that was two years ago, so that makes him fifty-three."

"Does he have a family?"

"I think I remember that he has a wife somewhere."

"Does he take dope, or anything like that?"

"*Him?*"

"It's just a question."

"I bet he'd drop dead if he saw the stuff, and so would my mother. Anyway, why're you so curious about him?"

"I was just asking."

"Do *you* smoke dope?"

I looked at him. I didn't want to give the wrong answer, and for some reason I sensed that how I responded was important.

"Well, do you?"

"Sometimes," I lied.

"I've got some. That's what I was showing you that first day, stupid."

I said nothing.

He glanced around us, evidently to make certain we were alone, then stepped closer. "You want some?"

"No," I said. And then, at the look of disappointment and dismissal in his face: "Maybe later."

Presently I said, "Where do you get it?"

"Shit," he said. "Stuff grows wild here."

"You get it wild?"

"No."

"Well, where then?"

"Around."

I didn't ask him any more about it, because I could see that he was beginning to feel pressed by all the questions.

"You want me to see what I can find out about old Lionel Egan?"

"Lionel? That's his first name?"

Russell nodded. "You didn't know that?"

"Lionel Egan," I said.

"Does it sound familiar?"

"No," I said.

"You made it sound like you'd heard it before."

"I never heard it before in my life," I said.

"Well, that's his name," said Russell.

"Wonder where he got the clown act?"

"You should see him do it."

"Is he any good?"

"Embarrassing."

I thought of Mr. Egan standing in the scornful laughter of children, and couldn't make the image come clear in my mind. He was, after all, the man sneaking up the stairs to Penny Holt's room each night. And I had begun to believe I heard her voice whispering in my sleep.

It *was* each night, too. I took to waiting up, listening for them. When I first heard his door open, I would scurry out of bed and sneak to the partition, crouch there, and try to make out what I could. His clumsy progress on the stairs would be followed by the sound of his small rap on her door. The door would open. I couldn't distinguish what she said to him, though I tried. After the door closed, I heard muffled laughs, bumpings, croonings, sometimes the strains of guitar music. And later he would come back down, always shushing her and trying not to laugh, and always being admonished by her that he ought not to wake the whole house.

One night I was crouched there, listening, and Mother spoke from behind me. "Thomas?"

I almost cried out as I turned, gasping, my back against the wood of the partition.

She was standing in the entrance to her room. "What're you doing there?"

I got to my feet, shaking, half naked, in my Jockey shorts.

"Huh?" I said. "What?"

"Thomas?"

I said nothing.

"Hey," she said, approaching me. "Do you know who you are? Say your name." And I received the pleasant little shock of understanding that she thought I was sleepwalking.

"Yes," I said.

"Tell me. Say your name."

"Gene Autry," I had the presence of mind to say.

She took my shoulders and led me back in to my bed. "Do you have to go to the bathroom?"

"Bathroom," I said.

"Well do you?"

"No."

"Are you awake now? Thomas, are you joking with me?"

"What is it?" I said.

I crawled into bed and she pulled the blanket over me, then kissed the side of my face. "Sleep," she said, caressing my forehead. "It's all right."

The following morning at breakfast, she told everyone that I had walked in my sleep the night before.

"Well, that explains the noises I've been hearing," Mrs. Wilson said.

"He's never sleepwalked before," Mother said.

"It's just the change in surroundings," said Lionel Egan, looking at Penny and then looking away. "I've seen it happen before."

"I've heard it's dangerous to wake them up," said Mrs. Wilson.

"I think that's right."

"Well, I didn't wake him," Mother said.

"I don't remember anything," I put in.

"That's true, too," said Mrs. Wilson, who then seemed vaguely puzzled by her own words.

Though I was constantly looking at images of Penny in my mind, I found it very hard to look directly at her, knowing what I knew, and when she was near, my strongest impulse was to remove myself. I felt much the same way around Mr. Egan, too. Twice he asked me if I wanted to come along with him for one of his clown shows. I couldn't refuse him quickly enough. The second time, as we stood out on the unfinished porch, he gave me a look. "Do I scare you, kid?"

"No," I said.

"You seem nervous around me."

"No, sir."

"Maybe you're just a nervous-type kid."

Russell was there, too, and we both watched as Mr. Egan got into his car and drove away.

"Ever see his room?" Russell said.

"Just from the open door when he comes out sometimes."

"No, I mean the stuff he has *in* his room."

I thought for a second that Russell was talking about dope. "No," I told him.

"Weird stuff. From all over the world. You know, shrunken heads and native spears and shit like that."

"I haven't seen it," I said.

"Lot of weird shit."

"Did he show it to you?"

"Hell, no. He wouldn't do that, no. I saw it when Mom went in there one time, looking for more dirty movies."

"Did you see any of the dirty movie?" I asked.

He smirked. "Yeah. Right. In *this* house."

In the next moment, something else occurred to me. "Your mother snuck into his room?"

"She has a key to every room in the house."

"Did she find anything?"

"Nah."

"Could *we* get into his room?"

"I did that sort of thing once," Russell said. "I got caught. Never again."

Later that day, when Mr. Egan came home, I managed to head myself in the direction of our apartment as he was going to his room. I came partway to his door, trying to think of something to say to him, and he turned to face me.

"Did you want something?"

"Nothing."

"What do you want, kid?"

"Nothing," I said.

He shrugged and went on. When he opened the door he looked back at me again. "Anything?"

Again I said, "Nothing."

"Okay, so quit staring. It's spooky."

"Yes, sir."

"Jesus," he said. "Did your father teach you that?"

I didn't understand what he meant.

"No, I'll bet it was your mother."

I said, "I wasn't staring."

"No," he said. "That 'sir' shit."

I let this stand.

And now he nodded, as if deciding, and spoke to himself: "The mother. Without a doubt." He went into the room and closed the door.

When I started down the stairs, Penny was there. "Oh," she said, stepping around me. "I'm sorry."

"No," I said. "My fault."

She paused. We were face to face. I had never been so close to her, and I felt my heart pounding in the bones of my jaw. "I get these terrible headaches," she said.

I said, "I'm sorry."

"Sweet. You're sweet."

"Thank you," I managed.

"Good," she said, then smiled.

It struck me like a bolt of electricity that I was being dismissed. I almost tumbled down the stairs to get away, and I heard her voice, simply greeting someone, Mother or Lisa, it was hard to tell. She had already forgotten me. Outside on the porch, Russell was tearing a sheet of shingle up and sailing the pieces into the street.

"What's the matter with you?" he said. "You seen a ghost or something?"

"I don't know what you're talking about," I said.

"Okay."

"Well, I don't."

He shook his head.

"Where'd you get that?" I said, indicating the shingle.

"It was laying in the yard."

I couldn't quite catch my breath.

"Man, what is it with you?"

"Nothing."

Mr. Egan came out then, wearing his painting clothes. A dab of the clown makeup remained on the side of his face, like a place where he had cut himself shaving. "Look at the mess you're making," he said to Russell. "Who's going to clean that up?"

"Aw, save your breath," Russell said, stepping down off the porch. "I'll get it."

Now Mr. Egan and I watched him go out into the street to retrieve the pieces of shingle.

"I wouldn't go around with that kid if I were you," Mr. Egan said.

I went inside without answering him.

He worked on the porch during the warmer hours of each day, but it was becoming clearer all the time that he wouldn't finish the job before real winter set in. Mornings now, a thin frost showed on the ground, like a scintillate coat of the paint with which he was trying to cover the porch. Each night, I heard him make his way up to Penny's room, and I lay awake until he came back down. I was burning with imagining what they were doing up there, and all the next day I forgot other things, thinking about the vigil I would keep that night.

We did not go to the prison, and though Mother went almost every day, it began to seem that Father was away on one of his tours of duty. She brought us news of him: he was healthy, his attitude seemed better. He appeared somewhat more relaxed. I think of her now, sitting in the big room with him, holding his hands across the table, trying to recognize him, trying to gain back something of the old feeling for him.

I read somewhere that the collapse of whole civilizations probably happened without the particular knowledge of anyone involved: those thousands of people going on with things while life as they knew it disappeared forever, everybody going on anyway, in the belief — the necessary conviction — that nothing unusual is taking place.

And doubtless it is less than original to say here that a marriage is civilization in miniature.

The walls were crumbling. And my father sensed it.

Sometimes he phoned the house to say hello to us, and it was like all the times when he'd called us from some other country, some other place where people valued him for his qualities, for one version or another of the things usually listed in his yearly evaluations while he was in the Air Force, those bloated accounts of virtue that he would read to Mother aloud, the two of them laughing at it all, at the distance between the descriptions and the realities, and my father would hold up the report and say, "In short, I'm an honest-to-God saint." And they'd both laugh. "Think they'll promote me?" he'd say.

And Mother would nod. "How could they not promote you?"

"Easy," he'd say, "I think they've got one of the other guys as actually being God himself."

"Can't get promoted over God," Mother would say, and they'd laugh again.

But now there was not much laughter when he called. Whenever he spoke to me, he would ask about Mother. "Is she taking care of herself? Is she getting enough rest? She looks tired to me, son. Have you noticed that she's tired a lot?"

"No," I'd say. "We're just all busy."

"Does she get out at all except to go to work, or see me?"

"We're fine," I'd say.

Once he said, "Son, you know if she has any kind of social life?" and in his voice I had heard a quiet and quite helpless faltering that made me want to shout at him.

"She and Penny go to the movies once in a while," I said. "Nothing else."

"Nothing else at all? There's nobody she's made friends with at work?"

"I think they're mostly older women."

"Nobody she can just be herself with?"

"She's fine. She has a good time with Penny."

"And she gets out to a movie now and then?"

"Right."

After a pause, he cleared his throat and said, "They show movies *here* now. All a couple of years behind."

I was silent.

"Is Penny nice?"

"Yes," I said.

"Are you taking care of your mother and sister like I asked you to?" This was something he asked me every time we talked.

"Yes, sir," I said, and I'm afraid I didn't do a very good job of getting the boredom out of my voice.

"Thomas, I'm sorry. There's not much to think about in here."

"I know," I said.

"I take that back," he said. "There's too much to think about."

"I'm watching out for them both," I told him.

"Good."

"Well," I said. "Lisa wants to talk to you."

Lisa would be standing there shaking her head, and Mother would push her gently from the back, forcing her to the phone.

"Hi, Daddy," Lisa would say, sounding younger than she ever did talking to me or to Mother, or to anyone else for that matter.

The rooms of Mrs. Wilson's house had begun to seem familiar. Things were happening at school which for a short while occupied my attention: Russell had let everyone know that Father was in the pen — his expression — and though there was less curiosity than you might imagine (the prison was, after all, one of the central establishments of the town), I still felt badly singled out. And when, each afternoon, Mother pulled in front of the school to drive me home, I was somehow ashamed of her. The hot anger at myself which resulted from this feeling did not prevent me from hurrying into the car and urging her to pull away as though I were being chased. She never said anything about this, and yet I'm fairly certain she understood what was going on: it was like her not to want to make things any worse than they were.

The weather had grown cold, and in mid-September the first snowfall hit. A storm deposited six inches on the ground in less than an hour, then moved off, leaving a bright icy day in its wake. At the same time, the news was full of war protests in St. Louis, Chicago, Detroit, and other cities. That afternoon, when the first reports came in, Penny Holt paced and muttered to herself, her hands deep in the pockets of her jeans. "They won't get away with it," she said. "This is supposed to be a democracy."

Mr. Egan had been painting the porch, wearing a thick parka, now spattered and smeared, which he had left heaped in a furry pile by the front door. "No, they won't get away with it," he said. "They'll pay a fine for disturbing the peace."

"Who?"

"Uh, these — well, these people —" he stammered.

"Agitators and communists," Mrs. Wilson said.

"You don't have to be a communist to hate that war," said Penny.

"What I say is, 'America, love it or leave it.'"

"How does that translate into killing people in Asia?"

"Your country knows what's best. And I can tell you right now, I won't have a communist in my house."

"I'm not a communist, Mrs. Wilson — how can you say I'm a communist?"

"Because you're against the war."

Mr. Egan, I saw, was looking at them each in turn with a stricken, beleaguered expression. I thought he might begin pleading with them to change the subject.

"I know when someone's betraying my country," Mrs. Wilson went on. "I don't need to know anything else about them. They might as well be communists if they aren't."

"I'm not a communist," Penny said. She stared at the television, her thin arms folded tight under her breasts. My fascination with her had reached a point bordering on pathology, especially since Mr. Egan's traversings of the stairs seemed to have stopped: I had begun spying on her during the days now. Russell was with me in this, too, though it was not the same with him. At least I don't think it was. I believe his curiosity must have been somehow healthier.

"I think everyone should get along," Mr. Egan said now.

I sat on the sofa and watched Penny's beautiful one eye grow narrow with anger, and with something else, too.

"All right, one doesn't have to be communist to be against the war,"

Mrs. Wilson said. "Of course, the thing about this country is that you're free to say anything you like. And it doesn't cost you a thing to help the communists by agitating against the war. And helping them is what you're doing. Nixon said as much on the news the other night. He said these protests help the communists."

Penny looked at her, and then, to my surprise, indicated me. "This young man's father is in jail because he disagrees with the war, and it's cost him everything."

Mrs. Wilson glanced at me, and I looked down.

"Nixon," Penny went on. "Jesus God. The only man in the country worse than Johnson."

"I won't discuss it anymore," said Mrs. Wilson. "I have my beliefs and I can't help them. But I certainly didn't mean to hurt any feelings."

"Well," Mr. Egan said, "one thing I promised myself never to do anymore, and that's argue politics. I think that's the best policy."

"That's what's wrong," Penny said. "People are dying or going to jail and you don't want to argue politics."

Mr. Egan's features seemed about to disarrange themselves. "You're absolutely right, there," he managed. "It's a terrible thing."

The news had gone on to the weather, the threat of more snow. Another storm was staggering toward us over the Rockies.

Mrs. Wilson went out to Food Mart and returned with five bags of groceries. Russell and I brought them in. The sky to the west was a strange violet color I'd never seen before.

"It's going to blow like hell in a few hours," Russell said.

We stood gazing at it.

"Your father really go to prison for protesting the war?" he said.

I looked at him. "He went," I said. "He was in prison *over there* — a POW — for thirteen months."

"Jesus."

I put my hands in my pockets and shivered.

"So they put him in jail over *here?*" Russell said.

"This is another thing," I said.

"Bad?"

I nodded.

"He was protesting the war?"

Again, I nodded.

He said nothing for a few moments. He was turning it all over in his mind.

"I don't like to talk about it," I said.

"Damn," he muttered. "That eats it."

The air stung my face. "I'm cold," I said.

"Shit," he said, "you ain't seen nothing."

Of course between the two of us, he was the one telling the truth.

The first real storm swept over us a few hours later — less snow this time, but the blast of arctic air that carried it was like something stripping away all the world's warmth. It was as if the sun had died at the very rim of the sky, and was now nothing more than a dead gray disk, barely visible through the cloud cover.

The snow blew like desert sand throughout the night, roiling under the streetlamps so you couldn't tell whether it still came from the sky or was being kicked up from the ground. I felt it all like an inner chill, since I knew the difference between what Penny Holt — and now Russell Wilson — thought about us and what the real story was.

Late the next evening, I spoke with Mother about it. "Penny thinks Father went to prison for protesting the war," I said. "I let Russell think so, too."

She looked at me as if I'd coughed or sneezed or dropped something, then she looked away. She was lying on her side in bed, propped on one elbow with a magazine open in front of her. She had been taking magazines over to the prison for Father to read, and she would look through them first, wanting, I realized much later, to have something to talk about.

"Did you hear me?" I said.

She said, "Keep it down."

"Well?"

She looked toward the open door, beyond which, in our room, Lisa lay in the dimness, trying to go to sleep. "Lisa?" she said.

Nothing.

"Mrs. Wilson was talking about communists —" I began.

And she put one finger up to her lips. There was a creaking on the stairs. Mr. Egan again, making his slow progress up to Penny's room. It was all I could do to keep the recognition from bursting out of me in words. Mother looked at me in that cool, measuring way she sometimes had. We waited. We heard a knock at Penny's door, and Mr. Egan's voice, low. It was impossible to separate the words, but there was a pleading in them. In another moment, the stairs creaked again, and he was on his way down. His door opened and closed. When it was quiet, Mother said, "I hate this house."

I was quiet.

"So," she said. "go on. Mrs. Wilson was talking about communists."

"Right," I said. "And I didn't know what to say. I was afraid she'd ask me something about it."

"Tell me what happened."

I repeated the scene of the previous afternoon as best I could, and she kept signaling for me to speak more quietly. Twice we stopped to listen for movement outside on the landing.

"Well, just let it alone for now," she said when I had finished.

"What if I can't?"

"Look," she said. "Your father's a veteran. He served over there and was decorated, and they treated him terribly, and he doesn't owe them one single solitary thing."

I couldn't quite understand this, and she saw it in my face.

"Let people think what they want."

Neither of us spoke for a time.

"So," she said finally.

"Okay," I said.

"It's not what you think, Thomas."

I didn't say anything.

"I can't help what people assume about us."

"No," I said.

"Well, your father knows about it, too."

Again, I was quiet.

"Maybe there's going to be some changes," she said, then seemed to catch herself up.

I waited.

"Don't look at me like that."

"What changes?"

She shook her head slightly. "Why don't you go on down and watch some TV or something."

"What changes?"

Now she sighed. "I don't know yet."

"Is he coming home?"

"Home," she said incredulously.

"Here," I said.

"We'll talk about it."

"Is he?"

She said, "I don't really know any more than you do, you know."

"You go over there every day."

"I just sit in a room with him."

"Well, what were you talking about?" I said. "These changes?"

"We've already been through a lot, haven't we?"

"Is that what you meant?"

"Look," she said, "I'm tired. I wish I hadn't opened my mouth."

"Just tell me," I said. "You can tell me."

"It's almost six months," she said. "He'll be eligible to get out on parole after that."

"Right after?"

"That's what I don't know."

"Will he come here?"

She looked down at her magazine. "Of course."

"Then what?" I said.

Turning a page, she seemed not to have heard me.

"Then what?"

"Then we'll have to make some changes." Her eyes were swimming.

"Will we go back to Minot?"

"Thomas, I don't want to talk about all this now. It hasn't even happened yet. It's not even sure yet."

"You sound like you don't want it to happen," I told her. I had spoken before I'd had the chance to think. It had simply come out of me, and now that it had, I was not sorry. I wanted to know what was going on in her mind.

For a moment she was silent, still turning the pages of the magazine. Then she looked at me and seemed about to smile. "I can't believe you would say a thing like that to me," she said. "Get out."

"I didn't say anything," I insisted. "I'm just trying to understand."

"Go," she said. "I'm tired of talking. I've had enough of talking. I don't want any, any, any more talk. Please, Thomas."

I went into the sitting room, then on through to our bedroom, where

Lisa lay with her arms clasped behind her head, staring at the under-side of my bunk. The house was quiet. Even Mr. Egan's TV had stopped. In the other room, Mother was making up her bed. I got undressed; I didn't want any more talk, either. Crawling into the top bunk, I lay on my stomach, listening to the small sounds she made — little murmurs of distress, a throaty cough.

"Thomas," Lisa said.

"Go to sleep," I told her.

We didn't exchange another word that night.

The storms kept coming, one after another, and the wind-driven, sculpted snow was as high as the downstairs windows. No one could go anywhere. On the news they had begun advising people not to go out without attaching themselves by a rope to their houses: a man north of the town had stepped out to take a bag of garbage to the end of his driveway, just in case anyone should be able to get around to collecting it, and on the way back to his house he had got confused and disoriented, lost in the dense swirling whiteness. He wandered in a small circle for crucial minutes, and by the time anyone got to him, he had lain down and was nearly dead. His wife and son dragged him back inside, where he remained in a shallow coma for several hours before regaining consciousness. Mr. Egan knew these people from his prison job, and spoke briefly to the wife over the phone after we saw the television report. He told us later that, according to the wife, when her husband awoke he looked around and said, "I thought some son of a bitch had moved the damn house."

We all laughed, even as Mrs. Wilson's dour expression turned from Mr. Egan to us and back again.

"Hey," Mr. Egan said to her, "it's the truth, Mabel." Then he turned to Penny. "Imagine it," he said. "Poor guy really thought somebody moved his house. I mean, I know him. He's not the kind of man who makes a joke."

"It's funny," Mother said.

He was still looking at Penny. "I never could figure a man without a sense of humor."

"No," Penny said. "It's true."

Mr. Egan's face brightened, and he seemed to expand from inside.

"Egan's got the hots for your mother's friend," Russell said when we had got out to the back part of the house — the sealed porch with its storm windows and doors, its look of a buried snow cave. "And so do I."

"He's way too old for her," I said. And I almost told him about the nocturnal goings-on of the two of them.

"I seen it happen with older guys than him," Russell said.

In the middle of the night, I woke believing I had heard the sound on the stairs to Penny's room. I lay absolutely still, trying to hear. She was playing music; the faintest drumbeat came through the ceiling. But I couldn't be sure she was with someone, anyone.

17

BEFORE THE END of that week, the cars parked along the street were nothing but a row of mounds in the blinding windswept dust of snow. We passed the time sitting in Mrs. Wilson's living room, watching her big RCA television, news coverage of the onset of winter. The wind howled all day at the windows and doors like something inimical trying to gain entry, and Mrs. Wilson asked that we keep only one light on per floor of the house, in order to conserve energy. Naturally, she wanted us all in one room as much as possible. The electric bill in the cold weather was beyond belief, she said. Mr. Egan shuffled in his slippers from room to room of the ill-lighted downstairs, clearly depressed: he'd missed three performances as a clown, and now the front porch would remain unfinished.

But there was something else bothering him, too, and I knew what it was. Whenever he came near Penny, she seemed actually to shrink — and her interest, her attention, went immediately elsewhere. Once I saw her get up and cross the room to keep from having him next to her on the sofa. He sat down slowly, paying a sort of theatrical attention to the throw pillow he had displaced, seeming not to notice what had happened; but his face was white. There may have also been the fact that he had intuited the true precariousness of his position in Mrs. Wilson's eyes, for just as Penny seemed to avoid him, he appeared anxious to keep out of Mrs. Wilson's way while still trying to make himself useful. He got a fire going and tended it, and as the number of logs ran down, he bundled up and went out for more. Mrs. Wilson seemed to monitor him, like one of those censorious study-hall proctors I knew at school. She sat in a corner of the living room with her hands neatly clasped at her waist, watching his every move. Her son lay on the floor in front of the chatter and flicker of TV, two fingers in his violet-colored mouth. I have an image of Mother and Penny sitting next to each other on the floor by the fire, talking in whispers like a couple of schoolgirls, and of Lisa arranged languidly near them, with a pad of paper open on her lap, trying to draw a face. It seems to me now that we spent several days like that, as if we were all waiting for the same thing.

This was when Mother and Penny began the friendship which was to count so heavily in our lives during the time we lived in Wilson Creek. Though Penny was perhaps twelve years younger, they had begun to discover that they had a lot of temperamental things in common. They liked the same kinds of books, the same movies and television shows. Penny had spent time as a teenager in Minnesota, where the winters were long and difficult, and like Mother she had developed an interest in ice skating and other winter sports. The same things made them laugh. Evidently Mother had told her some things about Grandfather Tinan, because when he phoned to say hello to us, she made a rueful face for Penny, and spoke to him with the other woman sitting there smiling knowingly at her. She even rolled her eyes at the ceiling. "We're all fine," she said into the phone. "You shouldn't spend any time worrying about us."

When I spoke to him, and to Aunt Elaine, I took pains to be pleasant, to let them know how much I missed them, and the big white house in Minot.

"You sound good," Grandfather Tinan said. "Your voice is lower, and richer — a nice baritone. I'll bet you've gotten even taller since I saw you."

"I don't think so, sir," I told him.

"How's school?"

"Just fine," I said, and then added, "I'd sure like to go get ice cream with you again."

"Pardon?" he said.

I repeated it.

"Ice cream," he said.

"We went to get ice cream for everybody."

"You did?"

"*We* did," I said. "You and me."

"Oh," he said. "Sure, I remember now." And it was quite obvious from his tone that he hadn't remembered at all.

"Remember," I said, not wanting to have to press it but finding myself doing so anyway, "that kid who was rude to us?"

"Oh," he said. "Oh, that. Right."

"It was fun," I told him.

"Yes, it was," he said uncertainly. And I let it alone, sick at heart. I was beginning to think there were separate organs of perception in the adult world I was about to enter and in the world where I still lived. Perhaps when I was older, I would remember with a different part of my mind, and the stream of my living wouldn't permit certain kinds of recollection.

"You been to see your father yet?" he wanted to know.

"No, sir."

"Well, maybe it's for the best."

"He's getting out soon."

"So I hear. Listen, I know I brought it up, but what do you say we talk about something else?"

"Okay," I said.

"You playing any baseball?"

"A little."

There was a pause.

"I got my hair cut," I told him.

"Good. That's good. You like it?"

"Too short," I said. "You know?"

"Well, one thing — it'll grow."

"Right," I said. "How about you?"

"Me?"

"You get yours cut?"

"Not recently." He seemed genuinely puzzled now. "Well, I better put Elaine on, to talk to your mother."

"Yes, sir," I said.

Mother talked a little about the six-month mark of Father's sentence being almost up, and then seemed to evade what must've been Aunt

Elaine's questions as to what we would do when the time came for him to return to us. "I'll let you know," she said, "just as soon as I know anything at all."

When she hung up, she went into the kitchen with Penny, to sit in its watery light and talk.

This was a Saturday.

That evening they watched a movie, and when it was over and Mother said good night, I followed her up to the door of her room and waited for her to notice me. She was taking the sheets off her bed, sighing, moving slowly. Finally she glanced over her shoulder and said, "Thomas, whatever it is, I'm tired."

"It was nice talking to Grandfather Tinan," I said.

She nodded. "Go on to bed, son."

"I miss him," I told her.

"Me too."

"What were you making faces with Penny for?"

"What was I — what?"

"When you were talking to him. You made a face."

She sighed. "Thomas, I'm sorry, but I can't account for every single minute of my day. I don't remember making any face."

"I was just curious."

"In what way? How could you be curious about a facial expression?"

"I don't know," I said. "It was like you were making fun of him."

"Oh, God," she said to the ceiling. "Go to bed, Thomas. No one is making fun of anyone. I promise."

"You like Penny," I said.

She merely stared now. "Yes?"

"You've talked about Grandfather Tinan."

"I haven't been keeping track."

"I just didn't like it," I said. "It made me feel funny. Like you were laughing at him behind his back."

"All right, if he calls again I'll go into a closet and shut the door. Now good night."

"I'm sorry," I said, barely able to control my voice. I thought I might begin to cry, and I turned away.

"Wait," she said, and moved to put her arms on my shoulders.

"Baby," she said, "I know you want so badly to keep everything as it always was."

I said nothing. I had a sense that she had seen right through me.

"I'm trying to keep it, too," she said, and kissed me on the forehead. "Okay?"

"Yes, ma'am," I said.

She smiled, but her eyes were all sorrow. "Maybe between us both — " She touched the side of my face. "Don't you like Penny?"

"Oh," I said. "I — oh, I like her —"

"Isn't there room for us to have friends?"

I nodded, and couldn't find the next thing to say.

"She's somebody I can talk to, honey."

"Yes," I said.

"And believe me, I'm not making fun of anybody."

"All right," I told her. I didn't want her to go on. It was as though my own feelings about Penny would come bursting forth if we said anything else.

She kissed my forehead again, then released me. "Now go."

"Good night," I said. "I love you."

"Me too, you." Her hands fluttered in front of her face. "You'll make me cry if you say another thing."

By Monday the sun was out, the plows had come through, the owners of the buried cars had gone out into the brightness and excavated them, and the town went on with business as usual, even though the sides of the streets were now lined by high, sheer canyons of encrusted snow. We went to school. We had three weeks of indoor activity, none of which is worthy of mention here, except to say that I could think of nothing else but Penny Holt. Most afternoons I sat in the downstairs living room, on the floor, while the television roared with Russell's cartoons and cowboy shows, pretending to concentrate on the homework in my lap but watching the women furtively — or I should say watching Penny. I watched her as she cleared the dining room table and waxed it, or polished Mrs. Wilson's silver tea set, or ran the vacuum, or dusted the surfaces around us. Sometimes I thought of asking her if I could do anything to help, wanting to ingratiate myself with her. And yet she continued to frighten me, too. Poor Mr. Egan seemed more and more distracted each day, more and more unable to keep still. My impression was that he had somehow got too close to her and then been rendered this way, turned into the hunched, discouraged figure I was always coming face to face with in the doorways of the house, as I sought reasons to be near Penny.

Remember, I was only seventeen.

Often when I could steal time alone in that little room Lisa and I shared in such mutual neglect of each other, I would lie in the tangled sheets of the bunk bed and think of Penny, of the smooth curve of her calves, her amazing skin, the soft down on her slender arms, her strangely beautiful face, her full murmurous voice. I would imagine myself climbing the stairs to her room at night, furtive, bearing some exotic substance which she craved and for which she would tolerate even the likes of me, and my whole body felt as though it might lift from the mattress and float away toward the ceiling. In school I lost track of entire blocks of time, daydreaming about her, seeing her in fantasies of crazy invention, as if my thoughts had been deranged by proximity to her; and the young girls whose society I might ordinarily have been seeking between and during classes seemed shallow and pallid by comparison, even the most charming of them.

"Oh, save me," Russell said one day as we stood on the closed back porch and watched her through the kitchen window. She was doing the dishes. "Look at those tits."

"Cut it out," I told him.

"But look at them," he said.

"You better shut up, Russell."

He grew more animated. "Oh, what's this, the movie about the young man defending the honor of his lady love from the low-talking villain?"

"Just quit it," I said.

He said, "Up yours. You think she gives a shit what either of us thinks?"

I didn't say anything to this.

"They don't give a shit what we think."

"Who?" I said.

"Girls," he said. "What do you think? Women." Then he walked off the porch and out into the yard, going on in the direction of the prison.

"Where're you going?" I said.

"None of your business."

I let him go. I went inside and into the living room, where Mr. Egan sat muttering about the weather, the lack of money, the paucity of things to do in Wilson Creek. "You know what cabin fever is?" he said to me.

"Guess so," I told him.

"I got it. I hate the cold weather. It's too early for it. You can't do anything outside except ski, and I hate skiing." He went off to his room.

Later that evening he showed up for dinner in his clown costume.

"What in the world?" Mrs. Wilson said. "You *couldn't* have a party on a Wednesday night."

"No," he said. "I'm just trying to feel a little different today."

"I wouldn't want to feel different," Penny said.

I looked across the table at my mother, who was watching Mr. Egan, her hands folded under her chin.

"I'm happy for you, Penny," Mr. Egan said. "Some people are satisfied with themselves as they are, that is true. It's an undeniable fact. And then there're also people who have to live with certain other facts." These words, spoken with such gravity, were unexpectedly comical. I could feel the effort to suppress laughter at the table, and then Penny did laugh.

Mr. Egan stood suddenly.

"I didn't mean anything," Penny said. "Come on."

"Do you think I'm amusing?" he demanded.

"You look funny. Aren't you made up to look funny? Isn't that the effect you want?"

"You can laugh at someone's suffering!" Mr. Egan's voice broke. "That's entertaining to you."

"I wasn't laughing at any suffering."

"Mr. Egan," Mother said, "you have your clown outfit on."

"I am aware how I'm dressed."

"All right," Mother said, growing impatient. "And what you said sounded just a little absurd coming from a face with a red ball for a nose."

"Perhaps you'll excuse me," he said, rising with exaggerated punctilio — I'm tempted to say the kind that one associates with clowns. He left the table.

"That man looks at dirty films," Mrs. Wilson said under her breath, as if by way of explanation.

When dinner was over, we watched television for a while. I had a lot of homework I was neglecting, and finally I excused myself and went upstairs to do what I could of it. I did my schoolwork at the small table in our sitting room. I hadn't been there more than a minute before Mother came in and put her hand on my shoulder. "I don't think I want Lisa to know yet," she said. "She's got enough trouble understanding all this, and time is such a big thing to kids that young — "

I waited. There was the slightest pressure of her fingers on my shoulder.

"Your father's coming home."

"Mom?" I said.

She nodded.

"When?" I said.

"Well, we don't know exactly when. But it's official now. It's only a matter of a few weeks now. And it could even be sooner."

I stood.

"Don't now — really. You can't say anything yet. I think I want to wait until I have a definite time before we tell Lisa."

"All right," I said.

"Oh, Thomas," she said, "there's so much that has to be straightened out."

I thought she was going to say more. But then she turned and left me there. And she didn't come back upstairs until well after Lisa and I had gone to bed.

The following morning as I was starting down for breakfast, I heard something I thought was a creaking in the hallway, and when I stopped to listen for it again, I realized that it was a human sound. It was coming from behind Mr. Egan's door. I thought everyone was downstairs, thought I had heard him come out and go down long ago. So I assumed his television was on. I went to the door, thinking that I would just step in and turn it off, and of course I was rationalizing a wish to look at his room, with its equipment for magic and its assortment of odd collectibles that I had indeed managed, over the past few weeks, to catch glimpses of as he came out or went in. I had seen an old flintlock musket and what looked like the spear of an African king — the thing Russell had spoken of — hung with strange black feathers; I had spied the head of a lion carved in bronze, and noticed a bow and hunting arrows on the wall. None of these things seemed important enough to him that he would mention them to us or talk to us about them — though I had recently witnessed him trying to explain to Mother the manly excitement of hunting with bow and arrow. He'd stood in the dining room with his hands out in front of him like someone clutching at air, his gut hanging over the top of his pants — it gave the lie to his every word — and he'd frowned, staring off at the imaginary quarry, and said with great drama, "You can't see your prey. You've been following spore only. But then, when the time is right, you close on the animal. You know he's there."

Now I tried the knob on his door and it gave, so I opened it, being careful, being stealthy, turning once, glancing back at the landing to be sure I wasn't watched. I stepped quietly into the room — and came face to face with Mr. Egan.

He was sitting on the edge of his bed, and I could see at once that he had been in some sort of distress. He wore none of the clown makeup, but his face was pasty white.

"What do you want," he said, nearly shouting. "Who do you think you are, walking in here."

"I didn't know —" I stammered, starting to back out.

He grabbed my wrist. "Wait a minute. What were you going to steal from me? You were going to steal from me, weren't you."

"It's a mistake," I said. "I thought your television was on."

"It is," he said, indicating a corner of the room where the small portable sat among icons from far-off places, shapes I had never seen before. On the screen, a round-faced man was reading the news; behind him was a big representation of a fighter plane flying through an explosion shaped like a star.

"I thought you were downstairs," I said.

"No. I'm upstairs. See? Upstairs, sitting here right before your eyes."

I said, "Yes, sir."

"I'm sitting here in the privacy of my room and you sneak in. I watched you sneak in here, boy."

"No, sir," I told him. "I thought your TV was on. I was just going to shut it off."

"You were going to sneak in here and turn it off. You were sneaking. I saw you."

I could think of nothing else to say.

"You're still just a kid, though. Kids sneak, don't they."

"I was going to turn the television off. Maybe look at some of these" — I indicated the room — "things."

"Your father's a thief," he said, sniffling, "isn't he."

I stared at him.

"Don't pretend with me. I know people at the prison. I was a guard there for a while, remember?"

"I'm not pretending," I said.

"So you've had to live with disrespect."

"No," I said.

"You've never had to live with disrespect?" he said.

I stood there with his hand closed tight on my wrist.

"You really haven't?"

"I don't know what you mean."

"I mean you've never had to live with disrespect."

"No, sir." It seemed what he wanted me to say.

He swallowed. "Ah. Christ. Don't call me sir."

"I'm sorry."

"You don't mean it, so why do it."

"I mean it. It's what I was taught."

He let go of me, then put both hands to his head. "Get out. Go on, get out."

"I was going to turn the television off for you," I told him. "I thought I heard the television."

"Shut it off," he said.

I did so, then waited.

"Shit," he said.

"I didn't mean any disrespect," I told him.

"You don't live with it."

"Sir?" I said.

He looked at me. "You got a girlfriend?"

"No."

"Why not?"

I shrugged.

"You like girls?"

"Yes, sir."

"Really like them?"

"Yes."

"I see the way you look at *her*."

"Who?"

"Show me the respect of not pretending you don't look at her, son."

I said nothing.

"You think she's beautiful, huh?"

"Yes."

"She walks in your dreams." His facial expression now was almost wild, as though he might begin screaming any second. "She walks in beauty, in your sleep. Huh?"

I nodded.

"Yeah. Me, too." He put his hands on his knees and sighed. "She talks to you, doesn't she? Does she talk to you? When I'm not there, I mean. It's all a game, isn't it?"

"Mr. Egan," I said, "let's go downstairs."

"You think I'm crazy, don't you."

I thought I shook my head.

"Don't stand there and stare at me. You think I'm crazy — go on and admit it."

"No," I said.

"Well, I *am* crazy." Then he whispered. "She let me into her room. She led me to believe certain things. You know what I'm talking about? She let me hold her —" He breathed, seemed almost to gasp, then sobbed. "Jesus. I never felt that way. I was a gentleman, like she wanted me to be — but she led me to believe it would — she played me for a sucker."

Presently he said, "You ever drink anything but that sweet stuff?"

"Sometimes," I said out of the pure pressure to speak.

"Hate the sweet stuff."

"Well," I said. I wanted to leave.

Again, he whispered. "She led me on. I never pushed myself on her. We were — it was perfectly friendly. I'm not a young man anymore, I know that. I told her that. Someday you'll understand what I'm trying to tell you, boy. It'll come clear to you. I'm a nice man. I am. I'm a thoughtful, nice man. I make little kids laugh. You should — you should see them laugh." He seemed to have forgotten for the moment what else he meant to say to me. "You ever see a flintlock rifle before?"

"No, sir."

"You're embarrassed, huh."

I didn't say anything.

"Embarrassed?"

"Mr. Egan —" I said.

"You think I'm an old closet queen or something?"

I hadn't heard the term. I said, "No, sir."

"Sure you do. That's what *she* thought."

"No," I said.

"How do you know that? If you haven't talked about me, huh? How do you know?"

"I just — sir, I thought you were downstairs and I was going to turn your television off for you. I don't know about any of this."

"You did that. You turned the television off."

"Yes, sir."

"You think I'm drunk now, don't you. At nine o'clock in the morning."

"I don't think anything," I told him.

"I used to hunt with a bow and arrow. You know that? I was an outdoorsman. Killed a big buck with one clean heart shot. Through the heart. One arrow."

"Must've been something," I said. And the helplessly automatic sound of it seemed to call him back to himself.

"Well, I'm not drunk." Again he sniffled, then he brought a handkerchief out of his pocket and blew his nose. "The fact is, I've been asked to leave."

"Asked —" I began, not understanding it, quite.

"That's right."

"You —" Again, I halted.

"I have a week to find other lodgings."

"Mrs. Wilson?"

"All of them," he said. "All the women. Your mother, too."

I said, "I don't think so."

"You can bet *she's* in on it."

"I'm sorry."

He blew his nose again. "Maybe they're going to need another room," he said. And he looked at me as if there were something we both knew about this.

"Pardon?"

"Well, isn't your father getting out soon?"

"I don't know," I lied.

"Sure he is. Model prisoner and all. And listen, son, they're just not in the habit of giving easy paroles after six months to protesters and draft resisters, you know what I mean?"

I was silent.

"I told Mrs. Wilson that, too."

Now, perhaps not so strangely, I hated him, with his misery, his wounded pride, his mussed hair and his pasty face. I was glad of any humiliation or disrespect he might've suffered at the hands of Penny Holt, no matter what had gone on between them. "What you said doesn't mean anything," I told him.

"No, that's right," he muttered. "It didn't."

I had moved to the door, my hand was on the knob, and I stopped again as he spoke.

"You don't think anything I say will be listened to, do you?"

"It's not true," I said. "My father is a brave man."

"Yeah. And he's a thief, too."

"You're wrong," I said, feeling the heat in my throat and behind my eyes.

"Convicted. Dishonorably discharged."

"Shut up," I said, moving toward him.

"Well, you were right. I am drunk."

"Take it back," I said.

"Shit, kid. We're not on one of your playgrounds."

"You take it back."

"Nobody listened to me, don't you understand? It doesn't matter what I say. I'm getting evicted, for Christ's sake. You've all got what you want. I tried to tell them about it. They wouldn't hear it, and the hero–war protester will come here and take my room. Think of that, kid. He won't be in with your mother. He'll be in here, by himself."

I took hold of his shirt and pulled, but he was too heavy, and then his hands closed tight on my wrists. He was surprisingly strong. He stood and moved me to the door, so that my back was against it. I smelled the whiskey on his breath.

"You still don't understand," he said.

"Leave me alone." To my own horror and dismay, I was about to begin weeping. He held me there against the door, then let go and turned, moving with a lurching motion toward his bed. "Shit, go on. Just get out, like I told you to in the first place. You think I have the stomach for this? I don't have the stomach for this. I entertain little kids, boy. I get them to forget what troubles they have laughing at me. You think I don't know they're laughing at me? You think I don't know that?"

"You don't know what you're talking about," I said to him.

He had his back to me. He had taken something from the small shelf above his bed and was turning it in his hands, looking at it. "Got to get some boxes."

"You've got it all wrong," I told him. "It's because you watch those movies."

He turned. "What movies?"

"You know," I said. "You know, all right."

"You mean the —" he stopped. "Oh, that. That was in July, boy. Mabel and I got over that — we've got to joking about it, in fact."

"I don't care. That's the reason. She told us she was thinking about it when we first got here. We weren't in the door five minutes and she was telling us about it."

He put whatever he was holding in his pocket. It looked like a string of beads. "Well, you poor son of a bitch. You think it matters."

"What?" I said. "I think *what* matters. I don't know what you're talking about. You're drunk."

"Just get out, will you? I'm sorry I said anything."

"Just because you couldn't get her to —" I didn't go on. He seemed now merely to be observing me.

"You think that's why?"

I couldn't say anything to this.

"They don't need a reason to kick me out, son."

I opened the door and stepped out into the hall.

"I was a guard over there," he called as I closed the door. "I know the way it is, how it runs."

I went down through the kitchen, the back way into the dining room, where Mother and Penny and Lisa sat eating cold cereal. Mrs. Wilson was already in the living room, drinking her coffee. The bright windows of that room made a shadow of her.

"What was that all about?" Mother said to me. "We heard you slam the door."

I wasn't aware I had done so. "Nothing," I said.

"What were you talking with him about?" Penny asked without looking up.

"He said he's being evicted."

"He is," said Mrs. Wilson from her chair in the living room.

"Why?" I said.

"Thomas," said Mother.

"Is somebody else moving into the room?"

For a moment no one spoke.

"Well?" I said.

"He's being evicted," Mrs. Wilson said, "because he's a sick, lecherous old man. That's why Mr. Lionel Egan the clown is on his way out."

18

THE DAY my father actually walked free out of Wilson Creek Federal Penitentiary came almost four months after Mr. Egan left us — well after Christmas and New Year's. Yet it seems to my unaided memory that no time at all passed between the two occasions. It's even possible for me to conjure an image of Father and Mr. Egan going by each other in the late afternoon light on the sidewalk in front of the house — the one leaving and the other arriving.

Nothing of the kind took place, though. And I have three separate journal entries to prove this to myself:

November 19, 1967
Mr. Egan packed a U-Haul with all that interesting stuff and left for San Francisco this morning.

January 4, 1968
We celebrated quietly that I'm eighteen. Father called from the prison. Grandfather Tinan and Aunt Elaine sent a card with money in it. I don't feel any different. Still don't even have a driver's license. Registered for draft. Medical exam was ridiculous.

March 12, 1968
M. brought Father to the house in car at five-twenty in the afternoon. From the window I looked out and the car was there, him sitting on the passenger side looking down at something in his lap. He got out. Very skinny and very quiet. Never saw him cry before. Can't think what else to say about it.

But before we get to that day, and what followed it, there are one or two other matters to describe. By the time my father did arrive, there was a feeling in the house that would have its effect on everything.

Some of this has to do with my mortal obsession with Penny. But it begins with Mr. Egan, whose last days as a tenant were troublesome and strained for all of us. Whatever else that odd man could do, he had an uncanny knack for discerning places where the people with whom he found himself were most vulnerable.

And he had apprehended Mother's complicated feelings about the impending return of her husband.

Each night at Mrs. Wilson's table, he behaved as though things were as they always had been, and to anyone not familiar with the situation he might've seemed pleasant, even kind. But his talk was poisonous. Why he chose Mother as his target I can only guess: in a way, Penny had chosen Mother over him, or at least that's how he could've seen it. In any case, through the whole progress of it Penny kept her silence, kept her eyes averted, her face expressionless. I watched her (I was always watching her, remember), and I watched Mother try to withstand the veiled, jaunty-sounding malice of Mr. Egan.

"I guess you're all looking forward to that day," he said late one night as we sat in the living room. Lisa had gone to bed. Russell was watching television in the private rooms off the dining room. "The happy father will be restored to his orphaned children."

"No one's been orphaned," Mrs. Wilson said.

"Except young Russell. And Penny, here."

"You know what I meant."

"But Mabel, if you consider the definition of the word —"

"No one's paying any attention to your definitions."

"Ah," he said. "The fault lies with me." He looked across the room at Mother. "You know, a lot of men find, when they leave prison, that they can't adjust to civilian life again."

Mother did not look at him.

"Yes," he went on, with a sigh. "They come out, and when they're reunited with their families, they find that everyone's changed. I'm certain that won't happen here."

Mother had been crocheting a scarf for Lisa. She let her hands down in her lap. "Excuse me, I have to count the stitches. I'm afraid I lost count."

Penny and Mrs. Wilson and I were quiet.

Mr. Egan addressed Mrs. Wilson. "It seems that the wives no longer feel quite the same about them, and then things've happened while they've been inside, too. Bad things which make it very difficult to adjust. A prison isn't really a very civilized place sometimes. Thank heavens it's not that way in this case."

"Why don't you keep your opinions to yourself," Mrs. Wilson said, and I saw Penny glance at her and smile. I had kept silent because I wanted badly to know, finally and unequivocally, the truth concerning Mother's feelings — I was confused and I needed clarity. I wanted to hear what would be said if she was forced into some statement about it all — the denial, which I hoped for, of what I believed I had also apprehended about her. Mother's obvious tactic, though, was merely to go on with what she was doing and ignore, as much as she could without blatant impoliteness, everything Mr. Egan *meant,* while appearing to attend — politely — to what he *said.*

"Of course each case is different," he went on. "But the pattern is familiar. I knew of a man who spent only a matter of weeks in jail, back when I lived near Dallas, Texas. And he came out to an entirely changed situation. His wife and three children no longer felt that they could be comfortable in his society, you know. And, uh, he sensed it almost immediately. And do you know what he did? What he did, he got into a pent-up rage and wound up battering some man in a bar over nothing. Broken bones and terrible concussions. The poor fellow he attacked almost died from it. And of course he was back in jail again. This time for a good long stay. Because, uh, what had taken place in the first stint —"

But now I interrupted him. I had looked at Mother's face and seen a single tear make its track down her cheek. I stood so suddenly that Mrs. Wilson gasped in startlement. "That's enough," I said.

Mother said, "Thomas."

"Sit down," said Mrs. Wilson, rising.

"Did I say something to offend?" Mr. Egan said.

Mrs. Wilson spoke to him. "It's entirely *my* doing that you were asked to leave. Do you understand me? I decided on it after I caught you looking at that terrible dirty film. *I* decided it and no one else. I was waiting until you finished with the porch, and you didn't even do that."

"Why're you saying all this?" Mr. Egan wanted to know. "Surely I haven't indicated any hard feelings?"

"I know what you're doing, and don't think I don't."

"Well," he said, looking at Mother, "if I've offended anybody, I heartily apologize."

"No one is offended," Mother said in a barely audible voice.

Later, she called me into her little room and asked me to sit down beside her on the bed. She had been crying again, and her eyes were streaked and reddened. It was past midnight and the house still vibrated with all sorts of sound: two different television sets — the one downstairs and Mr. Egan's portable — music from Penny's room above us, and the clatter of Mrs. Wilson in the kitchen, doing the night's dishes. I sat down, and Mother turned and put her arms around me. We were still for a moment, and I breathed the flower fragrance of her perfume, holding her.

"My young knight," she said.

I felt awful. "Maybe I should've spoken sooner," I said.

"No, you were fine. I'm very proud of you."

"I should've spoken sooner."

She let go, folded her hands in her lap. "Thomas, we've been through a lot together, haven't we?"

I nodded, though she was not looking at me.

"So much. And I know it's been hard for you and Lisa."

"It's okay," I said.

"No, honey. The thing I have to tell you — it's going to get harder. The — the trouble's really only just beginning."

"You mean because they're letting him out," I said. It was not a question.

She responded by saying something else. "When they sent him here, they also took away his livelihood."

"The Air Force," I said.

"Yes. They took that away. And now he has to try and find something else."

"Not here," I said. "Right?"

"I don't know."

"But we might be moving again."

The answer to this she muttered almost tonelessly, like a recited

passage she had been forced to remember. "I don't know that either."
Then she sat straighter, seemed to gather herself. "Anyway, I just
wanted to thank you. You've been fine, you know. You've done just
what your father wanted you to do."

"Is he going to be on parole? Like in the movies?"

She shook her head. "Nothing like that. He won't have to do anything like that. What's happening is they're running out of money or
something. Your father says they can't really afford to keep people
who aren't — dangerous — they can't keep them the full sentence.
And it's not just the prisons. Your father said he read that they're going
to start letting people get out of the service before their terms of duty
are up because the government can't afford to keep them if they're not
going to re-enlist. He said that was in the newspaper."

I waited for her to go on.

"Anyway, that's why we're not sure when they'll let him go. They
haven't settled on a date. But it's sure now."

"He's going to stay in Mr. Egan's room," I said, "isn't he."

Her gaze averted mine. "Maybe, for a while."

I said nothing.

"I'm trying to be as honest as I can with you, Thomas. Because
you've been honest with me."

"Why?" I said.

"I just told you why."

"No. I meant — Mr. Egan's room. Why?"

"I can't say why."

"Just say it," I said.

"Say what?"

"You don't love him anymore."

"No," she said, not looking at me. "You don't know —"

"Isn't that it, though?" I said.

"Well, I'm not going into any of that with you. That's between your
father and me."

"But you don't, do you?" I said.

"It's not that simple, Thomas. It's — you can't put it in do-or-don't
terms — black or white — people aren't that simple."

"But you know whether you're happy or not."

"No," she said, "no."

"Does he want to break up?"

"It's not a breakup. God."

"Well, what is it, then?"

"It's time to adjust and get to know each other again."

"You don't know each other?" I was honestly confused now.

She stood. "That's all. This is prying. There are things you don't understand."

"What," I said.

"You go on now. I just wanted to say you've been good through all this, and that there's more we're going to have to get used to. That's enough for one night."

"Tell me," I said.

"It's not something you just say out, like the movies. If I said it that way, it wouldn't be true. Stop putting words in my mouth, for God's sake."

"You can tell me something," I said. "You can say the words."

"I told you what I have to say. There isn't any more than that. You'll just have to try to understand."

"I don't understand."

"Thomas, please."

"I don't."

"Do you think I do?" she said, beginning to cry again.

"All right," I said. "I'm sorry."

"Just please." She motioned for me to leave.

"I love you," I told her, rising.

And she came to me and put her arms around me again. I don't know how long we stood there. But after a time we heard Penny on the stairs, and we moved apart. I went out to our little sitting room, and Penny walked in. She had put on a robe and slippers, and I could see under its hem the shimmering white of what she had worn on the train. She and Lisa had been putting together a quilt from some old clothes of Mrs. Wilson's, and she had just finished it. She wanted to show it to Mother. But the light in Mother's room was off now, and I knew she didn't want any company.

"She's not feeling well," I said.

Penny looked in the direction of the room. "Oh. Can I show it to Lisa?"

"I guess so — I mean, she's asleep."

"I didn't think how late it was," Penny said. She held up a fold of the quilt. "What do you think?"

It was a jumble of summery colors. In bright red block letters across it was the word PEACE.

"It's pretty," I said. And I wanted to say more. I wanted to think of something that would make her decide to stay. My mind was a featureless, barren desert.

"Okay," she said, turning. "Night."

When she was gone — that is, when I heard the click of her door closing — I went into the bedroom and found Lisa sitting up.

"Is everything all right?" she said.

"It's fine," I told her, and I thought of the burden of the knowledge I was carrying, feeling myself to be grown now, introduced into the complications of adulthood.

Of course, I knew nothing.

It now is necessary to construct another scene, and if my authority for this is bound up with later events, I offer it here purely as a function of the clock: this is the time when it most probably took place.

One rainy November afternoon Connie Boudreaux drives from her own job across town to pick up Penny Holt from a temporary job she'd got at a clothing store. It's the end of her first week, in fact, and the job will last through the Christmas season. Signs of the coming holiday are everywhere — the streetlamps are wound in wax holly leaves or hung with wreaths, and the houses glimmer with multicolored lights, which line the rainy eaves and wink in the windows. Patches of snow remain on the lawns, and piles of it flank the curbs. In front of one store a Salvation Army Santa stands ringing a bell, looking up and down the street. Connie pulls over in front of the store, as she has been doing all week, and waits for the younger woman to come out. The intersection a few feet beyond where she waits is jammed with traffic. Someone impatiently blares his horn. The wind sweeps rain at the windows and drives it in slanting sheets across the surface of the road. Presently she sees Penny's shape moving through the downpour. Penny gets in, talking about how difficult it is to get done with all the work by five-thirty. She shivers slightly from the chill, and the rain on her face makes it appear as though she's been crying. Connie turns the heat up, puts the car in gear, and waits to pull out into the tangle of traffic.

"You always think of me," Penny says.

Connie looks at her: perhaps she *has* been crying.

"When I got in," Penny says, "you saw me shivering and you put the heat up. Without my even asking."

"Oh, well — come on," says Connie.

It's a couple of days after Thanksgiving. Penny bends her head and mutters an incantatory something; it sounds almost like a prayer.

"What?" Connie says.

"Nothing."

"I thought you said something to me."

"No."

"What's wrong?" Connie says.

"Nothing. I was thinking about going back to Virginia."

"Okay."

"No, that's not true." Penny turns in the seat. "I can't believe myself sometimes."

Connie is silent.

"I wasn't thinking about going back. I was just saying that to get your sympathy. And — I think there's something wrong with a person who would do that."

"It seems pretty ordinary to me," says Connie. "I don't think it qualifies you for punishment or anything."

"I don't want to go to the house," Penny tells her.

Connie waits for her to continue.

"Do you mind?"

"I've got to."

"You wouldn't want to go somewhere with me?"

"Penny, are you all right?"

The younger woman wipes her face with a handkerchief, and doesn't speak for a moment. "When I feel like myself — I like to be, you know, I like to try things and be silly. It's like if I don't try anything, I'll miss it all. And I don't — I don't feel like anything bad's going to happen to me or anything like that." She pauses, frowns, seems to be trying to arrange the order of her thoughts. "But I wonder how people can seem so calm, you know? I wonder how they do it."

"It's just getting through," Connie tells her. "I guess." Then: "Why? What's upsetting you?"

"Nothing."

"When I was not much younger than you are, I used to think about my future and being happy — and it was like happiness was a place you could go to. Almost like that. But I mean I couldn't think of it except as just all one thing or all the other."

Penny turns to her. "I really feel bad that I was trying to get you to feel sorry for me."

"I don't know why," Connie says. "Most of us want as much sympathy as we can get."

"No, but that's not what I mean."

She waits again.

"I want you to love me," Penny says.

"Well, sure," Connie says, pulling out into the slow stream of traffic. The rain has let up some. "That's understandable."

"No, it's selfish."

"Oh, don't be ridiculous."

"It is. It's very selfish. You don't understand. I don't have anybody. I feel awful all the time."

"Well, you have us."

"What about when he gets out?"

Now Connie admits to herself the faint stirring of doubt about this conversation. She pauses a moment, and says, "What about it?"

"Well, you don't love him anymore."

"I never said that."

"You confided in me."

"I didn't confide that."

"You said you didn't know."

"I was talking about a feeling."

"But if you love him, then where does that leave me?"

Connie stares at her. "I don't understand," she says.

"He won't want me around." Penny says this in a sulking tone, moving her hands in her lap and staring down at them.

"That's absurd," Connie manages to say.

"Is it?"

"Look, you're not making any sense. He's not going to tell me who I can and can't have as a friend, because he's never done anything like that with me. Nor I him."

"I just — I don't want anything to change," Penny says. "I never want anything to change anymore. I've had enough changes."

"What's going to change?"

"Maybe *you* won't want me around."

"That's silly," Connie says. "You're being silly, now stop it."

They have stopped at a traffic light. The rain is swirling in the wind again, and the traffic light swings and sways on its intersecting wires.

"Will you hold me?"

"Come here," Connie says. And the two women embrace. They stay quiet for a time, and then Penny stirs, kisses my mother's cheek.

"I just get so scared sometimes."

"It's going to be fine. You're with friends now."

The light turns green, and Connie edges out into the intersection.

"It's like I'm so little, you know? And the rest of everything is just — huge."

"It's all right," Mother says, meaning to soothe her.

"But I don't have anybody now. I need you to be family."

"Well, so we *are* like family."

"Do you mean it?"

"Of course I mean it."

"I'm sorry. I'm scared," Penny says. "I'm very scared." And she nestles close again.

The traffic slows to a stop. Connie watches the water run down the windshield.

"I'm so afraid of hell," Penny says. "Do you believe in hell?"

"No."

"I do."

"Maybe I do too, sometimes."

"I should never have left Virginia," Penny says suddenly.

Connie gazes out the car window at the raining street.

"I should never have let Chummy talk me into it."

"Well, you're here now," Connie says.

"I couldn't have married Buddy — that was just so much shit. Buddy and I were done so long ago, it was stupid. It was all wanting to get away from stuff. The whole thing."

"Why go over all that now?" Connie says.

Penny doesn't answer for a few seconds. "When I get scared like this, it feels like I'm — stuffed with all the lies I told people to get here."

Connie edges the car forward, though the traffic is stopped now. She experiences a momentary sense of the magnitude of the younger woman's need for reassurance and affection. It stirs in her soul like a small fright, this awareness of the girl's fragility, which — only seconds later, as Penny sits forward and seems to come back to normal, chattering about the rain and Christmas — recedes into the background and is gone. The moment passes. Penny seems herself again. And Connie decides there can be no pursuing the subject with her, since the truth is that Penny seldom seems quite up to talking about herself. From the beginning it has been this way: while she has been happy to hear everything and anything Connie might tell her — seemed nearly avid for it, in fact — her own story, even now, has always been veiled in shy indirection, or casual dismissals. But something is working at her under the surface, and Connie knows it now.

It is knowledge she keeps to herself.

Just before Christmas, Penny came back from having driven Mother's car into town, walked straight up to our apartment, and knocked on the partition. "Hello, everyone," she said. "I've got news."

"We're here," said Mother.

We were in the sitting room, putting Lisa's homemade — and homely — decorations on the little potted pine Mother had brought up that afternoon. Penny strode in and admired the tree, while my breath caught in my throat. "It's so cute," she said. "Can I help make some decorations?"

"That's up to Lisa."

"You can help," Lisa said.

But Penny was already on to something else. She looked at Mother and said, "Don't you want to hear my news? Guess who I saw in town today? Chummy Terpin."

Mother stared at her.

"You remember —"

"Yes, of course."

Penny nodded. "Imagine. He followed me here, all the way from Leavenworth."

"What did you say to him?"

"Oh, I didn't speak to him, are you kidding? He was at the Burger Palace, standing in line at the counter. I saw him through the front window. I was heading in there to grab a bite to eat, and when I caught sight of him I turned around and walked away. I don't think he saw me."

"What would he be doing here?" Mother said.

"He's here looking for me," said Penny. "He followed me here."

"Well —" Mother began. Then she seemed to consider a moment. "The poor man."

"I wonder how long he's been here."

"He doesn't know this address?"

Penny shrugged. "Maybe he does. I don't know. I think he'd have come here if he did. I think he just knew I was on my way to Wilson Creek."

"You should've spoken to him," Mother said.

Penny shuddered. "I don't want anything to do with him."

"Yes, but you should've said something. Let him know it."

"Well, if I see him again, maybe I will."

"You're sure it was him?" I said.

Penny turned to me. "Oh, it was him all right."

"I wonder about his brother," I said.

Penny spoke quickly. "He's not interested in his brother where I'm concerned." This was not said proudly. It was a brutally simple observation. "No, he wants to come take me away."

"Maybe he knows the address here," Mother put in, "and he's just been too frightened to come forward."

Penny nodded. "But God, Connie — I don't bite."

"The poor man," Mother said. And the two of them laughed.

I had the distinct feeling they were thinking about my father. I said, "What's so funny?"

"You're right, it's not funny," Penny said, and then laughed again.

"Is this about Father?" I said.

Penny stared uncomprehendingly. "What?"

"Don't be absurd, Thomas," my mother said.

Before you take the wrong impression from this, let me hasten to point out that Chummy Terpin, if he ever was in Wilson Creek, and if

Penny did see him, never appeared at the house and was never mentioned in that context again. But I spent much of that night sleepless, thinking about him, imagining how it would be for a man traveling to a town because it happened to be where the woman he loved now lived. I thought it was something I might do (of course I knew I would, for exactly the same reason and with exactly the same woman in mind), and then I thought about how Mother had brought us all this way because Father was here. It seemed to me then that all my doubts and my imaginings — what I had taken from her expressions of doubt — must be wrong. I mean, I thought also that *her* doubts must be wrong. How could she not see how much he still meant to her, having put herself and us through everything we had been through to be in the town where he now was?

It would be Christmas soon. I looked out the window and saw that the snow had started again. It was descending weightlessly in the pool of soft light the window made, and I watched it for a while.

Then I knew that Lisa was awake, too. "Lisa," I whispered.

"What."

"It's snowing again. Come up and watch it with me."

She climbed up. We were quiet, watching the flakes drop out of the dark along the edge of the light. Finally she said, "I'm homesick."

"It'll be all right," I told her. And for the first time in months I believed it.

Christmas was quiet, and we celebrated quietly. Penny came down and stayed with us most of the day, working with Lisa on another quilt. The Wilsons kept to their part of the house, though Mrs. Wilson did cook a turkey for dinner, and we all sat down to that together. No one seemed very festive or much in the mood for talk. Grandfather Tinan and Aunt Elaine phoned early in the evening, and we thanked them for the box of presents they'd sent, lying about having kept it closed until Christmas morning (we had greedily torn it open when it arrived, three days earlier), and then, not much after this, my father called. He'd made presents for us, which Mother had brought back from her visit to him on Christmas Eve, and these we had saved for the morning.

Mine was a small carved baseball player, a coiled, muscular, chiseled wooden man holding a bat. It looked like a trophy until you saw the fine details that had been so carefully worked into it in miniature: the suggestion of pinstripes in the uniform, and the little craggy face, so delicately fierce, with its nineteenth-century handlebar mustache and its frown of concentration. I was astonished at the accuracy and sophistication of it, since I hadn't known Father possessed any talent as an artist. For Lisa he had fashioned an elegant lady in a floor-length dress, with a bun at the back of her head and ruffles on the ends of her sleeves. Mother showed them both around.

"Did you know he could do this sort of thing?" Mrs. Wilson wanted to know, holding my ballplayer up to the light. The flesh under her arm shook slightly.

"No," Mother said.

"Really impressive. He ought to make them and sell them. He could make money doing that."

"You know, I think maybe he could."

"I think they're better than that," Penny said. "They're art, and you don't sell art like — I don't know, like puppets or dolls."

"What do you think people buy in art galleries?" Mrs. Wilson said. "Goodness, girl."

"Well, I just mean you wouldn't make fifty of these in a week, you know."

"If he could, why not? The more the better."

We went on talking for few minutes about what Father might or might not do with this undiscovered talent, and then his call came through.

"Daniel," Mother said to him, "do you know we've been talking about how you could make money carving these things."

We all watched her listen to whatever his answer was.

"Well," she said. Then: "Well, okay. It was just a thought."

He asked to speak to me, and I wished him a merry Christmas.

"What do you think of your statue?"

I said, "It's something."

"You like it?"

"I love it," I said.

"It took me a month."

"It's so realistic," I told him.

"A solid month of close work," he said. "With a lot of failures. So

I'm real glad you like it, son." His voice sounded hollow, as if he were speaking through a tube, and once more I found myself casting about for something to tell him. "Let me say hello to your little sister."

"Yes, sir," I said.

"Oh," he said, managing it somehow, "I liked the book." It was what I had got him for Christmas, a history about Rommel and the African campaign. He went on: "Did *you* read it?"

"No, sir," I said.

"I'll give it to your mother. You ought to read it."

"Okay," I said.

"Well, let me talk to your sister."

I gave the handset to Lisa. And I saw that Mother was staring at me.

"Yes, Daddy," Lisa was saying. "It's beautiful."

"Here," Mother said to me, offering the ballplayer. I took it and smiled at her, and she said, "Put it where it won't get broken."

19

BY THE TIME of Father's release, the war protests in the Wilson Creek area were heating up. If little towns all across the country had lagged behind the cities, places like Wilson Creek were in a separate category: small, dependent upon federal money, inhabited primarily by government employees and their families, they posed a special set of challenges for those who wanted an end to the war. And now young people were coming into the area from other parts of the country, mostly the university towns of the upper midwest. A group of people calling themselves the Coalition Against the War had rented what used to be a Singer appliance store in the rundown part of Broad Street, near the train depot. They had a small printing press and had begun distributing broadsides and letters of protest, trying to organize draft resistance, and to spread awareness of the threat of the nuclear missiles in our back yard, to use their words. The television showed the constant presence of coalition members outside the prison, even on the coldest days. They carried big painted signs against the confinement of political prisoners and draft resisters. And there were also several gatherings outside the military base, with its high fences and signs forbidding trespass.

Mother said one night that the growing number of conflicts around the country had begun to be about something more than the war in Vietnam, or even the struggle for civil rights, which had been going on almost as long as I could remember. It seemed to her that the most vociferous of the protesters were out to transform the whole society, to ask ordinary people to accept an entirely different way of life. "They're not really interested in stopping the war, anymore," she said, "or else they'd speak to the people whose minds they want to change in something other than the street language they all use."

"You're talking like an Air Force wife," said Penny Holt.

Mother frowned. "My opinion has nothing to do with the Air Force. I want to stop the war. My husband suffered in it. And he came home and it meant less than nothing." And she started crying.

"I'm sorry," Penny said.

"No, really. I don't know what's wrong with me."

They were quiet for a long time.

Mother composed herself. "It just seems that everybody has an ax to grind. And it's all part of the same killing thing."

"Yes — you know," Penny said, brightening a little, "the — the values we're up against — they allow the war. Isn't it — I mean the whole thing, the whole Mommy and Daddy Workaday thing, while all these people are dying."

"People have to live, too," Mother said. "There's no reason to disrespect that. Mommy and Daddy Workaday are just people trying to get from one day to the next. Trying to be happy and okay, too."

"Oh, that — yes."

"It's hard to have the time to think about anything but getting along."

Penny watched her, as though she thought there might be more tears.

"I'm against the war," I said. "I'm with McGovern and McCarthy."

"I'm for Nixon," said Mrs. Wilson.

"I don't like his looks," Penny said. "He looks like he swallowed something that won't go down."

"He's going to be President."

"That doesn't make him handsome," Penny said.

These discussions seemed always to end with the same sort of exchange. There had been riots in the cities that summer; the war news was bad; the presidential elections were approaching and various national figures talked of law and order with all the piety of old-time religion. A new rage and a new hopelessness about everything seemed to be leaking into the atmosphere. It was reaching us, far away from the centers of strife, in a place like Wilson Creek.

The nearer we got to the time of Father's release (we knew the month now, March: Mother had brought the news home one night and cried, telling us both — as we cried hearing it, with relief and with happiness, too), the more anxious and irritable we all became. The rooms of Mrs. Wilson's house seemed to be contracting, and we couldn't get out of one another's way. Talk between Mother and Penny about what we were all watching on the news every night grew less flexible somehow. Several times they verged on quarreling over it all. In the aftermath of one exchange, Penny remained in her upstairs room through the evening, not even answering when Lisa went up and knocked.

It started with a call from Grandfather Tinan. When Mother spoke to him she called him Daddy several times, while yet again wrangling with him about where we would go and what we would do after Father's release. We had been seated at the table in the dining room, and after the call came in, Mrs. Wilson cleared the table while Penny, Lisa, Russell, and I went into the living room to watch television. A Sunday night, and the Beatles were going to be on *Ed Sullivan* again, premiering a new song. Russell had sprawled on his stomach across the sofa, so Lisa and I were lying on the floor, while Penny sat with her knees up in the easy chair by the window. She watched Mother, who stood in the entrance to the dining room arguing into the phone, and of course I was still watching *her*. When Mother hung up, Penny said, "You call him Daddy. That's kind of sweet."

Mother seemed not to have heard this. She walked into the room and sat in the remaining easy chair.

"Did you hear me?" Penny said.

Mother returned her look, then seemed to throw off whatever she had been about to say. She lay her head back on the chair and said, "I hate winters in this part of the country. I can't make him understand that I don't want to live in Minot."

"How old are you — and you call him Daddy?"

"It's just a word," said Mother.

"It's funny."

"No, I don't think so."

"You expect your own children to use 'Father.'"

"No."

"They call Daniel 'Father.' I've heard them."

"It's not insisted upon."

"Tommy is Thomas, and Lisa is Lisa. No nicknames."

"What're you getting at?"

"All these formal — I don't know — and you say 'Daddy' to your own father."

"So?"

"I don't know. I think it's funny."

"What's wrong with 'Daddy'?" Lisa put in.

"It sounds funny in a grown-up's mouth," Penny explained. "Don't you think so?"

Lisa shrugged.

"It's just the incongruousness of it."

"Icongru —" Lisa struggled with the word.

"That's what makes it funny," Penny said.

"All right, then shut up about it," Mother said. "We all understand that you find it funny."

A moment later, Penny rose from her place in the easy chair by the window and strode out of the room. We all listened to her on the stairs.

"I think she's hurt," I said to Mother.

"Well, let her be hurt, then. I'm tired of worrying about what she's feeling all the time."

I didn't want them mad at each other, because I had grown accustomed to having Penny in our circle: after Mr. Egan had gone, Mrs. Wilson and Russell moved off into their own sphere, not so much separate, but in some unspoken way distinct from us — from Mother, Lisa, Penny, and me. I felt this change like the purest distillation of hope, attending to the liquid grace of her movements, her astonishing skin, the shape of her hips, the fine bones of her eerily beautiful but flawed face. My father was coming back, and I knew it would almost certainly mean that we would move again. I was unable to think about this except in terms of what it might signify where *she* was concerned: she and Mother were friends; would she come with us if we moved, *when* we moved?

In other words, with my father about to be released from prison, and with all the unsettling complications I had sensed concerning this, I was worried about losing the chance to look at Penny Holt and hear her voice every day. It is possible that I might even have accepted a delay in my father's emancipation if it meant we would remain in her society that much longer.

The stupendous self-centeredness of this still has the power to astonish me.

I said, "There's no use being mad at each other."

Mother gave me a faintly disgruntled glance. "Well," she said.

"Want me to go talk to her?" I asked.

"No."

"Why don't I go talk to her?"

"Stay out of it, Thomas."

I turned and concentrated on the television. And later, after Lisa had gone up and knocked on Penny's door and received no answer, I said, "Maybe something's wrong."

"Nothing's wrong," Mother said. "Don't be melodramatic."

"I'm not being melodramatic."

"Thomas, please."

The look of exhaustion in her face stopped me.

I know that visits to the prison were badly draining her by this time. Each day she had to walk through knots of people with signs and placards, people whose searching appraisal of her made the skin along her hairline crawl. And she had to face her husband across the table in that big gray quiet room, both of them fearing that nothing would ever be the same.

My father had begun to press her. *When did you start feeling different about us, Connie?*

Don't. Please, Daniel. I don't know what you're talking about.

You must have felt it shift at some point?

I swear I'll get up and walk out of here.

I love you, Connie.

Don't say it that way — like a — like a challenge.

I got scared I was going to lose you.

No. Stop it.

I felt it long before here.

Will you please.

It's true. I felt it a long time, honey.

I won't listen to this.

That's why I did it, though. That's why I did all of it. I thought if I could just, you know, take you places and give you nice things —

I said I won't listen to this. Now stop it.

I'm sorry.

Don't apologize. For God's sake, what're you doing?

I'm trying to tell the truth. We loved each other, didn't we? We were great together.

Yes. Oh, yes.

But you stopped feeling it. You didn't feel the same, and I didn't want to admit it to myself. That's the truth, isn't it?

It isn't the truth. I don't know what's true anymore.

I went too far, didn't I, Connie.

Will you please stop. There's no sense going over all that now. That's over. You're getting out soon.

I'm sorry for everything.

Daniel.

I can't imagine living without you and those kids. I don't know how I've done it. I don't know how I've done it.

It's in the past now, Daniel.

The worst part.

Yes.

I feel all broken inside.

It'll get better, you'll see.

I feel such a distance between us.

We just need some time.

I never should've let you see me here.

Will you please just stop talking about it.

I know. I have to take hold. God, the thing is, honey, I just can't seem to take hold like I did in Nam.

We just have to take hold.

I'm scared. I am incredibly scared. I don't have anywhere to go.

Of course you do.

No, I mean — work. Something to do. I was in the Air Force, that was what I did. That was my work. They don't have survival equipment in civilian life.

You'll find something.

Honey, why can't you look at me.

* * *

I think of him, the last night in his cell, only hours away from being released. He has witnessed and been subject to all the various coercions: the clandestine drubbings by guards, the random beatings administered to the luckless member of any of the several subgroups of inmates by members of other subgroups, all of these things encouraged or abetted by the casual abuses of dignity contained in the very rules of the institution itself, rules which more than anything else require a careful study of the various planes one cannot cross without permission of the guards, who are capricious and who know how to draw the rules tight, how to enforce the letter of any law. And he has managed to get through every brutal level of it, taking as stoically as possible during the slow course of each bad, hard day what was meted out at the business end of the nightstick or the whip, the belt with its brass buckle or the rubber pipe or the plain doubled-up fist — taking it all and keeping his temper, as he had managed to do on the other side of the world five years earlier, when it counted for something, when he was the prisoner of an undeclared war in a strange country and could dream of someday going home. Now, just as he's about to be released from this second confinement, he realizes that he's only entering another strange country. Home has been taken away forever. He's about to walk not only out of prison, but out of what has for most of the last twenty years been his livelihood, the shape of his whole working existence. He has never felt more alone.

More snow came, and the coldest part of winter settled over us like a white cowl. Everything seemed to pause.

And the big day drew near.

Lisa and I were told not to question Father concerning anything remotely having to do with the past nine months of his life, or, for that matter, our own. We were to keep from disturbing him or troubling him in any way. Mother looked at me and said she expected me to understand this, and to help Lisa remember it.

"I'll remember it," Lisa said with an exasperated sigh.

"Well, see that you do," Mother said. "He's been through enough." She wanted the way smoothed. We were to treat his return as if he had come home from one of his temporary duty assignments.

I lay in my bunk the night before she brought him home, unable to sleep, wondering what we might find to say to each other, and entertaining fantasies of introducing Penny Holt to him, wanting, in my prodigious selfishness, to gather her into the family somehow. She moved through my fitful sleep like a hallucinatory shape born of fever, and she was all I saw in the days spent in the closed windowless rooms of the old castle, as we called it, daydreaming my way through the dull passages of high school. I wasn't even mildly interested in my classmates, and I'm pretty certain I made no impression on them at all except as someone who seldom spoke, and was seldom spoken to.

Oddly enough, the first time I was alone with her for more than a few nerve-stricken mumbled polite phrases took place on the morning of the day Mother brought Father home. I'd heard the car start, had stepped to the window of our apartment to look out at the street, and watched Mother drive away between the two tall ridges of packed snow, heading for work. She would leave there early to drive to the prison, where Father was scheduled to be released precisely at five o'clock. I watched her pull out of sight, and then I went out on the landing, hesitating at the top of the stairs. I heard voices in the kitchen, and started down. But then Penny's door opened above me, and so I stepped back up onto the landing, waiting for her to descend. It was Lisa.

"Oh, hi," she said.

"What're you doing up there?" I demanded.

She shrugged. "Penny's up there. I think we're going to make another quilt." She went on down to the living room. I waited. I could hear Penny closing the door to her room. She descended slowly, and I made as if I were on my way out of our apartment.

"Hey," she said, "I guess today's the day."

"Yes," I said.

She started past me.

"Penny," I said.

She stopped, one hand resting lightly on the railing. It was, I think, the first time I had ever said her name directly to her that way, and something about it felt almost too personal, like an intimacy we had been trying to avoid. I received an image of us falling into each other's arms, and had the good sense to suspect immediately that it was just my own skewed perception of everything.

"Do you —" I began. "Do you — think we'll move away?" I meant the pronoun to include her, but she took it the other way.

"I hope not," she said.

"There's — there's something else," I told her.

She waited.

I could think of nothing reasonable or calm. My mind had buckled, it seemed, and I was preparing to begin faking some sort of attack when I heard Russell laugh down in the kitchen. It was as if that sound, with its flavor of the house's daily business, would close off the chance for me to speak. In my sudden haste to say anything at all I blurted out something about wishing she would come with us wherever we went.

She had taken one step down, and now she came back up. She took my wrist and led me a little way toward Mr. Egan's vacated room.

"Have you been mad at me or something?" she said.

I was astonished. "No," I said.

"Is it that you don't like me?"

"No," I said. "Oh, no, I do."

"I thought you and Mr. Egan — I don't know —"

"It's not true," I said.

But she was already on to something else. "I hope you don't move."

"Me, too," I said. "I want us to stay together."

"You think he'll want to take you all away?" It took me a heartbeat to realize she was talking about my father. "I don't — I don't know," I got out.

We were now facing each other outside the open door. "I think Mrs. Wilson lets me stay here because of your mother."

I looked down the hall toward the landing, and the little rise, with its partition, which led into our apartment; I could see where her stairs began. For a breathless, guilty few seconds, I thought of myself crouched behind that partition as Mr. Egan snuck by me. It was as if something of that guilt were showing in my face.

"I won't have anywhere to go," she said.

"You can stay with us," I told her.

"No, I mean —" She stopped.

I said, "You could come with us."

"Did your mother say so?"

"It doesn't need anybody saying it."

"She *didn't* say it."

"Not in so many words."

"Then how do you know?"

We were face to face, close. *Oh, Penny.* I might've spoken it out loud. On the underside of a wooden shelf for books which Mother had put up above my bed, I had written in pencil, *To Penny with all my love, Thomas.* In the mornings, while Lisa slept, I lay staring up at it, dreaming of somehow, someday doing something or producing something which I could inscribe in that way, with those exact words. *To Penny with all my love, Thomas.*

"How?" she said.

"I don't know," I said. "I want you to stay with us."

She seemed to consider this. Then she shook her head, apparently dismissing it. "I think your mother likes me a lot. Do you think so?"

I thought of the assumptions she had made about why my father was in prison, and this stopped me.

"I want us all to stay together," she said.

"Yes," I said, with all my heart.

"Does she talk to you about what they'll do?"

"Not much," I said.

"I'm so tired of going from place to place."

I said, "Me, too."

Now her expression was slightly incredulous. "You all won't stay here long. You'll go back to her father."

I didn't know what to say.

"There's no choice — is there?"

"I guess not," I said, though I didn't really know one way or the other. In any case, I was happy to be talking to her like this, one adult to another — though when I look back on it, much to my surprise it feels as if we were two children whispering in the dark of a hiding place.

"I think I made a mistake," she said.

I waited.

She looked away, then back. "Does she say anything about me?"

"Mother?" I said.

"Yes." It was almost impatient.

"She doesn't tell me anything," I said.

"It feels like we're so close sometimes, you know —"

"You're one of the family," I said, and then felt as though I had said too much.

She touched my cheek.

"Penny," I said.

Her hand dropped to my shoulder. "You're sweet."

"No," I said. "Really. Lisa loves you."

"Lisa's sweet."

"We all love you," I got out.

"God," she said, looking up and down the hall. "I can't imagine Mrs. Wilson letting me stay, just me." She was shaking. "I get myself into trouble. Everything goes so wrong all the time."

Fleetingly I had the impression that she was referring to what had transpired with Mr. Egan, and that she knew I had spied on them.

But then she said, "Maybe I should've gone ahead and stayed in Kansas."

"No," I said.

And it was as though I had called her back from something. "Well," she said, and patted my shoulder again. Then she went partway down the hall and turned. "Here's hoping."

"Right." I smiled at her, realizing almost immediately the stupid look I must have shown her: for she hesitated, seemed about to ask me something more.

After she went downstairs, I hauled myself directly to our rooms, into the little bathroom with its oval mirror over the sink, and tried to duplicate the smile, wanting to see myself as she must've seen me. And there it was, my hopelessly muddled adolescent face with its bony inconsistencies and its mottled skin, smiling dumbly. Certainly no woman could possibly see anything in that look but the moronic consent of an idiot.

And yet Penny had spent time with someone like Mr. Egan, whose features I judged, even in the present extremity, to be less appealing than my own.

Deranged as I now was, it even crossed my mind that I might ingratiate myself with her by offering what I knew quite well Mr. Egan had had to offer — despite Russell's outright dismissal of the possibility that Mr. Egan would be in possession of dope. And I remembered that Russell had spoken about having some himself. It seemed a perfectly simple proposition to ask him for a little of it. But that was daydreaming. Later that morning, when I saw Russell, I asked if I could have one of his smokes, and knew I wouldn't stop there.

I could not quite believe myself.

He pulled out the pack of Tareytons and handed me an ordinary cigarette. We were standing by the frozen creek. I'd found him trying to chip through to the bed of rocks beneath it, purely out of fascination at the thick ice. The day had been sunny and windless, and it didn't feel cold enough to keep ice that solid and dry.

"Every year it gets me," he said. "It's the same. Every year I can't believe the whole thing all over again."

"I meant the other kind of cigarette," I managed.

"What other kind? I smoke Tareytons."

"You know," I said. My voice almost gave way.

"Oh." He stiffened. "Those."

"Well?" I said.

"I'll have to see."

"I thought you said you had some," I said.

"I don't have any." He spoke in a tone which told me that he had never had any.

"You said you did, Russell."

"Well, I had one. Once. You know?"

"You lied."

"Maybe I was goofing with you a little."

"All right," I said. "Do you know where I can get some?"

"I bet some of those protesters over at the prison have it," he said.

"I thought you said it grew wild around here."

"Right," he said. "In this." He indicated the bluffs of frozen snow around us.

Presently he said, "I guess you heard them talking about it too, didn't you?"

I stopped. "Who?"

"Penny and your mother. They were talking about it."

"When?"

"I don't know. A while ago."

"What were they saying?"

He shrugged. "They were talking about it."

"Well, like what?"

"Like, you know — what it does to you. How it makes you feel."

I couldn't speak.

"That's all," he said. "I guess it could've even been something else they were talking about."

"What did my mother say?"

"Nothing."

"She must've said something."

Again, he shrugged. "I didn't listen that close, man. I heard them talking and Penny said something to her about grass, and I started trying to hear what else, and I figured they were talking about it, that's all."

I watched him walk along the creek bed, and then I went up onto the back porch, too confused for the moment to do much of anything. In the kitchen, Mrs. Wilson sat at the table, breaking bread up and dropping the pieces into a big aluminum bowl. She barely noticed me as I entered and took my boots off, then strode past her to the hall and on up to our rooms.

I found Lisa in the sitting room reading a magazine. "Where's Penny?" I said, trying to sound as calm as I could.

"I don't know."

I stepped out onto the landing and made my way up the stairs to Penny's door. It was quiet. The whole house was so quiet. I knocked twice. Nothing. Then I retreated, trying not to make a sound.

Lisa was waiting for me, standing in the entrance of our apartment. "Penny got another temp job," she said. "She won't be back until tonight. She's all upset she won't be here when Mother brings Daddy home."

20

WE HAD BEEN WAITING at the window since five, when we knew Father was to be released, and even so I didn't see the car pull up. I turned and faced into the room to ask Mrs. Wilson if he would have to pay a separate rent. The question had come to me with a little jolt of my nerves, as if I had received some bad news: there was so much I hadn't thought about. Mrs. Wilson had spent more than an hour in Mr. Egan's old room, making up the bed and cleaning.

"Why, yes," she said about the rent. "I couldn't do it otherwise."

Lisa said, "Two rents?"

I looked out and there was the car, with Mother on the driver's side and my father sitting hunched over in the seat, as though attending to something important in his lap. Lisa, having also seen them, had already started for the front door. I remained by the window and watched him get out of the car. He glanced at the house, and then at the window where I was. For perhaps ten seconds he looked right at me, and he appeared to falter a bit; it was only the faintest movement backward, like a momentary loss of balance. Mother had come around the car and now she took him by the arm. He turned as though surprised to see her there, and the two of them came up the walk through the deepening gray dusk. Behind me, Mrs. Wilson said quietly: "Go on out and greet him, son."

I went to the door. They were walking up the porch steps, and Lisa waited at the top, her arms outstretched. She made a little jumping motion, up and down, and her small voice carried out on the chilly stillness. "Daddy."

He reached for her when he was on the step below hers, lifted her high and held tight, saying nothing.

"Daddy," Lisa said. "Daddy, Daddy, Daddy, Daddy."

I kept a few paces back, just beyond the plane of the front door. Mother stood to one side, and now she gestured for me to come closer. I took a step forward. Father had come up onto the porch and was standing there, his arms wrapped around Lisa. Then he held her back from him, looking at her, asking for kisses. I thought of Mr. Egan's room and wondered if my father knew yet where they were planning for him to stay. In a way he was like Mr. Egan now, and there was something of Mr. Egan's desperate look about him — the way the older man had seemed on that day he caught me sneaking into his room.

"Big kisses," Father said as Lisa clung to his neck. "Oh, my sweet baby, you've got so big. You come all the way to my chest." And he looked over her shoulder at me. His face grew serious. "Son," he said.

I nodded and strode forward to offer my hand. He patted Lisa's shoulders, reached beyond her to take hold. He squeezed, and I squeezed back.

"My boy," he said. Then, pulling me toward him: "Come here."

We embraced. I breathed the odor of something cedary. The cloth of his coat collar was damp from Lisa's breathing on it. I don't know how long we stood like that.

"Daniel," said Mother, "this is Mrs. Wilson."

"Sir," Mrs. Wilson said.

"I'm in your debt," he told her, letting go of me.

"You have a wonderful family, sir."

"You've been very kind to them."

"No — they're good tenants," Mrs. Wilson said. She took her son by the arm, just above the elbow. "And this is my son, Russell."

Father reached and shook his hand. "Glad to meet you," he said.

"Glad to meet you, too," Russell said.

We all filed inside and gathered in the living room. It took a moment for us to settle. He sat in the big easy chair near the fire, with Lisa sitting at his feet, and me across from him on the sofa. He kept looking from one to the other of us, as though he couldn't quite believe we were real.

"Well," Mrs. Wilson said, "your room is clean and ready when you are." She turned to Russell. "Come with me," she said to him.

Russell protested, but she managed, without much fuss, to make him see that we must be left alone. I was never sorrier to see anyone leave a room. I think we all felt the need of someone to stand between us for a time. When they were gone we had a few moments of awkward silence, and then Father shifted in the chair, put his hands over his eyes, and began to cry. He cried quietly. We sat very still, watching this. Lisa touched his knee, then took her hand away.

I thought my heart would break.

"I'm sorry," he said, trying to master himself.

I looked at his hands, at the way his hair was smoothed back and shone with something, some substance they had made him use at the prison. His coat was old Air Force issue, blue and frayed at the collar. He wore boots, and I saw the dull, unpolished toes.

Mother said, "Children, perhaps you should go up to the room —"

"No," he said. "Please. I'm okay. I'll be okay, Connie."

She turned to him. "It's done now," she told him. "You're home."

He sobbed, keeping his face covered. He ran one hand through his hair. "Ahh. Jesus."

Mother gave him a handkerchief, and he wiped his eyes with it, then dabbed his forehead. "It's burning up in here," he said, looking around the room.

"Let's go upstairs," she said gently.

"Get these prison clothes off," he managed. "Right. Jesus."

Lisa and I followed them up to the landing and part of the way along the hallway to Mr. Egan's old room.

"There?" he said, looking at her with brimming eyes.

"Your clothes are in the closet in there," she answered without quite returning his look.

He moved off down the hall.

"We'll wait for you in here," Mother said, indicating the entrance to our apartment.

"Right." He went on, stood for a moment in the open doorway, then stepped inside, turned, and looked at us. "Well," he said, half nodding. Then he closed the door.

I looked at my mother.

"He needs some time," she said, low.

We went into our own apartment and sat waiting for him. No one spoke for a while. We didn't even look at one another.

"Are you getting divorced?" I said abruptly.

"Thomas."

"Well, are you?" Lisa said.

"Both of you be quiet."

"We have a right to know," I said.

"When we know, you'll know."

"You mean you might be?" I said. I was frightened now, for the evenness of her voice, the lack of any emotion in it.

"Just be quiet, please."

We waited. In a few minutes, we heard the door to Mr. Egan's room. Father came to our entrance and looked in. No one moved. Perhaps the better part of a minute went by before he stepped across the threshold. At least, it felt that long. And then Lisa ran to him again, threw her arms around his waist.

"Daddy," she said.

"Hello, baby."

"Mrs. Wilson will have dinner ready in a few minutes," Mother said. "I hope you feel like roast chicken."

"I can smell it," he said. "It smells wonderful."

Mother moved over on the couch. "Come sit."

He did so. The four of us were then grouped around the coffee table, like people sitting stiffly at a party in someone else's living room.

"I can't believe I'm out of that place," he said. "That last few days was like a lifetime."

"It was that way here, too," I managed.

We all fell silent. No one seemed quite able to look at anyone else. Father cleared his throat, ran one hand over his mouth. Then he looked at me. "Your mother tells me you've been a very big help to her."

"I tried to be," I said.

He nodded, looking away. "I would like to apologize to this family — to all of you — for what I put you through."

Mother murmured something I couldn't hear.

"I'd still like to say I'm sorry, Connie. Everybody's — you've all been through it, and I know that. And I wanted to say I'm sorry for it." He paused. "I hope you can forgive me."

He looked at me now, and I could not have spoken if my life depended on it. Then he squeezed Lisa's shoulder. "This little girl's happy to see me."

Lisa smiled.

"I'm happy to see her, too," he said, and his voice broke. "I'm happy to see everybody."

Again we were all quiet.

"Well," he said, rising, "I'm going to go get a shower. Wash the smell of the last year off me."

Mother walked with him out into the hall, but she returned almost immediately. "Thomas," she said. "He has some things out in the car."

It wasn't much. A duffel bag full of clothes, a few books, including the one I had bought him for Christmas. Its pages were bunched and wrinkled, as though it had been dropped in water, or on a muddy street. I carried it all into the house and up the stairs. The door to the room was open, and I could hear him in the shower. I put the duffel bag on the floor by his bed and set the books on the nightstand. Something about the simple sound of the shower made me pause, and then I knew what it was: the sound itself, mixed with the faint odor of his shaving lotion, had called up other days in other houses. We were going to begin our lives again. It came to me in that moment that I was very, very frightened for us all.

Over the years, I have put together a version of what they must have said to each other on the drive home. I know that it was only then that Mother could manage to tell him that he would be staying in Mr. Egan's room. I'm sure she told him it was just for the time being. I'm sure she believed, or anyway hoped, it *was* for the time being: what she knew for certain, what troubled her, was that she couldn't bring herself to be abruptly thrown back into intimacy with him.

Probably he began by talking about Minot, which he had been bringing up more and more as the time of his release drew near. I can hear him telling her that he doesn't see any other choice, that much as he hates the idea and knows that she hates it too, Minot, and some job her father might arrange, is what they must accept as the next move.

And I can hear her telling him no. "No, I can't do it. I can't go back there and do that. There's got to be something we can do here — at least until something else comes up. I like my job, it pays fairly well. We can make it. You can find something here."

"I won't find anything here, Connie. I'm just out of the town's prison. They won't give me anything here."

"How do you know until you've tried?"

"Well, I know."

"I can't go back to Minot," she tells him. "It was hard enough just visiting on the way here."

"I don't see what else we can do."

"We can make a life for ourselves somewhere."

"Where?" he says. Then, as if to himself, "Where."

"I don't want to live in Minot, and I don't want to depend on my father's money, either. That's the mistake we always made, Daniel."

"No," he says. "The last time — the mistake I made was not going to him for money."

"But it put us in that frame of mind — that we could always get some money somewhere, money that we didn't have and weren't going to be able to earn."

"Well," he says, "I've learned my lesson. But I can't earn any money here."

"We have to stay in the Wilson house at least until these kids have a full year in school. Then we'll decide."

"Hey," he says, trying a joke. "Are you taking over here?"

It angers her unreasonably, and she can barely control her voice. "I've done this on my own, and I'm not going back from it."

"I never asked you to go back on anything."

"Minot would be going back," she tells him.

"Okay," he says. "Minot is out."

And when he begins to talk about how things will be, living in a boarding house through the spring and summer months, somehow she manages to get out that he will sleep in a separate room. Her explanation of this fact falters and is less than exact, since she hasn't really been quite able to explain the matter of it to herself.

Of course, he doesn't understand — it is entirely possible that he's literally unable to grasp what she's telling him.

She pulls the car out of the prison entrance and onto Route 11. She's watching the road and he's watching her. "I don't —" he says.

"Please don't jump to conclusions," she tells him.

"Connie," he says. "You mean — I'm in another room?"

"You've got to try and understand," she says.

He's quiet.

"It's just until I can sort things out."

"I knew it. I told you myself — I told you weeks ago that you'd —" He doesn't finish.

She's quiet.

"All right," he says. "You want to sort things out. What things?"

"Please don't take it wrong."

"How am I supposed to take it?" he says, angry now.

"I just need a little time."

"It's been nine months."

"That's not what I mean."

"No," he says. "This started way before I got arrested."

"How can you say that," she says, "after what I went through to come out here?"

"Well, that's what I'd like to know, Connie. Why you did that. What in the world made you come out here."

She's trying not to cry. "To be with you. To be near you. To go through it with you."

"You want to know something?" he says. "The first day you came to see me, I knew you were going away from me. I said you were. All those miles you traveled to get here, and you were going away."

"I'm *here*," she said. "I'm sitting right here. Can't you understand that I'd need a little time to adjust?"

He says nothing for a moment. "You never needed any time to adjust before."

"Everything's different," she says. "*You're* different. Don't you see how we can't just go back to the way it was?"

"I need us to be able to go back to the way it was," he says simply. "Before any of it. I need you. You don't know how much."

"I can't," she tells him. "Not now. Please understand, Daniel, we've been through so much."

"Why did you come here?" he says. "I would like to know why you came here."

She hesitates. It's as if she's attempting to frame an answer, and when she speaks now it's almost with tears. "I — I told you."

"You felt sorry for me."

"No. God!" she says in an exasperated tone. "I was sorry. But not like that — it wasn't like that. I wanted our family back."

"Well, that's — that's what I want," he says, trying not to give way inside.

"Oh, please," she says. "Please can't we just talk about this later? We're almost there."

"So that's it, then?" he says. "No appeal?"

She doesn't answer.

"So I have another sentence to serve," he says.

"This is not about you," she says. "Can't you see that?"

He says nothing. He stares out the window at the passing country-side, the distant cloud-capped mountains, the snow fields, the sinking sun which sends streams of color along what looks like the wide, white edge of the world.

When we went downstairs for dinner, Penny was there. She wore a dark blue skirt and a white blouse with ruffles down the front. She was leaning on the frame of the entrance to the dining room, sipping coffee and talking to Mrs. Wilson. "Hey," she said to Mother, "where is he?"

"He'll be down."

"How is he?"

Mother gave her a look, the kind one gives to express exhaustion and anxiety.

Penny sipped the coffee.

"I don't mean anything by this," Mrs. Wilson said, "but I just want it known that I won't tolerate any trouble."

"There won't be any trouble," Mother said in a quiet voice.

Mrs. Wilson went into the kitchen and began bringing the food out — a steaming platter of roast chicken and potatoes, with carrots and celery. We all took our places around the table, and Mrs. Wilson began dishing out the portions. No one said anything, and we were all watching the entrance from the hall, waiting for my father to come down. We had lived in that house for seven long months; sitting around that table in the evenings was a familiar thing, these people — Mrs. Wilson, Russell, Penny Holt — were familiar people, nearly like family, and yet I felt estranged from them, felt the pressure of being with them, as though they were people I had never met in my life, and the walls were the walls of an all too public place.

We heard him on the stairs. Everyone was transfixed, until Mother said, "Can we please not make him feel like we're watching him?"

So we were all in an artificial hubbub as he entered, and I believe I'm the only one who saw him in the moment he appeared from the hall. There was such suffering in his face that I felt as though I had deprived him of his dignity. I looked away. He came around the table and took the only empty chair, directly across from mine. He had put on blue jeans, and a red-checked flannel shirt Mother had given him the last Christmas we were in the officers' quarters at Andrews. His eyes wouldn't settle on anything, and it occurred to me that I didn't want him to speak; I was afraid to have him speak.

"Mr. Boudreaux," Penny Holt said, "your courage is an example for all of us."

This seemed very badly out of place, sounded such a false note that Father looked at her, then at Mother. He moved his hands in his lap. "You're very kind," he said. He was apparently not quite certain, even now, that it hadn't been a joke.

I felt the weight of the lie on my stomach.

Mrs. Wilson ate in silence, and I wondered what she must be thinking — what deal had been struck between Mother and her. For a long while, it seemed, no one said anything.

"This is very good," Father said about the chicken.

Mrs. Wilson acknowledged this with a small, deprecating wave of the hand.

I wanted to ask, What are we going to *do* now? When are we going to go back? But I kept quiet. It struck me again, as if for the first time, that we were not returning to the Air Force.

In the next instant, with that odd prescience he sometimes seemed to have, Russell cleared his throat and said, "What're you all going to do now?"

"Be still," his mother told him.

"It's all right," Father said. Then he smiled, looking around at everyone. "Is it always this quiet?"

There was now tremendous pressure to speak. I felt it like a heaviness in the very air. I said, "I hope we don't have to move again soon." Though in fact, at that moment I wanted us to be far away from that exposed-feeling room, from those people who did not really know us — even Penny, who sat eating her meal in silence as if she were alone.

"You don't want to go back to Minot?" Father said.

I couldn't look into his sad eyes. "Minot's fine," I told him.

"We are not going back to North Dakota," Mother said.

He murmured, "It was just a question."

Russell had been talking low to his mother, and I overheard the phrase ". . . paint the porch."

Russell looked at Father. A shiver of desolation shook through my soul. So not only had he moved into Mr. Egan's room, he had assumed Mr. Egan's place in the house. I couldn't stand this thought, and I must've shown it, because my father edged over to get into my line of sight and said, "Son?"

"Yes, sir," I was just able to say.

"You look pale." He smiled.

"I'm fine," I said.

"A man has to pay his own way," he said.

I nodded. But I was very tired of hearing what a man is and what a man has to do. Another long silence followed. Penny coughed once. Russell cleared his throat again. Lisa sat with her small hands in her lap, having barely touched her dinner. No one said anything, and the slow minutes passed.

When I was finished, I took my empty plate into the kitchen and set it on the counter, then went up the back stairs to the hall outside his room and our apartment. He had left his door open. The coat and the clothes he'd worn were lying across the bed, but the light was too dim to see much else. I saw the books on the nightstand, and there was a vase with one flower in it on the dresser. I strode into our apartment and, hearing someone ascending the stairs, hurried into Mother's room, acting on an inexplicable need to get out of sight.

I knew who it was. The heaviness of the footsteps was unmistakable.

"Thomas?" He'd come to the partition.

I said, "What," and stepped out into the sitting room.

"Can I come in, son?"

"Sure," I said, hearing the false casualness of it and hating myself.

He entered the room, glancing around at the furniture, the walls where Mother had hung pictures. He hadn't noticed any of it earlier, and he was taking it all in. "She always has had a touch," he said.

I nodded, though he wasn't looking at me.

"I guess she's talked to you about things," he said.

"Not really," I told him.

He sat down at my side, his hands on his knees. "Man," he said. "It's kind of hard to know where to start up again, you know?"

I nodded once more.

"How's school?" It was what he had asked me, each time, on the telephone.

"Fine," I said.

"You quit playing the guitar, huh."

"Yes, sir." This was also something he knew.

"Well," he said, "it's good to try a lot of different things."

I couldn't find anything to say to this.

"When I was your age, you know, I wanted to fly planes. I joined the Army Air Corps because I thought I could work it some way — get the training. Then I just sort of found out I liked it. Working the flight line, you know. The — the pilots, when they were hung over, used to come to us to get hundred percent oxygen to breathe before they logged their time in the air. There was a lot of camaraderie and joking then. But you felt that you were helping somebody stay alive, helping him work the parachute, and the survival kit. Your work was doing that, and it mattered, some. Even Nam, you know — you weren't particularly killing anybody. You were helping guys stay alive."

I waited for him to go on.

"Well," he said, "I guess you don't need to hear all this."

"No," I said, meaning to tell him it was all right. He took it as agreement, and stood.

"Well."

"It's fine," I told him.

"We'll have to do something together when the weather eases up," he said. "Get to know each other again."

"Yes, sir."

"Maybe throw the baseball around."

"I'd like that," I told him.

"That Lisa." He shook his head, rubbed the back of his neck. "It's like I was never gone."

"She missed you," I said. "So did I."

"I missed you too, son. I missed both of you worse than I can ever say. But I — you know, I simply couldn't have you see me there, in that place."

"No," I said.

"You understand, don't you?"

"Yes, sir."

"And Lisa too?"

I nodded.

"She's got so tall from when I remember her." He'd said the same thing when he got back from the first imprisonment, the one in Vietnam. And perhaps we were both thinking about that now. He went on, sighing, "I've been behind bars in two different countries." He shook his head again. "Lord."

I said, "I love the ballplayer you carved for me. I have it on the shelf in my room." I couldn't remember if I had told him this, and yet I must have. But it didn't matter. He was pleased; he sat down again.

"You know, it's not that hard to do. It takes a long time and it's trial and error, but I was amazed. It's like I can see the shape before I start to carve it, you know? I made a lot of them for the other guys —" He looked off. He was so far from the man who once stood in the doorway of the house at Andrews and threw my record albums out into the summer dark. I wanted that man back. "Anyway," he said, "I made a lot of them. Animals, and people. A lot of different people. I did one of Kennedy for a guy. And then five other guys wanted one, too. I got tired of doing Kennedys for people, though."

We heard a commotion on the stairs.

"Here comes Lisa," he said.

She came in and walked over to stand between his legs. Her arms rested on his shoulders. "Mother wouldn't let me come up here."

"Well," he said, "here you are."

"Oh, Daddy," she said, "I'm so happy." She kissed his forehead. "I missed you so bad."

He was patting her back. "I missed you, too, my big girl."

I saw Mother come to the entrance, then step back. A moment later, she was there again. I believe she understood that I had seen her. We traded two knowing glances, one accusing, the other refusing to accept the accusation. I could not help the way I felt.

". . . so I drew it on my notebook," Lisa was saying, "and Kelly saw it and laughed."

Kelly was a friend she had made at school who lived all the way on the other side of town, and who called to talk to Lisa at least three times every day, seven days a week. Even Lisa would express weariness at this from time to time. The phone would ring, and when you answered it, a thin, breathy squeak of a voice would say, "Lisa, please," with all the imperiousness of queenly command impatient with delay, and with the fact that one had possessed the gall to answer and also not to be Lisa at the same time.

"Will you make Kelly one, too?" Lisa said, talking about her own little wooden sculpture.

"Sure," Father told her. "Soon as I get the chance."

"Mrs. Wilson said you might sell them," Mother said.

"I think you told me that," he said. "They're just dolls. I'd need a factory."

"They're more than that, Daniel."

"Not much more."

"They're wonderful."

"Well."

"Daddy," Lisa said, "will you read to me like you used to?"

"Sure," he said.

Lisa took him by the hand and led him into our room. Now Mother and I were alone. I fixed her with my eyes, and at first she did not look away.

We heard my father's voice. "What should I read?"

"This one," Lisa said.

"All right."

Mother got up and went out, and I followed. She was descending the stairs, at the bottom of which Penny stood.

"I was just heading up," Penny said to her.

They went on into the living room, and the sound of the TV. I knew Russell and Mrs. Wilson were there, too, and was assailed by the sense that I now had nowhere to go. I wanted to get off by myself where I could think.

Finally I settled for our sitting room, and the murmurous sound of my father reading to my sister.

"'. . . no one could understand what the king saw in her, or why he found her voice to be such sweet music. To everyone else she was quite ugly and her voice quite like the rasp of a toad.'"

I began to think about how it could be — how it was supposed to be. We were a family, and it seemed that we had given everything to keeping it that way. And now, when we might truly have it again, my mother was about to let go altogether. I stood. All around me were the signs of her effort to make this like home. I looked at the walls with the photographs of us in our many different houses and at all the stages of my growing up, and was visited by a prodigious urge to begin breaking things.

"Read me something else," I heard Lisa say. "This is childish."

I went out into the hall, and along it to the back stairs down into the kitchen. In the dark there, I looked through to the entrance of the living room, where the others were watching TV. I could see Penny sitting with her legs under her on the couch, and I could see Russell lying on his back on the living room floor.

Mrs. Wilson was talking. ". . . seldom see anybody from there, you know. So it's easy to forget it's where it is."

"I don't understand why he didn't talk about it a little," Penny said.

Then I heard Mother's voice. "He never was a big talker. He has always been very quiet, especially with new people."

"He said *we* were quiet."

"Well, we were."

"It'll take a while to adjust," said Mrs. Wilson.

I walked through the dining room and in to where they were. Mother only glanced at me as I entered. She sat on the other end of the sofa, also with her legs folded under her. There was about her the look of someone waiting for momentous news — someone who is doubtful about the efficacy of remaining still, and is accomplishing it only by an effort of will. In the big chair across from her, Mrs. Wilson had brought out her crocheting and was nervously counting stitches. The TV was a muted blare of gunfire and shouts, and its light flickered on her glasses. I sat down in the smaller chair against the wall, and when Mother glanced at me again I couldn't help showing my displeasure.

"What's the matter, Thomas?"

"Nothing," I said. I felt a sudden surge of rage.

"Something's the matter."

"No," I said.

"Aren't you happy?" Mrs. Wilson asked without quite looking at me. "Your father's home."

"No," I said. "He's not quite home."

"Thomas," said my mother.

"Well, I understand that," Mrs. Wilson said. "But he's free now. He's out of that place. That's the blessing."

I was quiet.

"He's reading to Lisa," said Mother.

Mrs. Wilson made a little murmuring sound of approval.

I got my coat and went out onto the front porch. The street was empty and still, and the dark sky beyond the naked trees was streaked with a silky radiance, a suffusion of the glow from the buildings of town and the stars' twinkling. It was bitter cold now. I walked out to the end of the sidewalk and turned to look at the house, a big shadow with lights in the windows, in the darker shadow of the big tree. I was trying to breathe, feeling the anger climb through me, and then Mother came to the door.

"Thomas?"

I stood there.

"Thomas."

"I'm going for a walk," I said. But my voice had faltered, and I had to repeat the last words. "A walk."

"Thomas, come inside."

"I'll be back in a little while," I told her.

"Where do you think you're going?"

"Leave me alone," I said. "Can't you?"

"Don't go beyond the end of the street," she said. "Please."

I said nothing.

"Thomas, please don't be this way."

"Who said I was going anywhere?"

"All right, then." She closed the door, and her shadow moved out of view of the windows. I stood there for a moment in the stillness, and then I walked down to the end of the street and on, toward the lights of Wilson Creek's main thoroughfare. I walked quickly, wanting to get out of earshot. The wind moaned, racing across the open spaces. Traversing the bridge over the wide part of Wilson Creek, I saw the shapes of hills in the distance, and in that prospect, with the dark sky trailing its mist of stars down into the dim edges of the hills, I was aware of the ground I stood on as an infinitesimal part of the surface of a planet spinning through space, and I had an urge to grab on to something to brace myself; I may even have staggered slightly, the way a person will who, while walking on a street between tall buildings, looks up and, seeing the clouds move, experiences for a dizzy instant the sense that the buildings are falling. I had been in so many different parts of the country, I was so used to changes, yet a change was coming that I was not going to be able to accept, and I knew it.

I passed the railroad tracks and made my way along the row of closed shops on Main Street, looking in all the windows in an attempt, I now believe, to find some anchoring thing among those ordinary objects — the sewing machines and the hair dryers, the vacuum cleaners, the radios and the record players — something by which I might orient myself.

The wind shook a sign on the corner and lifted a piece of paper out in the street. I seemed to be the only person stirring anywhere, and I wondered if my presence had disturbed something elemental in the quiet night. But then a pair of headlights turned into the street a few blocks ahead of me, came toward me slowly, and swept off to the right, going up a side street. I stepped into the arched entranceway of the presbyterian church, out of the wind. The whole passage had become a problem: to keep from being seen. In a minute or two the slow headlights approached again, a policeman on his beat, cruising vigilantly. Hiding behind the stone column, I watched him go by, and when his small red taillights were no longer visible, I headed back up the street, toward the house. As I reached the place where the bridge gave forth to the creek bank and the land opened out to the far hills and the stars, I paused, waiting for the precarious feeling to come over me again. Nothing happened.

So much of what goes through us is fugitive.

Penny Holt was coming from the other direction at the end of the block. At least part of my delay in turning around had been the adolescent hope that she might follow me. The fact that she *had* followed me raised my blood. I had been cold, shivering with it, and in an instant I was sweating under my shirt collar.

"Where did you go?" she said breathlessly.

"Nowhere."

"You worried us." Her use of the pronoun seemed unnatural, forced somehow.

"Nothing to worry about," I muttered. The proper stance now seemed to be that of the brooding young man. I felt her watching me as we walked.

She said, "Everybody's acting different."

"I just went for a walk," I said.

We continued toward the house.

"It's scary," she said.

I stopped and looked at her. "What?"

She glanced toward the house, but didn't speak.

"What," I said.

"Nothing. The dark."

We walked on a few paces. But then she stopped again. "Penny?" I said.

"You're all going to go, I know it."

"You can come with us."

"No," she said. "It's silly."

"What's silly?"

She breathed. "You have your family. It's a family."

"Is it?" I said.

"Oh, but — see, Thomas," she said, her voice faltering. "I — I knew it was going to be like this."

"Like what?" I said.

"Nothing."

On an impulse I touched her shoulder, and she pulled away as if I had burned her. "No, don't do that," she said. But in the next instant she came close again, and to my astonished and heart-shaking delight she put her mouth on mine. We stood there in the cold, and her tongue went between my teeth, a surprise that almost stopped my pulse. I pulled her to me. We were all over each other; my hands were in her hair.

Then she pulled away again. "No, no," she said. "No."

"I'm sorry," I managed. I was strangely numb, and a little frightened, too. I couldn't breathe out fully. There was an odd, sharp pang across my upper back, like the lash of a whip under the skin.

She looked at me out of that brilliant blue eye. "It's going to be all right, isn't it?"

"Penny," I said, "I love you."

"Stop it."

I reached for her again.

"No, please — don't touch me. I'm sorry."

We were standing a few feet away from each other, and she seemed to be talking to herself.

"What?" I said. "What?"

"You mustn't touch me now — it's my fault."

"I won't touch you," I said.

"It's going to be all right."

"Yes," I told her.

"Oh, what if that were true?" she said.

"What if what were true? That I love you?"

"No. Thomas, I'm sorry."

"What?"

"Nothing." She was looking at the sidewalk.

"Penny?"

"Let's go inside," she said. "Don't tell anybody."

"No," I told her, thrilled. "Right."

"It's so awful to be alone," she said.

And again I wanted to put my arms around her. But I managed to refrain from doing or saying anything for a moment.

"I shouldn't have come out here," she said.

"I won't say anything," I told her. "Can I kiss you again?"

"Stop it," she said. "That was all wrong."

"It wasn't wrong," I said.

"Please — we have to forget it."

I said nothing.

"We have to forget it, Thomas."

"Okay," I told her.

"Good." She folded her arms tight about herself and looked at the house again. "We should go inside."

I said, "Whatever you say."

We started walking. I can't quite describe what my feelings were in this interval: an odd combination of stupefaction and avoidance, along with a sense of having stumbled into a zone of fear and madness. I still desired her, but now my hunger was tinged with a new something, an element of unreality that was somehow morbid, too, as though we had been playing a scene with each other over a corpse. We made our way along the dark street and then across the lawn without exchanging another word. It was as if we were returning to the vividness of being alive.

At the house, the others were still watching TV. Father and Lisa had joined them. Penny took off her coat and hurried in to sit next to Mother on the sofa, and Mother glanced at me when I went on to the stairs, starting up to our apartment.

"Thomas?" she called. I kept going. I had got partway up the stairs when she said my name again, this time from the foyer. I stopped and turned. She came to the foot of the stairs. "We're all down here, Thomas."

"I'm tired," I told her. "I'm going to bed."

"Wait." She walked up to me. "Are you all right?" She put the back of her hand against my forehead. "You don't have a fever."

"I'm fine," I said, turning.

But she followed me up to the landing. "Thomas."

I halted. "What."

"Hey," she said, "don't talk to me like that."

"I'm tired," I said.

"What's upset you?"

"Nothing."

"Honey," she murmured, "why don't you go back down and say good night to your father."

Abruptly I was angry with her; I wanted to hurt her. "Why should *you* be worried about that?" I said.

For a few seconds, we just stood there as if stunned, as if someone else had spoken and we had both heard it and didn't quite know what to do about it. Then she turned and started back down the stairs, slowly, like someone nursing sore muscles. Entering the apartment, I glanced back at her, there in the slanting light of the stairwell, one hand clasping the railing as she descended. I think I knew that I would carry that image of her in my mind all the rest of my life. Something was irreparably harmed between us, I was certain.

But I could think only of Penny Holt. And of course I couldn't go to sleep.

Soon I was hearing the confused jangle and uproar of the television. It came through the walls and divided my attention, kept me from falling off. I opened the curtain and looked out at the night sky again, with its tremendous webs of stars spun on the darkness. It began to seem that the noise of the TV was coming from out there in the distances. But then I fell asleep, and when sometime later I was awakened by the sound of Mother putting Lisa to bed, I saw the white oval of her face in the dimness, and didn't remember for a moment that there was trouble between us: all I felt was a rush of aching love and recognition.

PART FIVE

21

IN THE MORNING, my parents went into town to get Father's state driver's license and to follow up on several job interviews that had been set up as part of the process of being released from prison. They departed before we got on the bus for school. I watched them go down the sidewalk and get into the car, and I reflected with some unhappiness that they seemed quite accustomed to the new situation. A moment later, Penny Holt set out walking to her temp typing job down the street, after apologizing to Mrs. Wilson for not being able to help with the breakfast dishes and the housecleaning. She avoided all eye contact with me, and I had the unhappy suspicion that perhaps something like what had happened with me had happened earlier with Mr. Egan.

We — that is, Russell and Lisa and I — had our breakfast at the dining room table and then went out and rode our respective buses to our separate schools, Lisa to Edith Galt Elementary, and Russell and I to the old castle.

At school I looked at all the faces and wondered what it was about them that should seem changed. They were all the same; they were the faces of my daily existence in school, yet some part of me felt that they were not the same. I remember feeling this way for a long time after the night of Father's arrival in the house. Here's what the journal has to say about that first afternoon:

March 13
When we came home from school, Mother's car out in front of the house. He drove it back after getting license. He's in the living room when I come in, talking to Mrs. W. I see the crossed legs first where

he's sitting in the wing chair faced away from the entrance, and I hear something about hours. He leans up to look at me when Mrs. W says my name. Hey. I've got my books under my arm and he offers me his hand. I move them to my other arm and we shake. It's for her. We never shook hands like that. Mrs. W says I've grown taller even since being here, and he: This boy's quite a baseball player. Mrs. W isn't really interested in this. Nor me. It's like nobody's going to say anything about anything and we're just going to do it, go on through the days until they really split up. I don't know how grown-ups can stand each other if they have to spend their lives like this, in this stupid conspiracy not to say what's on their minds. I'm going to say what's on my mind. What does he do now? He smiles at me and then turns and sits back down and starts talking about jobs he might do around the house. How can they just let everything be so and not do anything about it? I hate it. I want to go somewhere else. I want us to get out of here, away from all these people and this place. Even without her. But I'm going to say it to her, say what's on my mind, and once and for all.

This last is about Penny, of course, and it is not a little surprising, since I kept most of my thoughts about her out of the journal: there are only a few coy, passing references to her, which ought to be some indication of the kinds of secrets I was keeping even from myself then. For in fact I saw a lot of Penny over the next two weeks.

I started looking for opportunities to be alone with her, paying attention to who was in the house at any given time. With Father returned to us, there was a great deal of activity, of going to and fro, and several times I even made my way up to her room. I'd lie across the foot of her bed and watch her pace at the window — she was almost never still — and we'd talk about goings-on in the house. I'd complain about the way Mother and Father seemed to be growing accustomed to their odd separation, and I'd plumb the depths of my feelings about having him staying in Mr. Egan's old room. I'd found it almost impossible to be near him. I couldn't look into his eyes or find anything to say to him, and this difficulty provided me with plenty to say to Penny.

She listened, without really seeming to. Occasionally she would come close enough for me to touch her arm or her hand, and there was always that small recoiling. Yet often she would put her hands on my shoulders, or brush the side of my face with her fingers. It was a secret, this new closeness between us, and the quality of a given day depended on whether or not I had been able to spend some time with her. When we were together, I felt grown-up and complicated, a man brooding over his troubled family. I was aware of myself in that role, and I never stepped back from it enough to see it for what it was: a kind of self-drama, with Penny Holt as an audience of one. We talked and idled the time away — or *I* talked; *I* idled the time away.

Sometimes, trying to follow my own determined promise to myself in the journal, I would try to say how I felt about her.

She wouldn't hear that, of course. And she was still very attached to Mother.

One afternoon, perhaps ten days after my father's return to us, I came home from school alone to find that everyone was gone to town — Mrs. Wilson and Russell to the dentist, the others to a recital of Lisa's. Penny had planned to go, but had got delayed at her temp job, and so had missed them. She was sitting in the living room downstairs, with the TV on and the sound turned down low. You could barely hear it.

I was so glad to see her that I almost dropped my books. "Hey," I said.

I had been striving to maintain this sort of casualness with her, as if our new situation had resolved itself and was firmly established at a vaguely platonic level. And yet I was continually aflame with the memory of having kissed her, and always looking for any sign that I might be allowed to take the next step.

"No one's here," she said.

I said, "Good."

She gave forth a little sigh. "Oh, Thomas."

"Well, I'm glad," I told her. Something of the breathiness of her voice as she said my name encouraged me.

"I promised Lisa I'd be at her recital."

"Lisa's fine."

"Stop looking at me like that," she said. But it was lighthearted.

"Let's go up to your room," I said.

"Thomas."

"Come on."

"There's no need."

I had never told her what I knew about her and Mr. Egan. I was tempted to now. But finally I lacked the nerve. It dawned on me then that even with the time I had spent in her company over the past few days, I didn't really know anything more about her.

"You're staring at me," she said.

"Tell me about your childhood."

This had the effect of drawing all the color in her face to the soft bones of her cheeks. "Oh, God. You're not interested in that."

I sat down on the floor at her feet. "Come on," I said. "I tell *you* stuff."

"No you don't. I don't know a thing about your childhood."

"What do you want to know?"

She smiled. "Everything."

"I can't think where to start," I said. "You start."

"Thomas."

"Come on," I said. "It'll be fun."

She drew her legs under her and put her hands up to her chin. "Well."

I waited.

"I grew up in a little cave by the sea . . ."

"Come on," I said. "I'm serious."

She stared at me, then seemed to decide upon something. And when she spoke, her voice was almost expressionless, as though she were reciting the words. "I'm not like you, you know. I mean I haven't lived in a lot of different places like you. It's all very dull and ordinary."

I got to my knees and faced her, my hands on the arms of her chair, and she stiffened, seemed almost frightened. I sat back on my heels. "You know, you're not that much older than I am," I said, smiling, trying to seem casual, even playful. But she was very still, and I had that feeling again, of a morbid unreality. "I love you," I said, flying in the face of it.

"You don't know anything about me," she said through her teeth. "Now back off."

I got to my feet and moved to the other side of the room. When I turned, I saw that she had stood.

"Thomas," she said, "the night your father got here. That — what happened. I wasn't — I wasn't thinking of you as *you*. Do you under-stand me?"

"No," I said.

"I was afraid."

"Of what?"

She was wringing her hands. "Everything."

This struck me as scene-playing. I said, "Ever since I first saw you . . ." But I couldn't finish. The expression on her face, the barely suppressed boredom tinged with exasperation, stopped me.

"I want to be friends with you," she said. "That's all it can be. You're only eighteen years old."

"So?" I said. "If you felt something —"

She had already begun to speak: "It — look, it doesn't have anything to do with you. Not the way you think. It isn't you."

"Is it Mr. Egan?" I said. I hadn't known I would say this.

"Who?"

I waited. I'm sure the challenge was in my expression. It was as if I had demanded an answer, and without having to go into it, she knew that I had witnessed Mr. Egan's nocturnal visits to her room.

"You can't believe that I'd — that he —" She stopped.

"Well?" I said.

Her good eye narrowed. "Mr. Egan had some grass. You know what grass is?"

I nodded.

"We smoked his grass. We opened my window and blew the smoke out of the top of the house. And when he got — when he started wanting to do more than smoke the grass, I cut him out."

"Look," I said, "I don't want to fight with you —"

"Are we fighting?"

"I'm sorry," I said.

"Tell me, Thomas. What did you think of me? What was it you thought you'd get, that you were so sure Mr. Egan had got from me?"

"No," I said. "That isn't it. This is getting all mixed up."

"*You're* getting mixed up."

For a small space, we were both silent.

"I want us to be friends," I said.

"Friends don't spy on each other."

"I wasn't spying. I heard him go up the stairs."

She said, "Jesus Christ."

"The stairs creaked," I said.

"Who have you told?" Her lips trembled as she spoke.

"No one." I held my hand up as if to take an oath, then realized the absurdity of the gesture.

But she wasn't looking at me now. "He offered the stuff to me. It made me feel easier about everything so I could — not worry so much. I thought I wasn't going to stay long anyway. And then it all changed."

"I didn't tell anyone," I said. "Really. I'm the only one who knows."

She said, "No, Mrs. Wilson knows. *He* told her."

I could think of no response to this.

"She put me on probation. She needs the money and it's hard to find boarders. But if I do anything else she doesn't like, I'm out."

"You're with us," I managed to say.

Her reply was quick. "I'm with nobody." She moved through the entrance into the foyer, then turned to look at me through the slanting beams of sun from the windows. Thick dust floated there, and her shape behind the light was almost spectral. "I didn't mean to hurt your feelings, Thomas."

"No," I said.

"Are we still friends?"

"You know we are," I told her.

That evening at dinner, she smiled at me from the other side of the table, as though we were conspirators in a secret game. Yet when I sought her gaze during the rest of the night's talk, she seemed not to notice me at all.

We went through the days. We were all being tolerant and careful of each other. The journal entry for March 23:

> *Driving lesson today. We went up to Route 11 and turned around. Parallel parking at the school for an hour. He hasn't found a job yet. The skin of his face looks too tight. Teaching me to drive, spending time with Lisa, doing stuff around the house to help Mrs. W. No life in him. They're just letting it go on. Seems almost normal sometimes. Mother asked Grandfather Tinan for some more money.*
>
> *They argued in nice voices about it. Awful. Him: I'll find something to do around here to make up the difference, Connie.*
>
> *And her: Well, just until you get settled into something.*
>
> *There's really no need to go to your father though. I know how you hate to do it.*

He wants to help.
But I know how you hate asking for it. Especially on my account.
I have no special problem asking for it on your account.
I didn't say I blamed you for it.
I said I have no special problem asking for it on your account.
Well, I know how hard it is on any account.
It has to be done.
Maybe something will turn up.
In the meantime, it has to be done.
Of course you're right.
Mrs W is there the whole time. And then tonight Lisa says to me How come you aren't mad? I am, I tell her. What makes you think I'm not? I don't like it, she says. I just don't like it. Are we just going to go the rest of our lives like this? I want to go home, I said. And she: Well, that's silly. We are home right now, aren't we?

What I had begun to notice was a faint but growing antipathy between Father and Penny — or, more accurately, a disaffection of Father's concerning her, which he expressed in small, casual-seeming comments to Mother. Mostly he was quiet, deferential to everyone. To me, he seemed hollow; there didn't appear to be anything left of the man I had known as my father. He spent his days brooding on his troubles, and he never seemed to hear what was said to him.

The entry for April 1:

Monday. Last night Pres. J announced wouldn't run. Mrs. W said Poor man. We didn't talk much more. But I saw Mrs. W watching Father. Now Bobby can get in, Mother says to P. And we can put an end to the killing. Father gives her a look — surprise mostly. How does she do it, how does he do it? Lisa refuses to be consoled, and won't allow Mother near her a lot of the time. It's warmer out. 40s. We got home from school and he was out on the porch, working the sander. I tried to talk to him. Nothing. Friendly, quiet nothing. I hate it. Takes me out driving. Serious, kind, but might as well be a stranger. Except he calls me "son." Never believe a blinking turn signal, son, some idiot could be tooling along and not know it's on, and you pull out and you've got a broadside, which is the worst kind of accident there is. People can survive head-on collisions sometimes, but not broadside. That's instant death, son. Mother comes home from work and he's sitting on the porch with the sander in his lap. I'm standing next to him. She says What a picture you two make.

Him: Just like you and your friend.

Exact words.
Mother: I don't understand you.
Him: A pretty picture.
Exact words.

For April 4:

MLK shot dead in Memphis. Fires set everywhere. Washington and Detroit. All over. We sat in living room and watched it on TV. Nobody said anything. I kept looking at Penny. Couldn't read her face. She keeps away from me like plague now. Even Mother noticed it. TV gets scarier. Talk of riots, casualties. Mother and Father held hands but like people bracing themselves in a disaster. Passengers on a jet that's about to hit. Lisa grows worse. Can't sleep alone anymore, crawls up every night no matter what I say about it trying to calm her. I feel sorry for everyone.

And the one from two weeks later:

April 21
Mrs. Wilson and Russell at church. Mrs. W says MLK's death did it. Scared. Whole country's gone mad. It's the war (P said). Makes an atmosphere for killing. Makes it easy. Makes life cheap. Not looking in my direction, not even a glance, when I say That's right. Father: Talk's cheap, too. Mother in a quiet voice agrees with P, and no one says anything else. We just watch the TV and it all unfolds like a bad dream. He talks to me about not waiting to get drafted, avoiding the infantry: You really don't want the infantry, son, no matter what. And Mother: He's not going to go to this war. I'm not giving up my son to this lunacy. Do you hear me? He's not going.

And Father: I'm just trying to make sure he doesn't wind up doing just that.

She: I won't let him, if we have to move to Canada.

He (almost under his breath): Well, that would be a move. Some kind of move.

Exact words.

She's quiet then. This is the first really nice day of the year. 60s and no wind. Not a cloud anywhere. All the snow's gone, even from the shadows of the houses. Buds on all the trees and patches of green in the lawns. Mother spends the morning helping P with another quilt. Lisa and I go to the foothills with Father to look at the crafts the Indians are selling. We look at this old man with dark, dark eyes, most wrinkled eyes I've ever seen on a human being. He's got the feather headdress on and also the ceremonial robe of the medicine man, Father says. Almost like he always was. But five minutes later staring off and not hearing anyone. Still no job. Talks sadly about these men, no jobs anywhere for them, nothing they can do, forced to try and make money off their old customs. He says, At least they know who they are and what is expected of them. Exact words. He talks to them, seems to know some of them, and we find out that one was in the prison with him. Father calls him Charlie, and introduces us. Charlie talks about how bad it all is. And Father says, I can't help wondering if I shouldn't go on back in. They won't let me back in the Air Force. Exact words. Later, he tells me it was a joke, a way of seeming to agree with Charlie.

And then there are these:

April 25, 1968
I watch the car pull up. Mother and Penny get out and walk toward the house. Father gets out slow on the driver's side and stands there staring at them. They laugh. Look on his face hurts me.

I take my road test in a week. Odd quiet in the car when we do the lessons. We don't know what to say to each other. I'm embarrassed for him. Everything is ruined. I'll get my license two whole years after everyone else, except Russell, who can't have his till he turns eighteen either. Grandfather Tinan calls and they watch her talk to him — Father and Penny. They stare at her.

April 29, 1968
Lisa refuses to go to bed unless I'm with her which means I go to bed when an eight-year-old does. They asked me to help them with her and now I'm in bed by eight o'clock every night. She's causing a lot of trouble. Never seen her so bad, and I think it's what she told me before: mad at them so she wants to take it out on everybody. He's painting the porch, wearing the apron Mr. Egan wore. Mother and Lisa pull in from Lisa's school. Him: Where's your friend?

Mother: Who?
Him: Jesus, Connie. Who do you think?
If you mean Penny, I guess she's at work.
You mean you don't know?
Come on, Lisa.
Did I say something wrong?
All exact words. I can't wait until I can drive my own car.

May 9, 1968
Drove to the prison on my own. Down Route 11. Hated it when trucks came in the other direction, still doesn't seem like they'll go by without hitting me. Grandfather Tinan called this afternoon and

when Mother told him about my license, he asked to talk to me. *Congratulations*, he says. Aunt Elaine got on and said so, too. Lisa scowled and refused to talk to either of them. It's extremely tense whenever they call. Today Father goes to his room and stays there. And afterwards he's quiet for hours. He wants to go to North Dakota bad. But she won't hear of it. And whenever the subject comes up, they get nervous and quiet. This morning he said *We can bring Penny along with us if that'll make any difference.*

And Mother: *What in the world are you talking about.*

Father: *I said if you want to, we could take Penny with us. If that's what's holding you back.*

And she: *Nothing's holding me back, Daniel.*

I left them and drove out to the prison, which is busier in the warmer weather. I saw many men out in the grass field beyond the last building. They were tossing a football around. People still walking around in front with placards.

May 12, 1968
Lisa up all night. Her dream again. No one else up. Do I think they'll stop this and be like before, and it's like she's challenging me, mad at me, too.

May 14, 1968
   Lisa: *Why don't they talk?*
   Me: *They talk.*
   Lisa: *They don't say anything to each other. Like they're just strangers in a train station or something. Like they have to try to be nice to each other and she says more to Penny. She's more like her own self with Penny, I swear.*
   Me: *Has Penny told you anything about me?*
   Lisa: *Like what?*
   I don't know.
   What about them?
   Nothing.
   Don't you think Mother's more like her own self with Penny? She's not like her own self with Father.
   That's what I said.
   Well, really, Lisa — what are they going to say in front of us? They don't talk right with each other at all and you know it.

May 19, 1968
Mother's birthday coming up. She said it aloud about how I was a year old in the Arctic Circle. He was taking a break from the porch,

almost finished the whole thing and getting the drain spouts and the
eaves and the gables too. He's talking more and more about moving somewhere, anywhere. Finding a place for us to live in Wilson
Creek if Mother wants to keep the job or if she doesn't want to
move away from Penny. Funny look on his face now when he talks
about how she doesn't want to leave Penny.

My job is a secretarial job, she says, I can do it anywhere. All
right, he says, all good nature, Then where?

Maybe Alaska, she says.

And he: Won't Penny freeze?

And she: Penny can take care of herself. I don't understand you.
You don't mean you would actually leave her behind.

What are you getting at, Daniel?

Nothing. Let's go to Alaska.

Very sweet.

And Mrs. W says, What about Alaska?

So they talked about it to Mrs. W, and later to P. He told the old
story, or started to. Thought he might even get the home movies
out. Strange this time, though, because the story wasn't about the
fight they had back then or about me either, really, but about the
terrible cold and having to live in darkness for six long months and
the oil business not panning out and all the money everybody lost,
what happened to their old friends.

He: I often wonder where they got to.

And Mother: They're probably not even together.

Both couples? That's pretty pessimistic, isn't it?

Well, maybe they are.

Probably not.

They all did nothing but fight the whole time, remember?

Well, but then we did a lot of fighting too, back there, didn't we?
Remember how discouraged you were that year?

I remember that, all right. How could I forget that.

But we had a lot of fun, too, didn't we?

I don't remember that being any fun. I remember I was depressed
all the time and not very good to be with, either.

You were fine, Connie.

Well, it was so long ago. Let's talk about something else.

And then Mrs. W: The young waste so much energy being unhappy.

June 1
I can watch Her again. I will. I don't care. Go ahead and look away.

June 3, 1968
Porch is finished at last. Mrs. W says we should have a celebration

about it. Awful idea. He takes no pride in it since it's all he could get, but she doesn't see it that way. He did good work, so she's insisting on the celebration. No hope of avoiding it. A cookout, no less. Hot dogs and hamburgers and beer. Whole idea like a humiliation to him and I can see it in his face as she tells him how she wants it. And anyway, quite clear all along that he can't shake himself out of his mood when he's around the others. But everybody wants to get into the act of celebrating. It becomes more bizarre by the minute. I can't write anything else now.

There is no entry for the following day, Tuesday, June 4, but it is the day I have come all this distance to describe.

I have a mental picture from that afternoon, a tableau: we are all out in front of the house in the cool, dappled shade, the murmuring sea sound of the trees as the wind stirs them. There's a smoking charcoal grill and a wooden table laid out with food for a picnic. The sun pours down through the small spaces between leaf and branch, and everyone is clean and healthy-looking. The light shimmers in their hair.

Anyone driving by would say we're one family.

It's the day of the big Democratic primary in California, the last hurdle for Bobby Kennedy.

22

IN THE NEWSPAPER that morning, a political cartoon depicted a book which was labeled *LBJ*, sandwiched between bookends labeled *JFK* and *RFK*. At breakfast, Penny said something about getting back to normal at last when Bobby Kennedy became president, and I saw Father shake his head. Even for what he had been through, he was still a military man. He carried himself that way. When Mother said she wished McCarthy would get the nomination, since McCarthy had gone against Johnson on the war before Kennedy had, Father looked at her almost sadly.

"What?" she said to him.

"I can't believe that's you talking," he said.

"It's me."

"You didn't talk that way before," he said.

"What way?" Penny said, flustered. "What's he mean?"

"They sent you over there," Mother said, "and they let you get caught. And it meant nothing. It meant less than nothing."

"It's a war," he said. "I've always been with my country when there was war."

"I thought he was against the war," Penny murmured.

"Let's talk about something else," said Mother. "Let's get off the subject."

"Listen," my father said, rising, "nobody wants a war."

He went up to his room. He was still there when we left for school, and he didn't come down when we got home. Mrs. Wilson was already preparing for the cookout. "I, for one, am going to celebrate the finished porch — a job well done," she said. She got Russell and me to take the folding card table out to the front yard and set it up. We did this without saying much to each other. And then we helped put the plastic tablecloth on it, the jars of pickles, mustard, and relish, and the chopped onions.

When we came in, Mrs. Wilson called to us from the kitchen. She was making potato salad while Lisa sat at the table cutting carrots.

"Open those cans of baked beans," Mrs. Wilson said to Russell.

He started on one, and I helped Lisa cut the vegetables. I could hear my father moving around in the room above our heads. I imagined him pacing, though the sounds weren't of the rhythmic kind that would indicate pacing. It was as if he were rearranging things, except that there was no sound of furniture being moved.

Presently Lisa pushed the rest of the vegetables toward me and stepped away from the table. "I'm through," she said.

"They're home," Russell said without looking up from his slow work on the cans of beans.

"I'll go see," Lisa said. "Thomas can finish."

Mother and Penny had indeed pulled up. We heard Lisa call to them, and then the screen door slammed.

Mrs. Wilson turned to me: "Go tell your father I need him to start cooking the hamburgers and hot dogs."

I went up the back steps and knocked on his door. Silence. I knocked again. From downstairs came the racket of Mother and Penny entering the house, their shoes on the hardwood floor and the reverberation of their voices in the tall foyer. They were laughing about something. They passed on into the kitchen, still laughing. My father's door opened. "What," he said. His hair was combed and wet. He was wearing a white shirt. There was no emotion in his voice at all.

I told him what Mrs. Wilson sent me to tell him, but found myself with the familiar sense that I couldn't look directly at him as I spoke.

"Come in here," he said.

I stepped inside the room. I had noticed before that it looked exactly the way it had his first day in the house: he had done nothing to make himself at home. This never failed to leave me with a sense of reassurance, since to me it was a sign that he would soon be moving into our part of the house. He closed the door and went to the chair by the bed, offering me the bed. I sat down, experiencing that queasy, butterflies feeling in my stomach: this was going to be something I would have to contend with — some revelation I wasn't ready for — and I received a passing intimation that he was planning to leave.

"It's a tough thing to ask," he began, studying the ends of the fingers of one hand. He bit the cuticle of a nail, looked out the window. "But I want a straight answer."

"Yes, sir," I said.

He looked at me. "Thomas."

"Yes," I said.

"It's hard to have any respect for me, right?"

For the moment I was unable to utter a sound.

"Well?"

"That's not true," I said. But it came too late, with the faltering voice of someone caught.

"No," he said. "Admit it, son. I'm hollowed out where it counts. That's what you think."

"No, sir."

"You can muster enough common respect for me to tell the goddam truth," he said through his teeth.

I was silent.

"Right?"

"Yes, sir."

"I know respect is something that has to be earned," he said. "I always believed that."

I nodded. I didn't know what else was required; I felt the immense anxiety of needing to find out.

"I don't have your mother's respect," he said. "I know that." He breathed out and muttered to himself: "Lost it before all this happened." Then he leaned back, as if saying this had given him some satisfaction. "You know when I lost it?"

"I respect you, sir," I said, and felt my mouth twist with the effort not to break down. I looked at the wall where Mr. Egan's spear had hung. A bare wall; the room was like a cell.

"I'm asking you something," he said.

"I do respect you," I persisted.

He nodded impatiently. "Do you know when I lost it, son?"

I said, "No."

"I lost it in Vietnam."

"No," I said.

He was shaking his head. "She was never quite the same . . . never the same after that."

I couldn't speak, but my expression refuted him.

"Well," he said. "You don't know. I know."

"She loves you," I told him.

"Jesus," he said. "I'm not looking for reassurance from you."

"Why —" I said, meaning to go on and ask why he was telling me these things now, and finding myself unable to continue.

He shrugged. "I came home pretty scared, boy."

Again, I couldn't look at him.

"I had a lot of trouble going to sleep in the nights. I had awful dreams. She had problems with that. She's — she's not very good about weakness, you see. She has never been very good about it. She's a lot more like her father than she realizes."

I didn't want to hear more. I didn't want to hear about his weakness.

"We kept a lot of it from you and Lisa," he went on. "But the whole thing started from there. My fault, kid. I made the mistake of thinking I could win her back, and things got a little extravagant. I was trying for that feeling we had when we were young — a reckless-ness, you know. Back when we were going to score big in the oil business and get out from under the old bastard's thumb."

"Don't," I said. "Don't — don't — please."

"Listen — I'm not telling you out of weakness now. That's the dif-ference now."

I had no idea how he wanted me to respond to this.

"She doesn't know she does this to people," he said. "I'm not saying she does it intentionally or with any meanness. It's something she can't help."

"What, then," I said. I couldn't help myself. I wanted him to tell me what he expected me to do with this information.

He said, "I just want you to know I didn't take those things for any personal gain — not for anything I wanted to buy. It was to show her, and it was stupid. And I paid for it."

"Yes, sir."

"I'm tired of still having to pay for it."

"Yes," I said.

"I don't want you to take it wrong when the time comes."

I stared at him, at the cold light of resolution in his eyes.

"I still love her, son. Just like I did when I was twenty-two years old." His eyes brimmed.

"Yes, sir."

"Stop sirring me. I'm talking to you like a man."

"Yes, s —" I stopped myself.

"I still love her and I'm going to fight to keep her, if I have to."

For an instant I had the sensation that he was enlisting my help in whatever he was deciding to attempt, and it was then that I felt the hopelessness of it. The full weight of the knowledge came down upon me that my mother was in the process of finding a way to leave him. It was all I could do to keep from showing him my distress.

"I want you to know," he was saying, "because it's liable to seem kind of harsh for a while."

"Yes, sir," I said, unable to help myself.

"I have to stand up," he said. "It's time to stand up a little. You probably understand what I mean, don't you."

I did, but I shook my head no.

"Well, you will, in time," he said.

"Yes, sir."

"I'm afraid I've let you down enough."

"No." This seemed too absurd to acknowledge. Mercifully he didn't seem to have heard me.

He said, "Are we straight?"

"Yes," I said, this time remembering to leave out the "Sir."

"All right," he said, rising. He offered me his hand. "We buddies?"

The word almost made me wince. "Yes."

"You won't say anything?"

"No, sir."

He shook his head. "She's been riding over me, son. And you can't let that sort of thing happen. I let it go for a while in the interest of peace, you know. This house being what it is. There's not much room for having things out in the open with the woman you love."

"No, sir."

"Okay," he said. "Go tell Mrs. Wilson I'll be down in a minute or two."

So it was afternoon now, and we were all out in front of the house. My father tended to the smoking grill, standing in the mottled, shifting shade of the big oak tree while Lisa and Russell watched him.

Penny Holt and Mother were in the foreground in the bright sun. Penny held a can of beer and Mother sipped from a glass of lemonade. Penny's immaculate skin was lightly tanned where she had been sunning herself, and I sat on the top porch step, watching her as I always was, actually feeling some small glimmer of hope in the fact that she had spoken to me about liking picnics as we started out into the yard — and vaguely tense, too, with that feeling of everything being in doubt.

Mrs. Wilson lounged in the metal porch chair behind me, her stockings rolled down to her big ankles. She called to my father, "I like my hamburgers charred, young man."

"Coming right along," he called back, a false note in his voice now, a fake heartiness.

The smell of charbroiled meat was on the air. Mother walked over to the table and, taking a pickle from a jar, popped it in her mouth. Penny had followed her. I saw Father keeping track of them. He was drinking beer. He was on his fourth can. He finished it and came up onto the porch to get another out of the cooler. From the table in the yard, Mother shielded her eyes with one hand and said, "Get me one too, Daniel."

"Why don't you come up here and get it yourself," he said. But he reached in and brought out one more in a shower of ice, and then stepped down off the porch, holding it out to her.

"Thank you," she said, and gave him a small puzzled smile. He walked away from her, back to the grill, where he had left Russell holding the metal turner. He opened his beer and drank down half of it in a gulp, then raised the can as if to offer a toast to Mother.

She raised her own can, and watched him drink. Penny watched him, too.

"Who wants a hamburger?" he said. "They're ready."

We all moved to the table to take up our paper plates, and one by one we filed by him for our choice of meat. Everything was festive and lighthearted. Mother strolled over to the base of the big oak and sat down in the shade, and Penny joined her. Mrs. Wilson brought her chair down from the porch, and Russell brought one, too.

"You'll want chairs," Mrs. Wilson said. "Russell, get the other chairs."

He did so, complaining to himself. I had not been asked to, but I helped him. Soon we were all seated in a semicircle under the tree, in the spotted shade. We ate, and talked about the food, the way the street was when it was buried in snow. We remarked about the cool weather, and how it was in summer.

"Sometimes in July, you'd swear you were in the tropics," Mrs. Wilson said. "The humidity comes in from that creek, and you can't find any relief from it. It's not the temperature, though. It's the awful humidity."

"It gets up over a hundred," Russell said.

"That's true. It's done that here."

"It was a hundred in Virginia when we were there," Lisa said.

"Not quite," I said. "Ninety-nine."

"It was a hundred and four here," said Mrs. Wilson.

"I don't remember it getting that hot," Father said. And it blew through me again that he had lived a summer here — a season doing hard labor, in fact. He went on to say he remembered the humidity, that he was not looking forward to experiencing that again. As he talked, Mother and Penny were shoulder to shoulder, engaged in their own conversation about other matters, and when Penny laughed at something Mother said, my father turned his attention to them.

"Hey," he said, "how about letting us in on the joke?"

Mother hesitated. "I'm sorry?" she said.

"How about letting us in on it."

She glanced around at the rest of us. "What," she said. "You mean what we were talking about?"

Penny said, "It was personal."

"Well, yes — all right. It was personal," Mother said.

"Personal?" Father said.

The two women regarded him.

"Personal."

"Yes," said Mother. "It really didn't have anything to do with anything."

"But it was personal."

She said nothing.

"Isn't that a little off, Connie? Trading little personal secrets like that with people around?"

"I didn't say it was a personal secret," Mother said.

"Well, if it's not a secret —"

"I don't think it's your place to worry about it right now, do you?"

"Oh, well — I see. It's about me being in my place."

No one said anything for a time. Then Lisa asked for another hot dog.

"Coming right up," Father said, rising. "Anything for my little girl." There was something pointed about the way he said this. At the grill he asked if anyone else wanted one. No one did. He walked over and handed the hot dog to Lisa, then sat down again.

Penny was saying something to Mother.

He looked over at them. "More personal secrets?"

"No," Penny said quickly.

"Well, tell us all, then."

"It's nothing," she said.

"I'm sure we'd all like to hear it."

"Daniel," Mother said, "please. This is not a schoolroom."

"No, really?"

Mrs. Wilson said, "I'd like to know how you'd feel about painting the eaves of the house, Mr. Boudreaux."

"I don't have any feeling about that," he said.

"You wouldn't be interested?"

"He's afraid of heights," Mother joked.

"No," said Father, shaking his head and looking down into his lap.

Mrs. Wilson hurried to change the subject. "Do you really think Bobby can be President?"

"Looks like it," he said.

"At least he came out against the war," said Mother.

Mrs. Wilson looked at Father. "You went over there — you saw it all firsthand. And you went to prison because you — well, you were against something they were doing . . ." She trailed off. It seemed to have come to her that she didn't really know anything about why my father had been in Wilson Creek. Perhaps something Mr. Egan tried to tell her, and that she hadn't believed, went through her mind. "Do you think Kennedy's right about it?"

He left a pause. He might have been considering telling her everything about himself. Then he said, "Like most military people, I hate war. But there are tigers in the world, you know."

"Yes," said Penny. "But who's the one with the stripes?" This seemed to have surprised her.

Mrs. Wilson said, "That's communist talk."

"No," said Penny, "it's not. I didn't mean it that way. It's loyal — the loyal — opposition."

"It may not be communist," Father said, "but it sure sounds disloyal."

Mother said, "What do we have to be loyal to? The Air Force?"

He gave her a look.

"Well, really, Daniel."

"I was talking about the country," he said.

"Okay, the country."

"You don't mean that, Connie. I don't know who you've been talking to."

"What is *that* supposed to mean?"

"I just mean that's not you talking."

"It's me," Mother said. "Whether you can hear me or not."

"Are you saying you're not loyal to your own country?"

"I'm loyal to my children. My loyalty stops there."

"What about me?" Father said.

Mother frowned, but said nothing.

"No," Father said, "really. What *about* me, Connie?"

She returned his look. "I meant my family," she said in a low voice.

"All right. Am I included in that?"

Penny said, "This is getting too personal."

"I was just asking my wife a question."

"Please," said Mrs. Wilson. "This is supposed to be a happy occasion. We're supposed to be celebrating a job well done here, and if you —"

Father interrupted, still staring at Mother. "Am I included in that lucky group, Connie? Your family?"

Mother had pulled up some grass, and was watching it drop from her fingers.

"Penny is," he said. "Right?"

She looked at him. "What're you saying?"

Penny stood. "Let's all stop this and play some croquet or something." Her voice quavered. "You must have some lawn games, Mrs. Wilson."

"There's a volleyball net somewhere," said Russell.

"Volleyball. Okay."

"Just making conversation," Father said to no one in particular. "Just wondering about the future."

"Be quiet," Mother told him. "You've had too much beer."

For a few seconds no one did or said anything. It was as if we were all waiting to see what would happen next. But then Mrs. Wilson stirred, got to her feet, talking about where she had put the volleyball net, and the inertia of the moment was broken; everyone was moving.

"Volleyball," Lisa said. Mrs. Wilson carried her chair back to the porch. Russell had run across the sunny yard to the falling-down shed against the side fence, and began working the combination lock on it. Lisa and Penny stood a few feet away, talking about where the game's boundaries would be. And I saw Penny exchange a look with Mother: a little furtive smirk of collusion at Father's expense. Then Penny turned her attention to Lisa again, and I watched her motions, feeling an abrupt stab of rage, still aching for her even as part of me had begun to wish she would go away. I was in a sort of wintry fever, a secret delirium, wanting to hold her and smash her at the same time. It was a very strange moment.

My mother and father were sitting under the tree, not looking at each other. He ate the last of his hamburger, and she said something to him. I knew what it was; I needed only to see the displeased expression of her face: *You ever do that again. Who do you think you are —*

And he spoke over her, still chewing the hamburger. He was almost cheerful: *It's over, Connie. All over. I've begged and sniveled and bowed my head for the last time. Do you understand, my darling? I'm through being the victim and the sad sack.*

And she: *Our private life is nobody's business —*

And he: *What private life? We have no private life.*

She: *I'm not going to have you parading everything before the oth-ers, and especially in front of the children.*

You're not listening to me, Connie.

I'm listening. I hear you.

All right. Good, then. Maybe you can hear this. I'm through being the beggar here, all right? That's what you need to know.

Nobody's asking you to beg.

You were.

No.

You didn't know it, and maybe you didn't want it. It's my fault, maybe — the whole thing. But it's over now. It's done and it's not go-ing to come between us anymore.

That isn't what's between us.

Yes it is. All the way. The whole time.

No.

Well, whatever. I'm through with it.

I wish it was just that.

People generally get what they want in situations like this.

I've told you.

Yes, and I'm telling you now.

It won't change anything.

I'm moving my family out of here, Connie.

Stop this.

Soon. I'm taking my family where they can have some kind of a life.

Back to my father, I suppose.

Maybe. I understand how you meant to hurt me with that, but until I get on my feet — just maybe. And he'll take us in, too.

You're not taking anybody anywhere.

You talk tough. Where'd you learn to talk so tough.

Stop this —

And you came all this way.

I won't listen to this.

I think I'm going to move back in with my kids tonight, too.

What are you saying.

You know. And if you feel you've got to be separate, maybe you'll have to be the one who moves out.

Oh, watch me.

Not interested.

He rose, walked to the grill, and closed it. Then he began clearing the debris from the table, stacking the plastic cups and the soiled paper plates and putting them in a big bag. His hands shook. Russell, Lisa, and Penny were working to put the volleyball net up. Mother strode to the porch and up the steps, on into the house. Mrs. Wilson, sitting in the shade by the front door, watched her go in, then looked at me with a question in her face, which I did not respond to. I walked over to where my father had begun to gather all the jars of condiments and sauce.

"Well," he said, without looking at me, "the battle is joined."

I could think of nothing in the way of a response.

"Here," he said, handing me a tin tray with glasses and silverware on it. "Take this inside."

"Yes, sir."

He began shakily folding the tablecloth.

When I came up the porch steps, Mrs. Wilson got out of her chair and opened the door for me, murmuring, "She went upstairs."

I put the tray down in the kitchen and then climbed the back stairs, making my way along the hall to the partition, the little stoop. She was just on the other side. I heard bureau drawers opening and closing. When I stepped up and looked in at her she turned, startled.

"What."

She was standing by the sofa with her small suitcase open before her. There were several pieces of clothing already folded in it, though haphazardly.

I said, "What're you doing?"

"Don't sneak up on people, for God's sake."

I repeated the question.

She hesitated. "Nothing."

"You're doing something," I said.

"Leave me alone, Thomas. It has nothing to do with you."

"Where are you going?"

This stopped her. She sat down on the sofa and put her hands to her face. "Please leave me alone."

"What is it with Penny?" I said.

She regarded me a moment. "Nothing."

"Penny's doing this," I said, "isn't she?"

"Doing what?"

"Making you act like this."

"Don't be ridiculous," she muttered. "What the — who the hell do you think you are —"

"He loves you," I told her. "Why can't you let him love you?"

She shouted at me. "Get out!"

I went down to the open front door and out onto the porch. Russell and Penny had put the volleyball net up and Father was tossing the ball at Lisa to let her try to hit it. He watched the house, too. Mrs. Wilson had joined them. I moved to the end of the porch and leaned on the railing to watch. My hands were shaking; I felt weak.

"Thomas," my father said. He looked calm now. "Aren't you going to play?"

I couldn't get my mind around what was happening, and I knew that whatever it was, it was only beginning. When Penny looked at me from the brightness and said, "Come on, Thomas," I climbed the rail and made a show of jumping down. (No trouble quite overtakes the vanity of obsessive infatuation.)

We chose sides: Father, Lisa, and Mrs. Wilson against Penny, Russell, and me. It was a very slow game, and very tentative, for Penny had all the difficulty one might expect, trying to play a game that required some peripheral vision. For a long time we were merely trying to keep the ball in the air. Now and again I saw her looking at the house, and I did so, too. Father was into the game, laughing at his failure to hit the ball, helping Lisa serve it, and trying to spike it when it wandered in my direction. We all knew something bad was under way, but we played on, into the beginning of twilight. Finally Mother emerged from the house, and moved to the railing. She called to Penny.

"Come play volleyball," Penny said with a sort of hysterical brightness.

"I'm moving in with you," Mother told her.

We all stood still in the dimness of the yard, waiting for her to say something else.

"Did you hear me?"

"Yes."

"I need the key to your room so I can put my things away."

"All right."

No one stirred.

"It's in my purse," Penny said. "In the dining room."

Mother left the railing. We heard the front door open and slap shut. Then it opened again, and she called from the dark: "Mrs. Wilson, Daniel will be moving out of his room and into our apartment with Thomas and Lisa."

"Mom?" Lisa said. Then: "Mom-eeeee." It was much like the scream she'd emitted the night they arrested Father. He took her hand and started toward the house. We all followed, Russell and Mrs. Wilson trailing behind, clearly uncertain what was expected of them. Penny ran ahead. She was in the house before anyone, and when I got there, just behind Father, I saw her standing at the entrance of the dining room, her hands working at her waist, talking to Mother.

"— I don't think this is the — I don't think —"

And Mother's voice: "Yes it is. It is. When did you think I'd do it?"

"Not like this, though. No, not — I thought we'd get a place."

"We have a place."

"Let me go," Lisa moaned.

Father held her tight, and turned away from Mother as she came into the room and tried to take Lisa. "Will you please give her to me, Daniel. She wants me."

He let Lisa down, and she immediately put her arms around Mother's middle.

"All right," my father said. "Leave us alone, please."

"You stay here, Penny."

"We have to talk this out," he said, "and we have to talk it out now."

"There's nothing to talk about. If you're moving into the apartment, I'm moving in with Penny. We already agreed to it."

He looked at Penny, then at Mother. "You agreed to it? What was it, a contingency plan?"

"We were talking about getting a place together," Penny said quietly.

Father turned to me. "Thomas, take Lisa out of here."

"I will not," Lisa said, holding on to Mother.

"Go on and take her, Thomas!"

"Yes, sir."

"Lisa," Mother said, "go with Thomas. I'm right here. We're right here."

Lisa screamed and fought, and it took all the strength I possessed to get her out to the porch, where Russell and his mother were waiting, like bystanders at an accident.

"Lisa," I said, "be still."

"I don't want them to gooooooo," she wailed.

"Nobody's going anywhere. Will you stop it? Stop it."

Gradually she calmed down. Or else she simply ran out of the energy to continue. She sobbed, caught her breath, and then she stared at the lighted window of the room where she had been dragged away from her parents. It was as if the light reminded her of this, and she started building up to another scream.

"Everybody's here," I said to her. "Be quiet and listen."

Then she seemed to realize what was happening. She gained control of herself and became very quiet. We were all straining to hear. The three of them were still inside, and the muffled, emphatic turmoil of their voices reached us in a jumble, without distinguishable words.

At last Penny emerged, walked to the top of the steps, and gazed out at the night.

"Well?" Mrs. Wilson said.

"Oh, I'm waiting for the sky to fall," said Penny. "I always am."

"What?"

"Dial the number and it rings," Penny said. "Every time."

"I won't have this kind of trouble," Mrs. Wilson said. "I really can't —" She frowned, watched Penny go down the steps and out into the dark of the yard. "What in the world —" She turned to me. "Do you know what that was about?"

"I don't know anything," I said as Penny's slender shape disappeared beyond the pools of light from the house.

"Everybody's gone crazy," Mrs. Wilson said.

A few moments later, Father came out. The door slapped behind him. He put his hands to his head and ran them roughly through his hair. Lisa hurried to his side, and he gathered her in. "Sorry for the commotion," he said to Mrs. Wilson.

She said, "I won't have this sort of squabbling."

He didn't answer for a space. "I'll be moving in with my family."

"And Mrs. Boudreaux?"

"I'm going to sleep on the sofa for now. I got her to see that I ought to be with our children more."

I went down the steps and around the house, looking for Penny. Russell walked with me.

"Go back," I said to him.

"Jesus," he said. "Everybody's gone totally nuts."

"Go on back, Russell."

"I just want to see where she went."

"Get out of here," I said. "Now."

"I didn't do anything." He stormed off in the direction of the back door. I heard it slam. But I was already walking on, toward the creek. Penny had gone to the back edge of the lawn, and she stood there picking a wildflower apart. The petals were white; they were what I saw as I approached her.

"What do you want," she said in an expressionless voice.

I said, "I wanted to be sure you're all right." It was a lie. I had gone there purely out of the need to know what we were going to be to each other now.

She tore the petals and dropped them. "You felt worried about me."

"Yes," I said. I almost went on to say, "I love you." I was barely able to keep it back. It was a reflex I controlled. I said, "What were you talking about back there?"

"Nothing."

"You scared Mrs. Wilson."

"I didn't scare you?"

"You always scare me," I said, trying to tease her back to something of our recent friendliness.

She tore the petals and dropped them. Nothing stirred anywhere.

"I think they've resolved it," I said.

She said, "I knew it would be like this."

"Like what?"

"Lonely."

"We're still friends."

"You were worried about me?" she said.

"Yes."

"Me?"

"Yes," I said.

"Not me." She sighed. "Something in your head."

"I don't get you," I said.

"You don't even see me. None of you do."

"I see you."

"No. You see what you think. I gave you what to think, too."

"I don't understand you."

"Don't you."

"No," I told her. "I *was* worried about you."

"Well," she said, "I'm glad *somebody* was worried about me."

I couldn't explain it, but I heard the sound in her voice of a disapproving lover, someone feeling ill used and lied to. I thought of this, and then dismissed it.

Presently she said, "Leave me alone. Can't you please leave me alone?"

Walking away from her, I was half hoping she'd call me back. She didn't. On the porch everyone was still gathered — everyone except Mother.

Mrs. Wilson said, "There's still the problem of the rent for your room."

"We'll keep paying it," said Father, "until you can get someone else. We're going to be moving out soon anyway."

"When?"

"We're going back to North Dakota. Connie's father."

"We are?" I said.

"When?" Mrs. Wilson wanted to know. "I've got to make up the income from these rooms."

"We'll wait until you can find other renters."

Penny had come to the base of the porch stairs, and now she started up. "Other renters?" she said. "You're leaving?"

"That's right," my father told her.

She looked beyond him, at the screen door, where Mother was now standing. "Is that true, Connie? You're leaving?"

"It's true," said Father.

"Let her answer."

"I don't have to take instructions from you," Father said.

"Now stop this," said Mrs. Wilson. "I won't have it in my house."

"Well?" Penny Holt said, still looking at my mother. "Is it, Connie?"

"I have to think of my children," Mother said. "It doesn't have to mean we don't see you again."

Penny turned to Father. "You simply exercise your power, is that it? You and her father." All her jitteriness was gone now, and in its place was a kind of heat. Her skin gleamed. She opened the screen door, stepped up into its frame, and turned to give my mother a look. Then she went on to the stairs, ascending them slowly as if she expected to be overtaken.

"I want this stopped," Mrs. Wilson said, standing with her back to us, supporting herself on the newly painted porch railing and trying to get her breath. "I want it stopped right now. Enough's enough. This is not right. I want peace. You agreed to peace."

We all moved separately into the house. It was as if no one was quite *with* anyone; even Lisa kept to herself, mincing into the living room and turning to watch us. It grew very quiet. For a few moments the only sound was the racket the insects made out in the night. Mrs. Wilson was shaking, doubtless from the effort of worrying about what might happen. She paid an almost frantic attention to the details of getting the house back to normal from the cookout, listing the tasks in a breathless voice for poor Russell, who seemed vaguely sorrowful, standing there with his hands on his hips, listening to her.

Mother said, "I'll help."

"Well," said Mrs. Wilson, with an air of having been rushed at, "you needn't."

"You put such a nice party together."

"Thank you."

They stared at each other.

Father said, "I'm going upstairs."

No one answered. When he was gone, we all spent a few minutes putting things away in the kitchen. The windows were black. The night bugs made an incessant hum and ruckus, and bullet-sized moths kept butting against the screens. Russell turned the television on, and Lisa joined him. Soon Mother and Mrs. Wilson were there, too. I went out onto the porch in the dark and sat on the top step. The night air was fragrant; it was a beautiful summery night. Behind me, I heard the noise of the television. Other houses on the street showed light in the windows, and somewhere children were playing. Their voices came to me on the breezes. The moon shone bright. It made a shade where the oak stretched its thick branches to the eaves of the house. The wind stirred the leaves. A moment later I heard Father on the stairs. He came straight to the door and out, without even glancing into the living room. He came to where I sat, looked out at the stars, drew a breath, then sat down.

"Nice night," he said.

I made a murmuring sound of agreement. I wondered what he wanted of me now, and I felt crowded by his presence. He was sitting too close.

"Anybody say anything?" he said.

"No, sir."

"There you go with that 'sir' business again."

"I'm sorry."

"Your mother didn't say anything?"

"No."

"She's up to something."

I kept silent.

"She caved in too quick. She's up to something, I'll tell you. I know her."

It was as if I had argued the point.

"The way she looked at me, boy. You don't know —"

It came to me that I didn't want to know. I felt that we had gone over some invisible line and entered a dark area where all the usual customs and applications no longer held sway.

"I know what she'll do now," he said. "She'll give me the passive treatment. The robot going through the motions."

"Don't," I told him. "Stop it, please."

He was quiet. He shifted his weight, then rose, walked down the steps to the sidewalk. He was in the moonlight, splashed with the shade of the oak branches. Out by the street, a couple walked by, talking softly. We heard the tripping syllables of a phrase, and laughter. They walked on, enjoying their quiet joke, whatever it was. "Be back," Father said, and headed out in the opposite direction, across the lawn, as though he were off to search for the place from which those strangers had stolen their lightheartedness and their comfort with each other, the magical source for it all somewhere in the night.

I watched him until he disappeared at the end of the street.

In the house, Mrs. Wilson and Russell were sitting in front of the television. Mother and Lisa had gone upstairs. I made my way up there, and found them sitting on Mother's bed.

"Well," Mother said in the tone of someone addressing the enemy.

"What did I do?" I said.

"Have you been talking with him?"

"Not much."

"What does he have to say?"

"He loves you," I told her. "He's hurt."

"That's what he said to you?"

"In so many words."

She shook her head, looking away. The light in the room was harsh, and made her skin appear sallow.

"So," I said, "is he moving back in?"

"You heard him."

"Are we going back to North Dakota?"

"Thomas, you were there when he told Mabel — Mrs. Wilson."

"Well," I said. "Isn't that — all right?"

She stroked Lisa's hair. "It's what we have to do. You want to go back, don't you."

It was not a question.

"Well?"

"Yes," I said.

"Of course you do."

"It's not a crime to want that," I told her. And I couldn't keep the anger out of my voice.

"Yes," she said, "well — it's just the way Penny says it is. He gets to use his power."

"He just got out of prison," I said, as coldly as I could. "I don't think he cares about using any power."

She said, "You don't know what you're saying."

"Yes," I said. "I do."

And she began crying. The tears just started running down her cheeks. There was no sobbing, no sound at all for a moment. Then she said, "I've tried. I've really, really tried."

"Why're you doing this?" I said.

"Please, go to bed. Go down and watch television. Do something besides hectoring me."

I went into my room and climbed into bed. I didn't even know what time it was. I lay there trying to put it all together in my mind. The house made its sounds, and I heard the television set downstairs, and then I dreamed that I was hearing it. I'd fallen off into a sort of exhausted sleep — like a lapse, a failure. Or at least that was how it felt when I woke up. In that instant I was breathless, startled. I had the feeling that I had let time get away from me, and that something awful would follow from this dereliction. In the quiet, I got down from the bed and saw that Lisa lay asleep in hers. The apartment was dark. Father was not on the sofa. Out in the hall, I saw that his door was closed. Downstairs, the television still made its small racket, and Russell sat in the silver shifting light of it, the only one awake.

"Hey," I said.

He jumped. "Oh."

"Did my father come back?"

"I wouldn't know." He was still angry with me, and turned back to the television.

I didn't have the energy to deal with him now, so I went outside, to the top step of the porch. The night felt cooler. I was beginning to believe that Father had come back and gone into his room, when he appeared from one of the little ponds of light under the streetlamps. Seeing him, I had a sense that he'd been waiting for me to come out. He crossed the lawn again and stopped at the base of the steps.

"You're up late."

"Yes, sir."

He shook his head. Oddly, he had the demeanor of a man who has been locked out. "Well," he said, and looked off.

"Where did you go?" I asked.

He shrugged. "Walked, mostly."

We said nothing for a time.

"It's nice to just walk and keep going, you know? Be able to keep going. I walked through a lot of imaginary lines, son, and it felt good."

"Yes, sir."

"Everybody asleep inside?"

"I guess so," I said. "Russell's watching TV." But then the screen door opened behind me, and Mother stepped out in a robe and slippers.

"Connie," he said.

She padded across to where I was sitting, and said nothing.

"Nice night," Father said.

"A little chilly," she said.

"I've been walking."

She let this go by.

"I was telling Thomas, here, how it felt to be able to cross all those imaginary lines. Just keep right on going and no walls to stop me."

"So," Mother said, "what stopped you."

He gave forth a small sighing laugh. "Right. Well, you know, that's — there's my family to think of."

"I didn't mean that the way it sounded," Mother said.

"Well," he said. Then he was quiet.

"How —" she began. "How far did you walk?"

He looked off in the direction he had taken. "Oh, on into town and out the other end. Past the train station." He paused, ran his hand through his hair. "I remember when they brought me in there. Right at sunset — a pretty day. What a thought to have at a time like that, but I remember thinking it was a pretty day. Everything was gold, you know, in the light. Way the light gets at sundown on a clear day. The grass, what there was of it. Just — gold. The — the windows. And — and I saw how everybody else seemed so much at home. You know — the people in the station. Ah. So much at home. Guys who were delivering me. The guy behind the counter. Everybody so comfortable, and — at home. That was the awful thing, I guess. They were all so — and you know none of them seemed to appreciate that they were home and could go around like they wanted. And I was coming here to be an inmate. I'll tell you, I sweated that first few days, really sweated. And it was tied up with what was going on in my mind, I guess. This — this trapped feeling. I just sweated worse than anything. Worse than Nam, even. I couldn't wear anything without getting it clammy with sweat. Without even lifting a finger. I don't know what it was. The strain, I guess." He put one foot on the bottom step, his hand on that knee, then swayed forward a little. "My clothes — everything. Just soaked all the time."

"You were always so careful of how you dressed," Mother said.

"Yeah, they — they cured me of that." Again he looked off into the night. A slight breeze moved his dark hair, made it stand up. "I'd count off time in my head." He laughed softly. "Adding and subtracting all day. Just like in Nam, really. In Nam there wasn't any time to think. Someone was always haranguing you. Here, I had plenty of time to think."

"You've been through a lot," Mother said. "I know."

"It wasn't easy for me to say all that," he said. "I think it deserves something more than that kind of polite observation."

"I'm sorry," Mother said.

"Yeah," he said, looking down at the hand on his knee. "Well, we've all been through a lot."

It was almost as if we had come through it now and were on the other side of it: we could be philosophical.

"I guess you can't help what you feel," he said, shifting, standing back a step. He put his hands in his pockets. "I'm aware of it."

"Thomas, why don't you go inside," she said.

"Ah," he said. It was almost like a cough. Then: "Let him stay."

She was silent. She stood there with her arms folded tight.

"When I was a kid," he said, not looking at either of us, "my father used to talk about my mother's — troubles. He'd get himself into one scrape or another with her — he didn't have much patience with people who gave her grief about her drinking. At least that was the way he was in the beginning. He'd get tangled up in some brawl or other, defending her. And then he'd bring her home, and he'd explain it to me. He'd say, 'Son, there's a kind of person who just can't make his own soul behave, and your mother's — like that. She wants life to be bright and good, and she spends everything of herself trying to make it that way — only her spirit won't let her rest. It does things inside her that she has no control over.' He was trying to tell me about all that spending and wasting and scrabbling after things to make the something inside a person stop driving, stop hungering all the time for more. Once you give in to it, well, it just never quits."

"I'm going in," Mother said.

"I'm just explaining to you that I understand," he said.

"I'm chilly, Daniel. I'm shivering. I thought you were talking to Thomas."

"I deserve better than that, too."

"All right," she said.

He muttered, "It *is* getting cooler."

She bent down and kissed me on the cheek. For some reason this surprised me. "Good night, son."

"Good night," I said.

She stood and faced him. "Good night."

"Sleep well," he said.

"Will you be sleeping in the sitting room?"

He said, "Maybe that can wait a day."

When she was gone, he cleared his throat and put one foot on the bottom step again. Then he stepped down, turned, and settled there. He had something in his hand, and he put it to his mouth and seemed to chew. Somewhere far off there was a siren, and behind us I heard Penny's voice. Father heard it, too. He threw whatever he was chewing out into the yard, then leaned back on his elbows and sighed, a long slow expiration of breath, almost like a gasp. "Your mother's strong," he said. "That's what she has." His voice was empty; it unnerved me.

"What're you going to do?" I said.

He looked back at me a moment. "Try to make things work some way."

"I don't understand."

He paused. "She never had anything apart — just hers. You see?"

I didn't see.

"She's the one who's strong," he said. "All those times I was gone, you know, I sort of wanted to be gone. Away from the whole responsibility."

"Stop it," I said.

Now the screen door opened and Russell leaned out, looking dazed, only half awake. "They shot Kennedy," he said.

We stared at him.

"Kennedy's been shot."

"Are you awake, son?" my father asked him. "Kennedy was shot five years ago."

"I'm awake. That's not the —"

"What's your name? Can you say your name?"

"I'm not dreaming or sleepwalking. They shot *this* Kennedy. Just now. Five minutes ago."

We were silent.

"I'm telling you they shot Kennedy. Bobby Kennedy."

"Bobby."

"In California," Russell said. "Five minutes ago."

I stood, and Father came up the steps. We filed into the house. On the television screen, newsmen were recapping the latest catastrophe in the national life. Russell and I, Mother and Father and Penny gathered in a semicircle before the hectic, surreal glow. Before long, Mrs. Wilson walked in from her rooms, having heard the urgent sound of the voices. She started to question us, then was still while the voices went on talking — the speculation and the horrified reactions. I glanced at Penny; she was wearing those pajamas I remembered from the train. She had her hands over her mouth. No one spoke. Once I saw my father reach over and touch Mother's elbow; she turned, looked at him, and then looked away. A moment later, when Lisa stirred, she hurried back upstairs. Mrs. Wilson sat at the edge of her big easy chair and wept, holding a white handkerchief in one fist over her mouth, looking as though she were about to stand again, but not moving to do so.

Russell kept saying "Jesus, Jesus" over and over, and the aggrieved sound of his voice was profoundly irritating to me, like fingernails being scraped across a blackboard. Presently Mother came down again, having soothed Lisa back to sleep.

"I didn't like him," Mrs. Wilson said about Kennedy. "But my God. What are we coming to. What are we coming to." She seemed to realize then that she had addressed this to my father, and she stiffened, holding the handkerchief to her mouth.

"Maybe he'll be all right," I said.

"He's a goner," said Russell.

"You be quiet, Russell," his mother told him. "You don't know what you're talking about."

"They shot him in the head."

"Stop it."

"Well, even if he lives he'll be crippled, probably," my father said. Penny sobbed.

"But I'm afraid the boy's right," Father said. "He won't live. Not shot in the head like that."

Penny turned and started upstairs. "I can't watch this." She was crying. Mother followed her.

"Why didn't the Secret Service —" Mrs. Wilson began, then fell silent.

"He went back through the kitchen," Russell said. "It wasn't even planned."

"What're we coming to — oh, my Lord, what're we coming to, what're we coming to . . ."

"This has been a terrible, terrible day," Father said.

But the day was far from over.

The news grew worse in the next hour or so, and finally Mrs. Wilson struggled out of her chair. "Russell, you'll never make it up for school in the morning."

"It's the end of the year," he said. "They're not doing anything anyway. All the exams are over."

"Russell."

"Whole world's falling apart anyway," he muttered.

"Please keep it down," Mrs. Wilson said to us.

Father turned the television off. Mrs. Wilson sobbed again, and started through the hallway to her rooms, Russell following her.

"Jesus," Father said.

We climbed the stairs slowly, almost side by side. On the landing he stopped us by putting his hand on my shoulder. "It's going to be tough for a while."

"Yes, sir."

"There's no love lost in Minot."

"Grandfather Tinan wants us to move back there," I said.

He nodded. Then smiled. "Nevertheless." He followed me into the apartment, and I was aware of the strangeness of having him there.

"I'll just look in on Lisa."

We went quietly across the sitting room and into where she lay in a fold of sheets, looking tossed and forlorn. The moon shone through the window and limned her face. Her hair was matted to her forehead; she was glowing with some riot in her dreams, and she looked feverish. "Is she all right?" I said.

He kissed her forehead. "Yes, cool as a cucumber." He adjusted the sheet at her neck, then kissed her again. I stood watching this, and then suddenly I put my arms around him. I hadn't known I would do so. It hadn't been our habit to be very demonstrative, and I think I surprised him a little.

"Hey," he said. He patted my shoulder blades.

I turned from him clumsily, pulling the blankets back from my bunk.

"You all right?" he said.

"Yes, sir," I managed.

"I know," he said gently. "I know, son."

Somehow, out of the tatters of what this day had been, I was gathering the sense that things might improve for us at last: we could return to Minot and start again as a family. This passage in our lives was finally ending. It occurred to me that more than anything else I wanted to go back to Minot, away from the bad feelings of this house.

"Well," he said. "Night."

"Night," I said.

He moved to the doorway of the room, and apparently he saw Penny emerge from Mother's room. Perhaps Penny seemed like a ghost to him at first, in those white pajamas. I heard the small sound of alarm and consternation that rose in his throat at the sight of her. And then I heard Penny's voice: "Oh, you scared me."

There comes a moment in the pathology of a night like this, with death in the air and all the long built-up suspicions and angers working in the soul; the world has conspired to seem just as chaotic and frightening as the poor lone spirit's own little history, and something snaps.

"What the hell is this?" Father said. "What're you doing in there, anyway? Don't you understand it's over?" And he started toward her. "Goddammit, you don't belong here anymore. You're the one causing all this mess. Get out — get out of here."

From the doorway of my room I saw her, a silver-white shape in the dimness, edging toward the entrance of the apartment, her back to the partition. He was a darkness, coiled, moving slowly at an angle to cut her off.

"Don't you touch me," she said. "You stay away from me. Connie, tell him to leave me alone."

"Daniel," Mother said from the doorway of her room.

"Don't you remember where you live?" Father said. "Get out. Get out!"

"You can't order me around," Penny said. "You're the one who doesn't belong here."

Father jerked a small table out of his way, and the lamp there fell and shattered. She screamed, and Mother shouted, "Daniel!"

For a brittle instant, no one moved or spoke or even quite breathed, and then Lisa woke, crying. It was as though we were all listening to Lisa, who moaned and then said, "Penny?"

This seemed to strike something through my father. He said, "You — goddam you —"

Penny bolted to the entrance of the hall and out, and he started after her in the sound of Mother's shouting: "Daniel, no! Stop! Stop it!" They scrabbled up the stairs to her room, and Mother followed them. The whole house was quaking with noise now — shouts, screams, more breaking glass. The floor shook from the force of the struggle, and I made my way up to where they were, realizing with a sick-feeling swoon that part of me wanted to see Penny hurt, wanted to watch as she was humiliated or beaten. I felt the thrill and recoiled from it, reaching the top step and somehow managing to propel myself into the room. What I found there sent a roar up out of my throat. Mother lay on her side by the open closet door with her hands to her face, crying. Penny had fallen across her bed, and Father loomed above her. He had torn the pajama top open and now held her arms down, his knee pressing against the fleshy outside of her thigh where she'd crossed one leg over the other to protect herself. "Thomas!" Mother shouted from the floor. "Stop him!"

All this in a single flashing instant. And then I was grappling with him, my father, moving with him in a terrible staggering dance, our shadows pitching crazily on the walls under the single wildly swinging ceiling light, my hands on the hard bones of his shoulders, and all around us the cries and shouts of the others, as now he surged upward, seemed to lift out of my grip, something inside me spilling over, and suddenly I was in a weird floating space, looking through gauze, hearing another kind of roaring. I couldn't focus my eyes and I was astonished to realize that I was no longer standing — the floor was punishing my back, and across the span of it I saw Mother rise, still crying. She scrambled to me, kneeled, and lifted my head. I looked into her face, and briefly I believed that I had spoken to her, but no words had come.

And then it was over, whatever it had been. I saw my father in the doorway, breathing like a runner; I observed the light on his gleaming arms, the tight musculature there. He hesitated, then stepped over Russell, who was on his stomach in the doorway, having tripped running up the stairs. I stood and moved with Mother to where Russell was also standing now.

Father descended without looking back. Penny remained on her bed, the blanket thrown over her, crying but without much sound, her face into the pillow.

"Are you all right?" Mother said to me.

"Yes, I think so."

"Your nose is bleeding. You're bleeding."

"I'm okay."

She turned and reached for Penny's hand, sitting on the edge of the bed.

"Get away," Penny said. "All of you. Please."

"Go on," Mother said to Russell and me.

"All of you," Penny said.

We made our way down to the landing, where Mrs. Wilson stood with her arm around Lisa. "I won't have this," she kept saying. "I won't have this."

"Where is he?" I said to Mother.

Russell started down to the living room.

"I don't want any more, please," Mrs. Wilson said, following him. "I want everybody out — everybody. I'll get a job at the prison."

Mother knelt and put her arms around Lisa, who seemed too dazed to notice.

I started down the hall to Father's room.

"Thomas. Leave it alone now. Stop it — you're bleeding."

So I came back and went into the apartment and tended to myself. The bleeding had mostly stopped. My shirt front was covered; it was as if someone had splashed the blood on me. I combed my hair, put a clean shirt on, and then went past Mother and Lisa, who had lain down together on the couch in the sitting room.

"Where are you going?"

"I don't know," I said.

"Leave it alone, Thomas."

"I can't sleep," I said. "I'm going downstairs."

"It's the middle of the night."

"There's the assassination coverage." I said this with a kind of brutal evenness of tone.

"Thomas, for God's sake."

"Please," I said. "I'm all right."

Downstairs, I found Mrs. Wilson sitting at the dining room table, staring into space. Russell had turned on the television, which showed five people discussing the sick society. The phrase was used two or three times by one of them — a thin, reedy man in a black suit whose lower lip drooped while he waited to speak, as if pulled down by some invisible weight in the skin.

"Kennedy's still hanging on," Russell said.

I went out onto the porch, where Father was sitting alone on the top step, his hands resting on his knees. He stared at the street, as though waiting for someone to pull up.

"I know how you feel about her," he said without turning around.

I said nothing.

Now he did turn. He studied me a moment, then went back to watching the dark street.

"Anybody could see it. I didn't mean to pop you."

We could hear Mother's voice now as she tried to get Penny to open her door and talk. Penny asked to be let alone.

"Goddam you," I said to my father's back. And in an odd way my anger was for two things: what he had done, and what the fact of it had made me feel in that harrowing minute before I got to the top of the stairs. I said the words, but it felt all wrong. It felt like something I'd been given to recite.

"You're an upstanding boy," he said. "So was I."

I was silent.

"Well, I was once. Christ — I didn't mean to hit you like that."

I was standing just outside the door. "God," I said, starting to cry.

"Go on inside, son. Nobody's that bad hurt."

I left him there and went back up to our rooms, where I found Mother sitting on her bed with Lisa. We had come so far, we three. We had been through so much together.

"Come here," my mother said.

And I went to her. I sat down and allowed her to put her arm around me. We were quiet. Now and again Lisa made a small sobbing sound. We heard the house settling down, and at last Father's footsteps on the hall floor and the stairs. He came to the landing and hesitated, then went to his room; the door there opened and closed. Mother leaned back, adjusted the pillow behind her, and I lay back with her. Lisa had begun to snore, but this was not restful sleep. "Turn the light out, Thomas."

I did so.

"Try to sleep," she murmured.

The day ended this way.

23

I WOKE IN rose-colored light, with a searing ache at the back of my neck. Mother's elbow. She lay on her side facing me, her arm under my head. Lisa was curled up into a tight ball on the other side of her, facing the wall. Extricating myself carefully, I put my shoes on and padded through the sitting room, expecting to find my father there. Sometime during the confusion of the night before, Mother had cleared away the signs of violence. I went out to the landing, where I paused, hearing someone moving around downstairs. With all the stealth of a burglar, I crept up to Penny's door, which, surprisingly, was ajar. I knocked softly, barely touching the wood with my knuckles. "Penny?" I murmured. Nothing. Gently I pushed the door inward, and its slow sweep revealed the unmade bed, the room's disarray — pieces of broken glass on the floor with scraps of paper, and one crushed paper flower. I stepped in and opened the closet; it was empty.

As I descended the stairs into the foyer, I saw Father going out, closing the front door. He was carrying a duffel bag over one shoulder. I hurried down to catch him. He had paused at the base of the porch steps, setting the bag down at his feet and looking at something on his wrist, a bruise or a superficial scratch. The noise I made coming out startled him. He looked almost sheepish.

"Where're you going?" I said.

"That's a good question."

I came partway down the steps. "Her room's empty."

He nodded. "I saw her leave. It gave me the idea."

I sat down; I might almost have fallen.

"Listen," he said. "Last night — that's — I want you to know I never did anything like that before. Rough a woman up that way. I never raised a hand to your mother."

I might've acknowledged this with a look, I don't know. I meant to say something, but I didn't have the words. I think I meant to say that I believed him.

He walked up the steps to me and reached over to touch my face. His hand shook, his touch was tentative. "Jesus. You've got a bad bruise there."

"It's all right," I said.

"Listen," he said, "don't ever — don't ever do a thing like that, son. That — last night. That was wrong. A woman — a woman shouldn't be treated that way."

"No," I got out.

"It was just that — seeing her like that. Coming from your mother's bedroom at that hour — and she'd been — it felt like she'd been chipping away at us ever since I got here."

"She wanted to be a part of the family," I told him. I was astonished to hear myself talking about her in the past tense.

"Well," he said.

"Where did she go?" I asked.

"Took a cab somewhere. Probably the one I'm waiting for. I saw her go. Even tried to tell her I was sorry, but — well, you can't blame her. I don't blame her."

"But," I said, "you don't have to go now."

He tilted his head a little, and seemed almost amused, but when he spoke his voice was broken-sounding. "No — I guess it wasn't ever her or me. Just — just felt that way."

I didn't know how to answer him.

"You remember that story your mother tells — how we met — how the two of us met. How I was what she didn't know she was looking for, all those years ago?"

I nodded.

"Well, maybe that's how it was here. With Penny."

"I don't understand," I said, though now I thought I did.

He seemed to consider this, then to decide against saying more.

"You're just going to leave?"

"I've got an old Air Force buddy in Seattle. I can stop there for a while, anyway. Clear my head. I've got just enough money to get there and tide me over a day or two while I look for something to do."

A cab pulled over in front of the house, the shadows of the leaves riding up its polished surface, and I thought of running inside to sound an alarm. He must've seen it in my face.

"I left a note for her, son. Believe me, this is best for now." He stepped down to the walk and lifted the duffel bag, then turned to look at me again. "Shake?"

I hurried down to him. His handshake was solid, but with nothing of the challenge I had felt in it at other times. "Try not to think too bad of me," he said, his eyes brimming. "I'm not always a son of a bitch."

I watched him go down and throw his bag into the trunk of the cab. The cabbie was the same one who had brought us here from the train station those months ago. My father opened the door on his side, and waved to me. "I'll be in touch soon."

"Yes, sir," I said, or tried to say. But my voice caught. He waved again as the cab pulled away from the curb, and I held my hand up, waving, until it passed out of sight beyond the last crossing street.

Inside, the house was quiet. Father's note was in a sealed envelope on the dining room table. I held it up to the sunlight at the living room window, feeling wrong, yet compelled to try reading it anyway. But the paper wouldn't yield up the words, and finally I put the note back on the table where he had left it. Soon Mrs. Wilson emerged from her rooms.

"Oh," she said when she saw me. "I thought you might be — well, never mind." She picked up the note. "What's this?"

"My father left it."

"He's left?"

I nodded. "Penny Holt, too."

"Together?" she said incredulously.

"No," I said.

She blew air from her top lip and started through to the kitchen. "I've got to get a *job*."

She put cold cereal and milk out, then returned to her rooms to rest. For a few minutes it was quiet again. I sat eating a bowl of cereal, then went into the kitchen and washed the bowl and spoon. Mother came down from our apartment with Lisa in hand and quietly read Father's note, her face as impassive as the face of a statue. Then she folded it and placed it in the pocket of her blouse.

"Penny's gone, too," I said.

"I saw."

"She leave a note?"

"There's no note."

"What did he say?" I asked, indicating the folded paper in her pocket.

"He says I don't want him here. And he's right."

"Tell me," I said to her, "what *do* you want?"

"I want my life back," she said in a calmly defiant tone. "I want some peace from always having to be asked what I want." Then she busied herself with Lisa's breakfast.

We stayed home from school, and spent the day in a sort of torpor. In the afternoon the announcement came through that Robert Kennedy had passed away in California. There followed statements of regret from various dignitaries and celebrities, several of whom talked about the recurring national tragedy.

"Whole country's sick," Russell said.

We watched the repeated images of pandemonium and death, grief and shock. The sun at the windows gave way to a shadowless gray, and soon it was raining, a soft cold drizzle. The sky was a pallid sheet of sparsely faceted cloud. In the evening, Mother called Grandfather Tinan, and talked about coming home.

The following few days are a blur in my mind. I know the Kennedy funeral was on one afternoon, but I don't recall that I watched much of it. What I do remember is a strong reluctance to be with anyone over that time, and in this I was not alone; we all moved through the house with the circumspection of strangers.

On the evening of the third day, Father telephoned from the road. He was in Spokane. He wanted us to know he was all right, and that he was thinking of us.

"You taking care of your mother?" he said to me. It was hard to believe he wasn't calling from the prison.

"When are you coming home?" I demanded.

There was just the faint static of the wires for a moment. "We'll work it out, son."

I handed the phone to Lisa, who was reluctant to talk. When Mother got on again, he must've apologized, for she said, "You've come to that a little late, haven't you?"

I watched her face.

"Well, we're moving back," she said. "Probably in July or early August. There isn't really much choice, is there."

Then he said something else, which made her turn away from us, hold the handset close, and speak low, so that we couldn't hear her. When she hung up, I said, "Well?"

She said, "Oh, Thomas — will you please stop watching every move I make? Your father and I are separated. He's on his way to Seattle and I'm going to be living in Minot. That's exactly how things are now, and I don't know any more."

I lacked the courage to ask her about Penny. And in fact only Lisa seemed at all curious.

"Do you think she went back to Kansas?"

"No," I said.

"Do you think she's still in Wilson Creek?"

"No."

"Then where?"

"I don't know."

Lisa said Mother had told her that Father would eventually be joining us in Minot. And so when the opportunity presented itself, I confronted Mother with the information. We were sitting in the living room together. Mrs. Wilson and Russell had gone off to bed. Lisa had fallen asleep while lying with her head on Mother's lap.

"Lisa says Father's going to join us in Minot," I said.

She sighed. "I suppose so. I don't know. You know as much as I do about it."

"Well, but — is he?"

"What did I just tell you, son?"

"But you don't want him to."

"Thomas, please." The look on her face was almost stricken. "Oh, can't you understand a little — can't you see what this has been for me?"

I couldn't look at her. And I have come to believe that if I had said something kind, if I had sought something other than an answer from her about everything, she might have volunteered some expression of her true feelings; she might have told me the truth about them: how they were mixed and muddled and muddy with need, with worry, with the wish that things could go back to the way they were before — and with the perdurable hope of somehow finding love again amid the shambles the years and troubles had made.

Perhaps a week later, a taxi pulled up in front of the house and a woman struggled out, looking around with the tentativeness of a person entering exotic surroundings. She held a black bag in both hands, and when the cabbie asked for his fare she opened the purse, stared myopically into it, fished out a few coins, and handed them to him. He gave her a look of intense scorn, turning to get back into the cab.

I watched all this from the front porch. I had gone out there to try and cool off. Mother and Lisa were off at the post office mailing a birthday package to Aunt Elaine. Mrs. Wilson and Russell were in their own rooms, where they had spent much of the last few days.

The cab pulled away, and the woman came gingerly up the walk. I stood to greet her.

"Is this Twenty-six Jewett Street?"

I told her it was.

She came up the stairs. "Hello," she said. "I'm Margaret Barnes." She touched my open palm and then took her hand away, looking past me into the house. "I'm Penelope Holt's aunt. I've — is she present at the moment?"

I explained to her that Penny had gone.

"Oh, my. Oh, good Lord."

Then Mrs. Wilson spoke through the front door screen. "Are you here to look at a room?"

"No, I — I'm afraid I've come all this way for nothing," the woman said. Then she smiled, repeated her name, and that she had hoped to find Penny here.

"Come in," Mrs. Wilson said, hurrying out to grasp her thin hand and giving me a censorious look, as though I were guilty by blood association with my father. As, in her mind, I suppose I was. I followed them into the house.

"Can I get you something — anything?"

"A glass of water."

"Please, sit down."

Margaret Barnes sat primly at the edge of the sofa, her purse on her lap. I doubt that I have ever seen a narrower or more elongated face on another human being. Though she was probably well past forty, her hair was teased high and dyed bright blond, and seemed too much for that small thin face to support. She wore a tight skirt, a small pearl necklace, and dark horn-rimmed glasses. Deep lines on either side of her mouth ran down into her chin and neck.

I had taken a seat across from her, and we were studiously trying to seem incurious about each other. In the kitchen, Mrs. Wilson was struggling with the ice tray.

"Do you live here alone with your mother?" Margaret Barnes asked me.

Her voice startled me a little. "No, ma'am. I mean yes — that's — Mrs. Wilson's not my mother."

"Did you get to know my niece?"

This seemed an odd question. I could imagine myself saying *I was in love with her*. It sounded absurd; I simply nodded.

"You don't know where she went."

"No, ma'am."

"Yes, well — I don't really know her very well myself."

I'm sure the effect of this showed in my face.

"I'm only running an errand for her father."

"Her father," I said.

"Yes?" It was a question.

"Excuse me — did you say her father?"

She nodded. Mrs. Wilson came in with three glasses of ice water on a glass tray. I took mine and thanked her.

"Yes," Margaret Barnes said as she took her own from the tray. "I was just telling this nice young man that I don't know Penny very well. You see, I live in Ogden, and — this is just what I was afraid it would be. The girl's father is in poor health. Diabetes, you know. Trouble with his legs. And he's been trying to locate her for a good long time now. And I was supposed to come here and confront her face to face. She sends him letters, you see. From various places she's been. But she won't allow any real communication. It's very strange. And since I have a grandson near here, my brother wondered if I'd just come see her for him."

"Did you say her father?" said Mrs. Wilson. "I thought —" She looked at me. And for a moment, no one said anything.

"What about her mother?" I asked. "She said she lived for a while with her mother in Virginia. In a trailer court."

"No." Mrs. Barnes looked puzzled. "Her mother passed away when she was a baby."

Again we were quiet, and again Mrs. Wilson and I looked at each other.

"My brother and I haven't seen each other in more than ten years, actually. We keep in touch when we can, of course. And I know the girl's been a heartache to him."

"She told us her father died at Pearl Harbor," I said.

Margaret Barnes's face was unaffected by this news. "Well, he's been trying to get in touch with her. And she sent him a letter from this address. Not too long ago. Here, I have the letter. My brother sent it to me." She reached into her purse again and brought it out. I stood to take it from her, and it must have seemed that I grabbed for it. Mrs. Wilson said, "Here, give that to me, Thomas."

I opened it and read the words *means to be a real family* before Mrs. Wilson took it out of my hands. "She was my tenant, after all," she said. She read it slowly.

"Now can I see it?" I said.

"I'll let your mother see it first, Thomas. And she can decide."

I excused myself and went out on the porch, fuming. I felt like a chastened little boy, and I hated Mrs. Wilson for putting me in that position.

There was a breeze now, and the sun-flecked shade moved. Up the way, I saw Russell shooting baskets with some other boys. And now Mother pulled up with Lisa. I went down the steps of the porch to meet them.

"Is everything all right?" Mother said as I approached.

"Penny lied to us."

"What?" She pushed the hair away from her forehead.

"Her aunt is inside with Mrs. Wilson right now. Sent by her father. And she never lived in any trailer court with her mother, either."

Mother looked at me with something of the expression of a person trying to decipher a puzzle.

"Go see," I said.

Later, I read Penny's letter:

Dear Dad,
I've waited all this time. I wanted to write you from some nice place and say I'm happy now, so you would know it and we'd be through with it all. It's not that I don't love you. But I can see now what it means to have a real family and I'm writing you to say that much. I've met a wonderful woman with children and I am very dear to her. I am part of her life, an important part. Please don't worry about me and I'm sorry if I worried you.
I'm happy. You be happy, too.

Penelope

We were not to learn much more about her. Margaret Barnes knew nothing of Chummy Terpin or of his incarcerated brother, and there wasn't much she could tell us about who Penny had been before we ran into her on the train. But finally there were indications in the woman's talk: unwitting intimations of the life Penny must have had growing up. Gradually a picture emerged of an austere, quiet household, steeped in the gloomiest passages from the Bible. A place where a girl with spirit might suffer for her very nature. Margaret Barnes sipped Mrs. Wilson's ice water and spoke through her tight, darkly lined mouth about the sort of physical discipline a child like that requires, and how a man couldn't let himself be fooled by coquettish smiles and feigned affection.

I remembered how frightened Penny had seemed when Father arrived in the house. I imagined her in another town, already making up another past for herself, for someone else.

The day after Mrs. Barnes's visit to Wilson Creek, I wrote Buddy Terpin at Leavenworth prison, explaining that Penny had lived with us, that she had gone off (I left the reasons up to his imagination), and asking if he might write me with anything that he felt he could tell me about her and about where Chummy might be. I had done so out of a kind of reflex, not wanting to leave any possibility unexplored. To my surprise, the answer came quickly:

> Dear Sir,
> I have not seen Penny Holt in five years. John Terpin is my brother all right but crazy. I have not seen him since I came to prison & don't wish to. Last I heard he was living in Virginia.
> Sincerely,
> Buddy Terpin

I wrote him back, telling him how Penny and his brother had been on their way to visit him at Leavenworth, and giving him the version of things which Chummy had provided. His answer was a little slower in coming this time:

> Dear Sir,
> Have not seen my brother in I don't know when. I am doing time for flight across state lines to avoid prosecution for armed robbery. Never saw anybody else. Went around with Penny Holt in high school and then lived with her for a month if that afterward before I went in the army and don't know whatever happened to her since. But know my brother is crazy and take it from there. John was born crazy and spent time in bughouse for it. Please do not write me anymore as it is hard for me to write.
> Buddy Terpin

I showed these letters to Mother, of course, but we didn't really talk about them. She shook her head and seemed resigned. "I don't know, Thomas."

"Don't you wonder where she is?" I said. "Who she was?"

"I can't worry about that now," she said. "I have to worry about getting us back to North Dakota."

I suppose now I wanted to know whatever I could about Penny, not because of the things she had done with me or said to me — since my feeling for her was already evolving into something else, a part of that sensation one experiences when dreaming of the evanescent and mysterious obsessions of youth — but because of the obviously profound effect she'd had on my parents.

* * *

Father returned to us sooner than he'd expected. He'd got all the way to Seattle, and then decided to turn around and come back — since we were going to Minot after all, he said, and since Penny Holt was gone. It wasn't good to be so far from everyone. He would sleep on the sofa in the sitting room. He was so calm about it, and apologetic. He would give Mother whatever she asked for in terms of the separation.

"I just want some time to be quiet," she said to no one in particular.

He slept on the sofa, then, and we waited to move. During the days, they worked together packing our things, sending boxes to Minot, and helping Mrs. Wilson arrange for the transfer of the leases. Mrs. Wilson brought prospective tenants through from time to time to look at the rooms. Mostly she talked to people on the telephone about them.

One morning shortly before we left Wilson Creek for good, I got out of my bunk and walked into the sitting room to find that the sofa there hadn't been slept on. In almost the same second this realization came to me, I heard my father cough in the other bedroom. I didn't want to know what they had said to each other to bring about this change. The curious thing was that after the months of worrying about it, I felt only guilty embarrassment now, as if I had spied on them.

24

WE RETURNED to Minot. We lived with Grandfather Tinan and Aunt Elaine, and Father got a job working as a custodian in the courthouse. He carved his wooden figures, giving them away sometimes and selling them when he could. Occasionally, the adults would start talking about the Air Force, and Father would get out the old films. But he and Mother were different with each other — polite, even, and vacant. One day Grandfather Tinan walked out of the house and took off to marry his woman friend. We got a telegram to that effect, and a promise that we would all love her when they returned from their sweet honeymoon on the Mediterranean. The whole affair sent Aunt Elaine into a fit of lasting rage, and the blue mark that had blossomed on the skin just above and to the side of her right eye always represented to me that particular crisis. There were no such marks on my mother and father. They entertained no fury or passion about anything, it seemed.

Grandfather Tinan brought his wife and her three children to live with us, and very soon after that, Father and Mother put a deposit down on a small house in the same neighborhood from which the new Mrs. Tinan had come. . .

But I was gone by this time, having joined the Air Force. And I was not one of those who joined to avoid being drafted. I could've had a deferment. I could've started college; Grandfather Tinan would gladly have paid for it. But I was restless and badly dislocated inside. None of the usual things had any taste for me, and when I happened upon the opportunity to get away on my own, without depending on any-one for anything, I took it. I even served a tour in Vietnam, though I didn't see any combat. Through eleven months I worked as a typist in an air-conditioned HQ personnel office in Saigon. Nothing required the slightest bravery from me, though I was frightened all the time anyway. I worked my shift and returned to the luxury of a hotel room, where I spent most of my off-duty time drinking Johnnie Walker Black.

I wrote home sometimes. But it was hard to find anything to say. I was spending a lot of time drunk. If I had adventures, they were only vague mental rumors in the blind and terrible mornings.

Toward the end of that year overseas, I received a letter from Mother which stated, quite simply, that she was staying with Grandfather Tinan again. "I'm not happy about it," she wrote. "But then I can't really help the choices anymore, and maybe I never could. Your father might've already written you. Lisa's with me, and she spends weekends with him. It's all amicable. How much I miss you," she went on, "I lie awake nights wondering what you're doing and if you're all right, and is it really as safe as you say it is. Please try to write more often, I know you're busy, dear. But I worry."

My father didn't write.

That winter, driving north at high speed through Des Lacs National Wildlife Refuge on Route 52, he lost control of his car; it veered off the road and plummeted into Upper Des Lacs Lake. The lake was not quite iced over at the time, and the car sank. No one seemed to know what he had been heading toward or fleeing from.

I flew home, and landed in the snows of Minot. Aunt Elaine picked me up. She looked years older than she was, but she had the same energy, the same commanding and somehow exacting pride. Lisa was tall and willowy now, with that gawkiness of movement some girls have just before they turn into young women; her grief had made her pale as ashes.

"Oh, Thomas," she said, putting her arms around me, breaking into tears. Aunt Elaine stood by quietly. I stroked my sister's hair and found myself unable to accept that we had reached this pass. It was hard to believe that Father wasn't still going on in the rooms of the little house they'd sent me pictures of after I'd left for the Air Force.

They drove me to Grandfather Tinan's house, where Mother stood waiting in the light from the door. She looked haggard, beset — and beautiful, too. She held her arms out and I walked into her embrace. We rocked back and forth there in the doorway. I was home, and my father was dead, and I couldn't think of anything I felt like doing with my life.

Grandfather Tinan was there, with his wife and the other children. His hair was even longer than it had been, and he had a tremendous fluidity about him now, as though nothing could be more comfortable than to inhabit that seventy-one-year-old body. He would live another fourteen years; that night, he looked as though he might live forever. And I felt a pang of resentment for the new bloom of health and good feeling in his face. It was his new marriage, of course, but I couldn't help wondering if he didn't feel some increment of gladness about the late facts of his daughter's life.

We sat down to dinner, and when he said the grace his voice quavered. "Father in heaven, we thank you for the safe return of our son. This family that has already had enough of sorrow humbly asks forgiveness for our sins, and rest for our departed, amen."

I realized then how far from the truth my perception of his feelings had been. He looked down the table at me, and his eyes shone. "Welcome home, boy."

I said, "I'm glad to be home." The words sounded almost foreign to me.

As had become my habit by that time, I got fairly drunk, and when everyone else had gone to bed I sat up with Mother a while. We drank more wine and watched a little television; the news came on. The war was going badly. Finally she got up, switched it off, and returned to her chair. I was reclining in the deep cushions of the sofa, my legs stretched out, my glass propped on my thigh with one hand while I unbuttoned the collar of my shirt with the other. I still wore my dress blues. I had the jacket open, the tie undone. She sat opposite me in a wing chair, her shapely legs crossed.

"Well," she said. Then she sighed. "I'm so relieved you're home."

"I was never in any real danger," I said.

We were quiet. I caught her staring at me almost warily, as though she were waiting for me to say something unpleasant.

"I keep seeing him on that morning in Wilson Creek," I said. "Getting into that cab. I can't make his face out the last time I saw him. I can't remember what we did or said — I was so preoccupied with myself."

"Don't," she said. "Don't do that, son. That isn't what he'd want."

"Where was he going?" I asked.

"Nobody's been able to find out." Her chin moved slightly, and I knew she was trying not to cry. "I hadn't seen him or spoken to him in a few days."

I drank the wine.

"The police say he was going more than a hundred miles an hour. He just had it all out."

"Maybe the accelerator got stuck," I said.

We were quiet, then, a long time.

"Guess who I ran into last April?" she said.

I waited.

"Penny Holt." She looked at me.

I sat forward.

"Elaine and I went to Lincoln, to the opera. It was some promotional thing I got through work, you know. We drove there, and we were standing outside the theater, and she came down the street. She was with some people — two other women and a man. They all came strolling by us. Can you imagine?"

"Did you say anything to her?"

"I wasn't going to. I mean, I decided not to, but she saw me and came over. She wanted to know how you were."

I drank the rest of my wine.

"We talked for a few minutes, mostly about what she's doing now. She has a job she likes. Friends. She seemed fine. Happy, and busy. But you know she told me she was married, and I saw a look on one friend's face when she said it, this look of surprise and puzzlement, and — I don't know — I knew it wasn't true. She was always such a helpless liar."

"She say anything about — that last night?"

"She asked how Daniel was. She seemed sorry to hear we were separating."

"Jesus Christ," I said. It had just raked through me again that my father was gone.

"Such a strange girl," said my mother.

We didn't say anything for a time, and perhaps we were both think-ing about Penny Holt.

"Did you ask where she went when she left us?"

"She volunteered it. She said she went to stay with Buddy for a few weeks. Visiting him in the prison, like I visited — I mean like it was, you know — at Wilson Creek."

We looked at each other.

"A helpless liar," she said again.

"I think the word is 'hopeless,'" I said.

"No, I don't think she can help herself. And I think she does it with all the hope in the world."

"I don't understand what she thought she was doing with us," I said. "How she picked us to come to."

Mother smiled and shook her head. "On the run, I guess."

Presently she said, "Lately, you know — I've been thinking a lot about Alaska."

I waited. Before me, the color patterns in Grandfather Tinan's carpet seemed to bleed into each other.

"I've even had that dream I used to have — you know — that I'm wandering around in some shadowy place looking for light. You know? And I wake up thinking I'm — thinking we're still together and I start to say something about it to him . . . It's like all the time between never happened, and just for that few seconds after I wake up I — I'm in love again." Her face seemed about to collapse. But then she straightened in her chair, and you could see her take hold again inside.

"I remember the story," I said. I was thinking of the home movies.

"I guess it's not so strange," she murmured.

Again we were quiet.

"I wasn't much older than you are. You know that? I stayed up all hours — God, I was a mess."

I watched her go over the memory of it. She really was quite lovely, still — past forty now, yet showing no changes at all.

"I sometimes think it would've worked out a little better if we'd stayed in Virginia and just waited for your father to come home," she said. She stared at the opposite wall, and I had the feeling that my presence no longer quite meant anything. She had been drinking heavi-ly, too.

"I'm drunk," I said.

"About the — the separation —" she said.

And I cut her off. "It's got nothing to do with me anymore."

She seemed then to be waiting for me to go on.

"That's just the truth," I said.

"Thomas, we couldn't come back from the night he had that row with Penny —"

"I said it's none of my business, Mother."

After a pause, she said, "I guess you don't think much of me now, do you?"

This surprised me. "Don't be absurd," I said. "Good God." I studied her a moment. She'd had too much to drink. She would never have said such a thing if she had been sober.

"I keep going over it in my mind," she said, "wondering what I could've done —"

I said, "What did he say to you that time — in Mrs. Wilson's dining room. After you both sent Penny out onto the porch?"

She shook her head. It was as if she were trying to reject some painful image in her mind.

"It all got done so quickly," I said. "Penny came out and walked around into the back yard and I followed her, and when I came back, Father walked out and said it was all settled. And you'd been so certain about moving out."

"He said he'd take you and Lisa away from me." She looked at the facets of light in her glass, the little swells of it in what was left of the wine. "It was simple. He said he'd charge that I was having — that there was something between Penny and me. Do you understand?"

"Jesus," I said.

"We had a very short, very serious discussion about it, and I decided to give him whatever he asked for."

"Then — when he came back — after it was all over and Penny was gone — you just — you decided to forgive him?"

"Oh, please. He was my husband. He was trying to do what I'd been trying to do, wasn't he?"

"And you forgave him."

"I tried to understand him. He was like a boy, trying to come off all tough. A lot of that had been taken away from him so brutally. And he — well, he was fighting for me, too."

"Was there something between you and Penny?" I asked.

"Oh, Thomas," she said with a sigh of deep exhaustion. "Do you really think so?"

"It was a question," I said. "I think there was something on Penny's side."

After a pause, she said, "The odd thing is, Wilson Creek was an attempt to save everything." She went on to tell me that there had never been any unusual physical affection between her and Penny Holt, and she just said it out plainly, in that tired voice, as though it were part of everything else. "I needed someone to talk to," she went on. "I was in such a turmoil about what I was feeling. And she was so easy to talk to. I *liked* being admired by her. The night Kennedy was shot, well, I felt that like a personal loss. And I think part of my feeling that way was that she was *watching* me feel it. She came to my room to cry, and really, Thomas, the two of us just held each other, like children in a storm. It was perfectly innocent."

"I was in love with her," I said. Now, after so much time, it sounded shopworn. And I added, "Or I thought I was."

She smiled. "No one failed to see that."

"Penny knew it, too."

"Well, she could hardly have missed it."

"I told her I loved her," I said.

"You did?"

A moment later, I said, "I wonder what she thought of us?"

"We were a family. We were trying so desperately to hold ourselves together. I think she wanted to be a part of that." Mother lay her head back on the cushion. "I suppose I could've asked her when I saw her. But it didn't, as we say, come up."

"Did you exchange addresses or anything like that?"

She shook her head.

"Why not?"

"It didn't, as we say, come up."

"She kissed me once," I said. "The night you brought Father home. I mean a real grown-up kiss."

"Lord — you were only eighteen. I think if I'd known that —" Mother paused. She seemed to come to herself, seemed to realize that it couldn't matter now.

"The night Father — when he and Penny —" I said.

"Nothing happened, son. He tore her pajamas, and that was all he did. He knocked me down and he hit you."

"No," I said. "I meant to say that I — that something in me wanted him to hurt her."

She took a drink. "Maybe that's natural."

"If it is, it frightens me."

She waited a moment. Then: "Shoulder it yourself."

"I'm sorry?" I said.

"Nothing."

Presently I said, "Did Penny talk to you about me?"

"Only to say how wonderful you and Lisa were. She was very fond of Lisa, too, you know."

"I'll tell you what I've been wondering about," I said. "I wonder why you let Father take you to the Caribbean in the fall of sixty-six. You must've known he was getting in too deep."

She was lying back, staring at the ceiling, and her eyes were dry. But something changed the light in them, a shadow crossing over water.

"Why did you let him buy you all those things?" I said.

Lifting her head, she sipped her wine, then lay back again. "What possible difference could that make now?"

"I want to know," I said. "It makes a difference to me."

Another moment went by before she answered. "I guess I just thought we'd end up asking your grandfather for it. Your father lied to me, you know. He kept the books, and he said we were all right. Then, he thought taking money from your grandfather was a humiliation."

"He kept the books, but you knew what the situation was, didn't you?"

"Not really."

"You didn't have an inkling that there was trouble?"

"I'm getting so sleepy, Thomas. This isn't the time. I don't owe any explanations to you. What are you doing?"

"We were talking," I said. "I wanted to know. It's my father —" And now I was fighting back tears.

"I'm sorry," she said. "I don't know — I didn't know."

"But you must've known, Mother — or else you wouldn't have thought about borrowing the money from Grandfather Tinan."

"Why is this so important now?" she said. "Can't you see it's finished, all of it?"

"I can't help wondering what it was all for," I said. "All the trouble we went through and everything that happened — if you and Father were going to break apart anyway."

Now she sat forward a little, and drew a breath. "Because I thought I could save it." She put the glass down on the floor between her feet and looked at me. "Because I didn't want to believe any of it, son. Not the least part of any of it. I told you, it was terrifying. He came home from Vietnam and he wasn't the same man anymore and I made up my mind I would last it out. Make myself last it out." Now she had begun to cry. "It took all that and more — prison, all that time — to make me finally believe that it might really be true, that what we had — that — that beauty — just wasn't going to be there anymore. And I couldn't stay with him then, could I? I don't know what he was doing on that road, Thomas. I don't know what he was doing."

What I'd had to drink was swimming in my head, but I got up and lurched across the space of bright carpet to her side, knelt down, and put my face in her hair.

"No one's to blame," she said, her voice high in her throat, barely a whisper through her tears. "We get such little warning about how we're going to change, my darling. But no one's to blame. There isn't anyone to blame."

I took her cool small hands in mine, and she wept softly into the blue cloth of my uniform.

There are just these few things left to say: I served the rest of my tour in the Air Force, and then mustered out and headed east, without much of an idea what I would end up doing. I was to take years to decide that life near the water, in something quiet like a bookstore, was what I wanted. Mother stayed in Minot, after all; she found a small house near Grandfather Tinan's, which she shared with Lisa and Aunt Elaine.

She still lives with Aunt Elaine in that little house. And though there have been times over the years when she has appeared to be on the brink of a serious romantic step with someone, she's remained with her sister. Whenever I get letters from her — which is rare enough, now — they are always chatty and full of news of the various projects she and

Aunt Elaine have lately undertaken. The latest is an attempt to change the strict zoning laws of their rural North Dakota county to permit the construction of a new hospital. She's sixty-three now, and passionate about her work on getting the law changed.

Father rests in that little country cemetery I visited with Grandfather Tinan all those years ago, and Grandfather Tinan is there, too. Whenever I think of them in that place, I also think of the nearly effaced stones, the names of children, of the aunt I never knew, who couldn't take things the way they were. And I recall the passion and anger the two men spent on each other over the twenty-odd years.

That winter night of my return from the war, Mother and I had said things to each other that we would never be able to say again, and after we had brushed away our tears, we kissed good night. We shuffled off alone to our separate rooms, where I believe we must have pondered the same thing, puzzled over the same thing before we slept: how it was that one singular human wish not to admit a change in the heart of feeling could have led to all that it had led to.

It was somehow as though we had been involved in a kind of game, a playing at life, an acting out. And it had gone its own way in spite of us.

That was how it seemed to me on that first night back from the war, waking, still half drunk in the dark, coming again into the knowledge of my father's death, hearing the sound outside of wind and breaking branches, the raving elements of the coldest night of the year, and the useless slaughter going on across the world.

My nightmares were not of the war at all.

I was only twenty-one years old. I had not even, as yet, been introduced to the woman I would marry.

Broad Run, Virginia
1989–1992